Palmetto Rising

Book 1 of A New Beginning

By Jonah Early

To my wife — thank you for your unyielding love, support and encouragement. The completion of this book would not have been possible without you.

You will always be my Princess.

PART I

Chapter 1

Los Angeles, California

The abandoned street front passed by in a blur, periodically illuminated by sharp bursts of red. There was no light anywhere except the piercing beam of the cruiser headlights. The streets were empty in this part of town, the stores vacant, and the residences boarded up and abandoned. It was dark and foreboding.

Detective Reginald T. Williams scanned the monitor for updates about the call he was responding to in Jefferson Park. He glanced for a moment in the rear view mirror, his eyes locking on his own blank stare. He shook his head in disgust. He knew what he would find at the scene. More senseless death, more hate, more racism. The incidents had been increasing in frequency over the past few years and now they were an everyday occurrence.

As the head detective on the special task force known as RIM, it was Reggie's protocol to be notified immediately, along with the primary responders, about any situation involving race conflicts. RIM stood for Racial Impact Mitigation, though he and others on his unit jokingly referred to themselves as the task force of 'Really Insane Men'. It wasn't too far from the truth. Los Angeles was now the national battleground for the emerging war between Latinos and African Americans and they were right in the middle of it.

To make matters more difficult, his team was underfunded, undermanned, and undergunned. But he didn't expect much more from a city that was bankrupt and struggling to maintain basic services. Hollywood's elite, the rich and famous, had relocated long ago to Nevada where there was still no state income tax. The resulting impact from the loss of the tax base had been devastating to California and particularly hard on the city of Los Angeles.

The neighborhood he was driving through used to be a bustling business district of small shops owned by African Americans, Koreans, and Latinos. Now it was considered a neutral zone, the area that divided the Latino and African American neighborhoods. Like many of the residents of Los Angeles, the shop owners had left in the last few years as gang violence and race clashes became more prominent. The final straw for many of them had occurred just eighteen months ago, when over three thousand Latinos and African Americans clashed on the main street in a bloody battle. The National Guard had been called in to restore peace, but not before more than five hundred people had been slain and another twelve hundred had been injured. Three days later, Reggie was assigned to the RIM task force, created in response to the increasing violence by an executive order of the governor.

South Los Angeles has been a hot bed for racial tension for decades. But it wasn't always that way. Predominately a middle income African American community since the Second World War, it was a prosperous, robust community that housed a hard working middle class. In the 1970's, a downturn in the economy greatly impacted the manufacturing companies in the area, resulting in the loss of many union jobs held by community residents. In addition, a growing influx of Latino immigrants into the area created competition for jobs. With fewer job opportunities, many African Americans turned to dealings drugs and involvement in illegal activities as a means to survive. By the 1980's, this repressed area had become known for its street gangs, violence, and poverty. All the while, the Latino population continued to thrive, as did their affluence. African Americans viewed the emergence of the Latino as a threat to their way of life. The Latinos viewed the African American as an obstacle to their pursuit of economic prosperity.

His mind jumped back to the argument he had with his wife the night before. Teresa was in tears, pleading for him to leave the RIM task force before he became a statistic, just like those that he was trying to save. The memory of her words struck him as if they had just been spoken.

"I buried my father because of racism! I don't want to bury you too! When are you going to realize that tempting death every day is no way to live?"

Her words were spoken out of true love and increasing fear, and he knew that she was right on many levels. Teresa had lost her father because of a senseless killing motivated by fear and hate. Her father, Pastor Darrell Powell, had been a minister of a small church located in South Compton. One of the first large clashes between the African American and the Latino communities occurred just two blocks away. He had taken to the streets seeking to shepherd and counsel youths from his congregation and unselfishly inserted himself into a melee of fists, bars and bats to protect a Korean delivery man who had been targeted by an enraged mob of black youths. One of the young men involved struck the pastor with the butt of a baseball bat directly in his nose, causing his nose cartridge to explode into his brain. He died instantly.

Teresa and her teenaged sister were devastated by the loss. With no other forms of financial support, Teresa was forced to drop out of the University of California and quit her internship as a congressional aide so she could work to support them both. Her dream of changing the world through politics had ended bitterly when it collided with the cold reality of necessity. Reggie didn't blame her for how she felt about his career, it was a natural response given what had occurred.

Reggie mulled over his conversation with Teresa, if only Teresa could understand the fire that burned in his heart for making this world safe for her and for others. If she could feel his passion to create a world where senseless crimes and the tragedies that resulted did not exist, she would feel differently. He knew that this was a gargantuan pursuit, but these ideals motivated him toward a purpose greater than himself. It was the reason he turned down a scholarship to Stanford Law School and instead chose to become a police officer.

It was only as a police officer that he experienced the immediate impact of his actions to protect the public. He had advanced rapidly through the ranks, earning medals and rewards for performance along the way. He even passed on a recent promotion to Captain, choosing instead to lead the RIM task force. Being a public protector was what he was designed to do.

The urgent voice emitted from his personal radio transponder shattered his moment of introspection. "Reggie ... donde estas?"

It was the voice of his Latino partner, Carlos Fierro. Reggie took a deep breath and clicked his microphone on. "I'm in route to the scene, Carlos. What do you have to report?"

Carlos voice was strained, "Get here pronto! We have a problem ... let me clarify ... we have Hell on earth."

Ten minutes later, Reggie arrived at the vacant building in the downtown area of Jefferson Park. The building looked just like every other building on the street, lifeless and desolate. Not a hint of its former glory or use existed. It had become a burned out shell with no windows, doors, or purpose. Reggie parked his sedan next to a flashing police cruiser and headed toward the building, not sure about what he would see inside.

There was no police barricade of yellow tape and officers to pass through. Neither the public nor the press ventured into this area of the city anymore. He instinctively felt for his pistol located in the shoulder harness under his coat. He was in a dangerous area and had to be careful. His wife's words echoed in his head again. For a brief moment, he thought that maybe Teresa was right. Maybe it was time for a change. But he quickly dismissed the thought. Enforcing justice was part of who he was and making Los Angles safer for her and others was the passion that motivated him.

He stepped inside the front entrance of the building and announced himself in a loud, commanding voice. "Reggie Williams on site. Carlos, where are you?"

"We are downstairs. Watch out for the third step, it is missing," Carlos yelled, his voice coming from somewhere in the basement of the structure.

Reggie turned on his flashlight and carefully made his way down the stairs to the next level. The floor was covered in dust and debris. The structure had been vacant for some time. He passed an old exercise bike, the handlebars bent at an odd angle and the base smashed in, as if someone had taken a sledge hammer to it. He steadied his flashlight and locked the beam on the frame of his partner Carlos, who was kneeling on the floor, writing in his notepad. Carlos looked up, anger evident in his eyes. Reggie approached Carlos, extending his hand to grasp his shoulder. "Hey man, que pasa? Are you ok?" he asked.

Carlos didn't immediately respond, instead he took his flashlight and swung it in an arc around the floor. Reggie's vision tracked the fluorescent white beam to several bodies strewn about the floor. The bodies of both men and women had been placed in odd poses, as if to ensure that anyone who saw them would know that this act of violence was done deliberately. Some of the bodies showed signs of mutilation and disfigurement. All of them were Hispanic. *What were so many Hispanics doing in the heart of the black district?* Reggie's struggled to make sense of the massacre he saw before him.

"These aren't the bodies of street fighters, these are normal people," Reggie said with astonishment. He directed his flashlight towards a female body that lay on her stomach with her back arched in the shape of a u. He could tell from her face that she was elderly, maybe in her seventies. The victim had been hog-tied, with her hands, feet, and hair tied together behind her body. Her neck had been slashed from ear to ear. Reggie quenched a fit of nausea. This was terrible.

"That is not the worst of it," Carlos looked at him intently, almost as if he was trying to determine if Reggie was capable of understanding what he was about to tell him. In the faint light cast by their flashlights, Carlos's youthful face was gone, replaced by a mask of dark shadows woven with concern. His eyes were what bothered Reggie the most. They were dark and solemn. To him, it appeared as if Carlos had aged twenty years since he had seen him just hours early.

"Show me," Reggie heard himself say. His mind was racing with the implications of what he had already seen. *What could be worse?*

Carlos walked him into another room that was adjacent to the main area of carnage. Attached to the wall, was another body. Large metal spikes had been driven through the man's hands and into the wood studs that framed the inside of the wall. A pool of darkened blood lay directly below the body. Reggie recognized the face of the man from recent television news reports involving unions and illegal immigrants. The man was Raphael Santoro, Director of the National Labor Development Agency. An agency of the Department of Labor Equalization, the NLDA provided business support services for unions throughout the country.

Raphael's body hung limp, his head cast down and to the side, his arms seemed overextended as if both shoulders had been dislocated. Reggie's shock turned to horror as it dawned on him what he was looking at. Raphael Santoro had been crucified.

Chapter 2

Greenville, South Carolina

Jasper Thorne was shown into the elaborately furnished study by an elderly black woman who introduced herself only as Moaney. The decor of the room brought back pleasant memories from his youth, when his parents were still alive. It reminded him of the coastal plantation where he grew up, a majestic home located on a bluff overlooking the rice plains outside of Georgetown.

Jasper seated himself in one of the two ornate chairs facing a large antique desk fashioned from black walnut. His eyes were drawn to the two adjacent walls where lush, burgundy colored silk curtains surrounded large mahogany trimmed windows. Directly in front of him, spanning a height of over twelve feet, were three picture windows, each consisting of two panes. The lower window pane could be raised to allow access to a covered patio just outside the room. Camel colored plantation shutters hid the top windows panes, but had been positioned slightly open to allow the sunlight to filter into the room in streaks of gold. The window glass was wavy and wrinkled from age, blurring the outside view into wavy streaks of color. The overall effect was calming. The room was peaceful, orderly, and purposeful.

Quickly, his mind began racing through the possibilities of what this meeting could mean to his campaign. He was about to meet with Whitaker Stanley, the wealthiest political socialite in the state. It wasn't so much financial support that his campaign would need, though that would not be discouraged. Jasper had personal wealth and money from his parent's estate, if he needed to supplement his campaign. What he really needed was Whitaker to publicly endorse his candidacy. If he could gain Whitaker's support, he would also gain the support of many high level political allies at state and national levels. There was no doubt this campaign would be different than his first, but he had confidence in his ability to win Whitaker over to his cause. Besides, he had a good track record as far as electability went.

Jasper had won his congressional election by a demanding margin over the long term Democratic incumbent. The fact that his opponent had been a staunch supporter of the Farm Equalization of Opportunity Act definitely played in his favor among his heavily rural conservative constituents. The legislation had been enacted in response to a massive outbreak of salmonella poisoning that killed more than three hundred people and sickened thousands. Thousands of farm and livestock owners in his jurisdiction had been impacted by the legislation which required licensing by the federal government for any person or corporation owning livestock for human consumption.

The effects of the legislation had been severe. The popular practice of raising chickens by an individual family for eggs and food basically disappeared overnight. It was now virtually impossible for a person to own a small flock of chickens due to the costs associated with compliance. In order to qualify for the license, the livestock owner would have to show the government tangible proof that all livestock was maintained in an environmentally and animal friendly manner and was processed for consumption according to existing governmental health and safety standards. Legislators that supported the law touted the importance of accounting for the country's available food supply, the standardization of food safety practices, and the importance of ensuring a competitive market place. The rural population, on the other hand, believed it was an infringement of their freedoms and had thus voted for Jasper.

He continued to sit in silence for another fifteen minutes, trying to steady his nerves and enjoy the serenity of the moment. Subconsciously, his hands rubbed across the soft felt on the arm rails. The rails were worn. He had not been the first to grace the chair awaiting an audience with Whitaker, nor would he be the last. Suddenly, a voice sounded from behind him, the words accented with a heavy southern drawl. "This is my favorite place to be this time of day."

Jasper rose from the chair and turned around, his heart rate increasing with a rush. Whitaker Stanley stood on the far side of the room watching him, studying the man who had invaded his private sanctuary. Whitaker's gaze seemed to penetrate his being, sizing him up, revealing his hidden secrets. The initial reaction was unnerving. Even so, Whitaker's eyes twinkled with an internal light and something Jasper could only describe as compassion. Jasper found himself liking Whitaker immediately.

"It is a pleasure to finally meet you, sir," Jasper said, rising to shake the man's hand. Whitaker's hands were small and weathered, but his grip was like iron. It was the grip of a man who knew he was in control of the situation. Whitaker released his grip and immediately walked over to a small mirror-topped serving table located in the corner of the study. The table contained a silver pitcher, a silver ice bucket, and a set of cocktail glasses. He filled a glass with ice and then poured a dark brown liquid into the glass until it was full. Jasper was suddenly conscious of how hot the room was getting. It was probably his nerves, but the room had been cool when he entered it. *Had Whitaker turned up the heat?*

"So Congressman ... for what do I owe the pleasure of your visit?" Whitaker asked. There was a hint of sarcasm in his voice.

Jasper spent the next ten minutes sharing his background and qualifications, specifically discussing his accomplishments as a freshman Republican congressman and his current activities on the Congressional Judiciary Committee. Whitaker barely moved, only nodding his head occasionally. Whitaker's gaze was focused intently on Jasper and he could feel the sweat beginning to break out of his forehead and neck. His underarms were already drenched under his tailored sport coat. *Was he connecting with this man?* The question echoed in the back of his mind as he spoke his closing statement, "Sir, I believe I can be the next governor of our great state and I want your support."

Whitaker took another sip of his drink before responding to the statement presented before him. "Son, are you aware of the revolution that is going on around us today? Do you know that our society is in an ideological death spiral caused by social, economic, and political influences that have been fermenting for years?" Whitaker didn't bother to wait for a response from Jasper. "You're asking to take a leadership position aboard a sinking ship in a fleet of ships that is plunging head first over Niagara Falls. What makes you want to do that?"

Jasper had anticipated this question and his response was measured, but full of passion. "Sir, I love this country. I cherish the principles upon which our country was founded and I strive daily to personify the freedoms for which so many have given their lives. I value the freedom to pursue a life of my own choosing, to be free of the control of others, and to create happiness for myself and those around me. If I were to do anything else, I would have no worth. I would have no purpose."

Whitaker's eyes locked on Jasper's for a moment, a look of approval flickered across Whitaker's face and then receded as quickly as it had come. Jasper felt he had made a connection, only he wasn't sure what it was exactly he had said that resonated with Whitaker.

Whitaker slowly rose from his chair and returned to the bar table to refresh his drink. Jasper suddenly realized his throat was parched. He thought Whitaker might offer him a glass of refreshment, but his hopes were soon dashed as Whitaker returned to his seat without even a glance in his direction. Whitaker studied him for another long moment and then asked casually, "Son, are you a Christian?"

"I was born and raised Catholic, sir," Jasper responded slowly, taken aback by the abrupt change in subject.

Whitaker raised a quizzical eye and took a sip of his drink. "Do you know the difference?"

Before Jasper could respond, Whitaker chuckled and asked another question. "Mr. Thorne, I don't mean to assume your ignorance but do you know the story of Adam and Eve?" His voice had an edge of anticipation.

Jasper responded rather abruptly, slightly offended by the question, "Sure I do. How is that relevant to our conversation?"

Whitaker paused, his eyes searching his for a moment, "My young man, it is the cornerstone of our conversation and the very heart of what is ailing our society today."

"You mean sin?"

"Sin? No, not sin. Though sin is the plague of humanity, it is too encompassing to be delegated to this event. I am talking about what happened when Eve offered Adam the fruit of the tree of the knowledge of Good and Evil."

Jasper was curious, but confused. *Why was Whitaker asking such a strange question?* He had to be careful how he proceeded. He needed Whitaker's backing and support, not only financially but politically. Over the past fifty years, candidates Whitaker supported had an election rate of over eighty five percent.

Jasper decided to play it safe, which in this case was to defer to the storyteller. "You have my full attention."

"The Bible tells us that in the Garden of Eden, Adam and Eve lived in constant communion with God. God would visit the Garden of Eden to fellowship with his creations. When they ate of the fruit, their direct union and fellowship with God was broken. Adam and Eve, and all humanity, were forever cast out of the Garden of Eden." Whitaker took a sip of his drink then continued, "The book of Genesis, those of the Old Testament, and the four books of the Gospel are about man's journey of redemption culminating in the death and resurrection of Jesus Christ. It is a journey with one aim — to regain eternal fellowship with God."

"Yes, I am familiar with the story," Jasper said still trying to figure out where Whitaker was taking their conversation. "But I am not sure about the relevance of the fruit?"

"The fruit …" Whitaker paused as if the subject was an afterthought to a more important topic, "well the fruit was simply the realization of self-will. God had given Adam and Eve free will from the beginning; however their realization of their choice to make decisions to obey or disobey God did not occur until they ate of the fruit."

Whitaker leaned out of his chair across the desk towards Jasper, "Why is the fruit relevant to our discussion as you so astutely asked?" He quickly reclined back in his chair, in the process grabbing his drink to take a long sip, savoring the silence of his captive audience. "Today, in our very government, there is a political faction that wants to banish self-will. They want to conquer our will to produce, our will to contribute, and our will to live. They want us to comply, to concede, and to follow." Whitaker's voice became very soft but offered a forceful edge. "Show me that you do not want the same. Show me that you will be a fighter for that which is the essence of mankind. Prove to me that you understand the true meaning of the fruit. Prove to me that you understand humanity's current plight. And prove to me that you understand our only hope. Only then, my young friend will you gain the support you so preciously covet."

Jasper paused, thinking through what he had just heard. *What did Whitaker really want him to prove? What did Whitaker want him to understand? Was the old, eccentric man even sane?* Before he could respond, Whitaker rose from his chair; his hands extended with open palms and walked over to the serving table. "Where are my manners, may I offer you a beverage?"

Chapter 3

"We must especially be aware of that small group of selfish men who would clip the winds of the American eagle in order to feather their own interest."
–Franklin Delano Roosevelt

Washington, District of Columbia

Mason Kelley glanced up from the menu he was reading to take a brief look at the two gentlemen sitting at the table across from him. "Crab cakes anyone? They really are the best in town," he said, nodding to the waitress who promptly came over to take their order. When she left the table, he turned his attention to the handsome, middle-aged man seated to his left. "Robbie, is your draft of the IPEA bill ready for introduction to the house judiciary committee?"

"A better question is do we have a majority on the committee?" Senator Harry Benjamin interrupted. The question was punctuated with a large burst of exhaled tobacco smoke.

The bluish cloud expanded to encompass the three gentlemen seated at a small booth in the rear of Martin's Tavern. It was the same booth where John F. Kennedy, as a Massachusetts Senator, had been sitting when he proposed to his wife, Jacqueline Bouvier. Situated a short distance from the capital in the picturesque neighborhood of Georgetown, Martin's was an ideal place for public officials to meet and discuss sensitive issues in a public forum. The ambient noise of the tavern made it difficult for people seated nearby to eavesdrop without drawing attention to themselves.

Harry was a large man with thinning white hair and a bulbous nose, most likely owed to too many bourbon cocktails. His skin was pale but his cheeks were flush red, accenting deep set blue eyes. He took another long drag from his Cuban cigar, taking a moment to enjoy the bold flavor before releasing the smoke slowly. Harry loved the way the smoke caressed his lips as he exhaled, not to mention the perfect buzz a fine cigar gave him.

He was so thankful the country had finally come to its senses and made peace with Cuba, if for anything, simply for the quality of their cigars. His wife had been chastising him for years about his habit, concerned about the impact on his health. At his age and after almost forty years as a senator, he had long passed the point of moderation in anything, be it personal or political. He believed that life was meant to be seized, savored and enjoyed. After all, once you die, there is nothing else.

"We have the Democratic support on the committee, but we need at least one of the remaining two Republicans to gain a majority," Congressman Robert Coolidge acknowledged. "We know that Douglass, Majors, and Beacher are untouchable on this matter," Robert said as he waved his hand in front of his face to disband a puff of smoke that had been aimed in his direction.

Robert presented a stark contrast to the Senator seated across from him. In his late forties, he had managed to maintain the physique and boyish good looks that originally helped him to be elected to Congress at the age of twenty-five, the minimum age to hold that office. He had wavy brown hair that tangled in its own tufts and a smile that displayed his perfect teeth.

"That leaves Goodman and the new kid, Thorne," Robert continued. "Goodman owes me several favors for past actions I have done on his behalf, not all of them related to his Senate duties. I am sure that he would prefer that some of those favors be buried and forgotten forever. The poor bastard will have no choice but to vote with us." The last statement was delivered with a devilish grin.

Mason knew that Robert could afford to be cocky. Despite his younger age and lack of tenure in his position, his influence and power was the main reason he was part of the elite trio seated at the table. He was one of the richest men in America, although he never earned a penny of his wealth.

Robert owed his wealth to the back breaking efforts of his father and grandfather who built a family business into a multi-million dollar global manufacturer of auto parts. Robert's father sold the company in a deal valued at eight hundred million dollars. The sole heir to his father's estate at the age of twenty,

Robert had used the money to create and fund multiple philanthropic organizations and institutes of social change in the country. To the public, Robert appeared as a generous donor and philanthropist, but he was actually the mastermind behind almost every large political demonstration, boycott, and public campaign that occurred in the country. Robert knew he had it all — money, power, good looks and the ability to use them all to his benefit.

"I want to make sure we are coordinated in our activities." Mason took a measured pause. "Harry needs to introduce the Senate version immediately after you gain approval to move it from committee to formal vote in the House. That way we can leverage the media frenzy that is sure to follow."

Mason knew that frenzy was a mild term to call the resulting chaos in the media that would be created by the introduction of the IPEA bill to Congress. The Immigrant Progress and Enrichment Act would change the direction of the country, not to mention make him one of the most powerful men in Washington. The legislation had been his brain child, conceived only with the assistance of the men who sat at the table. They and many others of similar mind believed IPEA was one of four key cornerstones that had to be in place in order for a new societal foundation.

The legislation would provide for illegal immigrants to become U.S. citizens on the condition that they joined a governmentally sanctioned labor union. If this legislation was successfully passed into law by Congress, millions of people would become instant citizens. He had calculated union membership would explode instantly from twenty percent of the workforce to more than sixty percent, and that was a conservative estimate.

In order to create the necessary volume of union positions, the legislation would make it a requirement for every company the government suspected of employing illegal immigrants to unionize their workforce. Only companies that managed to pass an exhaustive and costly procedural investigation to prove all their employees were legally employed would be excluded. The agricultural industry was the primary target of the legislation, as it would yield the majority of potential new citizens, almost two million if his current estimates were correct.

For him personally, IPEA meant power and control. In his current role he had direct oversight responsibility for every union organization in the country. Now he was authorized with much of the same powers of the Board, but also so much more.

He mulled his last thought over in his head. Sure he had power and control now. After all, he did have a position on the President's cabinet, which wielded plenty of influence, but IPEA would take it to a much greater level. The legislation would grant him expanded powers in his position, such as the express privilege and authority to grant a person citizenship. However, the real power would come from the expansion of unions and the people those unions controlled. Just as the president had the ability to marshal and control the military, Mason would have the ability to persuade the public through the direction of the union leadership.

"Can we get Thorne to join?" Mason said, looking expectantly at the two gentlemen. His question was met by silence.

"You need to be careful about Thorne," Harry replied, blowing another cloud of blue smoke. This one was aimed directly at Robert, almost as if to challenge him. "What do you really know about him? He has proven quite capable for someone with so little experience in playing the game."

"I have spent some time getting to know him on the Judiciary Committee," Robert responded. "He is a bright guy, but he is nothing special. He earned an engineering degree from the Citadel and a law degree from Washington & Lee in Lexington. Then for some crazy reason he joined the army as an enlisted soldier to fight overseas in the European Union Revolution. Four years later, he left the military as a decorated officer."

"That does not sound like your average guy," Mason interjected. "I understand there were some real nasty battles in that war, particularly when Germany was invaded. To start as a common soldier and finish as an officer with combat medals, this guy should not be underestimated."

"You're kidding right?" Robert objected, surprised by Mason's naivety. "Everyone gets medals these days for military service. It is the perpetuation of what was started in our school yards and on youth sports teams over a generation ago. Everyone gets a trophy no matter if you win or if you lose. Thorne is no different." He looked at Harry for confirmation. Harry had held the position of Chairman of the Senate Committee on Armed Services for the past fifteen years and had personally handed out hundreds of medals to members of the military. Harry nodded slightly in response.

"About the only thing he has done to demonstrate a higher level of competency was the fantastic story he created that got him elected. The small town boy who tragically lost his parents, went to war, and came back home to settle into a career as a small firm lawyer only to become disillusioned with the state of the country. His voters obviously were hopeless romantics who lacked true understanding of what is important." Robert locked eyes with Mason, "No, I am not concerned about Thorne."

"I don't care about how you feel, Robbie." Harry's normally calm voice was tainted with urgency. "What I care about is that we get the IPEA bill approved by your committee." He waived the now extinguished butt of his cigar in a threatening manner. "Your cockiness is going to be your undoing."

"Come now Harry. It hasn't failed me yet," Robert replied, the devilish grin back on his face. His grin had its desired effect as evidenced by the tension that left Harry's face.

Mason took the opportunity to take control of the conversation. "That's enough bantering gentlemen! We need to focus on the reason we are here. I still am concerned that key provisions of IPEA could be negotiated out of the deal. That would not bode well for our future plans."

Mason was keenly aware the real impact of IPEA could be completely mitigated if a key element of legislation known as Majority Compliance, was removed. Under Majority Compliance, industries would be assessed based on the amount of unionization. If greater than fifty percent of employees in any industry were classified as union, the overall industry would be classified as a union industry. Any new or existing business within that industry would therefore have to unionize its workers to comply with the majority in its industry. Majority Compliance would result in standardized wages, job classifications, and job responsibilities across an industry. This was perhaps the pinnacle provision to the IPEA bill. The government was never going to be able to create social and economic equalization among the citizens until it ensured that businesses employed and compensated those citizens in a fair, just, and equal manner. Majority Compliance and IPEA made that possible.

"If we do this right, we will have every public politician eating out of our hand, not to mention padding our pockets," Mason said. "After all, most people do what they are told to do, it is that simple. The people will belong to the unions. They will do what the union tells them to do. If we control the unions, than we control the country." *People are sheep. Most are just too stupid or too fearful to question authority*, he thought. That was why he and people like himself were needed to make decisions for the general population. "We, the intellectually elite, are the only people who possess the intelligence and savviness to effectively lead this nation."

Both Harry and Robert nodded in agreement, with Harry throwing back his bourbon in salute and flagging the waitress for another.

Mason took a moment to relish in the craftiness of his plan. IPEA was the best and most feasible solution to the problem of illegal immigration. Not only would it create "fair" wages and working conditions for many employees, it would raise the standard of living for the country to a common level. The economy would be positively impacted as millions of additional people would now be able to purchase additional goods and services due to earning higher wages that union positions provided. In turn, this would spark additional investment in small business and employment in order to support the increased demands of these new consumers. The unemployment level would drop and the government tax base would increase, allowing the government to continue to provide critical health and welfare services to its people and reinvest in the country's infrastructure. It would just get better from there.

Yes, Mason thought, *it was a masterful plan*. A plan only someone of his caliber, upbringing, and education could ever conceive. And with it in place, their revolution could begin.

Chapter 4

"I saw that evil was impotent ... and the only weapon of its triumph was the willingness of the good to serve it."
-John Galt, Atlas Shrugged by Ayn Rand

Georgetown, South Carolina

Jasper waited patiently in a cramped pew of the small church. There were a thousand other places he would rather be. Memories of various airports from around the world, an amusement park ride at Disney World, even the local neighborhood Starbucks, flashed through his mind to remind him of the countless hours he had spent waiting in lines. He chuckled to himself knowing that the thoughts were more a reflection of his boredom than of anything else. It didn't matter that he was waiting now, subjecting himself to this spectacle. He was here, after all, on a crusade for votes and this was yet another of the many battles he had already fought and of the many yet to come.

In his boredom, his mind wandered to reflect on the power that the federal government held today. Two hundred years ago, it was a different situation. Back then, the American population was passionate about their rights and freedoms. The average farmer knew his basic rights as a land owner and as a colonist. Therefore, the general population was much more actively involved in shaping public law and policy. Today, that responsibility was delegated to a chosen few who operated in clandestine openness in the seats of government. Sadly, the majority of people waltzed through life oblivious to the actions taken by their elected legislators, even though those actions were harmful. That was why he had left his legal practice and entered into politics. He had wanted to be one of the chosen who shaped the nation's policy instead of being one of the masses that was subjected to it.

It was a sunny October day in Georgetown, the oppressive summer humidity already forgotten. He had grown up in this town, but he seldom came back unless it was related to his political activities. A part of him missed the ambience and sense of community provided by a small town. It was in definite contrast to Washington D.C. where he spent the majority of his life these days.

The pastor's voice penetrated throughout the sanctuary forcing its way into the hearts of the congregation. The tense faces of the church members indicated his message was making its intended impact.

"Jesus died for the sins that you committed. I am talking about you individually, as well as every living human being past, present, and future. Jesus was crucified on a cross as a sacrifice for the sins that you committed yesterday, the sins you commit today, and the sins you will commit tomorrow. He gave his life because he loved you and knew that your sins had to be paid for because our holy God in Heaven detests sin and will not let anyone who has sinned enter His holy place. Jesus life was the purse. He gave it to all of us freely as a gift, a gift that we accept through repentance and belief in Him."

Jasper analyzed the pastor for a long moment. He always liked to critique public speakers and evaluate their strengths and faults as it related to audience engagement and interaction. Religious leaders, whether it was Martin Luther King, the Pope, or the pastor before him now, fascinated him. He marveled at how they could touch people at such a deep level and cause people to respond, to do things different, and to change. He knew Pastor Hank Mills was genuine. He had known him for as long as he could remember.

His father and Pastor Mills had served together in Vietnam on three consecutive tours of duty and had been the closest of friends since. When they returned, his father made the choice to remain in the military, rising to the rank of General. Hank had chosen to enroll in Christian seminary. Even so, the two families had remained close through the years.

Jasper recalled that every Thanksgiving his parents would take him to the Mills house for a day long feast. That was until the accident. Now, it had been almost twenty years since he had shared a Thanksgiving dinner with the Mills family. The brief sense of guilt he felt at that last thought quickly transformed into anger, though he wasn't sure who or what he was angry about. He always became angry when he thought about his parents and their senseless death. Maybe it was resentment that he was feeling. He did not know or care. He only knew that they shouldn't be dead.

The pastor completed his sermon and the organist began to softly play the hymn "Jesus is Calling". The pastor asked the congregation to stand, close their eyes, and bow their heads in preparation for the altar call.

Jasper didn't know why, but altar calls always made him uncomfortable. He wasn't sure if it was the event itself or the sharp words of the pastor that seemed to create a pressure on him. Either way, it didn't matter. Altar calls were not part of his upbringing as a Catholic so they were more of a spectacle to him than anything else.

The pastor was pleading now, asking those who were not eternally saved to come forth and accept the gracious gift offered by Jesus Christ. An old man in the pew in front him slowly stood to his feet and exited toward the center aisle. His footsteps were deliberate but shaky. The man proceeded down the aisle towards the pastor with cautious expectation. He was less than three feet away when he fell to his knees sobbing. The pastor was there by his side the moment his knees touched the ground, a pillar of strength with words of encouragement and praise for yet another lost soul. At that moment, with the pastor guiding him, the man professed his faith and belief in Christ as his savior.

Jasper could hear the man's muffled sobs in the lengthening silence between the pastor's last requests for more to come forward. The pastor pleaded briefly for another minute, his gaze falling directly on Jasper for a moment. Jasper held the pastors gaze, somewhat in defiance to his request, but also out of respect. God would not have any more souls this day. The pastor closed the service with a prayer then requested for everybody to remain seated. They had a special guest who would like to speak to the church. The young congressman from South Carolina took a deep breath and stood. It was now his turn to preach.

Chapter 5

Jasper stepped behind the church podium and surveyed the parishioners seated in the pews before him. They were mostly elderly couples and young families, but a few adolescent faces peered at him curiously. It was people like these parishioners who had elected him to a second term in Congress and given him the opportunity to earn his current appointment on the Congressional Judiciary Committee.

He had thought the committee position would allow him to directly shape public policy. Sadly, he soon learned that belief was just a charade. The liberal machine that had risen to take control of all three branches of the federal government had proven to be too strong. He was in the minority on the committee and as a result, his efforts served only to slow down the legislative process, not influence it. That was why he had recently decided to pursue a different course of action with his political career. It was the reason he was here today.

He opened his speech by thanking the pastor for the wonderful service, the church congregation for the opportunity to speak, and then shared a short joke that he would be brief in his speech, as he realized he was the only thing standing between the church congregation and Sunday lunch. That garnered a few chuckles from the audience.

"The majority of the population incorrectly believes that the Constitution of the United States specifically defines the separation of church and state," Jasper began. "This is because this belief has been hammered into their heads by politicians, lawyers, and activists in support of their own political agendas, not on the basis of fact. It is one of many incorrect beliefs about the Constitution that have been perpetuated over the decades. The First Amendment states that 'Congress shall make no law respecting an establishment of religion, or prohibiting the free exercise thereof.'"

Jasper knew most people were familiar with this clause, but he also recognized that most people lacked the historical knowledge of its true intention. Thomas Jefferson, the primary author of the Declaration of Independence and contributing author to the Constitution, believed the government was not to interfere with religion as religion was a matter that was solely between a man and his God. Errantly, the population began to believe government and religion should be separated, but in reality, it was meant to be inclusive. That is what the founding fathers had envisioned. A government that represented and protected the religious views of the people. He wished more people knew what he knew about the founding principles of the country. Sadly, most did not care.

He continued, "In short, our religious views should influence government, but government is not to influence religion. Never forget, this is your government, a government chosen by you, the people, for you, the people. That is why the Paysle -Thorne Act represents an important piece of defensive legislation." Jasper was extremely proud of the law he had co-sponsored with a liberal congressman from Tennessee. The legislation protected religious institutions from the federal government revoking their tax exempt status if the church were to engage in politically related activities or publically support political candidates. The fact that the public now viewed Japer as an advocate for religious freedom was the main reason he had chosen a church for this important speech.

"You have enjoyed the freedom of worship since the birth of our nation. Now, as a church, you have the freedom to influence the government by the campaigns you fund, the political issues you support and the politicians you vote into office." There was a brief round of applause from the audience. *Yes*, he thought, *he was reaching them*.

Jasper scanned the audience making eye contact with several parishioners before continuing. "Even with this legislative win behind us, several challenges face us. The purpose of our government is to establish law and justice, provide for the defense of the people, ensure domestic peace, promote the general welfare of its citizens, and above all, advocate and protect the personal liberties of the people. Today, as citizens, we can no longer trust that our government is rooted in these principles. The foundations of our country have become warped, misaligned, and are beginning to crumble. Our country is fast approaching a tipping point that could change life as we know it. Sadly, we can no longer trust that the fruit of our daily labor will be ours to enjoy. The government has decided that you are no longer working to advance yourselves; you are working to advance your fellow man. As noble as that cause is, it is fundamentally flawed and outside the original purpose of our government." He paused for brief moment. He could tell that he had the audience's full attention now.

"We have become a nation of laws, at the sacrifice of men, who are now hung on the cross of social justice," his voice rising in intensity. "My countrymen, I ask you to reflect on the issues that we face today in our nation. Our government debt is unprecedented and our nation is broke due to excessive spending to support social causes. Our manufacturing and industrial base, which was the envy of the world decades ago, is virtually nonexistent. Our borders are being overrun by illegal immigrants seeking a false dream of prosperity. They are lured to our country by liberal social programs and promises by our government to support them. Our own fellow countrymen, African Americans and Hispanics, are at war with each other throughout the country. They have been driven to racial violence by a lack of economic prosperity and a feeling that the other has taken something from them, like their job, their community or their social standing. Our situation is dire, and our federal government is the cause. Despite the efforts by those in government, who like me, seek to fight for the rights of the individual ... our government has taken us in a direction of servitude and dependence." He paused again, gauging the level of engagement of his audience. There was a hushed silence as his words sank in. His eyes found those of the pastor. Pastor Mills smiled slightly and nodded his head in approval, his face calm and poised, conveying an inner peace.

Jasper continued, "Yet, there is still hope for us and it is rooted in the foundations of our nation. A hope that our forefathers shared and ensured would be available to us today through the original design of our Constitution. You see, I believe state government represents the greatest and last defense against an oppressive federal government that has become harmful to its citizens. My hope therefore, rests in the power of our great state and in you the people who hold the power to elect our public officials. That is why today, I am announcing my candidacy to become the next governor of South Carolina. With your support, together we will defend our state, its people, and ensure that the rights of South Carolinians everywhere are no longer trampled upon! I am Jasper Thorne and I want to be your governor! I thank you for your support and for your vote."

Chapter 6

The sound of her voice sent an odd chill down his spine, leaving him with the feeling he had been caught doing something he shouldn't. He had heard her voice before, but he didn't recognize it. Jasper was still looking down at the floor, assembling his speech papers after he had dropped them when a rather portly woman from the church had hugged him a little too aggressively. "I'm sorry. What did you say?" He spoke without looking up.

"I asked you what church you attend?" the woman said again.

Yes, there was something familiar about her voice, Jasper thought. It was soft and seductive; her southern accent was evident, but not overpowering. "I don't attend chur—" his voice faded away as he rose from the floor and made eye contact with the young woman.

His first thought was that he had never encountered anyone so beautiful. She had shoulder length brown hair with shades of molten chocolate cresting the curls. Her skin reminded him of rose tinted porcelain, it looked soft and supple. She wore a white knee length summer dress, accented with a wide hot pink diagonal stripe that ran from her waist to her knee. The top of the dress was cut just a little lower than he expected to see in a church setting. Her body was petite, but she had more than ample curves and very sexy legs. Jasper stared at her quizzically for a moment. He was sure he had heard her voice before, but he had no idea from where. There was no doubt he would have remembered meeting this woman. She was gorgeous. Whatever the case, he knew in an instant that he wanted to know her better.

"You don't remember me do you? I must have really made an impression on you," she laughed. Her smile was infectious – her beautiful lips accented by soft pink lipstick and a small dimple on each side of her cheeks. She extended her hand. "Let me reintroduce myself, I'm Alexis. But you may remember me as Alex."

Jasper was at a loss for words. *No, it couldn't be.* The last time had seen Alex she had been scrambling up the trunk of the large magnolia tree in the backyard of her parent's home, disappearing into the thick coverage. That was more than twenty years ago. He was entering his freshman year in college at the Citadel and she was a rambunctious ten year old tomboy. No wonder he did not recognize her voice. It had been a very dark time in his life. He had consciously suppressed many of his memories of that time, and of the ones he still had, he did not like to think about.

"Now, where are your manners? Don't stand there speechless. You are a politician aren't you? Don't you types always have something to say?" She smiled again coyly as if she was toying with him and enjoying it.

Jasper was disappointed in himself for being caught off guard and cursed silently. He was always prepared for any situation. Things like this never happened. He looked her straight in the eyes, as he was reestablishing his composure. His next words came forcefully, as if pushed through a tight hole only to explode on the other end. "Alex! What a surprise. I would of never have guessed that was you. I mean, it has been more than twenty years. You look …" he continued to stumble over his words, much to his dismay, "… you look amazing."

"So I have been told," she responded matter-of-factly. She reached down to pick up a sheet of paper that slipped under the podium and handed it to him.

"Thank you," he said as he took the sheet from her hand. He noticed her nails were well manicured and smartly painted in a shade of hot pink. "So, what did you think?" he asked.

"Think about what?" came her cool reply. Her eyes we locked on his and they were amazing. They were deep brown, the color of polished walnut, yet they sparkled with an intensity he had not seen before. It was an intensity that seemed to challenge as much as it appeared to invite.

Jasper frowned, breaking contact with her eyes as he looked down and shook his head. He had to regain control. He was not used to being put off his game. "I was referring to my speech. But then again, you probably don't follow politics much do you?"

He could tell immediately that his words were taken as an insult since she flinched, as if stung. *Oh boy! I am really screwing this up, aren't I?* Maybe he should try a more humble approach. "Forgive me. I guess I never expected the tomboy next door to grow up to be so beautiful. I am honestly taken back. It is amazing to see you again after all this time."

He could tell his words had smoothed over the unintentional insult as a slight smile returned to her face. They shared an awkward pause in their conversation before Alexis spoke, a playful tone in her voice. "You have obviously done well for yourself over the years, Congressman. And yes, I do follow politics. In fact, I have been keeping a close eye on you ever since you entered the congressional race four years ago. I will have you know that I did not vote for you for your first term, because at the time, it was not clear to me as to what your guiding principles were. I did vote for you in the last election, after you established your voting record. But I am curious, why a man who does not belong to a church would fight for the rights of religion, considering it could paint you as fundamentalist."

Jasper was intrigued by her question. "It is what our founders would have done to correct an errant belief of our government. The founders knew that the presiding belief of the population was that God existed. Many of the founders were professed Christians. That is why Congress created an office of the Chaplain and each congressional session since the Continental Congress has opened with a formal prayer. Belief in God is also the reason that the Declaration of Independence contains five references to God — as the Creator, the supreme lawmaker, the source of all our rights, the supreme judge, and our protector."

Alexis nodded, smiling slightly. Jasper hoped he wasn't coming across too strong. He continued, "The separation of church and state, as we perceive it today, did not exist back then. Not only do the historical documents support this assertion, but the structure of the government tells us it was so. Sadly, today we cannot have religion and government in the same sentence. To me it is just another area where federalism is running rampart and must be stopped."

In-between interruptions from church members expressing their appreciation of his efforts in Congress or offering a word of advice on upcoming legislative issues, Jasper and Alexis talked for another fifteen minutes. Reluctantly, Jasper ended the conversation. "I have really enjoyed our conversation. You are really something. I don't think I have met anyone like you," his tone was sincere.

"Surely you jest, Congressman. I bet you have plenty of lovely ladies to keep you company." she bantered, her comment a statement more than a question.

Jasper was silent and continued smiling. *Why did he feel so comfortable with this woman?* "I look forward to seeing you again," he finally said. "I will have to contact your father and thank him. When I do I will be sure to ask him for your number."

"What makes you think I want him to give it to you?" she teased.

He smiled his best smile, "Because I always get what I want. I'll see you soon."

Alexis watched the congressman as he got into a black sedan and proceeded to drive out of the church parking lot. He waved to her as he passed by and her stomach leaped in anticipation for the first time in many years. She knew she was smitten with the young congressman, but only a little. She also couldn't deny that she was attracted to him. She shook her head and refocused, after all, thoughts like that would only get her in trouble. A hand gently touched her shoulder and she turned to see her father standing there.

"He has grown up to be quite an impressive man, hasn't he?" Pastor Mills smiled a broad grin that filled half of his face. "Well at the very least, he is very handsome."

Alexis blushed, embarrassed at being caught in a weak moment. Her father must have been standing there behind her long enough to know that she had been watching the congressman intently. "Oh Daddy, don't be silly. It was good to see him again. The last time we saw each other; we were basically kids with big ambitions." She laughed nervously and looking her father directly in the eyes, she asked. "Why did you invite Jasper to speak at our church?"

"Come, walk with me." The pastor took her hand and led her down the stairs to a sidewalk that led to the church playground. "I asked Jasper to speak at the church, because the Lord led me in that direction. You see, even though we haven't seen each other for several years, I have been keeping my eye on him. A long time ago, I made a promise to his parents to be his Godfather. The fact that they passed away shortly before his first year in college and he was already an adult meant that my obligation to him was limited. Even so, I approached my involvement as a commitment made before God, no different than I would my marriage. The relationship has been very much one way these past years, but I have kept my eye on him so that I could help him if needed. That being said, I have had very little direct contact with him except for an occasional Christmas card over the years.

Alexis shook her head. "I never knew that about you and Jasper. So tell me why you asked him to come here."

"It really was a simple choice," the pastor replied. "After my prayer time a few weeks ago, I was under conviction to contact him. When we connected, I had a long conversation with him about his beliefs about this country, the world, and the role of religion. I learned that I agree with him on most things, but more importantly, I became convinced that he was the type of individual that we needed in our government. He has a passion and a spirit that is lacking from our politicians today."

They stopped by an empty park bench and sat down pausing for a moment to watch a young boy chase another boy around the jungle gym. Two women chatted on a nearby bench while keeping any eye on the pursuit. "More importantly," the pastor continued, "Jasper has a solid understanding of our Constitution, the role of government and personal responsibility. When he asked if he could speak at our church, I figured that it would be a good opportunity for us to rekindle a relationship as well as influence some minds. I had no idea he was going to announce his candidacy for governor. I was caught off guard just like the rest of us." He searched his daughter's eyes. "What did you think of him?"

Alexis put her face in her hands, embarrassed. She had tears running down her cheeks. *What was wrong with her? Why was she uncharacteristically out of control?* She thought. Pastor Mills placed his arm around her, concern evident on his face, his voice was calm and reassuring, "Sweetheart, what is it?"

She turned and looked at him. She could see the love her father had for her, evident in his eyes. "Oh Daddy ... after all these years ... I don't know why ... but I think he is the one."

Pastor Mills embraced Alexis for a long time with a reassuring hug that only a father could provide. As he hugged her, he looked up at the bright blue sky above him, a slight smile forming on his face.

Chapter 7

Washington, District of Columbia

The door leading into the conference room was partially opened. Jasper tried not to notice the peeling brown paint that speckled the door, creating a patchwork of brown and grey. He was continually amazed that the facility was not kept in better shape and repairs were not addressed in a timely manner. The Capitol maintenance staff was large, well paid, and lazy. If it were in his power, he would fire every one of them simply for incompetence. Of course he knew that would never happen for many reasons, not only because he would never be in such a position, but because the Union and its labor laws were too strong. He shook his head in frustration.

Through the door, Jasper could hear a muffled voice from inside the room. He listened for a minute before entering. "Father, please forgive us. Please forgive all of us. We need you now more than ever. This country needs your mighty presence again. We need your people to rise up and to glorify you. We need you to be our purpose once again. We need your wisdom, your discernment, your leadership. Please Father ... please..." the voice trailed off into silence.

Even though he was more than thirty minutes late for this meeting, he waited for another minute before knocking and walking slowly into the room. Michael Matthews, the sole occupant in the room, was sitting at a rectangular, wooden table, intently scribbling notes on a pad of paper. A worn leather Bible lay open next to the pad, marked by a highlighter, scribbles, and an occasional coffee stain. Michael looked up when Jasper entered the room, fresh tears were running down his cheeks.

It was hard not to smile when you looked at Michael Matthews. He was a small, thinly built man with pale skin and bright blue eyes. In his late seventies, he still fashioned a full head of curly white hair, and that was what made Jasper smile. Michael's hair looked like a mushroom top and it would move animatedly whenever he talked or walked. It had earned him the affectionate term of endearment of "old slinky head" from his peers.

People never spoke ill of Michael Matthews. He was one of the most well-known, respected and connected people in South Carolina state politics. It had been a simple phone call from Michael that had solidified his meeting with Whitaker Stanley. Whitaker was a major potential donor to Jasper's campaign, but his endorsement was even more important. The ability to access high-level, influential people like Whitaker Stanley made Michael an asset not to be taken lightly, nor to be abused.

Michael had been his Chief of Staff for less than a month, but he had already proven himself more than capable. Jasper's prior Chief of Staff was capable, but lacked specific experience in the area he now needed most, running a campaign for governor. Michael was seasoned and he was widely regarded as one of the best in the industry. Over his career, he had orchestrated the successful campaigns of seven prior governors. If Michael had a down side, it was his religious zeal.

As an ordained Southern Baptist pastor, Michael took every opportunity to share his faith. Michael had even made religious activities a requirement for his position as Chief of Staff. Even so, Jasper knew he was fortunate to have a man of this caliber leading his campaign, even if it meant having to deal with a person who spent more time on his knees than he did in a desk chair.

Jasper thought back to the meeting three months ago to negotiate the terms of bringing Michael on his staff. Michael had asked him a personal question that had taken him by surprise, "Do you know the Lord?"

"What do you mean?" Jasper's response had been reactive and defensive. But he quickly recovered by asking, "How is that relevant to our discussion about you working for me."

"It is very relevant. You see, I have a belief that the nature of man is flawed. His heart, his very being, his very essence, is tainted with sin and the desire to sin. Therefore, a man is only as good as the principles he stands on, be they moral or ethical. Furthermore, a man's ability to lead others is directly related to his conviction to those same principles. To state it differently, a leader who lacks conviction cannot effectively lead, since he will fail when circumstances are dire and he abandons his principles." Michael pulled a worn pocket Bible from his jacket and waved it at Jasper. "My personal experience over these many years has led me to the conclusion that people who have gained a true understanding of God, His attributes, and His principles are better equipped to lead."

Jasper shook his head affirmatively, not sure where this discussion was heading, but intrigued by it just the same.

"The leadership of our country has taken progressive steps over the last several decades to minimize the role of God and religion in our society. Our government no longer values biblical guidance. We sneer at prayer in any form. We have become a nation that is no longer dependent on God, but on man alone. A nation that is dependent on itself alone is doomed to fail. I believe you are much like this world, yet I also see potential in you to learn and grow. One day, you will understand and embrace the importance of divine counsel and include it in your decision process as a leader. It is my hope that I will be able to help you truly know the Lord. For this reason, I will agree to become your campaign manager and current Chief of Staff. However ..." He paused briefly, "I have one condition that must be fulfilled."

"You have my full attention. What is your condition?" Jasper asked curiously.

"It is simply this one thing. You agree to meet with me once a month for a bible study until the election is complete." At the time, Jasper had thought it was an odd request, but he agreed to it. What harm could bible lessons create? After all, it was more important to have Michael as his campaign manager than anything else. Jasper had agreed to the terms, and now, it was finally time for his first lesson.

"I apologize for being late. Is everything ok?" Jasper asked.

Michael sat back in his chair and removed his glasses, pulling out a purple handkerchief from his pocket at the same time. He began to dab his eyes softly. "Yes. Everything is fine.

There are tough waters to navigate ahead of us and these past few months, I have been seeking the Lord for guidance on what to do. I am not sure I like the answer he is leading me to."

Jasper looked at Michael for a moment, an odd expression in his face. "If you say so — you're not going to start playing with snakes and convulsing or anything like that are you?"

Michael's laugh echoed through the small room. His white curls dancing on his head in response to the melodic sound. "That was funny, very funny, indeed," his voice softened. "But we have something important to discuss today." Michael's expression turned serious, "Please take a seat, Jasper. This will be a short lesson. Did you bring a Bible?" Michael's tone had also taken on a serious edge, but it was also familiar to Jasper. It reminded him how his father would speak to him when he had important parental wisdom to impart, like the time he received his first speeding ticket. Jasper's father had not been angry with him, but wanted him to understand the consequences of his actions and the potential dangers.

Jasper took a seat at the table directly across from Michael. From this perspective, Michel appeared more stately and wise. "No, I did not know I was supposed to bring a Bible. How about we use the one in front of you?" He responded curtly, slightly embarrassed at being unprepared. He hated being caught unprepared.

Michael did not react, almost as if he had been expecting that answer. "First lesson … you are not going to learn anything until you start to read the Bible. Everything you need to know is in this book. Second lesson, always bring your own Bible to a Bible study. That one should be obvious."

"I will be prepared next time." Jasper responded more politely. "I really was not sure what to expect from this meeting. It would help me to understand what we plan to do."

Michael set back in his chair and crossed his arms, studying Jasper for a moment. When he spoke, his voice had assumed a softer tone. "We are here to learn about God by reading about Him and studying His teachings. The Bible is not a collection of stories. There is tremendous personal insight and wisdom to be gained through the Bible that can be applied to daily life. Each time we meet, we will learn about a different topic and how it is relevant to your life. Today's topic should prove very insightful to you, if you are open to learn what the Bible has to teach you."

"Ok. Let's get started," Jasper responded.

Michael adjusted his glasses back on to his long, angular nose. "I will open the lesson with a simple question. I know you were raised Catholic. So what makes a person a Catholic versus a Baptist or a Lutheran or any other type of Christian religion?"

"I guess it is the doctrine I have been taught, along with the rituals and the teachings," Jasper responded, curious where this discussion was leading.

"Who says those doctrines that you believe are true?" Michael raised one of his eyebrows in a high arch as to punctuate the question.

Jasper shrugged. "I don't know. I assume they are valid because they are based on traditions that have been used for centuries. The traditions are part of my upbringing so I grew up accepting that was the way things were done."

"That is a good answer. Tradition is a key component of what I like to call the Structure. Structure can further be defined as the beliefs, practices, teachings and perspectives that a person prescribes to as part of their religion. It is synonymous with legalism or religiousness. Understanding the Structure is what our lesson is about today. Michael paused and took a deep breath as if to emphasis his next point. "Structure is pervasive in churches across our land today, and it is a path to destruction. You must be careful not to fall prey to the Structure. Let me show you what I mean …"

Chapter 8

"We have seen the technique of the 'Big Lie,' elsewhere employed by the totalitarian dictator with devastating success, utilized here for the first time on a sustained basis in our history ... We have seen the character of private citizens and of Government employees virtually destroyed by public condemnation on the basis of gossip, distortion, hearsay, and deliberate untruths ... The spectacle is one we would expect in a totalitarian nation where the rights of the individual are crushed beneath the juggernaut of statism and oppression; it has no place in America where government exists to serve our people, not destroy them."

-The Tydings Committee Report on McCarthy's Charges (1950).

The news ticker scrolled across the television screen, bright yellow words against a stark red background. "Yankees manager gives up $2 million salary because of fans." Aaron Mandon, the junior senator from New York, picked up the remote control and turned up the volume. The screen displayed a headshot of the manager of the New York Yankees baseball team; this year's champion of the American League. The Yankees had been favored to win the World Series since the beginning of the season and had been hailed as the best team since the 1950's World Series champions. That was until last night when they lost the seventh and final game of the World Series to the Los Angeles Dodgers.

The series had been extremely competitive, with both teams winning three games each. The seventh and final game was to be the tie breaker of all tie breakers. Only, the Yankees had been out played by the visiting Dodgers, resulting in a crushing loss made worse by the fact that it occurred on their home turf. Many of the fans, humiliated by the loss and anxious to vent their anger, took to the streets of the Bronx and began to riot.

The TV switched scenes to a video taken during the climax of the riot where fire and dark black smoke engulfed several store fronts. Police in riot gear carrying plastic shields were locked in side by side formation where they were slowly closing in on an unruly group of fans that were pelting them with stones, bricks, and the occasional baseball. Multiple storefronts in the newly renovated Fordham Road shopping district were vandalized, and several buildings had been damaged by fire before the police could restore order. More than one hundred people had been injured in altercations with the mobbing crowd.

Property damage and injuries would of been worse had it not been for the members of Local 45 Pipefitters Guild. They had been enjoying the game at their union office located down the street from where the riot had begun. When they had realized what was happening, the members formed a human chain across the street. Brandishing two foot pipe wrenches and other tools of their trade, they were a formidable enough blockade to deter the progress of the riot. National news coverage touted the action of the union members as one of the most heroic events by any organization in history.

The news returned to the pre-recorded interview that had occurred only an hour earlier. The manager of the New York Yankees was seated at a small table surrounded by several of the players dressed in uniform. Most of the players had their hands resting on his shoulders, and many were wiping tears from their eyes. A flurry of questions were being tossed at the manager from a large group of press crowded in front of the table.

Aaron turned the flat screen television off and turned towards the distinguished, older gentleman seated at a grand teakwood desk on the opposite side of the office suite. "Can you believe this guy? What an idiot! Why give up a salary like that because of a few fans that drank too much and got caught up in the moment?" He ranted. "What did he expect to happen when you lose the World Series? You wonder where people's motivations really lie these days."

"Did you see the damage caused by those rioters? They really tore up the Bronx. I have been fielding calls all morning on how the state is going to pay for it. The city is broke and refusing to offer anything." Aaron walked towards the desk and took a seat in a plush leather chair. "In the end, it's an insurance matter.

Neither the city nor the state can be responsible for what its citizens do. Luckily, those union members were there to quell the carnage." Aaron's ranting continued, "This will bode very well for the image of unions across the country. Very patriotic! By the way, I meant to ask you earlier, were any of our guys involved?"

Mason Kelly ignored the younger man's question on purpose, pretending to not have heard. He slowly finished reviewing his speech for the upcoming donors' reception and folded it into the breast pocket of his hand-tailored suit. Mason took a moment to rub the lapel of his jacket, enjoying the feel of the fine merino wool as it slid between his fingers. He had learned early on in his career that the best dressed person in the room usually commanded the most respect.

Respect from others had been something he coveted from his youth. Back then, respect had been a lot more difficult to come by. His friends had given him the nick name Runt, owing to his short height and rather small build. However, what he lacked in stature, he made up for in gumption, tenacity, and intelligence. People learned quickly not to cross Mason Kelley. To do so was not advantageous to one's personal health.

Mason studied the man standing across the room thinking about his question. Of course he had people involved. Riots do not start without instigators and he employed the best in the business. But that was only half of the equation, and he would never tell Aaron the entire truth. With only two years of experience as a U.S. senator, Aaron was too naive to understand the nuisances of political warfare and could not be fully trusted.

Mason knew that it was difficult to keep secrets in the halls of Congress, unless one held the leverage to make sure those secrets remained hidden. Fortunately, he had more than a quarter of a century of senate experience to perfect his craft and had been privileged to be mentored by some of the brightest and best teachers that had ever held governmental office. Teachers, who had planted, crafted, and harvested the seeds of past political events such as the McCarthyism movement, civil rights, the Vietnam War, and Watergate. The country was but a stage and its people mere puppets. What was needed was only the precise instruction of a director, pulling the proper strings to create the desired result. His experience had prepared him masterfully for his current role as Secretary of Labor Equalization.

Mason's phone chimed indicating an incoming text message. He glanced at the phone and chuckled. It was a message from Ron Stanley, Business Manager for Local 45 Pipefitters Guild. *Yes*, Mason thought, *the riot had succeeded in creating the intended outcome*.

"What is so funny?" Aaron asked.

Mason rose from his desk and approached Aaron, throwing his arm around his neck and giving Aaron a solid pat on the back as he ushered him towards the door. "Reality, my boy! Our perception of reality and how easy it is to control it. Now, let's go raise some money."

Chapter 9

"I believe that this nation is the last hope of Western civilization and if this oasis of the world shall be overrun, perverted, contaminated, or destroyed, then the last flickering light of humanity will be extinguished. I take no issue with those who would praise the contributions which have been made to our society by people of many races, of varied creeds and colors. America is indeed a joining together of many streams which go to form a mighty river which we call the American way. However, we have in the United States today hard-core, indigestible blocs which have not become integrated into the American way of life, but which, on the contrary are its deadly enemies. Today, as never before, untold millions are storming our gates for admission and those gates are cracking under the strain. The solution of the problems of Europe and Asia will not come through the transplanting of these problems en masse to the United States ... I do not intend to become prophetic, but if the enemies of this legislation succeed in riddling it to pieces, or in amending it beyond recognition, they will have contributed more to promote this nation's downfall than any other group since we achieved our independence as a nation."

-Senator Pat McCarran, sponsor of the Immigration and Nationality Act of 1952

Del Rio, Texas

By public consensus, "The Wall" is considered the greatest construction project of modern history. The twin barriers are separated by a twenty-five yard paved cement corridor. Together they spanned seven thousand miles of river bed, mountain top, and countryside along the Texas state border. Each wall has a minimum height of twenty-four feet and a minimum width of twelve feet. Constructed of steel reinforced concrete, the exterior wall has no breaks, gaps, or entrances. Entry is gained only through sealed access tunnels from the interior wall. The interior wall is also without gaps or breaks, though entrance ways exist on the inward facing side, away from the border. The predominant feature of the inside wall are the cubicle watch towers speckled every two hundred and fifty yards along the ridge of the wall. The deep black mirrored glass windows of each tower makes it impossible to see if anyone is inside, at the same time providing someone inside with unobstructed views of the exterior wall and the internal concrete corridor.

Both walls are peppered with closed circuit security cameras providing a complete view of the entire border that is scanned in real-time with the aid of several computer servers utilizing motion detection software. If movement is detected in any section of the border, the system will analyze the area, assess the movement, and identify any threats. Animals, sand storms, and movement caused by other natural events are ignored. Only when human motion or uniform movements are detected, such as caused by a car driving across the path of the camera, will the system alarm and send a live feed to a central command center where it will instantly be reviewed by Texas law enforcement officials. Since the system became operational, it has detected an average of eight hundred situations per day in which people attempted to cross the border, only to be repelled by the Wall and its sophisticated monitoring system.

Governor Doug Whorter surveyed the damage to the exterior wall with a disapproving scowl on his face. He turned to the state trooper who had been in charge of the command center at the time of the explosion and let out an exhaustive sigh. "This looks really bad. We are lucky there were no injuries." He paused to survey the structure again.

A fifty foot section of the outer wall lay in a mass of tangled steel and concrete rubble. The facing side of the interior wall was still intact, but barely. A darkened blast crater spiraled out from the location of the blast, extending over thirty yards into the neutral zone towards Mexico. Whatever type of explosives had been used, they were extremely powerful.

The governor returned his attention to the trooper, "Tell me what you know?"

The trooper pointed over the horizon toward a section of rocky foothills west of their location. "In that direction, we detected movement on the border shortly after sunset yesterday. Surveillance cameras picked up an individual carrying a large backpack walking towards the wall. Typically, this does not create much of an alarm situation on our end, because we encounter people along the wall all the time seeking a way to get through. But this individual approached the wall, removed his pack, and waited for about ten minutes. Then he walked away and headed back across the neutral zone." The trooper lowered the brim of his hat, "Five minutes later, the explosion happened. We are interviewing one of the maintenance crew who was in that vicinity only minutes before the explosion. Apparently, there had been an electrical failure and he had been dispatched to check it out. It was only luck that both he and the patrol sentry assigned to this sector were not in that section of the outer wall when the explosion occurred."

"Not luck, it was God's blessing," the governor responded, his steel blue eyes fixed on the trooper. "What happened next?"

"Sir, that is the strangest thing--nothing happened. I mean, nothing more from the zone. On our end, we initiated full lock down of the facility and assumed defensive positions in anticipation of further attacks."

"So no one attempted to cross into the border?" Whorter asked perplexed.

The trooper shook his head, "First responders were dispatched along with patrol personnel, to contain the breech and assess the damage, but it was twenty minutes before they arrived due to the remote location of the incident. Oddly, there was not a hint of activity from the border zone. The whole situation has me a little unnerved." The trooper adjusted his wide brimmed hat again and placed his hands on his hips, one resting comfortably on his pistol. "Why would somebody detonate explosives that only partially destroy the Wall and then disappear?"

"*Why* is a good question but the better question is *who?*" the governor responded. "This was not the work of a typical immigrant trying to gain access to our country. No, it was someone else. Someone who I fear has a much more malicious intent in mind. There are a lot of people in this country who do not like what this wall represents."

Authorized by a majority vote of the state congress, the construction of the Wall became an instant lightning rod of political controversy. In short order, Attorney General of the United States had sued the state of Texas, citing the power to enforce the borders was retained by the federal government. When the suit was upheld by the Supreme Court, Texas simply moved the construction of the Wall inland three miles from the border. A multi-decade project, it costs the state billions of dollars to complete, but it had achieved its purpose. To stem the tide of illegal immigrants into the state and increase the safety of its citizens. Whorter knew it had also achieved an unintended purpose. It had become a symbol of hope for millions of Americans who still believed in the founding principles of the country. A proverbial finger of concrete and steel aimed in defiance directly at the federal government.

After surveying the damage for a few more minutes, Whorter headed back to the helicopter that would take him back to his office in Austin. Terrorism acts like this would require a detailed investigation at both a state and federal level and he needed to begin coordinating efforts immediately. As the helicopter lifted, he took one more look at the large fissure in the Wall. The trooper's comments replayed through his mind. "Nothing more from the border zone." *Perhaps the trooper was asking the right question after all,* he thought. *Why would someone expend the effort to destroy a section of the Wall in such a remote area?* The lack of an answer to that question worried him. The attack was deliberate and that meant it had a purpose. Only for what purpose, and to what end, he was not sure.

He settled back into his seat for the flight back to the airport. There was not much else for him to do at the moment but to think about that question and to pray that they found an answer soon, before it happened again. Whatever was going on was not good. Not good at all.

Chapter 10

Georgetown, South Carolina

Alexis Mills strolled into the park, a large wicker picnic basket in one hand and a tightly rolled pink blanket held in the other. Her gait was measured and smooth, despite the high heels she wore that clicked sharply against the smooth concrete pathway. The weather was cool today; perhaps a sign that fall was beginning to lose ground to winter in the race of the seasons. She wore tight-fitting dark jeans that accented her long legs and a white cashmere sweater jacket pulled over a soft pink blouse. Her long brown hair was tied into a pony tail with a bright, pink bow. She knew she looked good, but she wondered what Jasper would think.

She quickly spotted him, seated under the shade of a large palm tree on a rustic wooden park bench. He was dressed in a casual navy sport coat, gray designer T-shirt and white linen khakis with closed sandals. *Very handsome*, she thought to herself, he was a little overdressed for a picnic, but she would manage that later.

The bench he was sitting on had seen better days, weathered by the moist and salty sea air that constantly blew in from the beach, only yards away. He began to rise as she walked towards him, only his pants snagged on the splintered wood causing him to have to twist his hips awkwardly to free himself. She laughed to herself. Her mother always told her that boys would always be boys, not matter how old they got. She walked right by him without a glance of concern. "Shame, Shame. Those are nice pants you're wearing. Come on this way. That is why I have this," slightly elevating her arm that couched the pink blanket. "I know the perfect spot where we can enjoy the beach in the shade and not have to worry about splinters, or ruining a pair of pants."

He did not say anything but followed her towards the beach. She led him to her favorite spot. Actually, it was her mother's favorite spot on the beach, but she had adopted it as her own. A large Magnolia tree sprouted majestically from the thin sandy soil. On one side, the tree crown expanded to cover a section of the cool green Bermuda grass, while on the other, the crown covered a section of the white sandy beach. In both cases, there was plenty of shade provided by the thick foliage and an amazing view of the water just yards away.

"I have not been to this place in years, not since the accident anyway. How did you remember it?" He opened the conversation as he assisted her with spreading the blanket below a large limb of the tree.

She liked his voice. It was deep, full, and offered a subtle accent that conveyed southern charm without pretentiousness. Having spent the last five years in Washington D.C. interacting with people from all over the country, she had become adept at identifying the origin of a person based on their accent. At the same time, she had become expert at controlling her own southern accent, learning to utilize it in a manner that would create her desired impact on those she spoke with, particularly judges and juries. At this moment, she wanted him to hear the charm of her natural voice.

"My family still comes here occasionally. Not as much anymore since Mom became ill and I moved to Washington," she replied, straightening a wrinkle in the blanket. "Dad really likes the view of the ocean. He would sit for hours under this tree writing his sermons. My mother always liked it because she could be in the shade of this tree and still feel the sea spray on her face. As for me, it has always been a place that reminds me of simpler times," she paused reflecting on a distant memory. "I remember coming here with you and your parents on many occasions. I would always be climbing this tree, or trying to catch a seagull, or doing something less than ladylike. I was such the tomboy." She noticed Jasper smile at her comment.

She gracefully unpacked the picnic basket and set out a large tray with an assortment of cheeses, grapes, cherries, crackers and a small tub of pimento cheese. "Go ahead and make yourself comfortable. I will be finished with this in a minute.

Please tell me that you're not one of those guys that need to be told everything to do," she prodded jokingly.

Jasper laughed in response, quickly kicking off his sandals and spreading himself on the blanket. He gazed out at the deep blue water and expansive beach line. "I had forgotten how beautiful this place is. I'm glad that you suggested it. This is a much better idea than coffee."

She turned to him and smiled. She really was glad he had called her to ask if they could spend some time together during his next campaign visit. "I will leave the governing of this country to you, if you leave the entertaining to me," she had told him.

Alexis could tell by his occasional glances at the wicker basket that Jasper was wondering what else she had brought. A southern woman was expected to be prepared for any circumstance. Not only was entertaining part of the culture of the South, it was a way of life. She had not had much time to entertain people with the demands of her job but loved when the opportunity presented itself.

Recently, her social life had been limited to the occasional outing with close friends, either dinner or a happy hour in the city. Dating was also infrequent, primarily by her choice alone. She was asked out nearly every day by random people she passed on the street or met in a store, but she would politely decline. The nation's capital was full of young, ambitious men who had their hearts set on conquering the world. It was also full of young men who were content to live off the efforts of others, who lacked self-discipline and achievement and believed in ideals of humanity without the understanding of what those ideals would require. For them, each day was a party without consequence and tomorrow would be dealt with when it became today. She had dated men from both spectrums and had found them all lacking. She was not exactly sure what it was they were lacking, only she knew they did not measure up to her standard. She had begun to think that no man ever would.

She looked up when she was finished setting out the spread and Jasper was staring at her intensely, his hazel eyes searching hers. "Is something wrong? Haven't you seen pimento cheese?" she joked trying to mask her uneasiness. Joking was the way she always handled situations where she felt a lack of control.

He shook his head, "No. I'm just trying to reconcile old memories of you as a tomgirl with the woman you have become. Beautiful does not began to describe you."

"For that, you are getting an extra serving of pimento cheese," she said, pretending to dig through the picnic basket again so he could not see she was blushing.

"Would you do me a favor and open this?" She said, hoping to take his focus off her. She tossed him a bottle of champagne which he caught easily with one hand.

"Nice," he smirked. "Are you sure that you want to be shaking this up?"

In a few quick seconds, the cork exploded from the bottle with a boom. Alexis gave a cry of delight in response. "I do so love a good bottle of bubbles," she gushed. In short order, she produced two crystal champagne glasses and laid them on the tray.

He filled each of the glasses and gave her one. As he held his own glass upward in the air, his eyes settled on hers for a brief moment. "A toast to the tomboy who went up this very tree so many years ago, and to the amazing woman she has become," he said cheerfully. They clinked glasses and took a long sip, staring in silence at the waves breaking on the shoreline.

Alexis turned to him, anxious to fill the silence, "Jasper is such an unusual name, even in the south. Is that a family name?" He smiled but did not immediately respond. He kept his gaze on the ocean, but she could tell he was reflecting on her question.

"Your question made me think of my parents," he responded softly, the smile returning to his face for a moment. "I miss them very much."

"I understand. I can't imagine what that was like to lose them when you were so young," she offered, placing her hand softly on his arm.

Jasper shrugged, "That was a long time ago." He took a long sip of his champagne. "Anyway, I was named after Sergeant

William Jasper, a Revolutionary war hero from the Second South Carolina Regiment of the Continental Army. As a boy, my father told me stories of the sergeant's heroics countless times but my favorite story was perhaps his most famous accomplishment." Alexis leaned in towards him, eager to hear his story.

Jasper continued, "During a ten hour siege on Fort Moultrie, the sergeant played a critical role in helping to repel the British from taking the port of Charleston. He risked his life to recover the South Carolina flag that had fallen from its staff and landed outside the fort. He recovered the flag, tied the flag to a staff and held it on the parapet of the fort to rally the colonists. He did this while British ships continued to bombard Fort Moultrie with canon and gun fire. My father always told me that Sergeant Jasper was a perfect example of courageous, patriotic, and inspirational people who built this country." Jasper looked at Alexis, his eyes searching hers, "Have you ever heard of him?"

She nodded affirmatively. "Yes. There is a statue in his honor in one of the squares in Savannah."

"I'm impressed," Jasper said approvingly, "I don't meet many people who know who he is, let alone know that he has a statue in Savannah."

Alexis could tell that he was genuinely impressed with her comment by the way he was staring at her. It was difficult for her not to blush under his intense gaze. "The statue is a reminder that he gave his life in defending Savannah from British invasion during the Siege of Savannah," she offered.

Jasper nodded in agreement. "Yes it is. Have you spent much time in Savannah?" he asked.

"Not enough. I love that city," she said. "Don't get me wrong, Charleston will always be my favorite city, but it can be a little proper for me. Savannah is like Charleston's naughty little sister who dresses up during the day, but parties all night. There is just something so seductive about Savannah."

Jasper grinned, "I have never heard Savannah described that way, but I have to agree with you. It has a unique feel for sure — there is no place like it in the world."

"Yes, that is true. I love to wander through the squares of that city," she said. "I could spend days walking the tree lined streets looking at the beautiful architecture. Something about Savannah resonates with me in a way I can't fully describe." Alexis paused for a moment and scanned the ocean as she took a deep breath, enjoying the smell of the salty air. She turned back to Jasper, "It's funny, but I have always imagined I would be married in one of the town squares." She suddenly giggled, "Oh! How improper of me to be talking about marriage on our first date! What kind of southern lady am I?" Alexis patted Jasper's hand softly. "Please forgive me," she teased, giving him a seductive smile.

He smiled back but did not say anything. He stared at her keenly as if he were trying to determine if she could be trusted. "So tell me, Ms. Mills. How did you end up in Washington D.C. working for a law firm?"

Chapter 11

His question caught her off guard. Alexis closed the lid to the picnic basket and moved closer to Jasper on the blanket. She picked up a cherry and delicately pulled it from the stem with her lips. A few seconds later, she spat the pit from her mouth, sending it flying ten yards into the air. "Score!" she yelled, throwing her had up in the air.

Jasper emitted a long, bellowing laugh, shaking his head at her in wonder. "So, you have not lost it have you? I remember when you used to challenge me to see who could spit the pit the farthest. I never was able to win." He ate a cherry himself, and then spit the pit in the same direction that she had launched hers.

Alexis chuckled to herself; it was obvious that his cherry pit fell far shorter than where hers had landed. "Nope, and you never will," she chided. "Now back to your question. We're not really a law firm. We are really a ministry that happens to provide legal representation to our clients as our service."

Alexis proceeded to tell him about how she found herself working for CLDA, known formally as the Christian Legal Defense Association. Her story began with her enrollment in the University of South Carolina because in-state tuition was the only tuition her family could afford. She told him how fortunate she was to find an internship at a local law firm where she worked twenty hours a week to help pay tuition costs. She had double majored in computer science and American history and had been an active member of the Tri-Delta sorority, serving as the chapter president in her senior year. He listened quietly, not interrupting. She felt comfortable talking to him, as if he was an old friend she had not seen in a long time, which was not too far from the truth. After graduating from a prominent Christian law school, she had returned home to Georgetown to take care of her mother. She had only been home a few weeks when she received a call from CLDA. The ministry wanted her to interview for a position at their headquarters located in Washington, D.C.

"The CLDA was founded in the seventies and has provided legal counsel in some of the most politically and religiously influential cases in recent history. If Christian beliefs have been violated or plainly ignored, the CLDA has been there as a stoic defender of the faith. Do you remember about ten years ago, a case where a private company was sued by an employee for having a display of the Ten Commandments posted in their lobby?"

He nodded his head, "I recall it went to the Supreme Court and they ruled in favor of the employee."

"Yes. My organization provided the legal representation for the business owner in that case."

"That must be really interesting work. What is it you do for them?"

"I have been a special defense attorney with CLDA for over four years," Alexis said as she helped herself to a cracker loaded with Pimento cheese.

"Special? How so?" Jasper asked.

"I specialize in cases that specifically deal with constitutional law. Lord knows the U.S. Constitution has been under attack for decades and in many situations, circumvented by our government. I know you see it … or at least I think you see it, based on your speech in church the other day," she probed. "What our founding fathers designed is ageless — it is unique in all of history. More importantly, our Constitution was crafted by a majority of men who held Christian beliefs and a high reverence for God. Did you know both the Declaration of Independence and the Articles of Confederation ended with specific references to God?" she stated proudly. "In the former, the founders used the statement, 'And for the support of this Declaration, with a firm Reliance on the Protection of divine Providence, we mutually pledge to each other our Lives, our Fortunes, and our Sacred Honor.' In the latter, the founders refer to God as —"

"The Great Governor of World," Jasper interrupted. "I have to imagine every day is a challenge for you and those you work with. You really have a tough job these days, not only defending the Constitution, but defending your faith."

"It is a tough job, but not a tough mission. It is my passion for what I am doing that keeps me motivated, even though it is an uphill battle. I just wish I did not have a battle on my hands at home as well," she sighed.

Jasper frowned. "Your father mentioned that your mother has been ill. I do not mean to pry, but how is she?"

"She is as good as can be expected. Her health had deteriorated greatly of late." She took another long sip of her champagne as if bracing for the discussion. "That is the reason I have been here in Georgetown for the past several weeks. I took a sabbatical from work so I could take care of my mother. You remember how my mother was — she was the outgoing one, so vivacious, so full of energy and always engaged with helping people. Always the tireless advocate for those in need in our church and our community ... she has touched so many lives." Alexis felt the tears welling up in her eyes as she thought of her mother. It was so sad what was happening to her.

"Five years ago, she was diagnosed with early stage Alzheimer's. Since then, her condition has become progressively worse. It is so sad to watch her become just a fragile shell of the woman she once was. When she was first diagnosed, I wanted to stay in Georgetown and take care of her, but Daddy was adamant that I go to D.C. and pursue my career. He felt strongly that I was needed to champion our rights and the beliefs of Christians in our country. We are fortunate that my father has had plenty of help caring for my mother from the church community."

"I am so sorry to hear that," Jasper said, a deep frown forming on his face. He remembered Alexis' mother as being a very kind and generous woman. "Is she currently taking medication?" Jasper asked. "I recall a congressional presentation a few years ago on a drug that was in clinical trials that was very promising in slowing the effects of Alzheimer's."

"You must mean Roxburin. My mother was on the waiting list to participate in second stage trials for that drug. Only it never happened." Her face tensed as she remembered the pain she felt upon learning that her hope for a treatment had been dashed. "Shortly after she was diagnosed, Congress passed the Medical Fair Pricing Act and the manufacturer ceased further research and development efforts."

"That situation was not unusual," Jasper offered sincerely. "More than half of the companies in the pharmaceutical industry went out of business, abandoning many promising medications and impacting countless sick people. But, I don't blame the manufacturers. There was just no profit to be made with the government mandating the pharmaceutical pricing structure. The legislation made it impossible for a company to recoup the heavy research and development costs associated with new drug development." Jasper finished another cherry and launched the pit into the air, this one landing very close to her first pit. She gave him an approving nod.

He continued, "In addition, almost all existing medications eventually lost their patents in favor of generic production. Manufacturers had to choose between producing as a public service for no profit or closing their doors. In either case, capitalism lost out," Jasper slammed back the rest of his champagne. "I am not very optimistic about the future of our country."

"Neither am I and I can't help but be angry at the government for what they have caused by excessive legislation. Not just for mother, but for society in general." Alexis said trying to contain the emotions that were stirring inside her again, emotions she had practiced suppressing with only limited success. She had to be strong when in public. She turned to look at Jasper. The muscles of his face were taut, his expression full of concern for her. She sensed that he shared her pain and that he understood her sense of loss.

"I am so sorry," was all Jasper said, but it was enough.

After a long pause, she offered in more cheerful voice, "I appreciate you asking about my mother. I am sure she would have liked to see you again now that you are all grown up and made a name for yourself. Who would have known you would be a congressman and possibly our next governor. I know Daddy is very impressed."

Jasper smiled, obviously pleased by her compliment. "Your father is a good man. I wish I had done a better job with staying in touch with people from my past like him and you. It is the people you have known that help make you the person you are today."

"You sound like a Hallmark card," she chided him, laughing. The champagne was making her a little giddy.

His response was suddenly sullen. "After the accident, I wanted to forget all about my prior life and anything that reminded me of it. That is why I never came back to Georgetown after I left for college. When your father contacted my office, I was not sure I was going to call him back. His name brought back so many memories. Even though I am stronger now, the memories are still painful." His voice became hopeful. "Anyway, I am sure glad I called him back, otherwise we might not have connected."

"Is that what we have done, Jasper? Connected?" she teased, scooting closer to him on the blanket. She drank the small remainder of champagne in her glass and began to wave the glass in his direction, obviously trying to get him to notice it was empty. He promptly filled her glass with more bubbles.

"So now you know my story. What about you?" she asked.

The chime of a grandfather clock broke into their conversation. "Let me check this." He reached into his pocket to remove his phone. "I told my staff not to bother me unless there was a serious issue."

"No problem. I will get you another glass of champagne." She had just begun to fill his glass when he touched her arm.

"I apologize, but I am going to have to ask that we save that next glass for another day." He looked genuinely disappointed. "That text was from my campaign manager. The union members of the Airport Security Administration have unexpectedly gone on strike. The airports are effectively shut down because no people or baggage can be processed through security. That means I will have to drive back to Washington."

"Do you have to go back tonight? It is almost a nine hour drive from here!" She knew her disappointment was evident in the tone of her voice and by the expression on her face.

"Yes, I have to go." Jasper responded reluctantly. "Tomorrow morning, we have the final subcommittee meeting to discuss the IPEA bill. I have to be there to influence the committee against it. I am the only one on the committee who seems to care about the potential ramifications of the proposed law. If IPEA is passed, it will change the way companies do business, potentially impacting their ability to compete in the global market."

Her disappointment quickly changed to concern. Jasper would be exhausted after a long trip and less than full night of rest. Besides, driving on the Interstate these days was an arduous task. The federal highway interstate system was in shambles. Continued lack of maintenance and repair caused by the absence of federal funding had resulted in large sections of the nation's highways deteriorating and in some cases, not drivable. Her concern changed to frustration. What was this country becoming? She let her frustration fade as she focused on Jasper. "Let me help you," she said, passing him his sandals.

He reached over, softly placing his hand on hers. He looked at her, a broad smile on his face. She hadn't noticed how attractive his dimples were and how they gave his face such serenity. She found his smile soothing.

"Thank you for an amazing afternoon," Jasper said. "I really could stay here all evening, but I must go. Let me make this up to you when you get back to Washington." With that, he raised her hand to his lips and gently kissed her hand. Still smiling, he rose and began to walk away.

She watched him as he walked down the path, the sun reflecting off of his sandy brown hair. She admired the way he walked — his gait was strong and determined. He was looking forward, not focused on anything but what lay in front of him. He was a man who knew he was going into a fight he may not win, yet faced his fate boldly, and excited for the challenge and the possibility to win against the odds. As she watched him disappear behind the trees, she suddenly felt very much alone. As much as she tried to shake the feeling while she packed up the picnic, she couldn't. She knew there was only one way she would feel better. She would have to see Jasper Thorne again.

Chapter 12

Washington, District of Columbia

Jasper walked quickly through the stark halls of the Rayburn House office building towards his office. The building was located adjacent to the United States Capitol and housed offices for the one hundred and sixty nine members of the House of Representatives. The building reminded him of a hospital. Unlike the Capitol and the Senate offices, this building lacked charm and character. There were no significant paintings, artistic sculptures, or lush cherry wood paneling. There were no majestic marble stairwells to traverse or sweeping views of the Mall. What the building lacked in opulence, it made up for in amenities lacking in the other congressional buildings, like a gym in the basement and an underground subway car to deliver him to the Capitol. The latter was a welcome relief today as winter had come early to the capitol city and with it had come a cold, blustery wind. Still, Rayburn House was a building devoid of charm and he longed for the familiar architecture of his home neighborhood in downtown Charleston, South Carolina.

With the upcoming Congressional recess, he would be home soon enough. The thought of being home in Charleston produced a strange feeling in him — maybe it was despair. In Washington, his days were full and there were always plenty of people around. At home, there was no one. He let the thought drop as he rounded the corner of the hallway and entered his office.

The doors to a public servant's office were always left open, just in case a constituent stopped by. His office, like most of the offices in the building, consisted of an entrance room and waiting area and a larger room at the rear which served as his formal office. The door to that room was now open and he could see Michael standing just inside the doorway, his arms making wild gestures aimed at other people assembled in the room. He headed straight for the room, but only made it halfway when he heard the voice of his administrative assistant, Abbey Elliston, coming from behind him.

"Well, hello to you too! You'd think with you barging in here, you take a moment to ask how I am doing. Just so you know, if I was any happier, I'd be twins." The look he shot her must have hit its mark, because her expression immediately changed to concern. "They have been waiting for you for fifteen minutes. What's going on?" He did not answer. If they had been waiting this long, chances were it was not good news.

Inside he found the two state senators from South Carolina, and four of the five state congressmen. There was a cornucopia of emotions expressed on their faces. Jasper knew these men well. He considered the senators personal friends and had spent considerable time working with the congressmen on legislative matters. He locked eyes with Trent Holloway for a brief moment. Trent was the senior senator in South Carolina and had been his father's college roommate. As a friend of Jasper's family, Trent had been Jasper's mentor as a freshman congressman and had become a close friend over the years. Trent's eyes looked pained. He just shook his head at Jasper in warning.

"Jasper is here ... the governor is also on the line." The voice of Michael Matthews barely registered in Jasper's mind. Jasper was struggling to make sense of the situation. *What could have happened to require the congressional leadership of the state of South Carolina to assemble on such short notice, let alone in such an ad hoc manner?* As his mobile phone rang, it was quickly followed by the ring of other phones in the room. He glanced at the phone before silencing it. It was Rich Penna, his primary journalistic contact from the USA Today. *What was going on?* He wondered, sensing the rising tension in the room.

The calming voice of Governor William McAdams filled the room followed shortly by the video feed as it was projected by the video conferencing system. "Gentlemen, there is a lot going on at the moment. We need to take a breath, turn off the cell phones, and talk. Are we private?" Matthews closed the door to the office in response. The governor looked at Jasper, "Jasper, I am glad you made it on such short notice, I know you were in the middle of the final committee review on IPEA. This is important and I want you to pay close attention as these recent events have significant impact on you now and on your future campaign for governor."

Jasper edged closer to the speaker phone. He had a deep respect for the governor. They had developed a close relationship since he had made his intention known that he wanted to run to be his successor. William McAdams was a fair man. He exercised wisdom and discernment in his decisions related to the state. He was a man you could trust, if you shared his view points. The press had demonized him through his tenure as incompetent and lacking in his ability to communicate effectively, citing his frequent use of slang and southern euphemisms. It was a gross misrepresentation. William McAdams was anything but incompetent. "What going on Bill?" Jasper looked back up at Trent, whose eyes were still locked on him. Only, it wasn't just Trent that was looking at him. Jasper had become the center of attention for the entire room.

"House Bill 122061 passed committee today." The response was direct and unemotional from the governor.

Jasper repeated the words *House Bill 122061* to himself but it did not register immediately. Since announcing his candidacy, Jasper had purposely begun to increase his awareness of activities in the state legislature, including proposed and pending bills. It was proving difficult to track the amount of legislation that was routinely introduced into Congress, let alone tracking legislative matter for the state of South Carolina. His mind struggled for a moment, recalling the bill, and what it was designed to do. Suddenly his stomach clenched involuntarily in a gag reflex that he did not expect. *No … no way!* He thought, *that was impossible! No one would ever take that bill seriously. How could it even be considered as real legislation?* It was a fringe bill, one that had been introduced to the state congress in one form or another for the past twenty years. It was ridiculous.

"I will infer by your silence that you are as surprised as the rest of us," the governor somberly stated. "The bill was approved less than an hour ago and news is just making its way to the wires. I think most of us thought this bill would be voted down quicker than water falls off a duck's back. Now we have to discuss what that means to us and our great state." The governor's last statement echoed in Jasper's mind. *What would the passage of this bill mean to South Carolina?* He did not even know where to begin. Things in the country were bad, but if this bill were approved by the state congress, it would create ultimate chaos.

"What was the vote count?" The very southern voice of Robert Hardy interjected. At age fifty-two, Robert had been in the Senate for only four years but had already proven adept at swaying the opinion of other senators, regardless of their political affiliation. He was the poster boy of a southern gentleman; handsome, polite, charming, and superbly dressed with an infectious smile. When he smiled at you, you could not help but smile back. Jasper glanced toward Robert hoping to see that smile now. It had been replaced with a scowl that gave Robert a troubled countenance.

"It passed sixteen to eight and that means it had significant support of both parties," the governor responded.

Jasper shook his head in disbelief. The possible implications of this news were enormous, not only for him and his campaign, but for the entire country. *Could it really be possible? Would the people of South Carolina actually secede from the Union for the second time?*

Chapter 13

Jasper looked around the room but everyone was still focused on him, their eyes telling him what they would not dare voice. They were concerned and it seemed that some of his peers were even afraid. To have both parties in a subcommittee vote to move this bill forward meant there was a deeper, more systemic issue at play. *How had he missed it? How had all of them missed it?* "That means that this may be a deeper issue than we thought," Jasper spoke, finally finding his voice. "Bill, you are the closest to the pulse of the state and the citizens. What do you think is driving this?"

Governor Bill McAdams removed his glasses and rubbed his forehead. "Well, if I knew for sure, believe me, I would be taking action to stop it. There are too many factors at play. I spoke with three of the delegates who voted for the bill and they told me basically the same thing. Our country is not the country it used to be."

"There has to be more to it," Jasper said. "We all agree that the legislation being passed by Congress and the executive orders being imposed by the president are destroying our country. We also know our state has suffered greatly in the last decade because of it. But something else is driving this."

The governor shook his head, "If I was a betting man, and I am not, my guess is the delegates think we are headed to Hell in a handbasket and they do not want to be along for the ride. I know these gentlemen personally. They are serious about state freedoms and they say they speak for the people of South Carolina. I fear they believe it is time to make a stand before it gets worse, before there are no other options."

"Bill, I mean no disrespect, but don't pee down my back and tell me it's raining!" Trent slammed his hands down on the desk. "Regular folks do not take action like this unless they are feeling real pain or expect it soon. What is going on down there?" his voice resonating with concern.

There was an unsettling pause before the governor responded. "Trent, you are absolutely right. It does me no good to keep you, the representatives of our state, in the dark." The governor looked to his left for a moment and nodded his head before returning his attention to the group. "Gentlemen, I am going to level with you and provide full disclosure about what I know. You will probably hear about this soon enough, but for now, what I am about to tell you is not to be shared to anyone outside of this room." Everyone in the room seemed to crowd even closer around the table, if that were possible.

"Nothing I said earlier was a lie. There is a growing dissatisfaction with our government and our people are becoming more vocal. You should see the e-mails from concerned citizens that I get every day. Even so, I believe that there is another matter driving Bill 122060."

Trent nodded his head in satisfaction of his astute assessment. The governor nodded to someone outside the range of the video screen again before continuing. Jasper wondered who else was there at the governor's office.

"Do you remember that killing of a Hispanic union official in Los Angeles a few months back?" Several people in the room nodded in acknowledgement. "Well, it is believed it was motivated by the IPEA bill. It appears the black population is very threatened by this legislation, despite what we are being told by the NAACP and other community organizations. There have been protests on a daily basis all over the state, some of them violent. Three days ago, a Latino woman was found murdered in Florence, South Carolina."

Jasper had been briefed on the story by Michael, but had little other details. At the time, he had figured it was another senseless killing.

""It seems that specific details of the investigation were leaked to a delegate on the subcommittee who apparently shared it with the subcommittee prior to them voting on Bill 122060," the governor continued. "The woman was the first Latino to be hired into the predominately black labor force at a cotton processing plant. She was found dead, hanging by a make shift noose and naked to the waist. A large hand written note had been scrawled into her back with a pen knife."

Jasper exchanged glances with Trent. They both knew where this was going.

"The note said TAKE OUR JOB, WE TAKE YOUR LIFE." The governor's voice cracked slightly. "The medical examiner thinks the woman was alive when the note was written."

There were various murmurs and gasps from the members in the room. Jasper rose from his seat upon hearing this unsettling news.

"Governor, this is not a political matter, this is about the security of our state," Jasper said, his mind having already processed the implications of the governor's statement. "We know that South Carolina's population is diverse with the breakdown roughly thirty percent black and twenty-five percent Hispanic. If there were a real uprising in retaliation to IPEA being passed, we could have Los Angeles all over again in our own backyard."

"That is not all of it," the governor's voice responded softly. "We have learned that civil rights leaders and community organizers have been advocating to their local communities that they permanently strike if Bill 122060 is passed."

That was problematic, Jasper thought. The majority of the black labor force was unionized, even though South Carolina was a right-to-work state. A strike could be devastating to the state's economy. Tobacco and soybeans farms, textile and chemical manufacturing plants, and food processing facilities would close their doors within weeks of a major incident. Worse, there wouldn't be anybody to fill the positions vacated by the strike, because other potential workers would be fearful of similar retribution. This situation was a tinder box that could explode any moment.

Jasper repeated the numerical title of the bill in his head and he suddenly recognized its significance. December 20, 1860 or twelve twenty-sixty was one of the most significant and controversial dates in the history of the United States. It was the date when the legislature of the state of South Carolina voted unanimously to secede from the Union. In an instant, it all made sense to Jasper. He knew why Bill 122060 was passed and why there was a majority, cross-party vote in support of it. The state legislature was taking defensive action in case conditions in the state went from bad to worse. Bill 122060 being passed by the state legislature was no longer a faint possibility, but a very real reality. Jasper nervously began to pace in the cramped room.

"Jasper, this is why this is going to be a dicey situation for you. Per our state constitution, any legislatively-referred amendment can go on the ballot if approved by a two-thirds vote of each house of the South Carolina State Legislature. Assuming that this bill is approved by both houses, it is still going to be up to the people to vote on it. That means as one of the gubernatorial candidates, you are going to have to choose a side on this issue." Jasper and several others in the room nodded indicating their understanding.

The governor's eyes narrowed, a stern expression forming on his face. "Jasper, this is serious. There is not going to be any middle ground on this issue. The people are going to vote for the candidate based on how they are going to vote on this bill. There is no way that we will not have a governor who is not aligned with the people on a matter as significant as secession." A moment later, the governor again acknowledged someone outside the view of the video screen. "I apologize for ending our discussion early. I have to attend to another urgent matter." He scanned the faces of the men in the room. "Gentlemen, I will be in touch." The video screen went blank leaving them in silence.

Trent Holloway stood up from his seat to address the room. His voice was strained, and he looked physically pained. "Gentlemen, this is grave news and I am sure we are all dealing with a range of emotions, but the bottom line is we can't let the state secede. This is not only about our state — it is about our country." He paused searching the faces in the room, "I regret that I am at an impasse on how to proceed. Does anybody else have a suggestion on what we should do?"

His question was met by a painful silence, before Michael Matthews spoke up, "I have a suggestion." They all looked at him expectantly. Removing his glasses, and setting them on the table,

Michael got down on his knees. "Gentlemen, I suggest we pray."
And together, they did.

Chapter 14

Jasper looked up as the door to the conference room opened. Michael entered, the look of surprise evident on his face when he saw Jasper already waiting for him. Jasper had been looking forward to this lesson and had arrived early even though his enthusiasm had been muted by the events of the past week. His entire staff was edgy and his office had been fielding phone calls from the press, constituents, and fellow congressmen at a dizzying pace since the committee approval of Bill 122060. Jasper was tired from the lack of sleep the past few days and by the looks of Michael, he was not the only one.

He logged off the game of online chess he had been playing on his tablet for the past fifteen minutes. He hadn't made a single move in that entire time. Jasper had been playing virtual games of chess with unknown opponents for years. Most of his opponents didn't seem to mind that it may be days between moves. It was typical of the types of games he played against RedBear17, his most recent gaming nemesis. Their first match had taken six weeks to complete and Jasper had lost badly. The next match had taken three weeks to complete and Jasper had finally won, but only narrowly. Recently, back and forth they had traded victories. By far, RedBear17 had proven to be the most challenging foe Jasper had encountered. Their competitive rivalry had proven both refreshing and intoxicating.

"We have to be finished by six, as I have another commitment I need to prepare for," Jasper stated. It was a demand more than a request.

Michael nodded knowingly, "Ah yes." A smile formed on his face. "Your lady friend. Very well then, let's begin with —"

Jasper interrupted him with a hand gesture. "Michael, I have been thinking about what you said about the structure that exists in our churches today. How tradition and compliance has become the focus, versus our relationship with God. I want to learn more about that."

Michael opened the Bible on the table and flipped adeptly to a section near the back. "Let's look in the Bible at a passage of scripture that was written by the Apostle Paul. Paul was an early leader of the Christian church and wrote more books of the New Testament than any other author. Interestingly, at one time in his life, Paul was known as a Pharisee, a title granted only to the most religious and zealous Jews. He followed the Hebrew laws to the letter and was a role model to the Jewish community. Paul later lost his status as a Pharisee when he converted to Christianity and became a believer in Jesus Christ."

Michael cleared his throat. "I will read aloud what Paul has to say about structure in the church. Beginning in the book of Philippians, in chapter three, verse five, Paul writes:

"*5Circumcised the eighth day, of the stock of Israel, of the tribe of Benjamin, an Hebrew of the Hebrews; as touching the law, a Pharisee; 6Concerning zeal, persecuting the church; touching the righteousness which is in the law, blameless. 7But what things were gain to me, those I counted loss for Christ. 8Yea doubtless, and I count all things but loss for the excellency of the knowledge of Christ Jesus my Lord: for whom I have suffered the loss of all things, and do count them but dung, that I may win Christ, 9And be found in him, not having mine own righteousness, which is of the law, but that which is through the faith of Christ, the righteousness which is of God by faith.*"

He looked at Jasper and asked, "What does that set of verses mean to you?"

Jasper shrugged his shoulders and stared at the floor. This was the first time he had really read a lengthy Bible verse and he found it confusing. Questions were forming in his mind, only he was not sure if he should ask them. *What did circumcision and God have to do with each other? Who was Benjamin? Why would Paul be so angry with Christians that he would seek to hurt them?* "I am not really sure what all that means and honestly it is a little hard for me to follow."

Michael sat back in his chair assuming a relaxed pose. "That is quite all right, Jasper. I understand this is new to you and I am sure you have questions. Those questions will eventually be answered as part of the process that all who seek to know God will go through. Let me help you to understand why this scripture is relevant to our discussion on Structure."

"In these verses, Paul is explaining that he was a man who was zealous for the traditions of his Jewish faith. In the Jewish religion, acceptance by God is believed to come from following Jewish rules and traditions. It was not until Paul came to personally know Jesus Christ that he understood he was wrong and that dependence on tradition and religious practices was worthless."

"I am still not following you." Jasper said shaking his head.

Michael rose from his chair and began to walk across the room, his hair bouncing gently with each step. Suddenly he stopped, turning to Jasper with a pensive look on his face. "Have you ever asked yourself why there are there so many Christian denominations?" Michael paused and then knowingly stated, "It is because man has taken it upon himself to define what are the correct behaviors and activities to obtain eternal life with God. Throughout history, people have broken away from traditional religious institutions and established different practices that they believed more accurately reflected a true relationship with God."

Michael continued with an illustration that he felt Jasper would be familiar with. "Martin Luther established the first Lutheran churches in response to disagreements with the doctrines and teachings of the Roman Catholic Church. Luther taught that eternal salvation is based on God's grace through faith in Jesus Christ, a belief clearly supported in the Bible but in direct contradiction to the teaching of the Roman Catholic Church, which believes it is based on personal works."

"That is very interesting. Why did they believe differently?" Jasper asked.

"The answer is quite simple," Michael responded. "Today, we have the Baptist, the Catholic, the Lutheran, the Methodist and the Presbyterian churches to simply name a few, because some theologian, at some point in time, believed in a slightly different doctrine, practice or teaching that they thought would properly lead them to eternal life with God." He paused and looked directly into Jasper's eyes before he continued, "If you follow the trail, it leads to the realization that structure is all about man still trying to be in control of his eternal salvation and his eternity. Man abandoned or added to God's infallible word to gain control — does this make sense to you?"

"Sure that makes sense. So what if there is a difference in belief? Is there any real harm in believing differently?" Jasper asked.

Michael frowned and shook his head. "My dear boy, belief is everything. The problem is that too many people are depending on the structure of their religion to determine their eternity. Let me show you what I mean." He sat down and deftly flipped the pages of the Bible to another verse of scripture.

"In the book of Mark, Jesus is speaking to a group of Pharisees and religious teachers, and we have an opportunity to hear directly from Jesus on this topic. As I mentioned earlier, the Pharisees were considered the religious elite of the Jews and they took great pride in their religious public displays, disciplines, and adherence to the historical traditions of Mosaic Law." Sliding the Bible across the table in front of Jasper, he tapped his fingers on a section of the page. "Here, you read verses six through eight in the seventh chapter."

Jasper nervously read aloud. "'*6He answered and said unto them, Well hath Esaias prophesied of you hypocrites, as it is written, This people honoureth me with their lips, but their heart is far from me.7 Howbeit in vain do they worship me, teaching for doctrines the commandments of men.8 For laying aside the commandment of God, ye hold the tradition of men, as the washing of pots and cups: and many other such like things ye do.'*"

Jasper looked up at Michael and asked, "So, Jesus was warning these Pharisees about this structure you have been describing but how does all of this really display itself in religious institutions today? I am still not sure why it is so important."

"At a boy! You are proving to be a quick study. I am glad you asked that question." Michael quickly reviewed his hand written notes. "Let me share with you a few examples from both the Protestant and the Catholic Church. There are some Protestant churches that believe it is a sin for women to wear pants. Others that believe you must only read the King James Bible and that all other forms of the Bible are corrupt."

"That is interesting. I am curious, which form of the Bible do you prefer?" Jasper interjected.

"Personally, I prefer the King James for the prose and the accuracy of the translation, but there are other Bible versions that I utilize as well in my studies." Michael said.

"What about examples from Catholicism?" Jasper asked.

"Yes, Catholicism." Michael took a deep breath, "Catholicism contains many traditions that were created by man. For example, did you ever go to a priest to seek forgiveness?"

Jasper nodded. "Yes, my mother used to take me to confession at our church once a month."

Michael paused for effect. "Did you know that is a tradition that is not supported biblically? It is structure that has been created by man and not found anywhere in the Bible. The Bible clearly states there is only one mediator between mankind and God and that is Jesus Christ. Because of Jesus Christ, you or any other believer can go directly to God to ask for forgiveness … you do not need a Catholic priest or anyone else to act as intermediary."

Jasper was silent as he processed Michael's statement. He believed what Michael was saying to him, he had no reason not to. Still it bothered him to hear it, just the same.

Sensing his concern, Michael added, "Another example is how Catholics treat statues of saints or Mary, the mother of Jesus, as sacred. The Old and New Testaments do not have any scripture pertaining to this practice. However, they do have scripture warning against worshipping idols."

"Are you saying that a statue of Mary is an idol?" Jasper asked with a hint of shock in his tone.

Michael nodded slowly in agreement. "Revering statues of saints or Mary was added to the practices of the Catholic Church in the early years of the church and became tradition. So what some would call tradition, others would call idolatry. In fact, when you review the list of the Ten Commandments published by the Catholic Church and compare it to scripture in the twentieth chapter of the book of Exodus in the King James Bible; you will find that the Catholic Church leaves out the second commandment, which is not to worship carved images, even those images of heavenly things."

Jasper shook his head in disbelief as he remembered a small statue of Mary that his mother kept on her bedroom dresser. He would often find his mother on her knees praying before the statue with a rosary in her hands but he never understood why. His parents were devout Catholics who went to church regularly, gave freely to charitable causes, and were good people. However, even though he had spent his youth involved in the Catholic Church, he really did not know what core tenants and beliefs the church was based on. If what Michael was telling him was true, how did he not see these evidences of structure growing up? *What else had he missed?* Questions were beginning to form as he contemplated this last thought.

"I have never heard any of this before." Jasper resisted. "Why is it not spoken of more often?" he asked somewhat challengingly.

A high pitched chirp interrupted the silence from Michael's watch. "Six o' clock. Our time together must come to a close."

Funny, Jasper thought, *he had not noticed Michael set an alarm at anytime during their meeting.* It amazed him how Michael always seemed to anticipate his needs.

Michel continued, "Before we leave, let me leave you with the application of today's lesson. First, don't look to the structure for the truth; for you will only find falsehood and lies meant to control. Instead, seek the One who is the source of all truth. God, and only God, will show you the way."

"You mean the Bible?" Jasper asked.

Michael nodded affirmatively. "Second, you must be aware of when the structure has become your goal instead of your relationship with God. Think about the scripture we read earlier about Paul. In Paul's mind, he was faultless because he followed Jewish tradition. He soon realized that the Jewish laws would not create the relationship he sought with God nor lead him to Heaven. Paul came to understand that true relationship and eternal salvation would only come through faith in Jesus Christ."

The lesson complete, Michael closed the Bible, stood up and walked out of the room, leaving Jasper alone to sort through the multitude of thoughts that were now colliding in his mind.

Chapter 15

National Harbor, Maryland

Jasper had decided to take Alexis to his favorite restaurant because of the view, but it didn't hurt that the cuisine was exceptional. The chef was a burly man, French trained and every bit as fussy about perfection as the countrymen he trained under. The chef knew how to make a perfect meal and Jasper wanted this dinner to be special. He was on a second date for the first time in a very long time, and he wanted to impress Alexis. The work of the people of South Carolina had consumed all of his time and all of his thoughts — that was until Alexis came back into his life.

The view of the Potomac River basin was beautiful. Looking to the north, one could see the majestic Woodrow Wilson Bridge spanning the river; and to the south, one could follow the river until it meandered out of sight, eventually to be consumed by the Chesapeake Bay. Directly in front of him, at the edge of the river, struggling to emerge from the sandy shoreline was a mammoth statue. This statue was the real reason he liked the view. Made of aluminum, and cast in five separate sections, it spanned over seventy feet. It was a statue of a partially buried man lying on his back, his exposed extremities and face barely peaking from the ground. The only exception being his right arm that reached forth high above the ground as if seeking to grasp something that could not be seen. The man's face was frozen in a scream of anguish, as if he was fighting against an immense force in an attempt to rise up out of the sand. On so many levels, he was that statue

A light touch of Alexis' hand brought Jasper's attention back to her. Alexis looked radiant. The elegant black cocktail dress she wore was accented with a pink rhinestone broach at the waist. Her brown hair flowed smoothly over her shoulders, wrapping around her neck and framing a pink amethyst that she wore on a silver necklace.

"Sorry. I tend do that sometimes. Just a lot on my mind," he said.

"Do what?" she responded, staring at him amusingly. In the flickering light of the waning sun, her eyes danced. They reminded him of pools of molten chocolate. She made him giddy.

"Become fixated. Tune out the world and get lost in a thought, regardless of where I may be," he frowned. "It is not very polite if it happens when I am with someone."

"Some people would say it would be a gift to have that level of concentration," Alexis said, taking a sip of her wine. "So what type of thought was so worthy of your full attention?"

"I was looking at that statue. It's called The Awakening and it has a very personal meaning to me." He looked toward the statue again.

She studied him for a moment, her eyes searching his, "What does it mean to you?"

He looked at her for a moment as if questioning her motives, but he wanted to tell her. "The original reason I ran for Congress was because I was frustrated with not being able to make a difference," Jasper paused contemplating his next words. "I mean I was making a difference within the sphere of influence I could impact, but I wanted to make a difference on a larger scale. I believed that the only way to make this happen was to be in Congress where I could influence legislative issues, represent the people of my districts, and influence other political leaders."

"So how is it working for you?" There was a hint of a smile on her lips as if she already knew what he would say.

"Though I had some success, the job has proven to be harder than I thought and not as rewarding as I expected it to be." He chuckled as he focused his gaze on the statue. Its face was now glowing faintly, reflecting the light from the full moon that was beginning to rise in the East. He studied the twisted grimace. It almost appeared as if it were laughing. "In fact, I have come to be very disheartened about my role in shaping the future of our country."

"Really, why is that?" Alexis asked, intrigued.

"I and those in Congress who are still fighting for the rights and freedoms of the people are like that statue. We are trying to do the right things, but we are buried under a governmental bureaucracy that has existed far too long, become far too strong, and strayed too far from the ideology that this country was founded on. We toss and turn, wrestling with an unseen foe, at times making what appears like progress, only to sink back under the mess of a system we call government. I will only do that for so long before I stop playing the game."

He looked at the statue again thinking about its personal meaning to him. "I am that statue. It represents my current struggle but also the potential that I can realize if I can break free and rise."

"So ... is your decision to run for governor how you plan to stop playing the game?" Alexis probed.

"Yes. I came to a point where I knew I had to either quit the game for good, or change the way the game is played," he chuckled. "Now with South Carolina secession a very real possibility, it looks like someone else has changed the game for me."

Alexis studied his face for a long time. When she next spoke, her voice had a tone of authority. "Have you ever wondered why some people are able to rise above their circumstances to become contributing and productive members of society, while others are destined to remain stagnant in a life of mediocrity, limited growth, and potential hardship?"

Jasper looked at her curiously. It was a very relevant question that he had thought about many times, but never discussed with anyone. He wondered what she would say. "Sure, at times." He shrugged his shoulders and added, "How do you answer it?"

She leaned into him, demanding his full attention. "I am driven to understand what makes a person different and aspire to improve their own situation in life despite the odds against their success. I propose the answer is as simple as personal accountability." She looked for confirmation from Jasper and he nodded, a slight smile forming on his face.

Alexis face became animated as she spoke, her eyes filled with an intense passion from within. "It is my belief that personal accountability is part of the essence of a human being that fills a person with a desire to live a meaningful and productive life. It is unique because it cannot be passed down from generation to generation, nor can it be taught, earned, inherited, or won. But it is real just the same."

"True," Jasper said in agreement.

"Those who lack personal accountability scorn it, but those that see it manifest itself in others, treasure it as precious," Alexis continued. "Accountability motivates an individual to pursue one's dreams for growth, fulfillment, and happiness despite the costs, sacrifice, and risk."

"The founding fathers of our nation are a good example of people who were personally accountable," Jasper interjected.

"Exactly! They believed it was an inalienable right for all to have life, liberty, and the pursuit of happiness. They did not believe it was the government's role to provide these things, only to ensure that freedoms existed in society to enable the obtainment of these objectives."

Jasper found himself smiling. He was not only mesmerized by Alexis' beauty, he was impressed by her conviction.

"Why do you think personal accountability is relevant today?" Alexis asked.

"Accountability is at the heart of the battle we fight between a dependent society and a free society," Jasper offered.

Alexis nodded in response. "Our politically-correct society would tell you that the Have-Nots are a product of a society that has left them behind. Have-nots could never develop their full potential for various reasons, be it because of the neighborhood they lived in, the quality of the schools they attended, the type of food they ate, the emotional traumas they experienced, or the poor paying jobs they were forced to take," she held her hand to her forehead in a fainting motion, soliciting a laugh from Jasper.

"Some might argue that society is wrong and I say that society is not only wrong, but that society is to blame for the conditions and circumstances that the Have-Nots use as an excuse for their condition." She said, tapping the table sharply with her index finger for emphasis.

"But what if the Have-Nots do not understand personal accountability?" Jasper asked.

"Accountability cannot be understood because it does not exist for the Have-Nots because our government has made them dependent." Her voice was laced with frustration. "Our government has shaped a society where instant gratification has become the norm and living responsibly for the future is an afterthought." She leaned forward for emphasis. "Why would the Have-Nots need to worry about the future when the costs for their transgressions are to be borne by someone else?" Alexis shook her head in disgust. "The fallacy is that the cost is left to those who planned and lived responsibly."

"That is a very sad but true statement," Jasper responded glumly.

"It is a simple cycle in my mind." Alexis traced a circle on the table cloth with her finger. "Personal accountability creates wealth. But that same wealth is then consumed by the government through excessive taxation and oppressive legislation in order to support a society devoid of the essence of what created it."

"You mean a society devoid of personal accountability?" asked Jasper.

"Yes. The cycle can only repeat for a limited time before it breaks down, as those who create wealth choose not to create or are driven to abandon this society in pursuit of another which would value and support their efforts," Alexis responded, glancing out the window for a moment. She was right, Jasper thought. He had often wondered what would happen if all the productive people in a society decided to form their own society and leave the Have-Nots to fend for themselves. It was an interesting possibility.

"I fear we are approaching the end of our country's cycle," she sighed deeply. "Our current society is all too willing to falsely bear the responsibility for a lack of personal accountability and it will be our downfall." She looked at Jasper, a slight smile forming on her lips. "That is why I am glad there are people like you left who still wish to fight."

Jasper stared at her for a long time, silent. He couldn't describe what he was feeling. It was a sense of acceptance, deeper yet, it was a sense of validation. Validation for what he stood for and for what he was trying to achieve. Alexis understood who he was.

He reached over and gently grabbed her hand, a smile forming on his face. "You are amazing!" Alexis blushed, obviously pleased by the comment.

As Jasper held the hand of the most beautiful woman he had ever known, he couldn't help but turn his gaze to the statue outside once again. Jasper studied the statue's dark outline briefly, confirming his belief about what the statue represented to him. The thought occurred to him that, like the statue, he was also a man struggling in anguish to rise against an unseen foe. Fortunately, he held the advantage. At this moment his foes had yet to realize he had awakened, nor did they know he was finally beginning to rise.

PART II

Chapter 16

Beaufort, South Carolina

The light from the single floor lamp dimmed unexpectedly, casting the room in a light brown hue. A few moments later, it flickered off only to come back on in an instant. Mack Jordon barely noticed. The cycle repeated itself countless times a day. It had been months since his apartment had reliable power. Mostly it was brown outs, but often times he and his parents would be without power for hours or even days. His neighbors played the victim card, complaining that the power failures where because they were in Section 8 housing and thus were always the first to lose power and the last to have it restored. He didn't argue. Maybe they were right. He didn't mind too much when power failed in the winter because temperatures in Beaufort were cooler and he and his folks could manage, but it was a different story in the heat of summer with no ability to use electric fans in the house. It could become downright brutal, almost like Hell on earth.

He smacked at a mosquito that had landed on his knee and scored a hit. *Crap!* He thought, as he checked the blood stain that was now on his white uniform pants. He flicked at the stain with his finger. It was just what he needed, something else for the boss man to yell at him about. He hated it here but he hated his job at the nearby plastics plant even worse. That mosquito must have gotten inside through the tear in the screen door. He wiped his hand on the paper towel he had been using as a napkin. His attention had been consumed by the article he was reading on his micro tablet and he had completely forgotten about the bowl of cereal he had been eating just minutes ago.

His micro tablet was his pride and joy; it offered the only means of escape from his dull existence. Over the past year, he had saved as much of his paycheck as he could spare to purchase it. To him, the tablet had become his ticket to higher education. He spent most of his free time using the tablet to read about current events, study various subjects, and absorb as much information as he could about the world that existed outside of Beaufort. He had read that studying a subject for two hours a day for two years would make you an expert and he believed it. In the past six months, he had completed several free online classes in IT security offered by a government-funded university. It was disappointing that the credits didn't count towards an actual degree, as he had completed enough classes to earn his bachelor's had it been a real university. That thought soured him. If he could have afforded it, he would have gone to college. Right now, he and his family could barely afford to eat. Fortunately the government provided free internet service to his apartment complex. As a result, he spent most of his time inside with the tablet these days. His parents didn't mind because it kept him out of trouble. They slept all the time anyway, usually doped up on pain medication. He had been the sole bread winner for the family because neither of them had held a job in over two years. It was fortunate that his union job on the assembly line paid decent wages; otherwise they would not make it for long. The welfare payments were few and far between these days and when they did receive a check, it was barely enough to buy groceries for the week. Maybe the union was good for one thing.

The article he was reading opened with the announcement that the U.S. House of Representatives had approved the IPEA bill and that the Senate was preparing to vote in a few days. Mostly, the article was about the new candidate for governor of South Carolina and his anti-union platform. Mack liked Jasper Thorne for that one reason alone. Sure he was a member of the union, but a reluctant member. Mack disagreed with having to pay twenty percent of his wages to the union for dues and other related fees. He had no idea what he got in return or where they spent his money. He was supposed to get specialized job training, the best benefits, and a retirement plan that the union managed. None of that was true.

Recently, he had read an article about a teachers union that invested all its members' retirement funds in the construction of a resort community along the Florida coast, without the knowledge of the members. A month after the resort opened, it was destroyed by a hurricane and deemed a complete loss. The union had not bothered to purchase insurance hoping they would sell the property shortly after it opened so the members lost all their retirement savings. That lack of accountability is what scared him about unions. There were always extra fees every month that never made any sense. Why did he have to contribute one percent to the family of some union member he didn't even know because they were on the bench without work. Maybe if things were reversed, he would appreciate that one percent, but that was beside the point. It wasn't his fault that they were not working. Most of the people on the bench were losers anyway. They didn't have jobs because they were slackers and no one wanted them. Each day on his shift, Mack had to work with slackers and he despised them. These slackers, both men and women, took extended smoke breaks, worked at half his pace, and constantly created problems for the company. Despite this behavior, these same individuals were never punished nor reprimanded in any way that Mack could see.

It frustrated him so much that there was so little accountability within the union. Even so, he felt powerless, like a slave at the mercy of the union leadership. He had to do what they told him to do or they would fire him. With the unemployment rate of more than twenty five percent, and jobs hard to find, he would be a fool to challenge the situation. *What could he do anyway?* He was just an assembly line worker, without any real power

Mack finished reading the article. His only audible response was a disappointing sigh, as he shook his head in frustration. *Why did the country want to pass legislation that would grant illegal immigrants citizenship if they joined a union?* He didn't get it. *Why shackle more people to a system that was corrupt and broken? Let alone, where were the jobs going to come from that these new citizens would be working?* This legislation was already creating issues at work. There were several Latino workers who were part of the union that had been advocating this legislation to the dismay of the rest of the workforce. He tried to stay out of the discussions at work, but it was difficult. He was aware of the growing violence caused in response to the legislation. His African American coworkers thought he shared the same sentiments of the general black population. Only they were wrong. The whole thing was wrong.

He gulped down a mouthful of soggy cereal as he read a short bio on Jasper Thorne. He liked the fact that Jasper presented himself as a Constitutionalist. Even though he had never heard the term before, he knew what it meant. The Declaration of Independence and the Constitution were two of his favorite historical documents. His other favorite was the Federalist Papers. He had memorized both of the former and spent considerable time studying the theory and philosophy of the latter. The level of ignorance of his coworkers about these documents amazed him. Like most of society, they no longer valued, nor understood the relevance of these historical documents. Few citizens today understood what this country had been designed to be nor how far it had deviated from its destiny. Mack knew he thought differently than the others and that is what frustrated him with his current situation.

He checked the time on his tablet. He had to leave soon to catch the bus to work. He spoke to the tablet: "Go to the announcement speech and display." The living room wall in front of Mack was peppered with text and light as a four foot by four foot display of the document appeared, created by a tiny projector in the tablet. Mack scanned the text of the speech that Jasper Throne had delivered when he announced his candidacy for governor. His eyes rested on the last paragraph of the speech

"Show video of the speech. Begin 'Yet, there is still hope for us'," he said aloud.

He heard the familiar voice of his digital assistant, "No video available, only audio. Do you have another request?"

"Play audio, begin as stated in previous request," he commanded.

The voice of Jasper Thorne filled the room. It was a strong voice of someone who believed in what he spoke. A compassionate voice that Mack felt he could trust.

"Yet, there is still hope for us. A hope rooted in the foundations of our nation. A hope that our forefathers shared and ensured would be available to us today through the original design of our nation. You see, I believe our state governments represent the greatest and last defense against an oppressive federal government that has become harmful to its citizens. Our state government, here in South Carolina, is my hope."

Lost in thought, Mack powered down his tablet and sat staring at the tear in the screen door. He no longer cared that he was going to miss the bus that was to transport him to the job he loathed. It was no longer of consequence. He didn't want to work for the union or anybody else in Beaufort. He felt odd, but strangely at peace with this revelation. For the first time in his life, he felt a sense of purpose. He knew what he had to do. Mack Jordan had to meet Jasper Thorne. He was the only person in the world he wanted to work for.

Chapter 17

"All war is deception."
-Sun Tzu

The Wall - near Laredo, Texas

The two men faced each other in silence in the small room located in the bottom floor of the interior wall. The room was very bright due to the extra LED lights that had been installed over the large table. Usually this room was used to review engineering documents, building plans, or equipment specifications. Today, it was being used as an interrogation room.

"Me llamo es Juan Paulo Martinez," he lied in a thickly accented voice. He did not look the man he was speaking to in the eyes.

"Habla English?" was the question Xavier had known was next. *Some people were so easy to read, so easy to manipulate*, Xavier thought. Xavier simply shook his head indicating that he did not. Brian Colbert, the chief maintenance supervisor for the South East Corridor turned away in disgust. Xavier smiled slightly enjoying the game.

The supervisor spoke to himself out loud, his frustration growing, "Why does this company continue to hire people who do not speak English?" *This is America after all. Shouldn't people who come to this country be required to learn the native language?* Brian thought. He turned back to Xavier, the spittle flying from his mouth as he spoke. "You people need to learn my language. My language! English!" He pointed forcefully at Xavier. "I am sure not learning your language or anybody else's. Comprende?"

Xavier just stared at the supervisor, visualizing the supervisor pounding imaginary hands against an imaginary wall in his head. Quickly, the supervisor steadied himself. "Wait aqui!" he pointed down at the ground. "No vamos."

Pretending to be confused, Xavier shook his head again. He watched as the supervisor left the room. He liked playing this game with people. People were so easy to fool. A person tended to trust in their own superiority over another, if they believe the circumstances were in their favor. In this case, a supervisor dealing with an employee whom the supervisor thought could not understand him. As long as you let people think they had a superior advantage over you, they were much more likely to expose weaknesses that could be exploited.

He laughed out loud without meaning too. He couldn't help it. He liked to see the supervisor so frazzled. Brian has a cushy job here on the Wall. Not much happened to create problems for the maintenance staff in this fortified facility, until recently. Now everyone was edgy. In the last four months, there had been five random explosions at different locations along the Wall. It was disappointing that Brian had interrupted his work on the sixth.

Xavier did not have any concerns. He knew why he was here in this break room, waiting on an interpreter. Brian had caught him in the act of installing a remote transmitter in an air conditioning control panel. Since Xavier's uniform indicated he was part of the janitorial crew, Brian had confiscated the transmitter and escorted him into this room for questioning. That created an unforeseen delay in the plan, as Brian was supposed to be in the inner wall section at this time, not the outer section. He had followed the same mission plan at other locations along the wall without a hitch. It was disappointing that something would happen on his last mission of the assignment that had the potential to expose him. Fortunately, this was to be the last job for him, at least for a few months. He was looking forward to sailing his yacht through the Caribbean until he received his next assignment. *Soon enough,* he thought. He just had to ensure he walked out of the Wall today with no major complications and without the authorities involved.

There were others just like him, creating chaos and havoc at others strategically chosen areas along the United States border. In the past six months, explosions had also occurred at several key border entry points including the Ambassador Bridge in Detroit and Rainbow Bridge in Niagara Falls. However, explosions were only part of the plan. Two months ago, four men in a small fishing vessel were apprehended by the Coast Guard agents along the Florida coast. When the vessel was searched, agents found a small dirty bomb capable of blanketing a five miles radius with radioactive debris. The unsuspecting men who had been transporting the bomb had been led to believe they were delivering a shipment of drugs to a buyer waiting on the coast. To ensure the Coast Guard found these men, the Coast Guard had been tipped off in advance to the location of the fishing vessel and that it may be transporting drugs. The incident had been successful in creating the intended results. Panic swelled in cities and towns along the Florida coastline buoyed by increased demands from the citizens and government officials to strengthen border security. When a similar incident was replicated on the West Coast, the hysteria took on a greater intensity. The country was quickly approaching a state of panic. It was all part of the plan, one much greater than Xavier was privy too.

Xavier waited patiently, calculating his next move. He was looking forward to continuing this game of deception. He had studied his employee handbook and knew the rules that the supervisor had to follow. Anytime an employee who did not speak English had to be questioned or disciplined, Texas law required a certified interpreter be present. This meant a delay of at least an hour as the sanctioned interpreter was located and brought in to question the employee.

Twenty minutes later, the interpreter arrived at the break room, earlier than expected. Her name was Selma Morez. She was of Latino decent, slightly overweight and comely. Xavier could tell that she was also agitated at having to delay her escape from the doldrums of work. He wondered what she did for fun. He guessed Selma spent her evenings reading Internet blogs about people who obviously had much more fulfilling and adventurous lives than her. The perfunctory interview was over in fifteen minutes and Xavier was allowed to leave. Selma confirmed his name, address, and employment information, all of which were lies. She had asked him the only relevant question that mattered, "What were you doing in the air conditioning control panel?" she asked in Spanish.

Making sure to look concerned and worried, Xavier responded in Spanish, "I was fixing a clogged toilet in that section and I noticed how hot it was. I could tell the air conditioning was not working and I was trying to fix it." His voice became more confident, he was careful to convey himself in a manner that could only be construed as prideful. "I know a little about air conditioning systems. I apprenticed as an air conditioning technician with Frio Aire, the largest air conditioning contractor in all of Mexico City. I found the problem. If Mr. Colbert would have given me more time, I would have fixed it for him. Did I do something wrong?" Xavier was careful not share any more information. What he had already said appeared to satisfy her and the supervisor. Ten minutes later he was escorted from the Wall. He had been suspended from his job until further notice for engaging in actions outside his job classification. The suspension was fine with him. It was going to be his last day anyway.

Outside the Wall, Xavier sat in the dilapidated Ford pickup truck he had purchased in the nearby town of Edinburg. He was free and in less than twenty four hours, he would be navigating through the crystal clear waters of the Caribbean. He took one last look at the structure that had been his project for the last six months. The Wall spread over the horizon before him, stretching from one end to the other as far as he could see. He laughed heartily. *People were so easy to fool*, he thought.

Five minutes later, he was driving down the road that would soon connect him to Interstate 35. Shortly after, he pulled over onto the shoulder and stepped out of the truck. He walked to the front of the truck and pulled up the hood, pretending to inspect the motor. Closing the hood, he looked back the way he had come. The faint outline of the Wall could barely be seen on the horizon. He reached for the pre-paid cellular phone in his pocket and dialed the number he had committed to memory that morning that would connect him to the backup transmitter he had installed in another electrical panel. He always had a contingency plan. Holding the phone to his ear he waited for his answer. Five seconds later, he saw a flash and a large puff of black smoke appear above the Wall in the distance, and then shortly afterward, he heard the muffled sound of thunder caused by the explosion. Xavier climbed back into the truck and proceeded on his way down the road, humming softly to himself. *Yes, people were so easy to fool.*

Chapter 18

"It was the labor movement that helped secure so much of what we take for granted today. The forty-hour work week, the minimum wage, family leave, health insurance, Social Security, Medicare, retirement plans. The cornerstones of the middle-class security all bear the union label."
-Barack Obama

Washington, District of Columbia

"... the skilled labor provided by a worker, performed in the structure of a managed force, creates the best desired output for all. Therefore, it is of utmost importance that we, a civilized society, change the conditions of our society to facilitate this objective. Right now, millions of workers are not realizing their full potential and our society is suffering as a result. We know this because the evidence is right before our eyes. We have a struggling economy, an unemployment rate that is at its highest rate in history, and a gross national product that is at its lowest level in fifty years. These conditions exist in our society today, not because of the worker, but because of the capitalist structure that you, the worker, have been forced to toil in since the founding of our country. Our predecessors in this same legislative body knew this when they passed the Clayton Act. They were visionaries who understood how to create progress in a society. They knew the labor of a human being is not a commodity or an article of commerce that can be manipulated at will so that others can profit. How can we know any different? How can we not act any different?"

Harry Benjamin paused and took a deep breath as he leaned forward hard on the podium. *Now it was time for him to close the deal*, he thought. The light reflected off a nearby television camera causing him to momentarily close his eyes, which had the unintended effect of emphasizing the relevance of this moment. Before him, senators from all fifty states and the newly minted state of Puerto Rico, several congressional aides, and news reporters from all of the major networks were watching his every move. Yes, now was the time to close the deal.

This speech was intended to reach the public more than it was meant to sway senators to vote in his favor. He already knew he had secured the votes needed to pass the bill. No, his concern was for the American people, more specifically, the existing union workforce. They were the intended recipients for this speech and he hoped they heard and received his message. It was vital that the existing union workforce fully accepted passage of this bill. The other pillars could not be built if this one did not first stand strong.

Harry and the others had anticipated some resistance by the union membership to this bill, but they did not expect race to be such a pivotal factor in driving that resistance. The increased violence and protests that was occurring from the black labor force had him and others very concerned. The killing of the union official in Los Angeles had created unwanted negative publicity for the legislation. Therefore, Robert and his minions were forced to expend unplanned resources and money to counter the undesired influence on the public. Polling suggested they still had the general public support for the legislation, but the incidents of racial conflict related to IPEA were increasing. Why didn't the black workforce realize how this legislation would benefit them? He did not understand why they felt threatened. IPEA would cement unions as the pillar of the economy, necessary and critical in every way to the functioning of society as we know it. All union members, regardless of race, would benefit from increased job security, increased wages, and increased opportunities for career growth.

Honestly, he was somewhat frustrated with the whole situation. The black caucus had agreed to support the bill, but with reservations. Even they seemed not to grasp the potential of this single act of legislation. Their lack of vision was probably due to their focus on themselves. A common argument they posed to him on many occasions was that IPEA would take jobs from black workers and give them to Latinos and other foreigners. There was some truth to their concern only because Latinos workers tended to be more willing to work the undesirable jobs and tended to be more productive employees in general. Companies were not ignorant of this fact and would seek to have a unionized workforce that was as productive as possible to help drive more profitability. As a result, there would be many black union workers who would find themselves competing for their positions and working harder than they ever had before to keep their jobs. *Progress was not without sacrifice*, Harry thought.

He looked into the camera that had been strategically positioned to provide a close up. He raised his right hand towards the camera, making a fist to ensure that the insignia on his ring could be plainly seen by the viewing audience. Many watching would not understand what the black letters carved into the gold signet ring meant, but there would be just as many watching who would. Arranged in two rows of four letters were the letters FEAA TEAN. The letters represented the cornerstone of the Marxist philosophy that he believed in and aspired too, 'From each according to his ability, to each according to his need.'

Harry continued, "Yes, we must act. We must act now to seize the future that can be ours." He scanned the audience. "Yet, I also know many of you are concerned about the impact of this legislation. Many of you have a belief that this law will take away jobs from the existing workforce and be harmful to the future of our country. Sadly, some people, driven by this concern, have resorted to violence." His expression softened but his voice remained stern. "First, let me plead for the violence to stop. This is your country! It is our countrymen and countrywomen who are the victims of this senseless violence. I ask of you, do not react out of ignorance and fear, but instead, seek to understand."

He extended his arms towards the audience, palms facing upwards, as if cradling an imaginary load. "IPEA is a game changer for all of us. It will propel our society to become the economic juggernaut of days long past. Only this time, everyone who is able to work, will work in comfort and security, knowing that his and her rights are protected and that they are being paid the maximum amount for their contributions." Harry paused for several seconds. These last statements had to be delivered perfectly to make the intended impact. His voice became increasingly intense as he spoke. "No longer will union positions be delegated to the class room, the factory floor, or to the field. No longer will employers be able to threaten workers with deportation if they complain about work conditions. No longer will the toughest jobs in America also pay the least amount. No longer will your employer be able to terminate your position as part of downsizing efforts." He lowered his voice, but maintained the intensity. "And that is just the beginning of the many benefits that will be provided to you. I urge each and every one of you to recognize and embrace the value IPEA will bring to you and your families. It is time that you, the worker, were given the importance you are due. Without you, we cannot succeed ... with you, we can only become what we were destined to be, the greatest nation on Earth." He raised his fist in the air in a gesture of victory. "Choose IPEA! It will be the best choice you can make, for now and for the future."

Six hours later, in the comfort of his luxurious brownstone townhouse in Georgetown, Harry watched the results transmitted across the video screen from his four poster bed. The Republican senators did their best to filibuster the vote, but eventually gave up, knowing it was a lost cause. The House version of the Immigrant Progress and Enrichment Act passed with a vote of 72 to 29.

"Let the games begin," he proclaimed loudly, soliciting a barely audible grunt from his sleeping wife. With that, he turned out the light and went to sleep.

Chapter 19

Los Angeles, California

Reggie shoved the stack of paperwork to the side of the desk. He was over it. Since the Santoro murders, his world had been in overdrive. It seemed that all he did these days was report upon report for some random bureaucrat involved with overseeing RIM.

It frustrated him that he and Carlos had hit a dead end on the Raphael Santoro case. Failure was not something he was familiar with and that was the only way to describe their progress thus far. They had not uncovered a new lead in the case in months. All the victims had been identified, evaluated, and investigated, but not a single connection could be made between any of them. He and Carlos had reached the conclusion that the victims were nothing more than a group of random souls with the unfortunate luck to be used for a sinister purpose. Carlos had equated them to pawns in a chess match who only purpose was to be used and discarded in order to achieve a bigger prize.

As for Raphael, it was not random circumstance that he had been a victim. It was clear that he was killed to deliver a message to the Latino and the African American communities. That message had been like the spark in a tinder box, igniting a firestorm of violence across the city. The Latino community had been enraged by the killing of one of their own. Raphael had been a prominent role model in the local Latino community and vocal advocate for passage of the IPEA legislation. Now he had become a martyr for the cause.

Since the murders, conflict between the two racial groups had risen to an all-time high. If Los Angeles had been bad before, now it really was insane. The continued conflict had intensified to the point that the National Guard had been called in to restore peace. They were having marginal success, but overall the city was in a full-fledged war.

The door to his office burst open, startling Reggie for a moment. Carlos ran over to the flat panel hanging on the wall and turned it on. "Jefe, you need to see this."

The television flashed to life. Displayed on the screen was a large structure on fire with smoke billowing profusely into the air. It took Reggie a moment to realize that he was looking at live footage of the Wall in Texas. "Another border explosion at the Wall?" he questioned not particularly interested by the event. "That is becoming a regular occurrence these days," he frowned at Carlos, not sure of the reason for the intrusion into his office.

Noting his apathetic reaction, Carlos motioned for him to continue to watch. "Espera," Carlos said. His eyes were locked on the screen and the look on his face told Reggie that he better pay close attention. There must be something else Carlos wanted him to see.

A news anchor appeared providing more details, explaining that the authorities were looking for a person of interest who had been found in an unauthorized area of the wall shortly before the explosion. An image of a middle aged man with a thin, angular face appeared on the screen. The man had a large, ragged scar running from his left temple and down the entire length of his face. His eyes were dark and sinister. Reggie leaped from his chair. He knew that face, the problem was he wasn't sure from where.

"Yes, Jefe ... you recognize the face, too? It took me a while to recall where else I had seen it." He opened the file that he had been carrying with him, removing a picture and handed it to Reggie. It was a picture of Raphael Santoro and Mason Kelley, the Secretary of Labor Equalization. The picture had been captured outside of the Los Angeles Courthouse shortly after a press announcement by Mason Kelley about the IPEA bill. As far as they knew, it was the last picture taken of Raphael Santoro alive. Reggie scanned the picture more closely, as he had on numerous occasions while looking for clues. Behind the two men were a multitude of supporters, some carrying signs, other waving Mexican flags. It was easy to miss the face, almost blending into the scenery. He pulled out a magnifying lens and looked at the face with the scar. There was no doubt about it. It was that same face staring back at him, the eyes as sinister as ever.

Walterboro, South Carolina

Jasper nocked the arrow and flexed the bow string slightly, feeling the tension. The rafter of red-headed turkeys were almost in range, oblivious to his position only thirty yards away nestled within a thicket of green fauna. The group was taking its time, foraging for food among the forest floor, greedily consuming bits of rotten berries, acorns, and the occasional insect. He never understood why a group of turkeys was called a rafter. It seemed strange to call a group of birds anything but a flock. *Well*, he thought, it didn't matter what they were called, the group would be minus one in a just a few minutes.

He adjusted his grip on his long bow. The bow was practically an extension of himself, custom made for his height, arm span, and draw strength. He had hand carved and tillered the bow himself from a stave of hickory several years ago. Back when he had more free time to pursue his hobbies, wood working being his favorite. Now, bow hunting was one of the few remaining luxuries he allowed himself. He found the peace and isolation of the wilderness was restorative and healing, a welcome refuge from the toils of his normal day.

It had been a grueling week of campaign activities that had culminated with his press conference yesterday at Battery Park. The conference had gone well from his perspective, but he disliked having to dodge the question that was asked of him by a reporter from the Post & Courier news agency. It had been a legitimate question, but one that he was not prepared to answer. The truth was he didn't know how to answer it. How does one answer the question, "Are you for or against the secession of South Carolina from the United States?"

In the end, his answer was based on his answer to a more complex question. What was the right choice for the people of the state? If he was going to be the leader the people of South Carolina needed him to be, he had to be crystal clear on his reasons in support or against secession. There was no opportunity to compromise his beliefs or his values. Compromise was only a luxury that could be afforded when a situation was not critical or when building the foundation of a larger, more strategic objective. The current situation of the state, let alone the country, did not allow for compromise. Now was the time for action. South Carolina needed a leader desperately and its citizens needed a leader who had a clear vision for the future.

What bothered him so much was that either alternative of the future required he trample on everything that he had defended all his life. That was the paradox Jasper had been wrestling with all morning and had been stewing over for the past several weeks. On many occasions, he had internally debated the logic in support of secession and the logic against it. In the case of the latter, how could he advocate for the destruction of a union that so many before him had sacrificed their lives for in order to preserve? Where was his honor to the oath that he had pledged as a soldier and the oath he pledged as a congressman to defend the Constitution of the United States against all enemies, foreign and domestic? By supporting secession, would he actually become the domestic enemy that he had sworn to defend his country against?

In favor of secession, he found the questions even harder to answer. Secession seemed a logical outcome for South Carolina to pursue given the past and recent actions of the federal government. The country today was far different than the country that the founders had envisioned it would be. It had deviated so far off track in so many areas in pursuit of equalization, welfare for all, and collectivism. Now, the government had become too powerful and there was little hope reform of any sort could be implemented. In just the last decade, he was amazed at the aggressive governmental policy that steadily encroached on individual liberties that had been sacred for hundreds of years. Even the holy grail of documents, the Constitution, had been emptied of its original intent. Like so much else, it too had become a victim of subversion, liberal policy and the liberal politicians who sought to make the law cater to the people, versus making people comply with the law. Jasper thought that a state would be justified in seceding if its people and its leaders believed their unalienable rights of life, liberty, and the pursuit of happiness were in jeopardy or worse, no longer relevant.

The debate in his mind came to an abrupt stop as a rather obese male turkey waddled into his target zone. Its bright red head bobbled up and down as it pecked on the ground, occasionally rustling it's dark brown tail feathers that offset its speckled white and black breast. It was a beautiful bird. Jasper rose slowly from his crouched position, simultaneously pulling back on the bow string with one hand until his bow arm was fully extended and the arrow was positioned in the center of the bow. He tracked the movement of the turkey for a few seconds, aligning the path of the arrow with his target. He waited patiently for his opening. Seconds later, the turkey presented its broad side as it turned to peck on a nearby plant. Jasper released the arrow gently, hearing the snap of the bow as the arrow cleared the rest and sailed forward. As the arrow landed with a thud in its intended target, Jasper was already thinking of the future. Not about secession, the election, or even his next date with Alexis. He was thinking about Thanksgiving dinner next November and what a feast it was going to be.

Chapter 20

Myrtle Beach, South Carolina

"How do you respond to allegations by your opponent that you are against illegal immigrants?" The news reporter asked, pushing the small microphone in the face of Jasper Thorne.

Jasper appeared not to be concerned by the reporter's question. He responded in a calm concise manner, making sure he made full eye contact with the camera. He was standing in the picturesque Battery Park. Over his shoulder stood the statue of Confederate Defenders of Charleston monument, a gift dedicated by the Daughters of the American Revolution for those who served at Fort Sumter.

"Let me be perfectly clear. I am not against illegal immigrants. They are some of the hardest working individuals in our country, who are only seeking a better life for themselves and their families. However, I am against the destructive immigration policies of our government that have fueled the problem of illegal immigration. Our immigration policies have failed and our process of integrating illegal immigrants into society is broken. We are told by our government that our current and proposed policies are meant to promote the greater human good and to create economic benefit for our country … only they don't and they never will. Instead these policies, like the IPEA bill, create division between people and lead us deeper into the economic abyss that we find ourselves in today."

"Can you provide an example of what you mean?" The reporter questioned.

"My opponent wants you to believe that IPEA will create jobs. I disagree. I believe it will cause the loss of jobs. Under IPEA, there will be cases where lower wage non-union positions will automatically become higher wage union positions. As a result when IPEA is implemented, the labor costs for many companies are going to increase across the board. Companies that can no longer deliver a profitable product or service because labor costs are too high will have no choice but take actions that will lead to job loss. We need comprehensive immigration reform to address current illegal immigrants as well as implement a solid method to control immigration in the future. At this point we have neither and what is proposed is detrimental to our country. That is why, as governor, I would fight against destructive federal legislation like IPEA."

"He is smooth. I will give him that." Derrick Baldwin reclined in the chair and glanced at his fishing line. Still no bites and they had been out on the water for almost four hours. Springtime had come late to South Carolina, which meant the speckled trout were finally on the prowl and starting to move into shallower water to feed and spawn. They were floating with the current about five miles off shore of Myrtle Beach. The boat rocked softly in the two foot swells, creating a rhythmic smacking sound as the hull rose and then fell back into the water.

"Smooth? He's a loser. Where else does a person get off being so self-righteous except in this backward state? I just don't get it," Robert Coolridge responded as he flipped the channel on the satellite video monitor to a baseball game. The New York Yankees were playing their season opener against the Texas Rangers and losing ten to two in the bottom of the sixth inning. The Yankees' season was expected to be a repeat of last year, considering the team consisted of the same players from last year's championship team. The only change was the replacement of the Team Manager. The Yankees were expected to win this game handedly; no one expected them to be losing to one of the worst teams in the league. Robert was surprised by the score. Not only were they losing, the Yankees were being thrashed.

"Excellent. That is what I like to see. The Yankees losing means DB is winning!" Derrick smacked himself on his leg in congratulations.

Robert held his tongue deciding not to respond. If there was an Achilles heel to Derrick Baldwin, it was his love of gambling. The man bet on everything. His obsession had made him the perfect hedge fund manager, by which both of them had profited millions. Even so, Robert had rescued Derrick from his own bad judgment on multiple occasions. Sure, Robert knew gambling was an addiction. He also knew that science had proven that people had a genetic disposition to gambling, but it didn't change things. He hated having to spend his money because Baldwin couldn't control himself or didn't care. Maybe Baldwin thought that Robert would always be there to bail him out.

Robert considered the situation further, and then stopped. It was too late to have reservations about the decision he had made. In the end, it didn't matter what he thought about Derrick's personal addictions. He and the others were too heavily invested to change direction now. Derrick was the man they were betting on and his gambling addiction made him the perfect candidate for the task at hand. Derrick was someone they could control at will and he would do exactly as he was told. All that mattered now was that Derrick wouldn't make a misstep to cost the election. Perhaps that was the riskiest gamble of them all. Robert took a deep swig of his beer. There was only one thing left for him to do and that was make sure Derrick bought into the plan.

"Derrick, we are a little more than six months from the election. How are you feeling about it?"

"I feel good. I think we have the right platform and our message is resonating with the citizens. We have the Latino vote locked and the polls indicate that the traditional Democratic voter is still planning to vote Democratic. If Congress can pass IPEA this month, we should see an increase of more than ten percent in the Democratic voting pool, assuming the illegals can find employment by Election Day. That should be enough to give us the win by a healthy margin," Derrick replied complacently.

"What are going to do if the South Carolina legislature decides to support secession?" Robert challenged.

"Are you kidding me? There is not a prayer that they will get that legislation passed. Even if they do, the people are against it. At least the people we have polled," Derrick shrugged. "The idea of a state seceding in this day and age is plain ludicrous. Not only is it impractical, it is inhumane. Even if a state managed to secede, how would it be able to cope with all the humanitarian needs of the people without the federal government?" Derrick watched the television monitor for a moment and cursed under his breath as the Yankees made a base hit.

"Most states are drowning in debt," Derrick continued, "including South Carolina. I will give the state leaders credit that they have managed to minimize their debt growth, but they are upside down like the rest of the country. There would be no way to support the people. The financial burden alone would sink the country in a matter of weeks." The fishing pole Derrick was holding flexed in his hand, causing him to jump. The tension was gone a moment later. He turned his attention back to Robert. "Just look at history and what led to the demise of the confederacy. In the end, it was finances. Throw in military action from the government, trade embargos, and just plain human idiocy in trying to govern a rouge state ... that is one deal I would not bet on, no matter what the payout."

"I am glad to hear that we think alike on that subject." Robert paused, choosing his words wisely. "Derrick, there is a reason I chose you as our candidate to become governor in this race. I think it is time you understood the bigger picture and the role that I, and others in the government, need you to play." Robert secured his fishing pole in a holder and turned off the television monitor. "That is one of the reasons I wanted to be out here, in the open water, away from prying ears."

Derrick turned his full attention on Robert, ignoring the twitching in his fishing line.

Robert spoke slowly, it was imperative that Derrick understood every word. "Despite what you believe now, there may come a time in the near future when the citizens of this country revolt against the government. Whether it is through protest, violent mobs, or secession, I am expecting we are going to have ramifications from the actions we plan to take."

"What are you talking about?" asked Derrick. "Who is this 'we' you are referring too?"

"There is a reason that we are not sparing any expense in supporting your campaign for governor," Robert grimaced. The truth was their spending was projected to significantly surpass their initial estimates, primarily due to the resilience of Thorne's campaign. That fact was a frustrating reality, only because it was his pocket book that had to cover the shortfall. "Derrick, we need you to win this election, just like we need the candidates in five other states to win their own respective elections for governor."

"Sure, we all want to win. Don't play games with me. Cut to the chase." Derrick demanded.

Robert continued calmly. "We are at a critical juncture in our nation's future. It is time for the government to take action for the greater good and longevity of our country. It is the only way we are going to create a more prosperous nation and solve all these issues that we have." He scanned the horizon, noting the increasing frequency of the white-capped waves. They would have to head back to shore soon, a storm was forming. He turned to Derrick who was still watching him intently. "Winning the governorship of South Carolina is essential to our overall success. The office of Governor has tremendous power in our system of government, though it is seldom exercised. Much like the president, a state governor has the power to propose, approve and veto legislation, issue executive orders, and appoint judges for the state." Robert tossed the dice, "Of greater importance to us and our mission is that governors have the power to control the National Guard and the state defense forces. Once all the governorship positions are secure, we are in position to take the next step."

"The National Guard? I am not sure I follow you completely. The president has the power to control the National Guard in a state of national emergency or on the voluntary agreement of the … governor." Derrick nodded suddenly understanding the relevance of Robert's comments. "I think I understand. Unlike the National Guard, the state defense troops cannot be called into federal service under the president. They are only at the command of the governor, almost as a last line of defense for the state. I know the ranks of state defense forces have swelled in the last years."

Robert asserted, "Yes, the state forces have gotten stronger. It would not be good to have a situation occur where the state's defense force and the state's National Guard where at arms against each other. We need to have a means of control. Many people are going to disagree and resist the actions the federal government will be taking and the potential for revolt will be very real. That is why we need to ensure we have a means to protect and defend. We cannot afford to have a rouge state use its people and resources against the federal government and our citizens."

Derrick nodded in agreement but remained quiet. Robert could tell he was processing the information he had just given him.

"Derrick, you and I have known each other since college. You know you can trust me. You and the other fifty governors, assuming all our candidates win their respective elections, will be the cornerstone of our new political structure." Robert stood up and balanced himself against the swaying boat. "That is why I need you to win this election. That is why your country needs you to win. The stakes are huge for our nation. They are even bigger for you." Robert flashed his best devilish grin. "You see Derrick, you and I will be in on the ground floor of what will come. We will be ushering in a brand new era in our country."

"You're talking about revolution?" Derrick gasped, almost dropping his fishing pole.

"I prefer to call it revelation," Robert responded curtly.

Derrick turned back to study his fishing line contemplating what he had just heard. Robert knew the payoff was too big for Derrick to resist; it was the gamble of a lifetime. Robert smiled as soon as he turned away from Derrick to inspect his own fishing line. He had been so intent on his conversation with Derrick that he had failed to see that he had hooked a fish. By the looks of the way his rod was bending, it was a good catch. Yes, it was a very good catch indeed.

Chapter 21

"Life is neither good or evil, but only a place for good and evil."
- Marcus Aurelius

Washington, District of Columbia

Jasper took his seat, leaning back in the chair as he rubbed his temples in an attempt to ease the pain. His head felt like a rubber band that was stretched to its breaking point and then some. Yesterday had not been a good day. The morning had begun with an announcement that the Senate had approved the final version of the IPEA bill. All that was needed now was for the president to sign the legislation for it to become law.

At noon, the news broke of a large explosion at the Naval Academy in Annapolis, Maryland just twenty-three miles from Washington D.C. A small motor craft, heavily loaded with explosives, had driven at full speed into the sea wall outside the Nimitz library. The resulting explosion destroyed a large portion of the sea wall and the east wing of the library. The details were still forthcoming on the incident, but forty people had been confirmed killed, several dozen more were either missing or wounded. Most of the casualties were students who had been busily preparing for final exams. Jasper had been very concerned when he heard the news for multiple reasons. The foremost being that a few of the faculty at the Academy were friends he had known since the War. He had made inquiries and had been relieved to learn that none of them had been injured in the explosion, but the incident still rattled him.

The worst news of the day, however, was when Alexis told him that she would be taking a three-month assignment in New York City. Though Jasper supported her commitment to her work, he was disappointed that they would be away from each other for so long. Their relationship had intensified over the past few months. What had started out as a few dates during the winter months had blossomed into full-fledged dating by the spring. Now, they made it a point to see each other weekly, despite his busy campaign schedule. They had become, in her words, *exclusive*. He didn't care what she called the two of them. All he knew was that he longed to be with her and it seemed that the time with her was never enough. He hadn't realized how alone he had been nor the extent of his social isolation. Alexis had changed everything.

"How is my prized student today? A little worse for the wear, it looks like," Michael chuckled. He had a yardstick in his hands and was tapping it rhythmically on the table, much to Jasper's chagrin. "Too many late nights with your lady friend?"

"I wish. We're still on a hand-holding only basis," Jasper's reply was half serious, half joking. It frustrated him that he and Alexis had not become physically intimate yet. She deflected his advances with a skill and deference that made him somehow feel good about being rejected. He didn't know how many times he heard her say something to the effect of "Jasper, honey … when the time is right, we will both know it. I want you badly, but our relationship must take its course. If I give in now, I will not be able to stop myself. My desire for you is that great. I am worth waiting for and you will be so glad you waited too." Perhaps it was the hope that one day they would become intimate that allowed him to accept her response and be patient. That day would not come soon enough in his mind. Jasper sighed, "But that is a story for another time."

Michael smiled approvingly. "She may teach you something, yet." For some reason, Jasper believed he was right.

"How was your trip to Charleston?" Jasper asked, reaching for the cup of coffee that Michael had waiting for him. Michael's knack for anticipating his needs was a skill Jasper had grown to appreciate in his Chief of Staff.

"Charleston was not as successful as I hoped," Michael responded, brushing a stray curl from his face. "Derrick Baldwin has quite the political machine in operation. He has weekly campaign events in every major city and is drawing huge crowds from the liberal base and the independents. It probably is due to the food certificates that he is giving away to anyone who attends. Not only that, he has gained the endorsement of the South Carolina Tourism Bureau, which has become a critical foundation of his job development platform. We have our work cut out for us."

"Food certificates? Do we know who is funding his campaign?" Jasper asked, surprised by the blatant attempt to buy public favor.

"We think that Coolidge may be the chief supporter and orchestrator. Baldwin and Coolidge were college roommates at Berkley," Michael said.

"That makes sense. They remind me of each other," Jasper wrinkled his nose in disgust. "They are like used car salesmen, only Robert is much better looking. Both of them make my skin crawl."

The mysterious Derrick Baldwin magically appeared as the Democratic candidate for governor just two months earlier. There had been other candidates in history that had come out of near obscurity to secure high level positions in state and U.S. government, himself included. That made Jasper weary. He couldn't effectively fight a foe that he didn't know. He was at a disadvantage for sure. Over the past three weeks, Michael had been compiling a great deal of information on Baldwin. Even though Jasper had learned plenty lately about his new opponent, it was not enough. And he was not particularly happy about what they had uncovered so far. Baldwin was definitely going to be a tough competitor to beat.

"I'll have the files updated with latest information first thing in the morning, in time for our briefing session. Right now, I want to focus on our lesson," Michael said, changing the focus of their conversation. Jasper nodded in agreement. He needed something to distract him from his daily ordeals.

Michael levied a serious look at Jasper and asked in a stern tone of voice, "Jasper Thorne ... are you a good person?"

Jasper muddled the question over in his head before he spoke. He had learned not to answer quickly with Michael because there was always a deeper meaning to the questions he asked. This was what made these lessons interesting.

"I like to think of myself as a good person. I don't commit violent crimes, steal, cheat, or do other heinous things. I contribute money to a few select charities and volunteer occasionally. I'm an ethical person, particularly at work, which very few can say around here. Sure, I have my faults, but relatively speaking, I think I am a good person compared to most." Jasper said. A moment later, a broad grin formed on Jasper's face as he realized his mistake. He knew he had fallen into the trap Michael had set.

Michael smiled knowingly, "Yes, you see the issue at hand don't you. Good is a relative statement."

"But there is a definite difference between good and evil. You cannot have one without the other." Jasper parried back, sure he was in the right. Michael was not going to get the better of him this time.

"Don't be so sure of that, my young friend." Michael stated authoritatively. The surety of Michael's statement made Jasper uneasy. He had a sinking suspicion this would not be like other lessons and he was right.

Chapter 22

Michael ruffled through his notebook. "Let's look at a scientific approach to this discussion to frame my original assertion that good is relative. Is there such a thing as a hot object?"

Jasper stilled a laugh. "Of course there is."

"Ok. Well is there such a thing as cold object?"

"Yes, there is. They are opposites of the spectrum, just like good and evil."

Michael nodded his head, causing a cluster of curls to spring down his face and then back again. "Well let's play this premise out. What makes an object hot versus cold?"

"The temperature of the object," Jasper responded casually.

"Yes, and temperature is really a measure of heat or thermal energy in the object. When we add energy to an object, its atoms and molecules move faster — increasing its energy of motion, or heat. Even objects which are very cold have some heat energy, because their atoms are still moving." Jasper nodded, he was well aware of this fact of thermodynamics from his engineering studies.

"We can measure the heat of an object by its temperature," Michael continued. "Scientific evidence confirms that there are increasing degrees of heat, based on the amount of energy in an object. For example, we can measure the small amount of heat generated by a match flame to the enormous amount of heat generated by the process of fusion that occurs in the sun. In fact, science has not been able to measure the outer boundary of heat, or to say it differently, science has not been able to determine a limit of the hottest temperature." Michael paused for a moment and scribbled something on his note pad. "Sorry, just a random thought I had to capture." Jasper chuckled slightly thinking that Michael was always working on multiple things at once.

"Now back to our discussion on temperature. Unlike heat, we really don't have anything that is cold. Cold is only a term we use to describe an object that has less heat. We can measure the temperature in an object to absolute zero, a level of four hundred and fifty eight degrees Fahrenheit below zero. Absolute zero is a total absence of thermal energy in the object or heat. We cannot measure cold because there is no such thing as cold; otherwise we would be able to go to greater degrees of cold than minus four hundred and fifty eight degrees. Therefore, cold is not the opposite of hot, it is just the absence of heat. Just like darkness is not the opposite of light, it is only the absence of it."

Jasper thought for a moment. He did agree with the premise though he had never looked at this issue from that perspective before. It was an intriguing viewpoint and very logical.

"So, based on what I just told you, is there such a thing as evil?" Michael asked.

"Of course, there is. We see it every day, in the example of man's inhumanity to man. It is in the multitude of crime and violence everywhere in the world. These manifestations are nothing else but evil."

"Perhaps, but it is my belief that evil does not exist … or, at least, it does not exist unto itself. Evil is simply the absence of good. Or as I like to think, the absence of God. It is just like darkness and cold, a word that we have created to describe the absence of something else. Evil is the result of what happens when one does not have God's love present in his or her heart. It's like the cold that comes when there is no heat or the darkness that comes when there is no light."

Jasper settled back in his chair, thinking through Michael's argument. It was definitely intriguing, but where was he going with it?

Michael continued. "So, let's take this analogy one step further. Let's say you take this yardstick and stand it vertically on the ground." He positioned one end of the yardstick on the floor and held the other with his index finger. "We will call the base of the yardstick where it touches the ground, evil. We will call the top of the yard stick, good. The yardstick symbolizes the spectrum of good and evil from a human perspective. Now, say we transpose the Ten Commandments onto the yardstick. If someone were to violate the commandment 'Thou Shall Not Kill', where would you expect to find that person on the yardstick?"

Jasper answered slowly, "At the bottom. The taking of a human life is one of, if not the most, heinous of crimes."

"Agreed." Michael pointed at the bottom of the stick. "So where would you place someone who violated the commandment 'Thou shall not tell a lie'?"

Jasper rose and began to pace, thinking through the question. "That is another subjective question. It would depend on the severity of the lie and its consequences. However, I cannot see a lie being more evil than murdering someone. I would place it midway on the yardstick."

Michael smiled, clearly enjoying this lesson. Jasper felt he was being set up for something big. "Yes. However, someone else may have a different opinion on where it should be placed on the yardstick. It is human nature to place those actions that violate moral values such as torture, rape, or murder at the base of the yardstick. While those actions that violate ethical values such as lying and stealing will tend to be placed in the middle of the yardstick. Using the yardstick analogy, it is easy to see how we quantify our own goodness relative to other people or our society. Now, where would you place yourself on this yardstick?"

Jasper didn't hesitate, "I know I am not perfect but I would place myself somewhere at the upper quartile."

"Fair. Where would you place a person like Mother Teresa?"

"Well obviously above where I would place myself. She would be closer to the top of the yardstick?"

"Why?"

Jasper paused. It was a good question. "I suppose I would place her there because of her extreme acts of charity, love, and selflessness. The greater good she did for humanity would make her a good person in most people's minds."

"So you are telling me that based on your own personal standards you are not as good of a person as she is?" Michael challenged.

"No, I guess I am not."

"So, from Mother Teresa's perspective, you would not be a good person, because you fall short of her personal standard of goodness."

Jasper scratched the stubble on his chin. He had forgotten to shave that morning. "Perhaps. But again, this is relative to a person's viewpoint on the subject. I could be a murderer and think I am a good person if I believed the murder I committed served the greater good."

"Well, does Mother Teresa deserve to go to Heaven more than you because of her goodness?"

"I think most of us deserve to go to Heaven, but we cannot determine that definitively by our own standards because our standards are tainted by our personal views. What we need is an absolute to measure against."

Michael looked at Jasper over the bridge of his glasses curiously. "What do you suggest we use then?" he asked.

"I guess we should measure ourselves against God," Jasper said, not really sure if that was the right answer.

Michael slammed his fist on the table, soliciting a crack of protest from the weathered table. "That's my boy!" he exclaimed. "Yes. It is God who is the one and only absolute definition of good. He is the measurement we must use to answer questions like 'Are you a good person?' and 'Who deserves to go to Heaven?'" Jasper couldn't help but feel encouraged by Michael's reaction.

"Let's use our yardstick again, but this time we are going to look at God's viewpoint on the matter. Imagine for a moment that we were sitting at the base of the Grand Canyon with our yard stick as we have already defined it. At the top of our yardstick, we have people who most would define as good people, be it Mother Teresa, the Pope, or Grandma. Now imagine that God was in an airplane flying over us and our yardstick at thirty thousand feet and looking down." Michael made a gesture as if someone was peering down into a deep well. "Now, consider that God has a different yardstick than we do and it is measured from the base of our human yardstick all the way to the airplane. If God is the absolute measure and he is the definition of good, we are a long way away from reaching his standard of goodness. From God's perspective, we are at the very bottom of his yardstick, just like someone who committed a murder would be placed on our human yardstick."

Michael reached for his Bible and opened to a page that was bookmarked with a red ribbon. "In God's sight, no one is good enough, not even those people that we would define as good people." He thumped his finger on his Bible. "Romans 3:23 states, *'For all have sinned and fall short of the glory of God.'* You see Jasper, it is our sin that makes us unworthy of Heaven. It makes us tainted and evil in God's sight. It causes us to be on the bottom of God's yardstick and His is the only one that matters from an eternal perspective. It does not matter how bad our sins are or how many times we commit a sin. Nor does it matter how many good works we do for others for we cannot earn our way into Heaven and cannot earn goodness in God's eyes. We will always fall short of his standard of goodness. So by this definition, no one is good and no one deserves to go to Heaven."

There was a long silence in the room. Jasper felt his heartbeat thumping in his chest. His first reaction was to argue that Michael was wrong, but something told him that would be useless. Michael's logic was very sound on the matter. "This is a new concept for me to grasp. I always compared myself, what I have achieved, and what I have accomplished against others. I have never looked at myself in comparison to God. If what you tell me is true, then how do I and others get to Heaven?"

"That will be in a future lesson. First, we need to understand the truth about sin and how ..." Jasper's phone vibrated in his jacket pocket, interrupting their discussion. He was going to ignore it, but decided to check the number in case it was Alexis.

He looked at the name displayed on his phone. That was odd, Jasper thought. *Why was Senator Holloway calling him?* He knew Trent was on vacation with his family at Hilton Head Island. "I need to take this," he said to Michael, who only nodded and begin writing more notes on his pad.

Jasper answered his phone in a jovial tone. "Trent ... for what do I owe you for the pleasure of your call? To interrupt your vacation to call me, you've either had too much tequila or this is very important."

"You're damn right, it is important, Jasper." Trent's voice was sharp and heated. "The president just issued an executive proclamation. It's unlike anything that's been done before and crooked'er than a three dollar bill."

"An executive proclamation? What about?" Jasper responded. Michael looked up hearing the concern in Jasper's voice.

Trent's next words were tainted with what Jasper could only describe as hopelessness. "You and I, along with millions of others, have just had our homes stolen by the U.S. government."

Chapter 23

"Ambition must be made to counteract ambition. The interest of the man must be connected with the constitutional rights of the place. It may be a reflection on human nature, that such devices should be necessary to control the abuses of government. But what is government itself, but the greatest of all reflections on human nature? If men were angels, no government would be necessary. If angels were to govern men, neither external nor internal controls on government would be necessary. In framing a government which is to be administered by men over men, the great difficulty lies in this: you must first enable the government to control the governed; and in the next place oblige it to control itself."

-Federalist Paper 51, Alexander Hamilton or James Madison

Proclamation 29230 was signed by the president at four o'clock in the afternoon, just eighteen hours after the terrorist attack at the U.S. Naval Academy. There was no prior announcement by the White House about the proclamation, nor any press invited to the signing. It had been orchestrated in complete secrecy. The White House Press Secretary had issued a press release that was direct and to the point. The president had declared a state of emergency along the U.S. border and established specific restrictions in Proclamation 29230. According to the Press Secretary, the proclamation had been executed in response to continued and increasingly more violent terrorist activities that had been occurring along the U.S. border over the past six months. The proclamation would facilitate the ability of the federal government to protect the health and welfare of the country's citizens from future attacks by allowing them to properly fortify and patrol the border.

The president's proclamation was simple in its nature, but powerful in its application. It established a formal governmental border zone along the entire U.S. geographical border. It extended inland by two miles, effectively making all land, buildings, and structures attached to that land the property of the United States government. Municipalities, corporations, and citizens who owned property inside the border boundary would still be allowed to occupy and utilize any buildings, homes, or other structures within the zone, but the government would have the ability to search, commandeer, and house troops in such property at will in support of patrolling the border.

Overnight, large coastal cities such as Miami, Baltimore, New York City, Los Angeles, and San Francisco lost large sections of their downtowns, marine ports, and key tourism centers to the expanded border zone. Up and down the coast, private land owners and small businesses owners suddenly found themselves no longer owning the asset that represented the majority of their wealth. Surprisingly and in relation to what had happened, the reaction of the public was muted. Those who were unaffected by the proclamation did not appear to care, and those who lived in the zone, but were struggling with upside down mortgages or foreclosure were almost relieved to have an excuse to no longer pay their mortgages. Others viewed it as a positive outreach of governmental power being used to protect them. But pockets of protest were springing up all over the country, particularly in the southern states.

"Alex, I really appreciate what you are doing for me. I also must apologize. This is not how I envisioned we would spend our last evening together before your trip to New York." Jasper tried not to let his frustration show. Alone together for the first time in three weeks at his condominium in Georgetown, tonight was meant to be a romantic evening. Italian wine, a nice dinner and nothing to concern themselves but each other — it was meant to be special in so many ways. Jasper was planning to tell Alexis how he felt about her and their blossoming relationship, only life was getting in the way — *again*.

"Can the president really get away with this?" he asked as he poured them another glass of sangiovese.

Alexis did not respond to his question. Her face buried in a mound of paperwork. Various legal documents and historical case records littered the coffee table and sofa, some in small orderly piles, others thrown haphazardly, as if discarded without a second thought.

He walked over to her and rested a glass of wine on a clear section of the coffee table, left open for that purpose alone.

"I am sorry, did you say something?" She ignored the fresh glass of wine, her focus absorbed by her reading of a legal summary of Korematsu v. United States.

He placed his hands on her shoulders and began to massage her neck and head. "Why don't you take a break for a moment? You have been at this all day," he pleaded.

"Oh, that feels good," she said, her body yielding to his touch as he loosened the tension in her neck. "Where did you learn to do that?"

"I have many secrets to share with you, but all in good time. Just sit back for a few minutes and let me do my thing." She complied willingly, giving over to his gentle but penetrating touch.

Jasper loved the feel of her skin. It was soft and silky and his fingers seem to glide right over it. He liked how she was responding to his touch even more. It made him feel good to provide her pleasure, even if it was only of a plutonic nature. He could tell Alex was enjoying it as well, she was emitting a soft sound, almost like a cat purring.

Ten minutes later, he concluded the massage and took a seat next to her on the couch. He was reaching for his glass of wine when she intercepted him. She moved closer to him, pressing him back into the couch. Her hands embraced the sides of his head as her head came within inches of his. Her brown eyes looked directly at him, searching. "You're a good man, Jasper Thorne. Thank you." She kissed him, first tentatively and then forcefully. Jasper responded, kissing her with fierceness, driven by his pent up desire for her but also with control that he knew that this would not go further. Her lips were lush and supple, perfectly matched to his. It was a long kiss, one that was over way to soon. It left him wanting more.

She broke away from him, returning to her side of the couch. "It is a good thing you're a good kisser, Jasper Thorne.

Otherwise, we would have to end this relationship right now," she chided him. Jasper smiled, agreeing with her.

"That massage was really invigorating and I really needed that. I was getting bored with all of this research." She took a long sip of her wine and then stood up, stretching briefly, providing him as much benefit as it did to her. "What is that smell?" she said, inhaling deeply. "It is divine. What are you cooking?" Alexis headed to the kitchen to investigate.

"Just a little recipe I picked up in Italy. I hope you like it. I have never shared it with anyone before," he said pleased that she was interested. Jasper had first learned to prepare the dish during the war while on a recreational break in Sicily. The key was to reduce the tomato, Greek olives, garlic and olive oil mixture to the correct concentration. Once the sauce was done, it was layered thick between thin layers of crumbled Parmigiano-Reggiano cheese over pasta and fresh vegetables. He was feeling pretty confident that she would be hooked from the first bite.

She quickly returned, blowing on a spoon that was filled with a deep red liquid. Jasper stared at her, thinking about how beautiful she was. Everything she did was sexy. "Oh my," she exclaimed, her face expressing a look of delight. "This is delicious. Not only are your fingers magic, you can cook too. Lucky me!"

"Wait until it has cooked for another thirty minutes," he exclaimed proudly. "It will taste even better."

"You learned this in Italy? When were you there?"

He was slow to answer her. When he did, his voice was despondent, "Back in the war."

"I know that you spent five years overseas in the war, but you have never shared anything with me about your experiences," Alexis said. It was a statement more than a question.

Jasper didn't bite. "It was another time and another place. There are more important things to discuss now."

She sat back down on the couch next to him. "Honey, you know I never mean to pry. I am only interested in everything that makes you the incredible man you are." Alexis stroked her fingers through Jasper's think hair, tickling him with her fingertips. "Now,

I don't want to know about every girl you kissed," she giggled, giving him a light check in the gut with her elbow, "but I do want to know about the things that shaped your life." She cupped his hands in hers. "I hope you will share with me those personal things about your past when you feel comfortable. You need to believe me when I say I will never judge you for what you have done. I really respect you." She paused judging his reaction. "Please understand that you can trust me with anything." Her voice was sincere and her eyes belayed the honesty of her statement.

Jasper was silent for a moment. Trusting others was foreign to him. Since his parent's death, the only person he trusted was himself. It didn't matter the circumstances. In the end, there was only Jasper Thorne to rely on, no one else came close. He didn't expect Alexis to understand so he didn't bother arguing with her on this point. "Thank you Alex ... I appreciate your concern and your honesty. Maybe someday, when I am ready." He changed the subject, "So, what have you been able to determine on the constitutionality of this presidential proclamation?"

Alexis seemed taken aback by the question for moment. Perhaps she had not expected to be shunned so quickly from an intimate discussion. But if that were the case, she did a good job in recovering, a moment later she was digging for her digital tablet under a stack of documents.

Once she found it, she paused and looked at Jasper. "There is a great deal to cover. Where do you want to begin?"

Chapter 24

Alexis' tone became very authoritative as she read from her notes. "By asserting that the federal government is now the property owner of the land and attached dwellings in the prescribed border zone, the president's proclamation has effectively neutralized the Third, Fourth, and Fifth amendments for those living inside the border zone. This includes you, since your residence in Charleston falls within the boundaries of the new border zone."

"No way! How is that possible?" Jasper exclaimed, his frustration resurfacing. He felt powerless to fight against the government's blatant disregard for his constitutional rights.

"The Third Amendment protects a property owner from having to house military troops in their property. Based on this proclamation, you are no longer the owner of your house, so the government could choose to quarter troops in your house, even during a time of peace," Alexis peered at him over the paper she was reading, gauging his reaction. "We have no prior case law to reference on this point, as Third amendment rights have not been called into question at any time in history before."

Jasper let out a long breath, trying to block out a mental image of a random U.S. soldier sleeping in his bed and helping himself to the food in his refrigerator. "Ok. So we have no precedence. That could work both ways, in our favor or against it," Jasper offered.

"True, but this is where it gets interesting," Alexis explained. "The Fourth amendment is completely usurped by this proclamation. Since the border zone is now an extension of the U.S. border, all people living in the zone or traveling through the zone are subject to search without probable cause. In addition, all homes, facilities, and forms of conveyance are subject to search. This complies with current border enforcement powers."

Jasper remained silent. He knew she was right. Within the boundaries of the U.S. border, the government had total sovereignty and could do anything it wanted. But that still did not give them the right to extend the size of the border boundaries at will.

Alexis continued, "Since the passage of the Immigration and Nationality Act in 1966, the government has had the power to conduct warrantless searches of automobiles and other conveyances within a reasonable distance from any external boundary of the United States. What went under the radar with the 1966 legislation was that the reasonable distance was determined by the Attorney General, who established the distance at one hundred air miles from any external boundary of the United States. That means, even before this proclamation, the government had to power to search your vehicle without probable cause if you lived within one hundred miles of the border."

"What? I have never heard that before. On what cause is such a search warranted?" Jasper questioned, not liking what he was hearing.

"Only if there is an assumption that your vehicle is transporting drugs, contraband, or illegal aliens. Immigration officers can also access any private lands, but not dwellings, located within twenty five miles of the U.S. border without warrant, but only for the purpose of patrolling for illegal aliens. Finally, the government has always retained the right to search people at the border. In essence, the government could argue it is not asserting any new powers that it did not already have, just that the span of the geography over which some of those powers are executed has expanded."

Jasper was impressed. Alex had presented the government's support for the president's proclamation in a concise, relevant, and factual manner. He bet she was amazing in front of a jury. "Even if we were to concede that the proclamation did not violate the Third or Fourth Amendments, it has to be unconstitutional when it comes to the Fifth Amendment. The proclamation is a blatant violation of eminent domain laws," Jasper argued. "Neither the U.S. government nor state governments can take private property for public use, without just compensation." Jasper paused, a thought forming in his mind as he reasoned through the situation. "Perhaps the government believes that they do not have to provide compensation because they are not evicting people from their homes and are allowing people to continue to use their property to conduct business and other related functions within the zone?"

Alexis shook her head, denying his statement.

"So you don't agree with that assertion? Let me pose another," he said, thinking through his next question. He loved when Alexis challenged him in debate. It didn't matter to him that he lost most of the time. She forced him to think quickly, logically, and with the intention to make an impact.

"So, does this mean that the government is now going to pay people's mortgages within the zone?" he asked. "It does not make any sense to me how they could hope to execute this proclamation, even if it were constitutional."

"Possibly, but I doubt it," she said. "My guess is the president and his allies did not think through all the issues and confusion that this proclamation creates. They probably just reacted to the perceived terrorist crisis and public concern for safety and hurriedly crafted a solution." She picked up another file and flipped through its contents and then tossed it back on the table. "I hope that is the case, anyway." She reached for her wine and slowly took a sip before letting out a long breath, "If this proclamation was an intentional, calculated action by the president, than I would say that we have bigger problems to deal with."

Jasper picked up a paper that had a list of various executive orders and proclamations that had been issued by past presidents over the past century. It was a lengthy list. "Does the president have any legal precedent to base this proclamation on?"

"As a matter of fact, he does. The ability to issue an order or proclamation has become an implied power of the Executive office, having been used by every president beginning with George Washington. The Constitution gives the president the power to execute the laws of the country. It specifically states that 'the executive power shall be vested in a President of the

United States.' Basically, if a proclamation or executive order is founded on the authority of the president as derived from the Constitution or an act of Congress, it has the effect of being law. In matters of national security, the president has almost unlimited authority to do what he believes is necessary to protect and defend the country, short of declaring war. Since terrorism is considered a threat to national security, this proclamation could be seen as derived from the president's authority under the Constitution.

"Interesting point," Jasper acknowledged. He had not considered the proclamation from that perspective. "Any specific examples of prior orders or proclamations that he could cite in support of his position?" he asked, hoping there were none.

"Great question but on that point, the president's position is probably the weakest. Although, he could try to support his proclamation by citing that it is an extension of the existing Roosevelt Reservation."

"The Roosevelt Reservation?" Jasper asked perplexed. He had never heard of it. The fact that Alexis thought the president could use it as a basis to support his proclamation was disturbing. He scooted closer to her on the couch. "What is it?" he asked.

"Not many people have heard of the Roosevelt Reservation and there is not a great deal of published information on it. Basically, the "Reservation" is a sixty-foot wide section of land on the United States-Mexico border that spans from California, Arizona, and New Mexico. It was created in 1907 by a presidential proclamation issued by Theodore Roosevelt as a protective measure against smuggling of goods across the border. When it was formally signed by Roosevelt, it established a formal border enforcement zone between the U.S. and Mexico that became federal property and remains so to this day."

"I should have known about that one, given my position on the Judicial Committee," Jasper said, reticently. It never ceased to amaze Jasper the things that he learned about the government and the questionable actions it had taken through the years. The average citizen was completely oblivious to the complicated web of governmental control that had been spun. "Remind me again," he asked, "how is a proclamation different than an executive order?"

Alexis picked up one of her note pads from the table. "They are basically the same thing; however executive orders tend to focus on governing actions performed by other governmental agencies and officials. Proclamations tend to deal with actions that affect private individuals, as is the case with this new proclamation. The framers of our Constitution never defined either one and neither has Congress to this point." She casually tossed the pad back onto the table.

"Do we have any legal recourse that we can take to challenge this proclamation?" Jasper asked. The answer to this question was the reason he had come to Alexis and solicited her assistance. He not only trusted that she would find the answer, he was depending on it.

"Well under our system of government, the legislative branch reserves the right to challenge any presidential proclamations or executive orders and strike them down, but it would require two-thirds vote of Congress. Alternatively, Congress has the ability to implement law in support of the executive order or proclamation, basically making it an established law," Alexis said for clarification, knowing that Jasper was well-versed in congressional procedures. She picked up another sheet of paper from the table. "As for the Supreme Court, there are historical cases were they have both supported and overturned presidential orders."

"Any relevant examples?" Jasper pushed.

Alexis nodded affirmatively. "Back in the 1950's, the Supreme Court overruled an executive order issued by President Truman that placed all steel mills under federal control. However, the Court did support the controversial Executive Order 9066, which ordered Japanese Americans into internment camps during World War II. In that case, the president executed his authority to protect the country, as a matter of national security from a perceived threat of espionage by citizens of Japanese descent. This is the precedent that has me most concerned. It could be used to support Proclamation 29230 more than any other, particularly if the public, Congress, and the Supreme Court view this as a matter of national security."

"If that happens, that would leave individual states rights as the last line of defense," Jasper said assuredly.

Alexis shook her head disapprovingly. "Not so. In 1986, the case of Chappel vs. the United States was one of the first cases dealing with eminent domain. The Supreme Court ruled in favor of the federal government stating that Congress may authorize the seizure of private property with or without any consent of the State, provided that proceedings to seize that property were conducted through the federal court system."

"But that is on the premise that Congress authorizes the action, which is not the case here."

Alexis simply smiled. "I wondered how long it would take you to reach that conclusion."

Jasper reached for his phone, a renewed sense of hope shown on his face. "I need to make a quick phone call. We have a team of congressional lawyers working on this issue and you may have just found the key we needed." His voice rose with excitement, "If we can figure out how to keep Congress from taking action in support of the proclamation, we may just have a chance in overturning it."

"No problem. Only, Jasper ... don't be long," Alexis acknowledged curtly. "I don't want you to burn your pasta sauce because I'm starving!"

Chapter 25

"I live in sin, to kill myself I live; no longer my life my own, but sin's; my good is given to me by Heaven, my evil by myself, by my free will, of which I am deprived."
  -Michelangelo

Greenville, South Carolina

Whitaker Stanley was seated in an Adirondack chair on his terrace overlooking the small pond on his property. The ghostly outline of the Blue Ridge Mountains could be seen in the distance. The terrace was shaded by a massive oak tree whose large limbs engulfed the sky as if trying to beat back the oppressive rays of the sun. Even so, the mid-summer heat was stifling. It was a very beautiful and serene setting that put Jasper at ease, despite the task before him. He had not spoken to Whitaker since their last meeting in November and had given up hope that he would become an ally in his campaign. Fortunately, Michael had maintained contact with Whitaker on a periodic basis, keeping him informed of the progress of the campaign. It was no doubt that Whitaker knew where his campaign stood and the fact that he was losing the race.

In the past month, Jasper had been steadily falling behind in the polls to Derrick Baldwin. Recent polls of likely voters had Baldwin in the lead by over fifteen percentage points, if one believed the media. The media, definitely in favor of his opponent, regularly insinuated that a vote for Jasper Thorne would be a wasted vote given the commanding lead Derrick Baldwin had achieved. However, polls conducted by Jasper's campaign had yielded a slightly different result, putting him within six percentage points of Baldwin.

There was still a great deal of ground to cover with only three months left until the election. If that were not enough of a challenge, the president was expected to sign IPEA into law this month, with an effective date of the first of October, the start of the federal government's budget year. His team estimated that new citizens created by the legislation could yield another five to ten percent gain of the vote in favor of Baldwin, assuming union jobs could be found for all those people between October and Election Day. That was his only saving grace. As far as he knew, those new jobs were not in high supply, union or otherwise. Even so, Jasper and his team knew they were behind and they also knew their time to close the gap was quickly disappearing. They needed a game changer that would not only drive votes his way, but drive enough votes to win the election under any circumstances.

When the campaign had started nine months ago, Jasper had been deemed an early favorite to win given his strong popularity as a U.S. congressman. His strong message about the importance of the autonomy of the state had resonated with many who took pride in South Carolina and its heritage. Also, Michael's suaveness in orchestrating his campaign and his connections had proved extremely effective, allowing Jasper to pick up endorsements from many major civic and community organizations. Jasper and his team were gaining momentum and it seemed that they would be sure to win the election. When Baldwin announced his candidacy for governor, several national organizations including influential agencies such as the American Civil Liberties Union, ARRP, and Planned Parenthood pledged public support for Baldwin's campaign.

Overnight the tide of Baldwin's campaign shifted. It seemed like his supporters appeared out of thin air and they included some of South Carolina's most prominent citizens. Baldwin's campaign supporters held rallies in the larger cities in the state, engaged in highly publicized community service activities in depressed areas and peppered the news and media outlets with articles supporting his ideals. They were fanatic in their crusade to elect Baldwin. The impact to Jasper's campaign was substantial and almost immediate. All of the effort by Michael and his campaign team had been neutralized in just a matter of weeks as Jasper's lead evaporated completely.

The fact that Jasper's campaign was vastly underfunded did not help his situation. What he needed was an influx of cash to counter the misinformation that was being circulated by Baldwin's campaign. Surprisingly, the eminent legislation of IPEA and the recent executive proclamation by the president appeared to have little impact on voter sentiment. Baldwin's campaign team was masterful at spinning these events as a benefit to the individual. The proclamation turned out to be easier for Baldwin to defend than Jasper had expected. Primarily because the government hadn't done a thing that Jasper could tell to interfere with anyone or anything within the border zone since the proclamation was announced. In addition, the press covered story after story of the progress by the government to control terrorism and how the proclamation had made it all possible. Jasper wondered what was really going on. Maybe there was some truth to the news stories. There had not been an attack on U.S. soil since the legislation took effect.

"So, Mr. Thorne, has the government taken residence in your house yet?" Whitaker offered with a chuckle, his gaze still focused on the horizon.

Jasper looked for a place to sit, but the Adirondack chair was the only furniture on the terrace and there was nowhere else to sit. No doubt a move orchestrated by Whitaker to make Jasper feel uncomfortable, just as he had done last time they met. Only with this meeting, Jasper wasn't nervous. This time he had nothing to lose. Gaining Whitaker's support was a last chance effort and they both knew it. It was time he put an end to the old man playing games with him. Jasper purposely moved into Whitaker's view, forcing Whitaker to look at him. Whitaker stared at him, looking amused.

"No, sir. Not yet. Things are, surprisingly … normal," Jasper said slowly. "But that doesn't change how I feel about what they did. It is not right and I will continue to fight against it." Whitaker only nodded and continued to stare at him.

Jasper met Whitaker's stare with a look of raw determination. "I am not going to waste your time. Last time we met, you challenged me to prove to you that I understood the true meaning of the fruit that Eve gave to Adam. If I was successful, you agreed to support me. I am here to answer your challenge and to win your support."

"I wondered how long it would take you to come to this point. I knew it was only a matter of time. Please tell," Whitaker Stanley scooted forward in his chair. The challenge had begun.

Chapter 26

Jasper concentrated on the words as he spoke them, making sure to place the correct emphasis where needed. He had only one chance to get this right. "You told me the apple symbolized the realization of mankind's self-will. I define self-will as one's ability to make decisions for oneself independent of any other person or entity in order to satisfy his or her own desires. Adam and Eve were created with the ability of self-will, but lacked the realization of how to use it. That was until they were placed into a situation where they desired something they did not have. When they chose to disobey God and eat the apple, because they desired it, they executed a choice to sin. Sin therefore entered the human race through the exercise of self-will."

"A logical conclusion, much of which I had already given you the information to reach ... so, what does it mean?" Whitaker demanded.

"What happened in the Garden of Eden demonstrates the power of self-will to define mankind, whether it be for the good or for the bad. What is a person but a reflection of the choices he or she makes and the actions he or she takes? One can choose to do evil, choose to do good, or choose to do nothing. One can choose to be self-sufficient, or one can choose to be dependent on others. One can choose to fight or one can choose to flee. These choices are all driven by individual will. Mankind's essence is therefore expressed through self-will. So even though the act of Adam and Eve eating the apple was a sinful act, and created separation between mankind and God, it was so much more than that. It was the moment of self-actualization for all of humanity. It was when humanity realized all they could be, and all that they were designed to become by the Creator. It was the full realization of mankind's potential to achieve their desires through the practice of self-will. In other words, it was the awakening of mankind."

Whitaker was silent, but his eyes were alive as he studied Jasper. Finally, after what seemed to Jasper to be several minutes, he said softly, "And what about the plight of mankind?"

"The plight of mankind is to live in a society that is governed with the objective of suppressing the expression of self-will." Jasper looked for a response from Whitaker, but Whitaker's face was blank, a mask of nothingness that made Jasper question if he were on the right track.

"Mr. Whitaker, I have come to believe that human beings are corrupt creatures, driven by their own selfishness." Jasper walked slowly in a circle around Whitaker's chair. "Therefore, the execution of self-will tends to be self-serving. Hence, we have one of the purposes of the structure of government, so that mankind's self-serving predisposition will not cause harm to others in the process. Humanity needs government or it will destroy itself. The problem is that systems of government can become corrupted by the very thing they seek to protect. This is what has happened to our country."

Jasper continued circling the chair as he spoke, "Driven by the desires of liberal ideologists, our government has been systematically reducing the liberties of the citizens, attempting to minimize their potential to achieve on their own accord. Why would government do this? The answer is simple. It is because individuals who are able to achieve above and beyond the common man are typically not dependent on our government. This fact is contrary to the objective of our current government, which is to drive our country to a state of equalization among the masses and have those masses dependent on government. Just look at what has already been attacked by our government on its path to equalization. If one seeks to publically express discontent with the government, he or she is labeled an extremist and possible danger to society. If one creates wealth, he or she is so excessively taxed that the individual is probably better off not having created that wealth in the first place. And, if one seeks to express his or her love of God in public, they are ridiculed and potentially subject to lawsuits enabled by a liberal judicial system that favors equality more than individual rights. We have become a society where our civil liberties exist only in word and not in action. This is a direct attack on mankind's execution of self-will."

Jasper analyzed Whitaker for a moment. He wasn't sure, but he thought Whitaker had a slight grin on his face. He proceeded to finish his point. "From history, we know that it is society, not the government, who suffers under socialistic and communistic forms of government. One will desire to create, but will only be allowed to create something sanctioned by those in power or something that is different than what was envisioned. One will desire to pursue a specific vocation, but be denied the ability to pursue that career by the government. One will purposefully seek to squander his or her potential and live off the output of others, with no adverse consequences because the government seeks to equalize his or her situation with that of general society. Those in power prosper financially and gain greater power, while the average person becomes confined and shackled under a system that will never reach its ideal state."

Jasper came to a stop directly in front of Whitaker. "You see Mr. Whitaker, I believe true equalization of a governed people can never happen. It goes against human nature. Individuals will always desire to possess something they do not have. Governments can implement laws and policies that will stifle individual self-will, but they will never extinguish it. It will always smolder under the surface, plotting, scheming, and waiting patiently for the opportunity to express itself. And that is what our and many other repressive governments fear, because as soon as self-will is expressed by a citizen, it shows the weakness of that government." Jasper had the mental image of a single Chinese man standing in front of large thirty-ton military tank, impeding its progress into Tiananmen Square simply by his small one hundred and sixty pound body. Jasper continued, "Self-will cannot be quenched because it is how each person expresses their individual essence. An individual will cease to be, the day he or she gives up self-will."

Whitaker came alive with a shout, "Bravo!" It was the first time Jasper had seen the man show any form of emotion. It gave him hope that he was making the right impact, but it also gave him pause for concern. He couldn't afford to make a mistake now.

The funding and influence that Whitaker could provide to his campaign was too important and too critical.

Slowly, Whitaker leaned forward in his chair, "And now, Jasper Thorne … tell me what is the hope of mankind?"

Jasper faced Whitaker with renewed confidence. He kneeled down next to Whitaker, his voice calm and commanding. "Mankind's hope is found in executing self-will in an environment that facilitates and supports the realization of what each individual wants to produce and to become, provided that those outcomes serve the betterment of self, fellow mankind, and society in general." Jasper wished Whitaker could feel his conviction about this matter. The hope he had just described was so personal to him. It was the hope of a society that he had always dreamed about. A society that he desperately wished was available in the world today. "In such an environment, those whose will is to be unproductive will not be rewarded. That is the environment that I will seek to create as governor of this state."

Whitaker shook his head negatively, causing Jasper to feel a pang of fear. He watched Whitaker anxiously. *Had he been wrong in his conclusion?* Jasper questioned himself. Finally, Whitaker said, "That is only part of the answer. You have answered the physical implication of self-will. What about the spiritual side of self-will?"

Jasper hesitated. He had not expected that question. Turning away from Whitaker he stared out into the countryside, his mind dissecting the question. After a short while, he turned back to Whitaker.

"Mankind's spiritual hope is also found through self-will." Jasper's enthusiasm was rising as he spoke. He was now sure he had the answer. "It is a person's reasoning that brings him or her to a point of understanding that he or she is not sovereign in this universe. When a person realizes that there is God, he or she is faced with a choice. One can choose to live a life relying on God, choosing to honor and serve God through one's actions or one can choose to live without God, a life dependent only on oneself." He observed Whitaker for a moment before continuing. The man was crouching forward in his chair, hungering for Jasper's next word. "I have learned that God's grace cannot be forced on anyone. Thus, it is by one's own will that one comes to accept the gift of God's grace and by doing so, assurance of eternity in Heaven. Therefore, even though self-will was the mechanism through which sin entered the world, self-will is also the mechanism through which mankind finds salvation. In the end, it is man's choice where he will spend eternity."

Whitaker nodded knowingly as if Jasper had answered correctly, however his next question stopped him in his tracks. "You have learned much in these past months about the nature of mankind. But what I want to know above all else, Mr. Thorne, is this one thing ... have you made that choice of which you just so passionately preached?"

Jasper tried to respond, but found that he couldn't speak. He tried to craft a suitable response, but it was useless. He wasn't sure. He had doubts. He had learned so much over the past year about his own spiritual nature. But he still lacked so much understanding. He couldn't answer because he truly did not know.

Whitaker looked at him for a long time, recognizing Jasper's inability to respond. "Your silence tells me much, Mr. Thorne. You will have my answer tomorrow." Jasper knew by the finality in Whitaker's voice that this conversation was over.

Chapter 27

"They told us that this plan would achieve a noble ideal. Well, how were we to know otherwise? Hadn't we heard it all our lives—from our parents and our schoolteachers and our ministers, and in every newspaper we ever read and every movie and every public speech?"

-Ayn Rand, Atlas Shrugged, Part 2, Chapter 10

Washington, District of Columbia

The champagne cork burst from the bottle with a loud pop, followed quickly by a spray of bright white foam. Mason Kelley held the open bottle proudly before the table. "Gentlemen, I present you with one of the last bottles of Dom Perignon in the world. I have been saving it for a special celebration and I can think of nothing greater than what we have accomplished." He poured three tall stemmed crystal glasses to the brim and handed a glass to the two other men at the table.

"What a shame that fine institution had to fall victim to the masses," Harry Benjamin lamented, his cigar in full blaze. The champagne house of Moet & Chandon had been destroyed during the European Revolution by a mob of unemployed dissidents who viewed the entity as a symbolic image of the upper class. Chanting 'Let them drink dirt!' they doused the vineyards in a toxic chemical and then set fire to the production facility and the surrounding grounds. The damage to the soil was so great that it was deemed unfertile and any attempts to plant grapes since the riot had ended in failure.

Mason stood up, "A toast ... to my fellow patriots! May our success not be measured by individual achievements, but by the historical significance of the plan we have chosen to pursue."

"Here, Here!" was echoed by the others. It was definitely a time for celebration. Earlier that morning, at a press conference specifically held in the White House garden, the president officially signed the Immigrant Progress and Enrichment Act into law. Surrounded by a crowd of illegal immigrants and government officials, the president hailed the legislation as the crowning achievement of his presidency and Congress thus far. The signing culminated with a military fly over while a choir of Latin American men and women sang the Star Spangled Banner. It was a historic moment on so many levels.

"Now that IPEA has passed, we can move forward into the next phase in our plan." Mason swirled his glass slightly and then inhaled the champagne's aroma deeply. "Elections."

"Well if you can get the president to do what we need him to do, then winning the elections should be a cinch," Harry responded. "Now that IPEA is law, it is simply a matter of execution, right? If done correctly, we should be able to have three to four million new voters by election time." He took a long drag of his cigar.

"Provided we find them jobs," Robert Coolidge added dryly.

"As you know, in the past six months, we have established immigrant processing centers in all major cities and along the borders. Tomorrow, these offices will open and begin processing our newest citizens. Fortunately for us, I personally wrote the majority of the IPEA legislation and was able to tailor it to our needs. In an obscure section of the legislation, I included language that would make it possible for unemployed illegal immigrants to gain citizenship as long as they are actively pursuing skill development in a union trade." Harry raised his glass in the direction of Mason Kelley. "Thanks to Mason, the unions have agreed to provide apprenticeship positions for one million people immediately following passage of the law. If people show up at the processing centers who are not employed, they will be funneled into these apprenticeship positions. That is the first phase and it is basically a done deal."

"That gets us part way there. What else is planned?" Robert asked. He had been purposely left out of the implementation activities for IPEA. His task of orchestrating fraudulent votes to sway the election results in their favor across the country was more vital and time-consuming.

"The second phase involves capitalizing on illegal immigrants already in the country, particularly those in the existing workforce," Harry said, his enthusiasm building. "Several organizations have been hustling to circulate communication within the major industries that utilize illegal immigrants to ensure that those illegals understand the process to citizenship. We have community organizers going house to house to inform illegal immigrants not currently working. We expect to process another two million people from these efforts before Election Day. Lastly, the icing on our cake will be the president's workforce treaty which he will announce in two weeks' time. Though open to the general public, we have taken measures to target this program towards illegal immigrants. Estimates are anywhere from two to three million additional citizens from this effort."

Harry had to admit that he was surprised when the president approached him and several other senior senators with the idea. The president tended not to do much of his own thinking. The Eastern Workforce Development Treaty, as it would be officially called, was an official U.S. treaty entered into by the president between China and India. In exchange for elimination of certain trade barriers on U.S. products, primarily automobiles and entertainment technologies, the U.S. would provide immediate jobs for more than four million skilled immigrants from these countries. The idea was actually brilliant. Both China and India were looking to reduce population levels and had a surplus of highly educated, skilled citizens. The U.S. on the other hand, needed increased exports of manufactured products to drive growth in the manufacturing sector and an influx of highly-educated, skilled labor to drive the president's infrastructure renewal programs.

As Harry understood it, the immigrant workers would participate in a program modeled after the Civilian Conservation Corps of the 1930's. Only this workforce would be a unionized workforce focused on civil infrastructure projects and urban renewal projects, which meant all of the workers would be eligible for immediate citizenship. Harry had recognized it as an opportunity that could bolster their efforts with IPEA and more importantly, serve their greater objective for the country. At Harry's request, Robert had already begun preparations to fast track the treaty approval process in the House of Representatives. "Do you know what is my favorite part of this whole scenario?" Harry continued, "They are all going to be voting for our side."

"Damn right! That is an awesome plan! " Robert Coolidge chimed in as he chugged his champagne. He never really cared for champagne and did not share in the novelty of Dom Perignon like his associates. He preferred beer, the darker the better. "I agree with you, Harry, execution is going to be critical. Not only do we have to ensure we pick up the new immigrant voters, but we also need to ensure that we cover our traditional voting base. This is where I have been spending my time."

"What is your assessment of the situation?" Mason asked.

"Our candidates are leading in the polls in every race. Now in some cases, we have helped to influence those poll results. We need Republican voters to believe that the race is already decided against them, and that the odds are too insurmountable for their candidate to win. We want them to think their vote would be wasted. Ultimately, we need them to stay home on Election Day!" Robert flashed a grin. "At the same time, we have to ensure that our own voting base does not do the same thing. We have already finalized our Voter Verification offices, the private non-profit organizations whose sole mission is to create larger voter turnout on our side for the election."

"How do you do that?" Harry wondered.

"The process will be simple. We are going to ensure that all voting stations have a specialized sticker that they will give to all people who vote. You have seen the stickers that say 'I Voted' before, right?" Robert patted his left breast pocket as if affixing a sticker to it. "This will not be any different, only in this election, the sticker will be redeemable at a local verification office for food and clothing vouchers. All registered Democratic voters will be receiving a series of communications through phone, text, video, and mail informing them about these verification offices and the benefits offered. Of course, the Republican voter will not be on the receiving end of any of these communications."

"Will that work? That appears pretty obvious that you are buying someone's vote," Harry interrupted.

"It sure will. Though there are federal and state laws against offering money, goods, or services for a vote, there is no law against creating motivation for the general public to vote.

"Aren't they one and the same?" Mason asked.

"Well, it comes down to a simple legality. It is illegal to provide payment to someone in return for voting for a particular candidate. It is not illegal to provide payment to someone for completing the act of voting as long as that payment is not tied to any particular requirement of that vote. Federal law provides exemption for some actions they deem to be 'facilitation benefits' such as busing a group of nursing home residence to a polling station so they can vote. Such actions are believed to facilitate voting without improper influence," Robert chuckled and grinned at Mason. He knew they were playing a dangerous game, but that was what made it so exciting. "As long as our Voter Verification offices are nonpartisan and provide vouchers for any voter, regardless of party affiliation, then it cannot be interpreted as creating influence for a specific candidate."

"You are walking a fine, fine line on that one," Mason stated.

"Are we stretching the truth?" Robert asked rhetorically. "You bet we are. But as long as there is no link to the candidate or any government agency, a private organization is free to do anything it wants to drive voter turnout. I have seen to it that anybody deciding to investigate the Voter Verification offices will hit a brick wall. Everything will appear legit and above board. Trust me," he stated adamantly, the smile gone from his face

"Thirty years in the Senate and who knows how many elections, and I never knew that. You never cease to amaze me Mr. Coolridge. Cheers!" Harry toasted.

"Don't toast me until we win the election. All of the elections." Robert's tone was harsh. "Otherwise, we are screwed. Even though we have been having a great deal of success, we are still encountering resistance and obstacles in Texas and South Carolina."

"Thorne?" Mason questioned.

"Yes. I am concerned about recent developments in that election race. In the last week, Thorne picked up a major donor, Whitaker Stanley. Directly related to that announcement, his campaign has collected more donations in the last week, than has been collected in the past four months.

"Can you neutralize Stanley?" Harry asked.

"Too late. The damage is done. Not only has his money flowed into Jasper's campaign, but so has his influence. Stanley is quite the adversary and extremely well connected in South Carolina. Outside of the state, he is a nobody. Inside, he is very influential. Stanley has placed his support behind Thorne and many other important people and organizations are beginning to follow suit."

"Well, what do you suggest we do?" Harry asked.

Robert ran his hands through his thick hair and then shook his head negatively. "I have not figured this one out yet. I need more time."

"I have a suggestion," Mason said. Both Harry and Robert turned to look at Mason expectantly. "I suggest a flanking strategy to help us win the battle."

"What do you mean?" Harry asked.

"If you can't neutralize the army, you need to neutralize the general. You need to take down Jasper Thorne. I know someone who can help, but it means I would need to let someone else into the circle, at least on this matter."

Robert and Harry shared a long look, sizing up the implications of adding another individual to their little conspiracy.

Robert spoke first. "That depends on who he is. Who did you have in mind?"

"Aaron Mandon."

Harry wrinkled his forehead in concern. "He's your boy, isn't he? I will only agree if his involvement is limited to helping us take down Thorne. Nothing more, nothing else."

Robert was quick to add on, "I concur. But what I need to know is, can we trust him?"

"I don't know if we have a choice and neither of you have any alternatives." Mason drained the last sip of his champagne and lifted the bottle to replenish his glass, only to find the bottle empty. He looked at Robert and Harry a frown on his face, "Can we trust Aaron? I think so. But then again, can you trust anyone anymore?" he posed sarcastically, which caused everyone to glance around at each other and then break into loud laughter. They all knew the answer. With the laughter taken as their sign of acceptance to his offer, Mason ordered another bottle of champagne. It really was time to celebrate.

Chapter 28

New York City, New York

Senator Aaron Mandon scanned the inside of the courthouse rotunda, trying to see over the crowd for the man he was waiting for. It was hard not to get distracted by the scenery on the large mural overhead. Built in 1927, the courthouse was a beautiful testament to early twentieth century classical Roman architecture. Designed in the form of hexagon, the centerpiece of the courthouse was the domed rotunda where he was waiting. Majestically expanding high overhead, the dome was painted with a mural depicting influential people from past cultures who had made significant contributions to law throughout history including John Marshall, Justinian, and Moses. The mural was aptly called 'Law through the Ages' but despite its beauty, Aaron never liked the rotunda. The faces in the mural seemed to be staring at him, as if the lawmakers were judging him, and it made him feel uncomfortable.

He tried to get a better view over the crowd by stretching on the tips of his toes, but it was no use. He hated being short. But what he lacked for in height, he made up for in muscle. He was a solidly built man, owing to hours spent lifting weights in the gym. He also had a handsome face and charming smile, at least that what the ladies told him. At the age of forty-five, he still felt like he was an attractive man. Most of his friends his age had beer bellies and had lost their hair, but he still had a full head of deep brown hair. And that gave him a great deal of satisfaction.

Aaron scanned the rotunda once again. It was filled with a frenzy of people, their voices echoing off the domed ceiling like endless whispers in his head. He wouldn't have expected anything less, given the importance of this trial. It was the opening day of arguments in the case of Fellow vs. the New York City Board of Education. The court session had just ended and based on what he had observed in the session, it was going to be a long trial.

An employee of the New York City Schools was the plaintiff in the case and had sued the New York City Board of

Education for actions that displayed hostility toward religion. She had been fired from her job for refusing to follow a supervisor's order that she not wear religious symbols at work. The supervisor was only complying with the requirements of a recently passed city ordinance. A lesser court had ruled in favor of the Board of Education, but the plaintiff had appealed. Now the case was being heard by the United States Court of Appeals for the Second Circuit which has jurisdiction over New York City. It was important that he be seen by his constituents as involved in matters that affected the rights of New Yorkers, which is why he decided to make an appearance at the trial today. The truth was he really could care less about the outcome of the case.

Aaron thought it was blown out of proportion. The Board of Education should have a right to establish proper guidelines for the dress of its employees. In addition, he believed government employees should be discrete about their personal religious practices erring on not wearing anything that would construe a religious affiliation. The line between Church and State was crystal clear to him, as it should be to everyone who had a brain. Religion has no place is public education, of that he was adamant. He was a firm believer if you couldn't prove anything through the scientific method then it should not be in the realm of consideration for educational study and discussion.

His eyes settled on an elegantly dressed woman standing a few yards from him. She was a knock out. He was tempted to introduce himself, but that wasn't his style. He was a senator after all and had certain standards of engagement with the opposite sex. He was used to women introducing themselves to him, not the other way around. He studied her for a few more moments. There was something about her that was different than most of the women he encountered in New York, but he couldn't place it. She was busy browsing through a note pad and talking on her phone. Maybe she was a reporter. If that were the case, he would need to be more discrete. Better he let one of his aides make introductions first, just in case. *Where was Jackson anyway?* He should have been back by now. Then again, Jackson was always late. What did he expect from an aid who was just out of college.

The work ethic of youth today was not like those of prior generations.

"Aaron!" he heard a voice yell. He looked through the crowd of people that had been circulating in front of him. A smile came to his face as he saw the face of the man who was following closely behind Jackson. At the same time, he felt a cold shiver run up and down his back. Franco Milano was a man he knew well, but also a man of whom he was very wary.

Franco Milano was tall, slender, and could only be described as intense. He had thick, oily black hair that shined with a white radiance due to a zealous amount of hair product. His eyes were dark and beady, and always in constant motion darting one direction to the next. It made Aaron annoyed anytime they spoke face to face because he never knew if Milano was actually paying attention. What scared him the most about the man was not his checkered past, but the fact that he had the uncanny ability to uncover secrets about people. That made him a dangerous ally and an even more dangerous foe.

"Franco, glad you could meet me here," Aaron said as they shook hands. "I have to catch the train back to Washington D.C. shortly and wanted us to connect about the assignment we discussed on the phone yesterday." He pushed his aide Jackson towards the center of the rotunda. "Jackson, give us some privacy, would you?" His aide nodded and hurried towards the center of the rotunda, where he proceeded to play with his mobile phone. Aaron shook his head. The kid was probably playing games instead of trying to do something useful for him, like returning e-mails.

He turned his attention to Franco, looking around to make sure they had some privacy. There was no one else around except the beautiful creature just a few feet away busy talking on her phone and writing notes. She was obviously preoccupied, she had not even glanced in his direction.

"Franco, you ever hear of the name Jasper Thorne?"

Franco thought for a moment and then shrugged his shoulders. "Jasper Thorne? Nope. Who is he?" His voice was deep and carried a heavy Brooklyn accent.

"He is an adversary that is causing us some trouble in a key race for governor of South Carolina."

"Does this guy have something on your candidate?" Franco asked, his black eyes darting to the ceiling and back to the floor.

"No. He is the opposing candidate," Aaron said flatly.

"I thought you had that race in the bag already?" Franco questioned, scratching his chin.

"We think we have the race in hand, but we can't afford to take chances. Thorne just picked up a large financial donor who is extremely well connected and highly influential," Aaron responded, looking around him again. "Already, we are tracking a surge in likely voters in his favor. He needs to be taken down now."

"So what are you looking for? Drugs, embezzlement, prostitution ... child pornography?" A devilish smile forming on his face. "I can plant it all," Franco said, tapping himself in the chest. "I'm the best." Aaron knew Franco was right. Franco reputation as an effective blackmailer was well known within certain clandestine circles and that is why he was the perfect person for this assignment.

"Something bigger, much bigger. We need something that will destroy Jasper Thorne's credibility beyond repair." Aaron looked around. The woman had not moved, but was silent now, apparently listening to a long conversation from someone on the other end of her phone.

"That will be tough. I need some time to pull it together," Franco hesitated. "What's the bounty?"

"You will be able to retire on this one. It is that important! In all the years we have worked together, this will be your crowning achievement. But I need you to be committed one hundred percent — no other projects but this one."

Franco nodded. "You have set the stakes high. This will be fun."

"One more thing." Aaron pointed his finger at Franco's chest. "Absolutely no juice until you're done. Kapeesh!"

Franco nodded again, only this time more solemnly. "Yes sir. I understand."

"Great. I will be in touch with more information shortly. Now I got to get going, my ..." Aaron felt a sharp tap on his shoulder, interrupting his conversation. He turned around to find himself face to face with the gorgeous woman he had been watching earlier. She was no longer on the phone, but still carried her phone in her hand. *Maybe she wanted to interview him*, he thought. "Excuse me, are you Harry Ashol?" she asked.

He smiled. What a fortunate set of circumstances that she would engage him. He could tell from the accent of her voice that she was from the New Jersey shore. "I am sorry. You must have me mistaken with someone else." He offered his hand. "My name is Senator Aaron Mandon. It is a pleasure to make your acquaintance, Miss...?"

"Wow, the resemblance is uncanny," the woman said, ignoring the question and apparently unimpressed by his title. "You really look a lot like a Harry Ashol I used to know. Oh well, my mistake." With a quick turn, she hurried away from the senator and towards the atrium exit.

Aaron Mandon watched her walk away, disappointed in the outcome of their short meeting. For a brief second he wished he was the Harry Ashol she thought he was. Oh well, Jersey shore women were not his favorite anyway. They tended to be overly dramatic, at least the ones he knew. He scanned the atrium, his eyes resting on a full-figured woman with long blond hair that was enjoying a cup of coffee alone on a nearby bench. Yes, that was more his style.

Alexis Mills walked away from the rotunda at a brisk pace toward the nearest building exit. She made sure she could no longer be seen by the senator before she touched her phone to turn the recording application off and placed the phone into her purse. She was furious over the conversation she had just heard. But she knew her anger was masking something greater. She was afraid. Deathly afraid. *What were they planning for Jasper and why?* She had to speak with Jasper right away.

Chapter 29

"If the Union is once severed, the line of separation will grow wider and wider, and the controversies which are now debated and settled in the halls of legislation will then be tried in fields of battle and determined by the sword."
- Andrew Jackson

Washington, District of Columbia

Jasper was sitting at his desk in his congressional office when his desk phone rang. It was an oppressive day outside with high temperatures and even higher humidity, which didn't help his progressively worsening mood. Things were just not going in his favor today. He clicked the mute button on the video display he had been watching, leaving the video on. He couldn't take his eyes off of it.

"Jasper here," he said, somewhat distracted.

"Jasper!!! Thank the Lord!!! I am so glad to hear your voice. I was so worried. I have been calling your cell phone for the last two hours. Why haven't you answered?" It was Alexis and she sounded panicked.

"Whoa! Slow down, honey. What is going on?" Jasper clicked the video off so she could have his full attention.

"Jasper, you're in trouble ... I mean your campaign is in trouble ... I mean both." Alexis seemed to be having difficulty expressing herself which told Jasper something was terribly wrong.

"I am fine, just a little tired. I am sitting in my office in Washington," Jasper's said, his concern beginning to intensify. "Princess, I can tell you are really upset. Take a moment and catch your breath." He had never heard Alexis like this, she was always polished and in control. If she was rattled, then something bad must have happened.

When Alexis spoke again, Jasper could tell she chose her words deliberately. "Jasper ... someone is trying to destroy your credibility and your campaign. I heard it myself from Senator Mandon."

"What?!?" was the only word that came to Jasper's lips. *What did Aaron Mandon, a senator from New York, have to do with his campaign?* He had only met the senator a few times at formal congressional functions. *Why would Alexis make such a statement?*

Alexis interrupted his thought process. "We just recessed from the court room and I was on the phone with my office to relay details of the opening arguments. I noticed this creepy guy staring at me. I mean I am used to being checked out, but this guy made my skin crawl. I had no idea he was a senator." Her tone expressed disgust. She paused and took a deep breath "Well, it was crowded in the courthouse rotunda, so I just turned my back on him and continued with my conversation. When I heard your name mentioned, I became concerned. Why would some creep in New York City be talking about you? I don't know what made me do it, but I started to record the conversation while I pretended to still be on the phone. These men were talking about hurting you, Jasper." There was fear in her voice. "Then I became very angry. I wanted so badly to confront them."

"You did the right thing, Alex. Now tell me what you heard them say?" Jasper's voice was calm and reassuring.

Alexis proceeded to share the details of the recorded conversation. Jasper waited until she finished, but he had already surmised the situation, and it was not good. He knew from his experience in the military that successful campaigns were well-coordinated and often included elements that were not easily connected until it was too late. There was something more significant going on than just his race for governor. Whatever it was, someone was willing to go to great lengths to remove any obstacles, and that included Japer.

"Honey, are you there?" Alexis' voice was concerned again.

"I am sorry Alexis. This is a great deal of unsettling news and I am just trying to process it." Jasper said. In an attempt to raise her spirits, he offered cheerfully, "I am so thankful that you were in a position to uncover this. At least we have an advantage on our enemy, whoever that may be."

"What do you mean an advantage?" She asked.

"We know that he is planning an attack. That means we can take action to protect ourselves versus being unknowingly flanked. I know exactly what I need to do. That being said, there are bigger matters before us that we need to be concerned about. Haven't you heard the news?"

"Baby, I have been in court all day," she said, the exhaustion in her voice becoming more evident as the fear dissipated. "Since then, I have been trying to reach you the last few hours, so I am not sure what is going on in the world."

"South Carolina voted to put secession on the ballet today," Jasper said flatly. His tone lacked any emotion. He wasn't sure how he felt about it, other than he knew it was a serious statement of defiance by the state's legislature.

"Oh, no!" Her voiced was pained. They were both silent for a long time. They both knew the implications of what had occurred and the impact it could have on both of them now and in the future.

"Michael and I have been fielding calls from the press all day. That was why you couldn't reach me. I turned off my cell phone to have a little privacy and to get some much needed campaign work done."

"I understand. Thanks for telling me that," she said gloomily. A moment later, she let out a brief cry of distress, "Jasper, I was really worried about you!"

"Princess, we are going to figure this out. Please do not worry. I can take care of myself." He wished she was with him so he could wrap her in a protective hug.

"I know," she said, but Jasper could tell she was not sure she believed him.

"I really miss you," he told her reassuringly.

"I really miss you too, Jasper," she responded slowly. There was a longing in her voice that made Jasper feel better.

"When do you think you will be home?" he asked, hoping it would be soon.

"I expect the trial to wrap up in a few weeks, barring no issues that extend the trial. I am really looking forward to spending some time back home. I really have been worried about my parents and it will be good to enjoy a slower pace of life for a while. New York is an amazing city, but it can really wear you out," she was sounding more cheerful.

"How about I call you in a few hours when I am back at my condo. I need to take care of some pressing matters."

They exchanged a brief goodbye and he hung up the phone. He sat at his desk silently for a few minutes mulling over their conversation and the news Alexis had shared. He wished he knew what it all meant. He clicked back on the video display, needing a distraction. A news reporter was at Battery Park in Charleston on a live news feed. In the background a young man was waiving the state flag of South Carolina amidst a crowd of cheering supporters. Jasper rose from his desk and opened a window, he needed fresh air. His actions only resulted in a wave of hot air filling his small office. "Why did it have to be so hot outside?" he roared. The heat and humidity was what he would have expected from Charleston at this time of year, not Washington, D.C. But then again, the Capitol had been built on a swamp. He wished at this moment the whole city could sink into the swamp and take him with it.

His eyes fell on the Bible that was on the shelf below the window he just opened. He considered it for a moment and then picked it up, returning to his seat. He thumbed through its pages, finally resting on a section midway. He opened the Bible and read the first few verses his eyes fell on.

"'Psalm 91 – My Refuge and My Fortress'.
¹He that dwelleth in the secret place of the most High shall abide under the shadow of the Almighty. ² I will say of the Lord, He is my refuge and my fortress: my God; in him will I trust. ³ Surely he shall deliver thee from the snare of the fowler, and from the noisome pestilence. ⁴ He shall cover thee with his feathers, and under his wings shalt thou trust: his truth shall be thy shield and

buckler. [5] Thou shalt not be afraid for the terror by night; nor for the arrow that flieth by day;"

For the first time since he could remember, he bowed his head and prayed to God on his own initiative. It was awkward at first, but he gave himself over the task. It was more like a one-sided conversation than a prayer, his pleas coming randomly and not in any logical manner. There was so much to pray for, so much that he needed help with. When he was done he raised his head and glanced at the clock. He had lost track of time and now was going to be late for his lesson with Michael. He hurriedly prepared his things and left the office, walking quickly down the hallway.

As Jasper turned the corner from his office, he was met by a tall, distinguished man dressed in a gray pinstripe suite blocking his way. "Mr. Thorne?" The man asked in a heavy Russian accent.

Jasper stepped back instinctively evaluating the stranger. The man was bald but sported a finally trimmed goatee that reflected hints of grey. His brown eyes were kind, but Jasper detected something else in them, hidden deep below the surface. Sadness or perhaps pain, he thought. The stranger must have recognized that he had surprised Jasper as he placed both of his hands in the air indicating he did not mean any harm. "I am sorry to surprise you, Mr. Thorne. You are Mr. Thorne, yes?"

"I mean no disrespect, but I am late for an important meeting. Please stop by my office and make an appointment with my assistant," Jasper responded beginning to walk by the man.

The man moved in front of Jasper again, blocking his way. "Mr. Thorne, I represent the Russian consulate. It is very important I talk with you."

"What about?" Jasper responded guardedly.

"Secession," the man replied coolly.

Jasper eyed the man warily, "You can talk with me while I walk. As I said, I have a meeting. You said you are from the Russian Consulate? What is your name?"

The man's response was brief and limited. "My name is Demitri. I am the Correspondent of Governmental Affairs for the Federation of Russia."

Jasper took the man's brief response as a clue and decided to keep his answers brief as well. "You've got five minutes. Why does the Consulate want to talk to me about secession?"

"No reason in particular," the man shrugged his broad shoulders. "We are just curious to understand what a rouge state, recently seceded from this mighty nation, would do to survive?"

Jasper stopped in mid-stride. He hadn't really thought about that, but it was an extremely relevant question now that secession was to be voted on by the citizens of the state. *What would happen in South Carolina post-secession?* Jasper thought. The enormity of that thought was unsettling. He started walking again, but this time maintaining eye contact with the Russian.

Noting the silence, Demitri continued, "Let's assume that the U.S. government takes a diplomatic approach to your new country, opting not to use military force. Maybe they implement a trade embargo and cut off supplies being shipped in and out of the rogue nation. How would your little symbol of American ideology survive, let alone grow and prosper?"

Jasper didn't like the Russian's humor, but knew the question was deadly serious. "It would need resources of all types, particularly financial."

The Russian nodded his head. "But the motherland would not be willing to provide those resources. After all, they are trying to destroy the rebellion."

"These resources would have to come from friendly states or from outside the U.S. entirely," Jasper responded.

The Russian nodded his head and then came to a stop. "I believe this is your destination, Mr. Thorne. It was a pleasure to speak with you." He bowed formally and then proceeded to walk down the corridor, leaving Jasper alone to contemplate the odd conversation he had just had.

Chapter 30

"This is a faithful saying, and worthy of all acceptation, that Christ Jesus came into the world to save sinners; of whom I am chief."
-The Apostle Paul, 1 Timothy 1:15, King James Bible

Jasper entered the conference room to find Michael waiting for him, a fresh cup of steaming black coffee sitting next to his Bible. Michael's eyes were blood shot and the fatigue in his face was evidenced by the tight creases in his forehead that were more pronounced than usual. Jasper knew Michael had been extremely burdened by the passage of Bill 122061. They had spent most of the day together, fielding calls from the media, formulating their campaign response, and strategizing on upcoming actions. Despite his obvious condition, Michael perked to attention when Jasper walked into the room.

"Ok, Michael I can tell you are eager to teach today. You have been dropping hints all week that we are going to be talking about sin," he plopped down in the chair adjacent to Michael. "But with the day I have had, I prefer to pass, and talk about a different subject. The last thing I need is a preacher telling me how bad I am and making me feel like crap," Jasper looked at Michael defiantly, but then softened his expression as he noticed Michael's haggard appearance. It had been an exhausting day for both of them. Jasper offered a quick smile trying to lighten the mood. "I know your day has been as bad as mine with the announcement that the Palmetto state may rise again."

"Yes Jasper, it has been a tough day," Michael exhaled loudly. "By the way, it is not from preaching that one feels guilt or as you so stately said, *'makes me feel like crap.'* It is the Holy Spirit convicting you about your condition. You need to learn how to pay attention to the presence of the Holy Spirit."

"If you say so," Jasper said skeptically. He hated when Michael made statements that he didn't really understand. Knowing they had both had a long day, he decided not to push the issue. "Well, should we get started?"

"Very well," Michael responded. "I have been thinking a great deal about the question you asked me last week on the flight back from Charleston from our last campaign visit. Not about the answer, for I know the answer, but how I explain that answer without becoming too theological."

Jasper took some satisfaction in Michael's statement. He had asked a simple question that he knew would be difficult for Michael to explain, "If God is good, benevolent, and forgiving, why would He kill people as he did in the Old Testament?" It had really bothered Jasper to learn about the killing, debauchery, and punishment that occurred in the Old Testament, much of it sanctioned or at least appeared to be sanctioned by God. He had asked the question because he wanted to challenge Michael for a change, but also because he truly wanted to understand the answer.

"So, have I put the mighty Michael Matthews at a loss for words?" Jasper smiled.

Michael shot him a look of displeasure. "My young man, I am never at a loss for words, if only people had ears to hear." Jasper suddenly had a bad feeling he was about to receive a lecture.

Michael continued, "As we learned earlier, sin by our standards is relative because we view it in degrees of severity. God views sin as an absolute. To Him, sin is sin because any and all sin is a violation of His laws and righteous standards. Do you remember what is the penalty of sin?"

"Death," Jasper responded with a tone of finality.

"Death," Michael echoed Jasper's tone. "So when God would sanction or directly cause the death and killing of people in the Old Testament, it was because they had sinned and disobeyed God. In Genesis, we learn that God created the Great Flood to rid the world of all humanity because humanity was evil. Let's read about it aloud.

Michael opened his Bible to the sixth chapter of the book of Genesis and began to read verse five:

"⁵ And God saw that the wickedness of man was great in the earth, and that every imagination of the thoughts of his heart was only evil continually. ⁶ And it repented the Lord that he had made man on the earth, and it grieved him at his heart. ⁷ And the Lord said, I will destroy man whom I have created from the face of the earth; both man, and beast, and the creeping thing, and the fowls of the air; for it repenteth me that I have made them."

Jasper frowned at Michael, "That is heavy stuff. I know the story of Noah and his ark, but to wipe out all of humanity?"

Michael nodded, "God also executed His judgment when He destroyed the cities of Sodom and Gomorrah because the people of these cities were corrupt, full of sexual debauchery, and pursued their own lusts. Still later, in the time of Joshua, God orders the death of various tribes of people that inhabit the Promised Land because they have sinned against Him and chosen to worship other gods. This cycle continues on throughout the books of the Old Testament, because God is constant in how he deals with mankind throughout history. When He performed these acts of seeming brutality, He was only executing justice and fulfilling the punishment required by His own law about sin. The penalty of sin is death."

"So you are telling me that in all these situations, God is not being maligned or evil, He is only acting as judge and sentencing appropriately for the crime that was performed," Jasper responded.

"Precisely," Michael sounded pleased that Jasper had arrived at the correct conclusion. "As humans, we have trouble rationalizing these judgments because we know that the taking of another's life is evil. That is why understanding God's perspective on sin is so important. There is no heavenly scale that measures good versus bad. Sin is always sin in His eyes and He will judge each of us for our sinful actions based on His standard, not ours."

Jasper considered Michael's words for a moment, "This is definitely making more sense to me ... not to side track our discussion, but I think you just helped me to understand the biblical basis for the justification of capital punishment and the defense against abortion. Under the former, we execute a person as a consequence of the crime that they committed because they violated the law and death is justified. Whereas, in the case against abortion, the victim is a living being who is innocent and has committed no crime, therefore death by abortion is unjust."

Michael nodded affirmatively, "Exactly, and I am glad you picked up on that insight. It is all a matter of justice. God is just and will always be consistent in how He handles justice. A parent is not evil when they punish a child for disobeying them, the parent is just executing justice. God is doing the same with us. Does that answer your original question?"

"Yes, it does. I understand the logic and the purpose, but it still seems an extreme approach to dealing with sin."

"Any more extreme than sending your *only* son to die as a sacrifice?"

Jasper wasn't sure how to answer. Michael had a good point.

Michael continued, "Most people know verse John 3:16, 'For God so loved the world, that He gave His only begotten Son, whosoever believeth in Him should not perish, but have everlasting life.'" He peered at Jasper quizzically, "But do you know what John 3:17 says?"

Jasper shook his head, indicating he did not. He opened his Bible and immediately turned to the verse Michael was referring to so he could read it himself. He read out loud, "'For God sent not his Son into the world to condemn the world, but that the world through him might be saved.'"

Michael spoke up as Jasper finished the verse. "In the Old Testament, sin was absolved or forgiven through prayer, repentance, and the act of the sacrifice of animals to God as an offering. This was done because God required the death and shed blood of the animal as the payment for the sin that was committed. Only a clean, healthy animal without spot or blemish could be sacrificed because anything else was unworthy of God. Remember, the penalty of sin is and always will be death."

"That sounds like a barbaric method of absolution, if you ask me. How come that tradition was not carried on by Christians?" Jasper asked curiously.

"The answer to that question highlights my earlier point regarding the continuity of God's eternal plan for humanity. Jesus Christ was fully human and fully God and lived a sinless life while on Earth. He was without blemish, without fault. When He was crucified on a cross and died, He became the perfect, sacrificial lamb. Since Jesus was the ultimate sacrifice for all of humanity, all the sins of the entire human race: past, present, and future were transferred to His account. Thus, as it was in the past, blood had to be spilt in order for the atonement of sin to happen. Only with Jesus' death and spilt blood, it was final and it was for everyone. This is the good news of the gospel of Jesus Christ."

"From an intellectual standpoint that makes sense, and I see the continuity of God you speak of. Yet, it is still confusing," Jasper said.

Michael closed the Bible in front of him. Jasper was not sure if Michael was frustrated with him or not, but his voice sounded resigned. "Jasper, over the past several months, we have studied many subjects in the Bible and learned much about religion. During one of our earlier sessions, you asked how you can be forgiven. I have given you the answer. You now understand sin and how God deals with it. You also understand the role Jesus played in helping man to be forgiven for his personal sins. We are all sinners, but there is hope for us because there is a path to redemption through having faith in Jesus Christ and what he did for us. As soon as you believe that, you can not only be forgiven, you can be saved for all eternity."

A few minutes later, Jasper was walking down the corridor towards his office. He didn't know why, but he was feeling a weight that he could not explain. Maybe what Michael had said about the Holy Spirit was true. Perhaps he needed to start paying attention. Only he wasn't sure what Michael really meant. How does he pay attention to something that he can't see, hear or touch? And even if he knew the answer to that question, he still had so many more questions, the chief of which being, what was he supposed to do?

Chapter 31

Charleston, South Carolina

Jasper walked briskly down Tradd Street toward Battery Park. He was hoping to arrive before the sun rose. Bands of crimson, orange, and purple were already forming and overlapping in the sky. He didn't know why, but it always seemed to him that the sunrise in September was the most beautiful of any time of year. He had been looking forward to enjoying a sunrise since returning to Charleston four days earlier, but campaign duties had required him in the office well before.

Walking through the streets of downtown Charleston was one of his favorite ways to relax. He had spent numerous hours admiring the unique architecture of the residences, many of the homes dating back to the eighteenth century. A few blocks ahead of him was one of his favorite areas in the neighborhood, known as Rainbow Row. Built directly on the harbor waterfront, the street contained a series of majestic row houses painted in various pastel colors. Local legend stated the houses were painted in the various colors such that the intoxicated sailors coming in from port could remember which houses they were to bunk in. Jasper didn't think there was much credibility to the legend, but it served to enhance the character of the downtown area. He glanced up at the bright pink eves of the Georgian style home he was walking by, noticing the contrast the decorative beams created with the lightening sky. The sun would be rising soon, he had better hurry.

Turning right onto Meeting Street, he slowed his pace. From the corner of his vision, he had seen a man suddenly duck into an alcove, apparently trying to avoid being seen. The warning from Alexis echoed in his head 'just promise me that you will take measures to protect yourself.' Jasper was never one to run from a fight nor did he like living in fear. Instinctively, he crouched into an alcove under an elaborate marble stairwell, waiting for his possible pursuer to pass by. He wished he had brought his 9mm but he had never felt the need to carry it while walking in his own neighborhood. Things were different now and he would have to be more careful.

Jasper listened for the footsteps. They came hurriedly, apparently his pursuer was concerned that his prey had escaped because he was no longer in sight. Jasper lunged on the figure as he came by the stairwell. In a single fluid motion, he wrapped his right arm under the man's right arm, while driving his left elbow into the man's upper back, forcing the man's weight back onto his left leg. He then drove his foot into the back of the man's left knee and pushed down. In seconds, he had the man on his stomach in a submission hold, his elbow applying intense pressure into the man's back.

"Why are you following me?" Jasper asked as his free hand searched the man's backside for weapons.

"Mr. Thorne!" the man screamed. "Wait — you're making a mistake."

"Who are you?" Jasper repeated as he dug his elbow further into the man's back.

"I work for you, man. Ouch!" the man exclaimed in obvious distress. "Please stop, you're hurting me."

Jasper eased up the pressure on the man's back. The man was not very muscular — he was actually quite skinny. *Not the typical build he would expect of an assassin*, he thought. *Maybe he was over reacting.*

"What do you mean you work for me?"

"I work at the campaign office as a volunteer and I need to talk with you," the man pleaded. "It is very important."

Jasper took a moment to pat down the front side of the man checking one last time for weapons and then offered a hand to help the man up from the ground. In the emerging light, Jasper was finally able to get a good look at the man's face. It was chiseled but youthful. Jasper guessed he was in his early twenties. He was African American and wore his hair closely cropped. He looked familiar, but Jasper could not recall meeting him before.

"Have we met before?" Jasper asked, still wary.

"Yes, briefly a few months ago," the man said, brushing dirt and gravel from his knees. "I just happened to be in the downtown campaign office inquiring about employment when you came in. You were in a rush. We shook hands but didn't exchange names."

Jasper had shaken thousands of hands since he started the campaign. He wasn't surprised that he did not remember.

"Sorry about tackling you and for the rough conduct," Jasper said. "I thought ... well never mind." He shook his head somewhat embarrassed by his treatment of his volunteer. "What's your name and why were you following me so early in the morning?"

"Jordan. Mack Jordan," The man offered his hand in greeting. Jasper shook his hand, noticing the scrapes in the man's palm caused from colliding with the concrete sidewalk.

"I have been sitting outside your house since four am this morning because it is urgent that I talk with you." Mack rubbed his shoulder, wincing in a bit of discomfort. "But I did not want to startle you, so I figured I would follow you until there was an opportune time to get your attention."

"Well it is a pleasure to meet you again, Mack," Jasper said sincerely. "What is so important that you thought it worthy of stalking me? Fortunately for you, I do not have bodyguards. Otherwise, you could have been arrested."

"Yes, I know, but please let me explain," Mack was shaking with urgency and excitement. "I work with the IT staff assisting with the technical aspects of your social marketing campaign. Things like mailing lists, donor database management, and website updates. You know man, all that basic stuff."

Jasper nodded. Michael handled the oversight of most of those activities so he wondered why Mack had come to him instead.

"I was updating addresses directly in our donor database because, well you know, it is quicker that way," Mack said. "Then I happened to notice a few of the non-essential data fields had strange symbols in them. This usually happens when an outside program interacts directly with a database, but does not use normal protocols."

"I am not following you. Why does that matter?" Jasper asked.

"Our system was hacked!" Mack exclaimed. "Someone accessed our database and stole the names of all of our donors."

"And you know this for sure?" Jasper pressed, not quite believing Mack's statement. Michael had assured him at the beginning of the campaign that they had state-of-the-art IT security protocols in place to protect all of the campaign computer systems.

"I took enough classes in IT security to know how to identify a hacked system," Mack confirmed. "If I had not been directly reviewing the database, I would never have seen it. I checked a back-up copy of the database from yesterday and those symbols were not there, so this happened in the last twenty-four hours."

"Did you tell anyone about this?"

Mack responded shaking his head empathically yes. "Every dude I could think of in the office, but they all thought I was crazy. So I decided to investigate the situation myself. I determined that the only fields that appear to have been queried by the outside program were the donor name, and their mailing and email addresses. There was other information that could have been taken, like the amount of the donor's contribution, the age of the donor, the credit card number, or the bank account information. Why take only those three items of information?" Mack tapped the side of his leg nervously. "It made no sense. A traditional hacker would definitely be interested in credit card or back account information. Then I figured it out. Do you know what four items of information are required to complete an online absentee ballot in the state of South Carolina?"

Jasper thought for a moment, having voted by absentee ballot himself a few years back. "I recall it is just your name, mailing address, email address and your state identification number, which for most people is their driver's license number. What does the absentee ballot process have to do with this?" Jasper asked.

"Whoever hacked into our system was a real pro, man. You have a good IT staff and they have some of the best security in place. Like I said, we would of never of known this had happened if I hadn't stumbled across it by accident. So if this is a pro we are dealing with, who is to say he or she wouldn't try to the hack the Department of Motor Vehicles. It would be easy to match the names and addresses to the corresponding state identification numbers."

"But even if that were the case, I am struggling to see how this plays out," Jasper argued. "Assuming that the hacker was successful, what would he be able to do with that information?"

"We have over forty thousand names in our database representing forty thousand people who we expect will vote for you. What if they weren't able to vote on Election Day?"

"What do you mean?" Jasper challenged.

"You politicians crack me up. You know so much, but also know so little," Mack smiled revealing a set of big, white teeth accented by a big gap between the two front teeth. "It's the machines, man. Three years ago the State Election Board replaced all the voting machines in South Carolina with computer-based machines. The new machines allowed for seamless integration with a central state voting database to eliminate the need for any human intervention, thus ensuring a more accurate vote count and minimizing the chance for voter fraud. The online absentee ballot system was also integrated into the new voting system. I know this because they changed them the year that I was first eligible to vote.

Jasper remembered his concern over the new machines while running for his second term as congressman. "I am still not following you," he said.

"You wouldn't know where I was going with this unless you read the technical specifications on the software that runs the machines, which I did. In order to minimize the opportunity for voter fraud, the software was designed to track when a vote was placed by a specific person based on name, email address, and either a social security number or a state identification number. If someone tried to vote twice, the system was set up to appear to allow the person to vote, but it would not record the second vote in the database since it already had a record of that person voting previously. The voter would therefore never know the "duplicate" vote had not been processed."

"That is very interesting. So how does this tie into our problem with the hacker?" Jasper asked.

"That's easy. Early voting started in South Carolina three days ago. If our hacker uses the information that was stolen, theoretically, they could place forty thousand absentee ballot votes in favor of your opposition. When your campaign donors showed up at the polls to vote or placed their own absentee ballot, their vote would be identified by the system as a duplicate and would not be counted. But your supporters would not know that their vote had not been counted and then you would find yourself with a forty thousand vote deficit."

Jasper felt his blood pressure rise. He knew he was in a nasty campaign, but he had never expected voter fraud to this degree. He had to know if Mack's theory was accurate.

"Why should I believe you? How do you know all this information?" Jasper wondered, genuinely curious. The young man's knowledge and resourcefulness was impressive. He liked Mack. He had gumption and it was evident, he was a producer.

"I read, man. I read all the time. If I am not working, eating, or sleeping, I am reading," Mack stated proudly.

Jasper grinned in response and offered his hand in thanks, "Mack, if you are right about this, I owe you a great deal."

Mack shrugged. "You're a cool dude. I believe in what you stand for. I want to work with people like you. You know, people who share my beliefs and ideals. If you could get me on your staff in a paid position, I would be solid."

They shook hands. It was a deal. "I will take that request under consideration. For now, we need to get the election office and contact the authorities. We don't have any time to waste." Jasper looked up at the soft blue sky that was now overhead. He has missed the sunrise, but that didn't matter. Something told him he had found an even brighter star to watch.

Chapter 32

"If a nation expects to be ignorant and free, in a state of civilization, it expects what never was and never will be."
-Thomas Jefferson

New York City, New York

Alexis approached the jury confidently. She had worn her sole couture suit for the occasion because today was about impression. The brown suit accented her body in a modest way, but highlighted her extremely athletic legs. Under the suit, she wore a bright pink shirt with ruffles around the neck, accenting her brown hair which curled over her shoulders. A wave of excitement rolled through her stomach as she walked. Closing the deal was her specialty and this moment was what she had been waiting for the entire trial.

She had examined the proceedings over the last three weeks as a sports analyst might analyze a boxing match; identifying the strengths and weakness of each party, identifying missed opportunities to make an impact, observing the reactions of the jury to the evidence that had been presented, and the statements that had been made or debunked. As she observed the trial, she had been preparing for her closing argument, utilizing the information she gathered to craft her message to the jury. This is what made all of it worth it. The long work hours, the time away from home, the time away from Jasper. It all came down to this one moment. This moment is where she shined.

The jury was typical for New York City, an eclectic mix of Italian whites, African Americans, Latinos, and Asians. Six of the twelve jurors were women. The selection process had proven challenging for both sides as each sought to out maneuver the other, hoping to result in a jury that was both demographically and religiously in their favor. The New York City Board of Education had sparred against her team for a jury that was indifferent about religion. Unfortunately, for Alexis and her client, the School Board had won the initial engagement. Four of the jurors were atheist, three did not aspire to any specific religion but believed in a higher power, two were practicing Catholics, one was Jewish, one was Buddhist and the last juror was a young woman who professed to worship a "god" that no one had ever heard of. Alexis was staring directly at that young woman juror now.

The juror was small in frame, with flowing brown hair with unkempt ends that had been pulled loosely into a pony tail. She had an attractive face if you could get past the nose ring and multiple cheek and forehead piercings. Alexis couldn't help but think how little humanity had progressed regarding its viewpoints on religion. She remembered that the apostle Paul is quoted in the Bible referring to a statue in the city of Athens that was dedicated with a simple inscription, "to the unknown God." If anything, in the last two thousand years, humanity had become less tolerant of religion, believing secularism was a more equitable and suitable characteristic of humanity. Even so, she felt confident she could reach this young juror and convince her to vote in favor of her client. But in order for her to win the trial, she would have to convince the atheist jurors to vote in support of something they did not believe. This trial was going to be her toughest test yet.

Alexis's client had filed suit against the New York City Board of Education for improper termination of employment based on religious discrimination. Her client, Martha Fellow, had been terminated from her position as a clerk in the Records Office after fifteen years of employment with the New York City School system. The grounds of the termination were based on her refusal to comply with a request from her direct supervisor to refrain from wearing religious symbols while at work. Martha thought the action was discriminatory because she had worn a cross on a necklace on the outside of her clothing every day for the entire term of her employment without a single complaint. Her case stated that the Board of Education had violated the Free Exercise Clause of the First Amendment. Lawyers for the Board of

Education had argued that wearing a cross was not a requirement of being a Christian and was therefore a promotion of religion. They based their defense on a recent city ordinance banning the use, application, and promotion of religious symbols and practices that were not a requirement of the religion in question.

"Your Honor, ladies and gentlemen of the jury," Alexis turned to the judge briefly and nodded at him and then back to address the jury. "At the core of this trial is a simple question. Does Ordinance 5578 violate the First Amendment rights of my client?" She scanned the jury assessing each juror's attention level. "For the past few weeks, you have been hearing testimony about this case. You have been peppered with case law, case histories, legal jargon, and opinion both in support and against the position of my client. The basis of our discussion has been focused on the constitutional right to freedom of religion provided by the Free Exercise Clause and the Establishment Clause found in the First Amendment. The former guarantees the free exercise of religion. The latter prohibits the establishment of a national religion by Congress or the preference of one religion over another."

She paced slowly in front of the jury, making eye contact with each juror for a second, but no more. A single second was just enough time to acknowledge the juror, but not enough time for the juror to feel uncomfortable. There would be time for that later in her closing argument. She continued, "It is my belief and the belief of my client, that Ordinance 5578 not only violates the Free Exercise Clause by suppressing expression of personal beliefs, it violates the Establishment clause by supporting one religious preference over another. My intent today is to show you how this violation of the First Amendment occurred. If I am successful, you will then understand that my client was unlawfully terminated from her position and you must then rule in her favor." She scanned the jury, searching for any indication of agreement but she did not find any.

"I am not here today to convince you that the defendant, the New York City Board of Education, discriminated against my client. In fact, I am not even here to defend the fact that my client was unjustly persecuted simply for wearing a symbol of her religion at her place of employment. This case is about so much more than this specific event. This case is about an issue that is more profound, more influential, and more expansive than you may think." Alexis walked towards her client and then turned to face the row of pews that were bursting with people who had come to watch the closing argument. The audience was hushed, listening to her intently. It was time to make her move. "What I am here today to do is to defend the God given rights of freedom, justice, and liberty that you, my client, and all U.S. citizens enjoy in this country," she said, her voice resonating with zealous compassion. "These very rights are systematically being taken away from you and me through codes, statutes, orders, and laws passed by our local, state, and federal governments. Laws just like Ordinance 5578; a law that is blatantly unconstitutional and is obviously hostile to the prosperity of our nation." Her comment received a murmur from the spectators in the courtroom.

She slowly walked back to stand in front of the jury before speaking again, mentally counting the seconds of her silence. "This issue at hand goes beyond our First Amendment rights of the freedom of speech and the freedom of religion. She stopped and stared at the jury. All eyes were locked on her. "Have the rights of my client been violated in this case?" She slammed her hand down on the rail of the juror box creating a loud echo in the courtroom and startling a few jurors in the front row. "You bet they have," she exclaimed, pointing threateningly at the jury.

Alexis walked over to her desk and picked up a single sheet of paper and returned to the front of the jury box. "I know some of you profess not to believe in God, deities, or a higher power. Some of you have no belief in the purpose of religion. In both cases, that is your right to believe the way you do. It is your freedom to believe the way you do because the Free Exercise Clause protects you. Under this clause, we are able to practice the religion we choose and to express ourselves as we choose." She nodded at the young women juror with the nose ring. "You are no different than my client, Martha Fellows, who chooses to wear a cross to express, not promote, her belief in Christianity," she paused again, surveying the jury one more time.

One of the atheist jurors was paying close attention and staring directly at her, an expectant look on her face. She was an elderly woman with a tragic past. She was a widower and had lost her only son shortly after child birth. Alexis recalled from the jury interviews that the woman was very proud about the fact that she was an atheist. Not bothering to couch her directness, Alexis stood in front of this woman and spoke directly to her. "You may be inclined to view this situation with my client as inconsequential. You may even be inclined to support the legal code passed by New York City that is being challenged. But what I want you to understand is that the decision you make today about this case has implications on the validity of your personal freedom tomorrow. It is your freedom to believe and to express that belief that is *really* on trial today!" She paused to let the last statement sink in. Now, it was time to close the deal.

Chapter 33

Her voice more forceful, Alexis confronted the jury, "Ladies and gentlemen of the jury, I do not pretend to know your level of understanding of Constitutional law. Nor do I assume that you are naive of current events that have challenged the legitimacy and boundaries of our Constitution. So I think it important to refresh your memories on the freedoms provided by our First Amendment rights, as those are the freedoms that are being challenged in this case today."

Alexis paced in front of the jury, "The Constitution established our current form of government, but it was the Bill of Rights, or the first ten amendments to the Constitution, that provided our true freedoms as citizens. You see, the Bill of Rights was necessary for the states to ratify the Constitution because many states believed the Constitution alone was not sufficient enough to protect the people from an oppressive government." Several of the jurors nodded, obviously knowing this historical fact. She continued, "Still, have you ever wondered why the very first amendment to the Constitution contained the rights it does? The First Amendment of the United States Constitution reads, and I quote:

'Congress shall make no law respecting an establishment of religion, or prohibiting the free exercise thereof; or abridging the freedom of speech, or of the press; or the right of the people peaceably to assemble, and to petition the Government for a redress of grievances.'"

The words came naturally to her; she had memorized them along with the rest of the Bill of Rights a long time ago. She purposely slowed her speech, giving direct emphasis to each word in the next question she asked. "What made these rights so important to our founding fathers that they had to be included in the First Amendment versus any of the other nine amendments?" There was a long silence as she assessed the jury. She could see by the expressions on many of their faces that they had never before considered the question.

"I have a possible answer. I believe it is because these rights have the most power to protect us from an oppressive government. Take the right of free speech, for example. You have heard the expression the pen is mightier than the sword. If citizens of this country were to lose their right to freely express their dissatisfaction with our government, its policies or its actions, or if the government was able to control and dictate what we read in the papers and watched on television, we would quickly become a nation controlled by the government. We would lose our ability to fight injustice and oppression and would soon lose other freedoms because we would lack a means to publically defend them. The rights provided by the First Amendment, therefore, are necessary to keep our federal, state and local governments in check." She turned to the judge, making eye contact with him for a moment. He held her stare. Judge Leonard was in his late seventies and had been presiding in this courthouse for more than thirty-five years. Though he was a smaller framed man, he was a man who commanded respect simply by his presence. She hoped that she was earning his respect at this moment.

"Now I ask you the same question, this time in the context of our rights. Why is the first right in our Bill of Rights the freedom of religion? It could of easily of been our freedom of speech, our right to assemble, our right to bear arms, our right to trial by jury or our right against unreasonable search and seizure of our property. All of which are notable and critical rights in themselves, but our freedom of religion came first." She noticed one of the other jurors who had professed to be an atheist, fidgeting in his seat. He was obviously not comfortable with the emphasis she was placing on the importance of religion in the Constitution. She had anticipated this reaction, but she still had to tread carefully. She needed all twelve jurors on her side and could not afford to turn one of them off now.

This was the moment of truth. Her argument would sink or swim based on how the jury responded to her next few statements. "If you look up the word religion in Webster's Dictionary, you would find this definition among a few others. I quote, 'religion is a cause, principle, or system of beliefs held to with ardor and faith.'" She rested her hands on the banister that surrounded the jury box and took a deep breath for impact. "So, by this definition, even the practice of atheism is considered a religion as it is predicated on certain beliefs and practiced by actions." The atheist jurors looked at each other, a bit confused. Alexis seized her opportunity, knowing that people where most open to influence when they were faced with information that caused then to doubt what they believed. "To support my last statement, I would like to read to you a couple excerpts from the formal definition of atheism provided to the Supreme Court of the United States in the case of Murray v. Curlett. For those of you who may not be familiar with this case, this is the case which banned the reading of the Bible and reciting the Lord's Prayer in public schools in 1963." As Alexis read, she held her notes out in front of her so she could also maintain eye contact with a few key jurors.

"Your petitioners are atheists and they define their beliefs as follows. An atheist loves his fellow man instead of God. An atheist believes that he can get no help through prayer but that he must find in himself the inner conviction and strength to meet life, to grapple with it, to subdue it, and enjoy it. An atheist believes that only in knowledge of himself and knowledge of his fellow man can he find the understanding that will help to a life of fulfillment. He seeks to know himself and his fellow man rather than to know a "god." He wants disease conquered, poverty vanquished, war eliminated. He wants man to understand and love man. He believes that we are our brother's keepers and are keepers of our own lives; that we are responsible persons and the job is here and the time is now," she said as she read from the case notes.

Alexis gently folded up the paper before she continued. Many of the jurors were now looking at her with odd expressions on their face as they puzzled through the logic of her argument. She began to see eyebrows arch and heads nod in the jury as people began to connect the dots.

"Your Honor, ladies and gentlemen of the jury ... I thank you for your time and attention. I close with this last statement about my client and about this case. Regardless of your viewpoint of religion, it is our freedom to pursue, worship, and practice the religion of our choice, free of government interference. It is our freedom to believe. Ordinance 5578 was implemented by the city with the intent of providing distinct and clear boundaries between religion and government but it is unconstitutional at its core because it violates the Establishment Clause by supporting the religion of atheism. The city government crossed a line by passing this ordinance and my client has been unjustly affected by their actions." Alexis scanned the jury and noticed several jurors nodding in agreement. "To vote in favor of the defendant and thus support this ordinance is to vote against the Constitution that serves to protect your very own freedoms. Unless we push back in protest and firmly establish the boundaries of our freedoms through legal action, the government will cross other constitutional lines and progressively reduce our freedoms. Is that the future you want for yourself, for your children, or for this country?"

Alexis paused for a long moment, making eye contact with each juror before proceeding. "You can choose to believe the information presented by the defendant in this case, or you can choose to believe the information that was presented by my legal team. In either case, you will be executing the fundamental freedom of belief. Are you willing to put that freedom at risk by voting for the defendant?" Her voice echoed through the courtroom. "If not, then there is only one choice in this case. You must vote in favor of my client to ensure that your freedoms are protected as well." Her argument concluded, Alexis turned and walked slowly back to her desk. She glanced briefly at the judge. She wasn't sure, but she thought he was smiling.

Chapter 34

Washington, District of Columbia

"Robert? It's Derrick," the voice said urgently, causing Robert to pick up the phone to turn off the speaker. Robert noted that Derrick sounded agitated. He *was probably upset because he lost a bet*, Robert thought. He hoped Derrick was not calling for money.

"What is it?" Robert said calmly.

"We have major situation developing down here. The police are at my campaign headquarters with a search warrant. They have reason to believe that my campaign was involved with voter fraud," Derrick cried, almost in a panic. "Sheesh!" he exclaimed. "Do I have anything to worry about here? I don't like what this insinuates."

Robert's pulse quickened. Something must have gone very wrong, but he couldn't let Derrick know anything. Derrick would give them all up if it would save his own skin. The less Derrick knew, the safer they all were. Robert took a deep breath and released it slowly, "Calm down, Derrick. Everything is fine and there is nothing for you to worry about. I will have a lawyer at your office in the next thirty minutes to get this sorted out. Let me make some phone calls and I will call you back later."

"You better get this straightened out, Rob. I won't have a chance to win this election if the people suspect my campaign was involved with voter fraud," Derrick said, regaining his composure.

"I will have this taken care of. You just keep your mouth shut. Don't talk to the press. Don't talk to anyone without counsel present. Are we clear?" He didn't wait for Derrick's response and hung up the phone.

Robert pressed the button for his secretary. "Debbie, get me Dan Huskins immediately. Tell him it is an emergency."

A minute later, his phone rang. "Danny, please excuse my interruption, but I have an urgent favor that I need your assistance on immediately." Dan was an old friend, but that was not why he was calling him. Dan was the Deputy Director of the FBI and the only person he could trust to find out the truth. Fortunately, Dan also owed him several favors. "The Charleston police department has apparently opened an investigation into voter fraud in the South Carolina governor's race. As we speak, the police are at the Democratic headquarters with a search warrant. I need to know the details behind the investigation, specifically what the police suspect and more importantly, what they know."

He listened intently to Dan's response. "I don't care how you do it; just find out what the story is. This has huge implications for our candidate in South Carolina. Not only that, but I fear if the investigation is not contained, it could expand to other states, which would then make it a federal matter. The Bureau has too much on its plate already. We need to get ahead of this, not only for me, but for you too."

Dan's response gave him encouragement. "Thanks," Robert said. "You are a good friend. I will look for your call within the hour. By the way, please call me on my secure line." He hung up, already thinking about his next move to contain the situation.

Fifteen minutes later, Dan called him back to debrief him on this situation. It was worse than he thought. The authorities had confirmed that the South Carolina central voting system had been compromised. They were still working out the specific details of the breadth and extent of the electronic voter fraud, but it was already apparent that it was significant breach. Authorities had confirmed that several thousand absentee ballot votes had been cast by people that were on Jasper Thorne's donor list. All of the votes had been cast for his opponent, Derrick Baldwin.

Robert placed his cellular phone down and opened his desk drawer, removing another cellular phone he rarely used. He quickly dialed a number. *Come on! Answer the phone*, he thought. After the fourth ring, he heard the hearty voice of Harry Benjamin.

Not bothering to exchange pleasantries, Robert broke the news to the Senator. "Harry, there is an investigation into voter fraud going on in South Carolina. The authorities have found evidence of hacking into the State's central voting system, specifically the absentee ballot database."

"How is that possible?" Harry asked.

"I am not sure," Robert admitted, "we have been doing this for years, all over the country, with no problem. Something else must have happened?"

"What are you going to do?"

"We have to start damage control on this immediately," Robert responded. "If the general public begins to distrust the integrity of our voting system, and other investigations occur in other states, our whole agenda is screwed."

"Keep me posted," Harry said and then hung up. Robert knew it was time for him to act. Fortunately for both of them, managing public perception was his expertise.

Two days later, the story of election fraud in South Carolina was national news, but only for a day. Robert had worked feverishly through his extensive network of media contacts to float the theory that the hacking of the central voting system was done by North Korea as a mechanism to both influence and control the election. His efforts had paid off, at least for now. He had cited both real and fictitious examples of cyber attacks on state voting systems that had been successfully thwarted, emphasizing the integrity of the electronic voting systems that existed in almost every county and city in the country. Regretfully, he had to exchange some favors with a few key congressman on the House Committee of Foreign Affairs to motivate them to publicly support his imaginary scenarios, but it had worked. He hated to be indebted to someone else, particularly if those debts were not monetary, but the cause was more vital than his personal agenda.

Public opinion polls conducted in the coming days indicated that the general population believed the scenario being promoted by the media. After all, foreign countries such as Russia, China, and even allies such as Great Britain, had been hacking into the IT systems of American corporations and the U.S. government for years. That gave Robert some breathing room. By the time the official investigation would conclude and any information pertaining to the exact nature of the crime would be released, the elections would be well over.

Even so, he was disappointed and a little concerned that they had lost a huge advantage in the South Carolina race. That very week, the governor of South Carolina issued an executive order requiring all voters to present a valid state or government picture identification in order to vote at the upcoming election. The state legislature supported the measure fully. Robert had been counting on the previous requirements which allowed people to present utility bills, paycheck stubs, or even a library card as a valid form of identification. The new requirement would definitely create complications to his plans.

The frontal strategy to ensure they won the election had been dependent on unhampered access to the polls. In addition to the false votes gained through the absentee ballot process, and the legitimate votes of recently minted citizens, he had counted on at least fifty thousand falsified votes cast by his "volunteers." The "volunteers" were people who were hired by his various organizations to execute specific actions, whether it be to march in a picket line, protest outside a store, or illegally vote. Unprincipled people were always willing to make an extra buck; it was a trait of human nature that he counted on. Because of this, there were hundreds of thousands of "volunteers" ready when needed. His agents were already preparing the list of long term care residence, recently deceased, and those citizens working abroad who identities would be temporarily taken over by the "volunteers." Historical probability proved that most of these people, at least those living, did not vote. Therefore, votes cast by his "volunteers" would have been an upside to the general tally. Now, none of that was possible. The healthy voter margin of more than twenty percent that he had anticipated had been basically eliminated. That meant he might actually have to rely on the general population to push the tide in his favor and that thought scared the hell out of him. Jasper Thorne was much too resourceful of an opponent to leave the election to chance.

To make matters worse, he did not have confidence that Aaron Mandon's lackey would be successful in discrediting

Thorne. That meant Robert needed to fortify the plan with something more impactful, something he could count on with all surety. It was time to place some personal pressure on Jasper Thorne. He wanted Thorne second guessing his race for governor. Better yet, he wanted him to drop out of the race entirely. But to make that occur would require a different, more personal sort of pressure. Fortunately, he knew just who to call to make that happen.

Chapter 35

Austin, Texas

Governor Doug Whorter reviewed the most recent security report issued by his Attorney General. *Funny*, he thought, *there had not been an incident at the Wall in more than four months.* The random bomb attacks along the wall had become such a frequent occurrence and then suddenly nothing. Maybe the fact that authorities now had a visual identification of the terrorist had deterred future activities. But he didn't feel very confident about that conclusion. One person, acting alone, would not have been able to execute the series of attacks with precision that occurred. There had to be others involved and that meant that the state was still in danger.

Jeff Ruger entered his office; his face was tense — as if he was bearing the weight of the world. That was a rather common state of mind for his Director of Public Works. Jeff took his job seriously to a fault. Unlike seasoned veterans of state government who had learned to go with the flow of things, he was a high strung perfectionist who tended to wear his emotions on his sleeve. Still, he was very good at his job and had been instrumental in coordinating their security response efforts along the Wall the past several months.

"What is it?" Doug barked. He was always tough on Jeff, more than he should be. It was probably because he knew the man could take it and would treat him the same way if their roles were reversed. Jeff had earned his respect, but that didn't mean he had earned a pass.

"I have confirmed that construction crews from Fort Hood arrived at two different sections of the Wall this morning. Each of them has a small armed military escort. The sections are Denver City and Socorro. Laughlin Air Force Base has also dispatched construction crews to Big Bend National Park and to Del Rio. Based on the reports of the vehicles and machinery, we believe they are preparing to tear sections of the Wall down at those locations."

"What?" Doug exclaimed. "You got to be kidding me? Under whose authority?" Doug asked pointedly.

Shrugging his shoulders, Jeff responded, "Who else but the United States Government." The statement was said with a heavy hint of sarcasm in his voice. Past liberal administrations had always been somewhat hostile towards Texas. Not only for the conservative nature of the state and its government, but because of the Wall. However, the current administration has intensified the hostility into a full-fledged hate campaign. Doug had a hunch it was because the president was the son of illegal immigrants. To the president and other liberal leaders, the Wall was the manifestation of conservative ideology and individual state rights run amuck. What this same administration would never admit is that the Wall had successfully and unequivocally done the job it was designed to do — keep illegal immigrants, terrorists and drug traffickers from entering the state and ultimately the country. Since the Wall's construction, drug-related crimes per capita in Texas were now the lowest of any state in the union with the exception of Alaska.

Doug pursed his lips for a moment and a mean scowl formed on his face. "Those bastards!" he cursed.

Jeff ignored the outburst and continued with his report. "Border security spoke with a foreman of one of the construction crews. The foreman stated that he was under contract by the Army Corp of Engineers and was to remove a section of the internal and external wall. The cleared sections were to be graded and a gravel road constructed. The only border barrier to be left barring access the country is supposed to be some rickety ass wooden gate and a guard shed purchased from Home Depot." Jeff scratched nervously at his neck before finishing his report. Doug hated when he did that, it meant bad news was coming. "The crews are also supposed to construct a small building that the foreman called simply a processing center. The crews have been instructed to work overtime and do whatever is needed to complete the project in less than a week. Whatever the government is up to, they are in a heck of a rush to complete it."

"What are they up to?" Doug said thinking aloud. "There are already border stations at the intersections of the main access roads through the wall. Why open additional access points?"

"Maybe it is because they are expecting a higher volume of traffic than can be handled at the current border stations," Jeff posed, now rubbing his chin nervously. "It would make sense with the so called processing center they plan to construct. Perhaps they think that now IPEA has been passed, more immigrants will come here seeking jobs."

"That is only part of the story and we both know that." Doug said, rubbing his own chin. He stopped as soon as he realized he was doing it. "They have wanted this Wall taken down for decades and it appears that they now have as good as an excuse as any to start the process."

Doug and Jeff stared at each other in silence for a long while. They both knew that something like this might occur. Technically, the Wall was in the Border Zone established by the president's executive proclamation meaning that the Wall was federal property, but only if you believed the executive proclamation was constitutional. Unfortunately for the United States government, Governor Whorter did not.

Doug pushed a button on his phone console and it rang audibly through the speaker phone. It was answered on the second ring. "This is Commander Bryson. How may I help you, Governor?"

"Greg, I'm here with Jeff Ruger. You know that scenario you and I have discussed? Well, it is time to put it into action. There is a situation occurring which requires the services of the National Guard. Your boys are loyal to the state, right?"

"They will do what I tell them to do. We are all prepared to do what we believe is right for our state and its people. In the end, I am in command and the final responsibility for the troops and what they do falls on me. My men are just following orders."

"You know that we are talking treason here?" Doug added.

Jeff reached across the desk and pushed the mute button "What in God's creation are you doing?" he asked, his face full of alarm.

"The same thing I would do if someone broke into my house and started destroying my property." Doug stood up, placing his hands on his desk and leaning forwards towards Jeff in a confrontational manner. "I'm going to fight back and I am going to kick some real ass!"

Chapter 36

Charleston, South Carolina

Jasper was so exhausted he felt like he could fall asleep standing up. The decadent food and heavy wine he and Alexis had just consumed did not help matters. They had been celebrating her return and her trial win with a lavish dinner at one of the few remaining upscale restaurants in Charleston. It had been over two months since he had last seen her. To say he had been looking forward to their evening together for weeks would be an understatement.

He had been able to cope with not seeing her by maintaining his focus on his campaign. The past week had been specifically hectic as he had crisscrossed the state to visit the major population centers. The days had been long and arduous, filled with campaign events, fundraisers, and key meetings with state and corporate leaders. He had only returned home to Charleston that afternoon, with scarcely time to shower and dress before Alexis had arrived. In some respects, her absence had been a positive thing. Their relationship had blossomed on a mental and emotional level through their long distance interactions in a manner that neither of them had expected. Jasper felt an intimacy with Alexis that he had never experienced with anyone else in his life. It felt good to be with her and better to hold her in his arms.

It was a beautiful warm autumn night, with a light breeze blowing steadily. Jasper loved the fall season — it was his favorite time of year. To him, it was a time for new possibilities to take shape. Possibilities, that once formed, would hibernate through the winter only to emerge in full glory in the coming spring. He and Alexis settled in on his patio couch, his arm around her and her head nestled into his chest. He loved the smell of her hair and the feel of her skin. Despite how tired he felt, Jasper had been waiting for the right moment to ask her a question that had been on his mind since his last lesson with Michael. Now that they were alone, he felt better about asking it.

Recently, Michael had taught Jasper about the encounter between Nicodemus and Jesus in the Book of John. Nicodemus was a Pharisee who had sought after Jesus in the secrecy of night so that he could ask him questions about spiritual matters. Michael had used the story to discuss the concept of spiritual rebirth and why salvation was necessary in order to have a true relationship with God.

He tickled the back of her neck gently with his hand as they stared into the courtyard. "Alexis, there is a question that I have been meaning to ask you ... but I feel a little awkward asking it.

"Jasper, baby ... you can ask me anything," she said supportively, her sensual southern drawl more pronounced than usual. "I'm a big girl."

Jasper stroked her hair for a moment before speaking. It was such a strange question to ask someone. A little unsure of himself, he finally asked, "When were you saved and what happened to lead you to that decision?"

Alexis lifted her head and stared up at him, trying to discern his motive. She did not say anything at first. Jasper thought for a moment that he had overstepped his bounds with the question. Jasper couldn't help feeling awkward. Catholics didn't talk about being saved, at least the ones he knew. It felt like he was asking Alexis when she joined the neighborhood cult. Any reservations he had about asking her the question faded when he saw the gentle smile form on her face.

"I have been waiting for you to ask me that question," she said softly, but Jasper wasn't so sure based on the sound of her voice. It was unusually timid and she scooted away from Jasper to the opposite side of the couch. She looked at him, her brown eyes searching his, seeking assurance, "Promise me that you will not disrespect me for what I am about to tell you."

Jasper leaned over to her and gently kissed her forehead, "I promise." He searched her face for another approving expression, but Alexis was looking away, her gaze focused on a faraway time.

She reached over and grabbed his hand. "You may think that you asked me a simple question, but the answer is not that simple. Being saved or coming to Christ or being born again, whatever you want to call it, well it is a different experience for every person. But I do want to tell you my story, the whole story," she frowned. "It was a dark time in my life and I have done my best to forget about it." Jasper could tell that she was uncomfortable. She was couched on one side of the sofa in a protective posture, seemingly removed from him.

"I was seven years old when I first professed my faith in Christ during children's Sunday school. I did it again two years later at a church retreat. At the age of thirteen, I still wasn't sure I was saved, despite being in church my entire childhood. I think my father was aware of my doubts, because he would frequently bring up the topic of salvation and emphasize how the evidence of salvation is a changed heart and overtime, a changed life. I didn't feel any different, I was still the same tomboy brat I had been four years earlier, only I had become increasingly more rebellious against authority, school, and the church," she said softly.

"There had to be a lot of pressure on you, growing up as a preacher's daughter," Jasper said sympathetically.

Alexis did not acknowledge his comment. "At that time, my mother and I had a horrible relationship. My mother couldn't understand why I acted the way I did and I couldn't understand why she wanted me to be like other girls my age. We barely spoke to each other but when we did our conversations would end with me cussing at her until she broke into tears. My father would punish me, of course, but that didn't change anything. I hated my parents, I hated my life, and I wanted nothing to do with church. Obviously, I had more than enough difficulty with the rules my parents placed on me and the last thing I needed was some "spiritual" entity who I could not see, could not hear and did not know for certain existed, telling me what I should do and not do."

Jasper chuckled slightly at the last comment. "I am sorry. But I have had the same exact thought before."

Alexis nodded slightly, nervously twirling a curl of her hair. She continued, "At the age of fourteen, I met Mateo. I was sitting alone in my school cafeteria when he asked if he could sit with me. He was cute and I didn't have any friends of my own, so I invited him to join me. He was so easy to talk too. We decided to skip the rest of school that day and hang out down at the beach. He was from a troubled home and felt like a family outcast, just like me. I learned that his father would beat him regularly when he was drinking, which was almost every night," her voice suddenly subdued. "When I think back, I believe that he was such a loner because part of him believed the awful stuff his father would tell him. His father would berate him about how pathetic he was, how he was a waste of a life and how he would never amount to anything." The way she conveyed the story of Mateo made Jasper sad and angry. No one should have to suffer that type of verbal and physical abuse.

Jasper listened intently as Alexis shared her story, hanging on her every word. "That day was also the first time I smoked marijuana. It provided me a means of escape from the reality of life and the pain I was experiencing. Within a few months, Mateo and I were experimenting with much heavier stuff." She flashed a quick glance at Jasper. "You see, I trusted him. He didn't try to change me ... he was the first person I felt accepted me for who I was. He only wanted to spend time with me. We soon became closer physically, and just like with the drugs and alcohol, we did begin to experiment with more intimate actions. We never had sex, but I am sure we would of, if ... ," her voice trailed off to a whisper.

Jasper held her hand firmly, seeking to reassure her. "It is ok. Please tell me what happened."

"At the end of that school year, my father received my report card and told me that I would be starting preparatory school the next fall, even though he was not sure how we would afford it. When I saw Mateo the next morning, he had a large cut under his left eye, and his right eye was swollen shut. His father had been unusually rough on him the previous night. By noon that day, we had hitched a ride and were heading to Charleston. We were both convinced we were running away forever," she smiled briefly at the memory.

"We had been in Charleston for only a few days the night it happened. It had been rough — we slept wherever we could find shelter, stole food and clothing, or whatever we needed from wherever we could. That night we hooked up with a group of guys who promised drugs and alcohol and we partied at an abandoned warehouse. Later in the evening, after the partying was done and all of us were basically passed out, I woke up to find one of the men on top of me with his hand covering my mouth. He was trying to take my pants off and I could tell that his were already off. I struggled under him as hard as I could, beating my hands against him to no avail." Alexis's voice broke and Jasper saw tears began to run down her cheeks. Jasper felt his blood pressure rise as he pictured this scene in his mind. He gave Alexis hand another reassuring squeeze, "You don't have to do this, Alex."

"I tried to scratch his face, gouge his eyes, anything to cause him pain, but he was stoned and wasn't fazed. I remember him drooling on me as we struggled. Eventually he managed to pin my hands above my head. He soon had my pants off while I struggled in silence. I couldn't believe what was happening to me. The next thing I know, Mateo was screaming and hitting the man with a fury that I could only describe as pure, unbridled rage. I was stone sober by then and watched helplessly as the other men ganged up against Mateo. One of them had a knife and stabbed Mateo in the stomach, while the other two held him. It happened so fast. The next thing I knew, Mateo and I were alone. He was on the ground thrashing and writhing in pain in a growing pool of blood. I tried frantically to stop the bleeding, but there was nothing I could do," Alexis shivered. "Mateo died in my arms that night." Her tears were streaming down her face as she relived the moment.

Jasper handed her his handkerchief, but he wasn't sure what else to do. He finally said, "I am so sorry. That must have been horrible to go through."

Alexis wiped her eyes. "I found myself alone, not knowing where I was, or what I was going to do. I was so distraught and I remember this consuming feeling of complete hopelessness. Not only was I grieving over Mateo, but these horrible thoughts were going through my mind. That I was a failure, that I had hurt my parents, that they couldn't possibly love me anymore. That somehow I had gone off track in my life and would never recover. That no one would ever need me. No one would ever love me." She sobbed for a moment, the words coming hard. "That Mateo would still be alive if it were not for me."

Jasper's heart ached for Alexis and the pain she was reliving. He wished there was something he could do, but he didn't know what. He just held her hand and listened.

Alexis's wiped the tears from her cheeks. "I don't know how long I lay there, writhing in my despair in the dark, sobbing over Mateo's dead body. And then it was like someone lifted a veil off of me. Only it wasn't light that I saw, it was a song that started playing in my head. It was the song my mother would sing to me when I was frightened." She began to sing softly,

"Are you weary, are you heavy hearted?
Tell it to Jesus, tell it to Jesus.
Are you grieving over joys departed?
Tell it to Jesus alone.

Do the tears flow down your cheeks unbidden?
Tell it to Jesus, tell it to Jesus.
Have you sins that to men's eyes are hidden?
Tell it to Jesus alone."

Jasper had never heard Alexis sing before. Her voice was melodic and soothing. Alexis paused before continuing, collecting herself. "That song penetrated through the cloud of my despair. I started to call out for Jesus to save me with every ounce of my being. I knew that He was my only hope. Jesus was the only one who still loved me despite the wicked things I had done and the hurt I had caused."

More tears began to fall down her cheeks as she remembered the moment, but her voice had taken on a strong, inspirational tone. "For the first time, I truly realized and valued my dependence on God and understood what his gift of salvation meant. I knew that there was forgiveness in him for all my sins if I just believed and accepted his gift. I emptied my heart to God at that moment, confessing all the things I had done against him, against my parents, against others, and against myself. What was amazing about the whole experience is that as I emptied all my concerns, fears, and sins through confession, I felt myself being filled with the most amazing sensation. It was like having a living, pulsing energy inside of me. It wrapped me in warmth, protection, and love. Jesus had heard my cry for help and he had truly come to save me."

Alexis turned to Jasper, her eyes were red and she had mascara smeared across her left cheek. "So now you know."

Jasper pulled her onto his lap and hugged her protectively. She nuzzled against him, "What are you thinking?" she finally asked him.

"I am thinking how grateful I am that you are in my life," Jasper responded sincerely. "Thank you for sharing your experience. I know it was difficult," he paused for a moment, staring deeply into her eyes. "Alex, as long as I am in your life, you will never be alone. I care about you. I ..." He struggled to say the next words. "I need you."

She squeezed him tightly. "I need you too!" she whispered. "It feels so comfortable with you, like I was made to fit right here in your arms." They rested there in each other's embrace, not saying a word, grateful to have each other to hold. A few minutes later, they were both asleep, still wrapped tightly in each other's arms. The last conscious thought to go through Jasper's mind was about Alexis and how it felt so right to hold her. No matter what, he knew one thing for sure. He never, ever wanted to let her go.

Chapter 37

Los Angeles, California

Reggie checked the name and address against the Homeland Security's citizen database for the third time. There was no doubt; the address for the location of the surveillance camera was a match. It was directly across the street from the residence of U.S. Congressman Jasper Thorne. His first introduction to Jasper Thorne had been through a Los Angeles Times article about the upcoming national elections covering key battleground states. There were several highly contested gubernatorial elections, the most interesting of which was occurring in South Carolina. The recent announcement of a state vote on the secession of South Carolina had propelled that race into the forefront and cast a spotlight on the two candidates for governor, one of which would have to deal with the election outcome. Now, Reggie couldn't watch late night news without hearing a story about Jasper Thorne.

Reggie laughed softly. Those people in the South were a strange breed indeed. *What were those people thinking anyway?* The idea of secession was plain ridiculous. When he had shared the story with his wife Teresa, she had agreed adding that the idea of secession was as crazy as his decision to stay in the RIM taskforce. Reggie half-jokingly responded that if she kept making comments like that about his job, he was going to secede from her. "At least then I wouldn't become a widow," she had retorted with a scowl.

"Damn that woman," he cursed under his breath. She always knew how to get the final word.

"Did you say something, Jefe?" Carlos didn't bother to look up as he typed away on his keyboard, typing one letter at a time with his index fingers. Reggie smiled, Carlos was a good cop, but he was a horrible typist. Last month, they had decided to move into an office together to increase their ability to communicate more easily and brainstorm ideas about the case.

Solving the Santoro murders had become RIM's primary focus since IPEA had become law.

The governor of California had personally told both of them that solving the Santoro case was the only way to restore peace between the Latino and African American communities, an impossible outcome to imagine given the chaos on the streets. Active militias of African American citizens now patrolled certain areas of Los Angeles under the premise that they were protecting the city from an invasion of illegal immigrants. Gang violence and bloodshed was a daily occurrence as Latino gangs continued to make raids into African American areas of the city in retribution for the Santoro murders. The governor had failed to offer any insight on how to address the situation, leaving it up to Reggie to solve. Regardless, Reggie was not sure his new office arrangement with Carolos was helping. "I was just mumbling to myself about having to make a trip to South Carolina," he lied.

"South Carolina? Why would you have to go there?" Carlos asked, surprised by the comment.

"Scarface," Reggie retorted with a growl. His response caused Carlos to suspend his typing and look up. Scarface was the name Carlos had given to the unidentified suspect associated with the last explosion at the Wall. Scarface was now the chief suspect in two high profile incidents. He was being investigated by the FBI for the bombings at the Wall in Texas after being positively identified as the same maintenance technician who had been found in the area of the very first attack. In addition, he was also the lead suspect in the Santoro murders, thanks to plain old-fashioned detective work.

Both he and Carlos had thought it strange that Scarface had been in Los Angeles at the time of the murders and even stranger that he had been photographed near Raphael Santoro. Even though there was no hard evidence to suspect Scarface had anything to do with the murders, it would have been freshman of them not to investigate any possible links. Their investigation had yielded fruit but also generated more questions.

"Diga me. What is going on?" Carlos left his seat and walked over to stand behind Reggie. They both starred at the strong handsome face displayed on the video monitor. The pensive expression on Carlos face changed to a smirk. "Look, Reggie. I know things are a little rocky with the wife, but looking at male porn on the job is not only going to get you fired, but you're going to lose a lot of respect around here," Carlos joked, slapping Reggie lightly on the back.

Reggie shot Carlos a look of pure disdain that immediately erased the smile from Carlos face.

Carlos knew when to back off. His tone more serious, he added, "You know I am behind you whatever the case. Now who's the white guy?"

Reggie couldn't help but smile, thinking about the pun that went unstated but was fully intended. Carlos could always brighten his mood, even in a sick kind of way. "His name is Jasper Thorne. He is a U.S. congressman and a current candidate for governor of South Carolina. Scarface has been taking siestas outside Thorne's house for the last three days."

"What do you think he is doing outside the residence of a U.S. congressman?" Carlos asked.

"Your guess is as good as mine. I am thinking he is tracking him, observing his comings and goings, but I don't know why."

Carlos tapped a spot on the monitor, pulling up a recent video of Scarface. "I wonder where he has been hiding?" That was a question that Reggie had asked himself multiple times in the last hours.

Only yesterday, Homeland Security had alerted him that a positive match for Scarface was identified in the NSIS database. The National Surveillance and Identification System, or NSIS for short, was the result of a program instituted by the Department of Homeland Security nearly a decade ago to combat terrorism. Since that time, a massive networked web of high definition video cameras had been installed throughout the country. The initial phase of the project focused on surveillance installations at major transportation centers, primarily airports, bus depots, train stations, and ports. Future phases expanded the surveillance network to cover both urban and residential centers within a five miles radius of all major cities. A little known caveat of the program was that additional surveillance systems had been installed near the residences of all active U.S. Congress members, Cabinet officials and members of the Supreme Court. In most cases, the locations of the cameras were unknown to those they monitored. That was by design and exactly what the government wanted.

Despite the periodic outcry of privacy violations that arose every year against NSIS, the system had proven very affective at helping authorities to identify, track, and apprehend suspected terrorists and criminals. NSIS had been instrumental in establishing Scarface as a prime suspect in the Santoro murders. Once they had uploaded a photo of Scarface to NSIS and entered their search parameters, it had taken less than thirty minutes for the massive technology application to run an analysis. Tens of thousands of hours of surveillance video gathered from thousands of cameras in the Los Angeles sector of NSIS were reviewed from a three day period before and after the murder. Three positive identification matches were found. The first was a photo from a camera at the Los Angeles court house on the same day Raphael Santoro had been photographed leaving the court house. That was a dead end. They already knew Scarface had been at the court house that day. The second match was a picture of Scarface entering a local neighborhood bank in Bellflower. The last photo match was of Scarface standing in line at a rental car office located at Los Angeles International Airport.

At first, the latter seemed to be a promising lead, but further investigation determined that Scarface had used a fake driver's license and stolen credit card to rent a car. Scarface could have driven his rental car anywhere, making geographic matching through NSIS difficult. A national search for Scarface in NSIS for the day he had rented the car had taken over a week to complete, but came up empty. That was one of the limitations to NSIS. Even with a supercomputer, the amount of data that had to be analyzed for a historical search of the camera network on a national basis was enormous. It was different with the real-time data feeds from the cameras. All feeds were processed through an extensive series of facial recognition algorithms in the system allowing for active monitoring of chosen individuals. Hence the reason Reggie had received the recent alert on Scarface being in South Carolina. Even though two of the recognition matches from NSIS had led to dead ends, they had learned something important about Scarface. He had the capabilities to successful forge a state driver's license including the ability to modify the ID chip that had become standard in all state licenses. That fact alone meant they were dealing with a professional criminal with expansive resources.

Fortunately, RIM had its own pros and their work allowed Reggie to directly link Scarface to one of the victims of the Santoro murder. Upon his request, one of his IT analysts had conducted a search of transactions using the fake driver's license number. The search revealed the license had been scanned as part of a banking transaction at the same bank where Scarface had been photographed. The time stamp for the banking transaction was five minutes later than the time stamp on the security video, collaborating the fact that Scarface had initiated the transaction. A detailed review of the banking transaction showed a check payable to William Shuck was cashed for five hundred dollars. William Shuck was the same name Scarface used to rent a car at the airport, again collaborating that Scarface initiated the transaction using his fake driver's license.

Though these developments were encouraging for the case, Reggie still lacked any evidence to link Scarface to the Santoro murders. Fortunately, Carlos had asked for a copy of the canceled check from the bank to review. Reggie recognized the name of the checking account owner as soon as Carlos read it to him. The account belonged to Martha Rodriquez. Martha was an elderly woman in her late seventies who had lived alone in the Bellflower neighborhood. Sadly, she was also one of the victims of the Santoro murders. It was pretty easy to connect the dots that Scarface must have killed Martha, stolen a check from her checkbook, and cashed it at the bank.

But even with this new evidence, they were not any closer to capturing Scarface or even identifying where he was. It was almost as if Scarface was a ghost. Not only that, Reggie had real concerns about the type of criminal he was dealing with. *What kind of man orchestrates a graphic mass murder, blows up part of the border wall in Texas and is able to elude a national surveillance system?* One thing he did know right now, he sure did not want to be Jasper Thorne.

Reggie stared at the face of Jasper Thorne on his video screen. The man had a quality about him that was appealing. It was in stark contrast to the other face veering at him on the other screen. That face made his skin crawl. Wait until his wife learned that he was heading to South Carolina to hunt down a mass murder and one of the most wanted men in America. He might as well pack his bags and not come home. Well, no sense dwelling on something he could not change. Right now, a man's life may be in danger and he was the only one in a position to do anything about it.

Reggie turned off the video screen and leaned back in his chair, contemplating his next move. "What have you got yourself mixed up in?" he said under his breath. The funny thing was he didn't know if he was talking about Jasper Thorne or if he was talking about himself. It didn't really matter, in either case he wasn't sure he wanted to know the answer.

Part III

Chapter 38

The restaurant was crowded, as was usual for the popular downtown meeting place. A flurry of waitstaff in white shirts bustled from table to kitchen and back again to support the large lunch crowd. It was an efficient operation and both the service and the food were better than most restaurants in the capital, at least in Harry's opinion. The five distinguished gentlemen in uniform who rose from the table directly in front of him did not raise a second glance from any of the nearby diners. Their presence was to be expected here.

Located across the street from the U.S. Treasury building and a half block from the White House, Old Ebbitt Grill had become the recognized watering hole for the governmental elite. It was common to see congressmen, senators, State Department officials and high ranking military officers indulging in the fine food and energetic atmosphere. Perhaps that was why Harry liked this place. It was a place where the privileged could interact with other privileged people. The military men walked by his table in single file. Each man wore a uniform jacket that displayed a broad range of colorful ribbons, insignias, and medals. Harry locked eyes with the last man in the group and received a subtle nod in return.

Harry knew he could trust David Walker to do what needed to be done. After all, he had personally sponsored David through his Senate confirmation for his position as Chief of Staff of the Army. Given the escalating situation in Texas, David was currently the most influential military officer in America. In the past week, the Texas National Guard had taken defensive positions along the border entry points, effectively shutting it down in a blatant act of rebellion against the U.S. Army's actions to dismantle the wall. The federal military escorts that had been sent with the constructions crews working on the border entry expansion project were outmanned and outgunned. Both the crews and the escorts had been forced to cease activities and retreat under threat of harm. In response, the Army had sent troop reinforcements to gain offensive positions along the border, surrounding the individual National Guard units from Texas. With the Army and National Guard in a standoff and tensions rising on each side, it was becoming an increasingly dangerous situation, particularly since heavy artillery was involved.

It reminded Harry of the international crisis that occurred at Checkpoint Charlie when he was just a young man. Checkpoint Charlie was the nickname of the infamous border crossing between East Berlin and West Berlin that was thrust into the world spotlight over a two day period in 1961. A dispute at the border escalated to a point where U.S. and Russian tanks squared off, separated by only a few hundred yards. Fortunately, a Russian tank commander made a decision to move his tank away from the confrontation. One by one, both Russian and U.S. tanks followed suit and the crisis was averted. He wasn't so sure the crisis in Texas would have a similar ending. One wrong move by either side could result in needless bloodshed and destruction. Though that scenario concerned Harry, it was not what worried him. His real fear was avoiding all-out civil war between Texas and the United States.

Harry recalled his conversation with David from earlier that morning about the military standoff and options to advert it. According to David, the president was fearful of this situation becoming a domestic crisis and favored ordering the U.S. military to stand down and the construction crews to halt work. Both he and David disagreed with the president. Pursuing this course of action would set a precedent across the country that was potentially harmful to their cause. With South Carolina little more than a week from voting on secession, the last thing they needed was to have an incident that would support and reinforce the powers held by each individual state.

The other problem involved the gubernatorial election in Texas. Despite their efforts, it appeared that Governor Whorter would win reelection by a large margin. This created a huge obstacle to their master plan of controlling the state militias; a situation they had hoped to avoid by having governors loyal to their cause in power. It was only two days ago they had all agreed the Governor of Texas and his cabinet had to be removed from power. It was a necessary action to support the greater cause. David's challenge was to sell the president on the need to arrest the governor, his cabinet, and the Commander of the Texas National Guard for treason, then institute martial law until new elections could be held. The caveat was that they needed the president to hold off on any action until after the elections. It was a risky proposition. Declaring martial law in a state had never occurred in the history of the United States. Then again, they were out of options and desperate times required desperate measures.

Harry turned his attention back to Robert Coolridge who sat across from him aggressively attacking a large bowl of banana pudding. "You ready to go?" he asked. Robert nodded as he swallowed a large spoonful of pudding. It amazed Harry that Robert managed to maintain a healthy weight, despite the rich food he consumed in mass quantities.

They walked down Pennsylvania Avenue towards the Capitol building, allowing their meal to settle but most importantly giving them some much needed privacy. "Robbie, I hate to say it, but I am a little nervous about how this week will transpire," Harry confided. "We have too many loose ends to tie up."

"I know you are worried about the situation in Texas, but whatever happens there, it is only of short term consequence. We will get through it," Robert said assuredly.

"It is not only Texas that concerns me. Aren't you worried about the situation in South Carolina?" Harry asked, less sure than Robert.

Robert shrugged. "I was really nervous when the voter fraud issue bubbled up. But we got it under control." He squeezed Harry's shoulder affectionately, "After all, *that* is why I have contingency plans."

"You mean Franco?" Harry glanced nervously at the FBI building to his left. He wondered if they knew about Franco.

"Franco?" Robert laughed. "You should know me better than that, Harry. Franco is only part of the contingency plan. I can't rely on some underling who I know nothing about. There is too much at stake." Robert stopped for a moment and looked at Harry. There was a slight smirk on his face. "Let's just say that I have taken additional precautions."

Harry's stomach soured. He knew what Robert meant. As much as he supported the cause, he would prefer that change came without violence. On the other hand, Robert preferred violence as a means to create change. Reluctantly Harry asked, "And those plans include?"

"I took the liberty of enlisting the support of our old pal Xavier," Robert said. "But it cost me a pretty penny, probably two, to get him to agree to the assignment."

Harry frowned. He knew what Xavier had done in Los Angeles and in Texas. If Xavier was involved, it was definitely going to get violent. The man was a brutal murderer. *What did Robbie have in mind?* He wasn't sure he wanted to know the answer but he just had to ask the question. "Level with me, Robbie. How does this play out between Franco and Xavier?"

"Despite my doubts about his abilities, Franco has uncovered an incredibly destructive piece of information about our friend Thorne. I don't know where Franco's sources came from, but I confirmed it. Tomorrow, we will leak the information to the press and they will take it from there." Robert had his normal smug look on his face. It reminded Harry of a man who had just learned he won a prize, even though he had rigged the results. "If this approach works, then Xavier's services may not be needed."

"That is encouraging. Why haven't you shared it with me?"

Robert shook his head. "It's nothing personal, Harry, but this information cannot be released until just the right moment. Besides, I like keeping you in suspense," Robert laughed, his charming smile brightening his face.

"You're an asshole but you probably know that too," Harry joked. It felt good to release the tension. If Robert had something damaging on Thorne, it was good news. It was even better news that Xavier's services may not be required. That last thought gave Harry pause. "What happens if the information does not create the intended effect?"

They passed the Navy Memorial, one of Harry's favorite memorials. His father had been in the Navy and had fought in World War II. Perhaps that was why he was so drawn to it. Maybe he just liked the simple aesthetics of the site, particularly in front of the memorial where there was an exact replica of the world's oceans carved into a large granite slab on the ground. Overlooking the granite sea was a statue of a young Navy midshipman called the Lone Sailor. Though just a bronze sculpture, the sailor seemed so alive, his face expressing wisdom that indicated he had already gained a lifetime full of experiences. His eyes looked forward to the horizon, seeing an unknown future, but his stance indicated he was willing to walk towards it and tackle it. There was a look of resolve on his face, a look of courage. Harry felt he needed some courage right now.

"As I said, it is important to have contingency plans. Xavier is preparing to take action and is waiting on my call. I will call on Xavier to execute his mission, but only if I have too," Robert reassured. "As I said, his services are very expensive and I hate spending money if I don't have too."

"I hope you are not planning any more violence," Harry said seriously. It was not a question.

"Only if it is required," Robert lied. "One way or another, Congressman Thorne will find himself having to make a very difficult choice." Robert shrugged his shoulders, "In the end, I will do what I have to do in order to take Jasper Thorne down." There was a tone of finality in his voice.

"What will Thorne have to choose between?" Harry pressed.

"The only things that matter to him," Robert said coldly. "Jasper Thorne either stays in the race, or he loses something very dear to him ... *very dear*." They continued to walk. Harry wasn't sure if it was the cold breeze that was blowing or it was the tone of Robert's voice. He pulled his jacket closely around him. He was shivering and he couldn't stop.

Chapter 39

Charleston, South Carolina
October 28th

Xavier watched from a distance as the handsome couple frolicked hand in hand down the boardwalk that bordered the harbor. It was a beautiful fall afternoon by others accounts, but too cool for his liking. The air had a hint of the winter that would be coming instead of the soft warming touch of the winds in the Caribbean, which he preferred. He strolled forward casually, keeping pace with the two people, but far enough away not to attract attention. He was getting bored with the routine he was observing.

The couple would stop for a moment, the man pointing out a landmark, or colorful bird, or an object of nothingness in the distance. The woman would respond by pressing herself tighter against the man and raising her head to give him a kiss. They would meander forward a little, and then repeat the process, only the next time; it was the woman who was pointing out a statue, or an obscure cloud or something else of little relevance and they would kiss again. They were obviously in love. *What fools they were*, Xavier scoffed. He had been in love once, when he was naive, foolish, and weak. He would never let it happen again — sacrificing his logic for emotion. *Never*.

Xavier had been back in the states for more than a week and it was already much too long for his liking. He knew he was a wanted man by the authorities and that meant he needed to complete this assignment fast and get free of the mainland as soon as possible. He rubbed the thick stubble on his chin. He hadn't shaved in two days. His hand unconsciously felt for the long scar that extended up the left side of his face. The skin was callous and bumpy, like a ravine roughly cut through an otherwise smooth and rolling landscape. The scar was a nasty but necessary reminder to the reality of his chosen vocation. Either he had to kill or be killed. Even so, with great risk came great reward.

Truthfully, the payout was the only reason he considered taking this assignment and forgoing his treasured annual ritual. Normally at this time of year, he was sailing his 38-foot Catalina yacht through the Caribbean, traversing from island to island with no schedule and no plans; only time to waste and the occasional island girl to seduce. Of course, a nine figure payoff would make most people give up anything they valued. But unlike most people, he didn't value possessions; he valued his time to experience life. At the moment, time was a precious commodity. The longer he remained stateside, the more chance that he would be discovered. Fortunately, he had lived most of his life keeping a low profile, a necessity to be successful in this business and stay alive. The bottom line was to be smart and always have your next move planned. If all went as planned, in a few days he would be sailing his boat out of Charleston Harbor and back to the Caribbean and have enough in his bank account to take a few years off.

Unlike his last visit to the U.S., where he had driven across the border at San Ysidro near San Diego, entry by boat was now the only method of getting into the U.S. without extensive scrutiny from U.S. Customs officials. Though his plan was to sail in undetected, he had taken precautions in case he encountered a border patrol or a coast guard vessel while at sea. He had outfitted his yacht with a legitimate South Carolina registration number, a U.S. Customs and Border Protection decal, and an American flag. On his person, he carried a fake passport that listed his place of residence as Charleston, South Carolina. His story would be simple. He was returning back to shore after sailing several miles into international waters to test a new sail and rigging in preparation for a trip to the Caribbean. Simple was always better than complex. The fewer details there were in a story, the fewer the chances that someone would doubt it. Fortunately for him, he had made it to the Florida coast near Melbourne undetected.

It had been an easy trip. Head due north for ninety miles from Freeport and then due east. The remainder of the trip was traveling the Intracoastal Waterway north until he landed in

Charleston. His current employer had rented a home for him on the water in the harbor so he could dock his boat privately. The home was located in the small town of Mount Pleasant, directly across the harbor from Charleston. Every detail had been made to facilitate his mission. A large suburban truck was at his disposal, various clothing had been ordered per his specifications as well as several specialty items ranging from technology hardware to firearms. The bar in the house had even been stocked with his favorite tequila, Patron Silver.

Though he did not care much for U.S. politics, Xavier understood the importance of his mission. It was Xavier's responsibility to make Jasper Thorne clearly see the futileness of continuing in his campaign for governor. He also knew that he was part of a broader plan to ensure that Thorne would fail in his attempt to become the next governor of South Carolina. His employer had shared with him the ongoing activities of another operative attempting to discredit Thorne publically. Time was running out and if the operative failed, Xavier was the contingency plan. He hoped he would have his opportunity. He relished the thrill of the hunt with these types of assignments. More importantly, this assignment promised to be quite challenging.

Xavier had been hunting Thorne the past week, analyzing the routine of his schedule. He would monitor Thorne's coming and goings from his home, the path he would take through the city as he walked to his campaign office each day and the route he followed when he was jogging through the historic district for exercise. It was only two days ago that the beautiful woman spent the night with Thorne. He took a picture of her when they left the house the next day, right before he broke into Jasper's home to rummage through his possessions and personal affects. That was when he had planted the bugs so he could record any conversations that were spoken. He wasn't sure what information he was likely to gain from any recorded conversations, but part of being a successful hunter was to understand the prey being hunted. To successfully manipulate an individual, one had to understand what made that person tick.

Xavier had done his research on Thorne and discovered that there were aspects of Jasper Thorne that were not much different than his own persona. Thorne was a loner for most of his life, which meant he was a selfish man at heart. It was most likely due to the tragedy that Thorne had experienced earlier in his life — Xavier had read about it in the intelligence dossier his employer had prepared for him. Oddly, Thorne appeared to hold himself to some high personal moral standard. He obviously cared a great deal about his reputation, owing to how he bitterly defended the relentless accusations about his moral and political character that had been flung at him throughout the campaign. The aspect that troubled Xavier the most was that Thorne was a resilient man. He would not break easy. That would mean Thorne would need a significant motivator to abandon his goal to be governor. Discovering that one motivator was really the real challenge of this mission.

He watched the couple cross the street and enter into a local restaurant. The man was stopped at the door by a young man who was exiting the restaurant. They shook hands, making introductions. The young man was obviously excited by the encounter. They soon parted ways and the couple was gone from his site. Xavier lit a cigarette and looked back down the boardwalk. There was another couple approaching him, hand in hand, but much older. They walked slowly and cautiously. *Perhaps they had been together as husband and wife for most of their lives*, he thought. He had no doubt that the man and the women had made their share of sacrifices for each other over the years in the name of love. After all, that is what people in love are supposed to do for each other. He laughed out loud. *Fools!* He thought. *They were all fools.* Love was such a strong emotion yet, it was an emotion that had an Achilles Heel. People in love could be manipulated. They could be coerced to do things they would not normally do if the object of their love was in danger.

Xavier flicked his cigarette on the ground and pulled the hood of his jacket securely around his face, making it difficult to see his face from the side. It was time to put his plan in motion and it was not going to be easy. Jasper Throne was a strong and cunning adversary. Xavier wasn't worried though. He always planned for the worst case. If the first part of the plan failed, then he would be forced to strike at Thorne's only weakness. He took one last look at the older couple, who was now sitting on a park bench catching their breath. The woman was fussing over the man while he sat quietly looking at her with a big smile on his face.

"Yes, Jasper Thorne, you have an Achilles Heel," he said softly, "and her name is Alexis Mills."

Chapter 40

Charleston, South Carolina
October 29ᵗʰ

Jasper ignored the flashing message on his monitor. It was the third invitation this week he had received from RedBear17 to start a new game. He was still smarting from the last bruising RedBear17 had given him when they had played a month ago. As tempting as it was to lose a few hours in a game of chess, he didn't have time, not with the election so close. The vibration of his phone on the desk put an end to his temptation to escape from reality. He answered it reluctantly, not bothering to look at the name of the caller.

"Jasper, are you someplace alone were we can talk?" He recognized the voice, it was Trent Holloway.

"Your timing is fortunate, Trent," Jasper said. "I just got back to my office at campaign headquarters. Michael is out getting the team some lunch so I have some time now. How are you?"

Trent hesitated before responding and Jasper heard him take a deep breath before he spoke. "Jasper ... I'm sorry. I ..." Trent stammered. Jasper could tell Trent was downcast, he didn't sound like himself.

"Trent, what is wrong?" Jasper asked concerned. He had never known Trent to be at a lack for words. There must be something really amiss.

"Jasper, I put myself in a compromising position a long time ago. Please believe me, there was nothing I could do. I'm so sorry," Trent said despondently. There was a long pause. "Just know I never meant to hurt you," Trent's voice trailed off.

"Trent... Trent!" Jasper yelled after not getting a response. "Tell me what is going on? What have you done?" His question was met with a dial tone. Trent Hollaway had hung up the phone.

Jasper dialed Trent on his cell phone. No answer. He dialed it one more time and it went straight to voice mail. Trent must have turned his phone off. *That is strange*, he thought.

Frustrated, Jasper dialed the cell phone number of Trent's wife, Trudy. Her sultry southern voice answered on the first ring, but it was her voice mail. He left a simple, but terse message stating he was concerned about Trent and would appreciate a call back as soon as possible. He hung up, not sure what else to do.

This behavior was completely out of sorts for Trent, a man who was usually jovial and making light of even the hardest situation. Trent's ability to be optimistic, no matter how dire the situation, was one of the many qualities that he admired in the man. He recalled the last time they had spoken, Trent had joked about how good it felt to go out in his backyard and piss on government property. Jasper shook in frustration. What had made Trent so upset that he felt he had needed to apologize to him?

His concern took his thoughts back to a time when his parents were still alive – back to his earliest memory of Trent. His father and Trent had just returned from a day of deep sea fishing and had been fortunate enough to hook a large tuna. They had prepared tuna steaks that evening and it had been the first time Jasper had tasted fresh tuna. Since then, Trent had become an important part of his life, offering guidance, support, and encouragement, even more so after the death of his parents. He remembered Trent had tried to persuade him to enter law school directly from college, but Jasper had chosen to enlist in the Army instead. After the war, Trent had called in some favors to assist Jasper in getting accepted to the law school of his choice. Trent had also been Jasper's primary advocate during his run for Congress and had personally guided his first campaign. Trent was much like a father to him and that is exactly how Jasper felt about him. *What had Trent done?* Jasper agonized over the thought.

His mind jumped to his gubernatorial campaign. He and Trent were supposed to campaign this week together in Charleston, Columbia, and Greenville in a last minute effort to push the vote in his favor. The race was a virtual dead heat. Even the left leaning news outlets were now saying it was too close to call. That meant he had a legitimate shot at winning. *Was Trent's phone call about not being able to campaign with him?* That would make some sense, but what did that have to do with being in a compromising position a long time ago? Things just didn't add up.

Rich Penna, the USA Today journalist poked his head around the corner of the doorway. He was dressed in his standard uniform, a tweed sport coat, brown t-shirt and tan khakis. An offensive lineman in college for Norte Dame, he was a large man. Seeing Jasper at his desk, his mass slowly filled Jasper's office doorway. Jasper liked Rich and considered him a friend. They had first met during a Congressional orientation session for new congressman. Rich had been writing a story on the effectiveness of congressional training programs but really Rich focused on how new senators and congressman learned to navigate through the red tape. Both of them were new to the circus on Capitol Hill, and for some reason they had hit it off. Rich had become as much as a friend as one can be with a journalist. Normally, Rich would flash his boyish smile when he saw Jasper, only this time there was an odd expression on his face. "Is it true?" he asked, somewhat tentatively.

Jasper was still mulling over the recent phone call from Trent but Rich would be a good distraction. Maybe Trent would call back in the interim. Shuffling through some papers on his desk, he offhandedly replied, "Hi Rich. Is what true?"

The reporter studied Jasper for a moment longer and looked at the video monitor lying dormant in the corner. "You haven't heard, have you? I suggest you turn on the video screen."

The tone in Rich's voice caused Jasper to immediately focus. As he reached for the television monitor remote, Michael burst into the room, his face flush red with anger. The curls of his hair seemed to be like flames dancing on a pit of coals. "If this story is true, you have a lot of explaining to do!" he threatened, shaking a long finger at Jasper. "I can't believe you never told me. How can I effectively manage your campaign when you keep secrets like this from me?"

"What in God's creation are you talking about?" Jasper yelled as he rose from his desk chair. He was definitely perplexed by the situation. *Why was Michael mad at him? What had he missed?* Trent's final words still echoed in his head, *I never meant to hurt you.*

Rich looked at Michael and shook his head incredulously, "He doesn't know yet."

"Know what?" Jasper snapped back, his frustration mounting.

Michael grabbed the remote from the desktop and turned on the television monitor, changing the channel to a national news station. There was a news alert ticker scrolling across the bottom of the screen. Jasper stared at the video screen in disbelief. In bright yellow words scrolled the words 'Government sources confirm Congressman Jasper Thorne responsible for deaths of more than 300 children in the European Union Revolution.'

Jasper looked at Michael and then at Rich. They were studying him, waiting to see his reaction to the news. Now, he understood why Trent had been apologizing to him. A trail of questions blazed through his mind. *Why would Trent expose Jasper's secret? To whom did he give the information and for what in return? Why would he choose to release his secret now versus any other time?* The thought that Trent had betrayed him was crushing. It was even more disturbing because Trent was his closest friend. Jasper thought that he could trust Trent with his life. Jasper fell back into his chair deflated. As he thought about the breaking news story, his hurt and frustration flashed to anger. He wanted to hunt Trent down, shake him by his neck, and beat the answers of out of him. *Why had he done this to him?* "Why!" He screamed out loud, slamming his fist into the desk.

Rich and Michel exchanged glances, obviously confused by his outburst. "I want to know everything," Michael demanded with a scowl. He slammed the door closed, causing the thin walls of the office to shake.

Jasper had never seen Michael angry. In fact, he had never heard Michael raise his voice. Michael and Rich obviously wanted answers and they deserved them. Jasper took a deep breath, steadying himself. He had to tell them everything. It was vital that they understood.

"Sit down," Jasper said solemnly. "This is going to take a while to explain."

Chapter 41

Rich and Michael dropped themselves into the two aluminum office chairs that represented the extent of the office furniture. They looked at Jasper expectantly. Jasper let out a long sigh, trying to formulate his thoughts and muster his courage. He had never shared this story with anyone else but Trent, not even Alexis. Now, he was about to tell his darkest secret to a man he had known for less than a year and a news reporter. He wasn't sure where to begin. He was not one to tell stories full of descriptive narratives that contained hordes of useless information. He believed in being direct and to the point. To be otherwise was inefficient and a waste of his effort and his listener's time. With a slight reservation in his voice, he began to tell his story.

"I will answer any questions you have, but hear me out first. I can explain everything," Jasper said, noting the scrutiny of Michael's gaze. The anger radiating from Michael was almost visible. "You both know I enlisted in the Army after college. People don't understand why I enlisted, as most college graduates pursue officer candidate school. I enlisted because I wanted to serve my country and because being a soldier is an honorable position. I also wanted to prove to myself that I could do it. After basic training, I kept proving to myself that I could do more. My second year as a grunt, I earned an opportunity to go to Army Ranger school. It was the toughest three months of my life, but I did it. After that, I graduated from Officer Candidate School with a rank of second lieutenant, just in time to see action in the European Union Revolution." He remembered how proud he had felt at graduation. After all the nights of studying into the late hours, intense physical training, and dealing with hard-headed professors, he had achieved his goal and proven to himself that he could do it. He recalled Trent had made a special trip from Washington, D.C. to Fort Benning, Georgia just for the occasion. *Why hadn't Trent called him back?*

Michael and Rich were listening intently as he relayed the story. "I did three consecutive tours of duty. I entered my third tour as a Captain and was placed in charge of a Ranger rifle company made up of four platoons consisting of one hundred and sixty soldiers. These men were some of the best infantry soldiers in the Army. Midway through my tour, my company was assigned to an airfield seizure in Rheinmuenster, Germany on the Rhine River. Our mission was to secure the airport, remove any resistance from the Muslim revolutionaries, and recover any weapons of mass destruction. It was a critical mission as the airport was the only remaining commercial airport in the region with runways capable of supporting our bombers and cargo planes. Three months earlier, a dirty bomb exploded at the other airport in the region located in Strasburg, France. It destroyed the airport and part of the city, not to mention killing over five thousand people." They both nodded silently, recalling the event. It was the first time a nuclear device had been used as a weapon of mass terrorism.

It was later learned that the bomb was meant to be detonated at the Louise Weiss building in downtown Starsburg, the seat of the European Parliament. At the time of the explosion, all five hundred and seventy four members of parliament were in session voting on additional austerity measures in a last ditch effort to avoid a fiscal collapse. For reasons still unknown, the bomb had detonated at the airport by mistake. It was apparently being smuggled into the country on a private jet and had exploded shortly after the jet had landed.

Jasper noticed that the redness in Michael's face was starting to subside. That was a good sign. "We had intelligence reports that indicated one of the two generals of the Revolutionary army was in personal command of the airport and unconfirmed rumors that he was in possession of another dirty bomb. This meant this mission had bigger implications to the war effort than providing a base to land aircraft." Jasper remembered receiving his orders for the mission. At the time, he was both excited and petrified by the news. He had been excited for the possibility to confront and capture a high ranking official in the Revolutionary army, but the possibility that a weapon of mass destruction could be used against him and his company filled him with fear. It wasn't a fear born out of self-preservation, but out of concern for the men and women he was responsible for.

"Fortunately, our team was successful in securing the airport with minimal casualties; however a team of the revolutionaries, including the general, escaped on foot during our assault. I personally led a team of six of my best men in pursuit, not willing to risk the lives of my company if the general did indeed have a dirty bomb and decided to use it in retaliation."

Jasper could tell that both Michael and Rich were mesmerized by the story. He continued, his confidence growing, "That evening, we found the general and the rest of his soldiers held up in a large picturesque manor home about five miles from the airport. Infrared surveillance told us that soldiers were not the only people in that house. There were children ... so many that we couldn't even get an accurate head count. My XO estimated there were close to three hundred children crowded in rooms throughout the house," Jasper looked down helplessly. "There may have been more," he said bitterly. As he reflected on the memory of the evening, a scowl formed on his face. He remembered the anger he felt at the general. *How dare he use defenseless children as a shield to protect him! This man had no courage, no honor, no ethics and no value for human life. He deserved to die.* He also remembered the conflict he experienced over the decision that faced him. *Could he afford to jeopardize the lives of those children in his attempt to arrest the rogue general? If he didn't stop them now, could a greater amount of people be in jeopardy from the dirty bomb, if indeed the general even had a dirty bomb?*

"The general must have known we had tracked him, because shortly after our arrival, one of his soldiers left the house and stood in the courtyard, yelling as loud as he could. When I have nightmares, I sometimes hear the words that man screamed." Jasper looked at Rich who had pulled out his notepad and was busily scribbling notes. "The man screamed over and over 'If you attack, we will kill the children. Let us go, or we kill the children.'" Rich's stopped writing notes and looked back at Jasper, his face masked in horror. Michael just shook his head in disgust.

Jasper took another deep breath, "The man just stood in that courtyard repeating that message, as if challenging us to act. I made the decision quickly at that point. There was no time to negotiate, particularly with a terrorist who would use human shields. If the general was in possession of another dirty bomb, we could not afford to let him or anyone else escape with it because there was no telling the damage he would do. Recovery of the bomb had quickly become our sole mission and if we killed a general in the process, it was icing on the cake. I had one of my riflemen shoot the man in the courtyard and the rest of us began running towards the manor house under cover fire. It was a calculated risk. We didn't have time to think at that point, we just reacted. Almost immediately, the sound of gunfire exploded into the air, but it wasn't aimed at us. It was occurring inside the house." Jasper closed his eyes for a long moment as Michael and Rich waited in silence. He did not want to have to relive the experience, but he owed it to Michael and Rich.

He looked at Michael. The man's face had lost its color and the look of fury had faded. In its place was a look of genuine concern. Reluctantly, Jasper continued his saga, "The assault itself was pure hell. My XO went down almost immediately as we reached the manor house. Two others went down minutes after we got inside. I took a bullet in the shoulder, fortunately it passed through and was not my shooting arm, but I was injured none the less. There were several hostiles inside, but my remaining team and I were able to systematically secure the manor house. But we were too late. Bodies of children littered the floors of every room we searched. There were bodies and blood everywhere. They were all dead ..." his last words trailed off. The face of a young girl with brown hair flashed in his head. Her eyes were lifeless and blank. She had been shot in the forehead at point blank range.

"Blood and bodies were everywhere I looked," Jasper grimaced. "They were all dead." Old emotions of rage, frustration and guilt began to surface and he shoved them back down, focusing on the story. "I went through each of the remaining rooms knowing that those children's blood was on my hands. It had been my call to storm the house and these children were dead because of it," Jasper paused for several agonizing seconds, collecting himself. "Shortly, my team and I came to the last room in the house. The general and whoever was left with him had to be in there."

Rich scooted forward in his seat, a look of intense concern on his face. Jasper wondered what he was thinking. He needed Rich and Michael to believe that he was justified in this situation. He took another deep breath before he spoke, "I took the lead – it was my mission. I was responsible and I wanted revenge for what this mad man had done. I threw in a flash bomb and stormed into the room immediately after it detonated. I don't recall how it all happened, but it was chaos. I threw myself against the rear wall as I scanned the room for enemy soldiers. I began to fire at the figures in the room. There were people firing back. My team came right in behind me, going in different directions as they fanned out in the room. There were only two enemy soldiers in the room and they went down quick. But the gun fire continued on." Jasper shook his head in frustration, "In a matter of seconds, all three members of my team were shot dead ... I was the only one left."

Chapter 42

Now, the memories were flooding back. They seemed so real. He could picture the room as if he were standing in it. The faces of his fallen countrymen lying in front of him, twisted in agony. The bullet holes that riddled the tan plaster walls. The broken shards of an ivory colored glass lamp that had exploded in the corner. Jasper struggled to keep focused on telling the story against the memories and emotions that had been resurrected. He gritted his teeth and continued, "The bullets had been fired from above and behind me. By the grace of God, I was protected by a thick wooden shelf that also kept me hidden. I quickly surmised that there must be a loft above the room and someone, most likely the general, was perched there in perfect position to take out anyone in the room. I don't think the general knew I was in the room because the gunfire stopped. A minute later, I heard him walking down steps that were located behind a closet door on the side of the room. The closet door opened and a man in street clothes stepped into the room. I knew immediately from the pictures I had reviewed in my mission briefing that it was the general."

"What did you do?" Michael asked his eyes wide with anticipation.

"I didn't have time to think, I just reacted. I shot the general three times in the chest at close range. He crumpled before me. I carefully cleared him of his weapon and checked his vitals. He was still alive, but barely. I asked him several times where the bomb was in both English and French, but he did not respond. A few seconds later, he was dead. It was then that I noticed he was clutching a small device in his left hand. I pried the device from his hands, thinking it was a weapon. But it was not a weapon, it was a detonator."

Both Michael and Rich exhaled in unison. "So you saved the day?" Rich ventured.

"Not exactly," Jasper responded. "The light on the detonator display was green. The dirty bomb or whatever device was on the receiving end of that signal had been armed."

Rich let out a squeal, which was odd for a man of his side. Michael just stared at Jasper intently, a look of shock on his face. Jasper shook his head, it was hard to believe the story himself and he had lived it. "I had no idea where the bomb was nor if I could do anything to disarm it. My demolition specialist had been killed in the assault. The only thing I could do was run. I ran from the house as fast as I could for thirty minutes. I must have covered three or four miles when I heard the explosion. I turned to see the mushroom cloud on the horizon, it was smaller than I expected. I took cover in a creek basin and waited for the shockwave to pass over, but it never came. The bomb had detonated, but its impact zone was very small. I learned later that the bomb destroyed everything in a mile radius of the manor home." He grimaced again, feeling a deep pang of guilt. "I was safe, but my men and those children — they were gone. Everything had been destroyed." The image of the young girl flashed in his mind again. "I barely made it back to the airport alive, given the blood I had lost from my gunshot injury. I almost wish I hadn't. I should never have returned alone. I deserved to die with those men ... *and with those children!*"

"Of sweet Jesus," Michael said, "You poor man. I would have never known you harbored such a tragedy in your life."

Rich nodded in agreement, but true to his reporter nature, he interjected, "What happened next?"

Jasper thought for a moment before responding, "After I received medical treatment, I briefed the commanding officer at base on the entire situation. I made sure not to leave out a single detail. I gave him full disclosure on exactly what had happened. Oddly, I was never asked to complete a written report of the event."

"That is odd," Rich commented.

"Since there was no evidence of the existence of the manor home, the children's bodies or the enemy soldiers, I was told to keep quiet until further notice," Jasper said. "A few days later, I was told to forget the event ever happened. It was in my best interest and the interest of the country, to avoid a potentially dicey legal and political investigation. The bottom line was I was commanded to keep silent in 'everyone's' best interest." Jasper remembered the conversation with the base commander. It had been brief and they had been alone together in the commander's office.

"They just expected you to keep quiet?" Michael asked skeptically.

"No, not exactly," Jasper said. "In return, I was going to be celebrated for securing the airport, killing a high ranking official in the Revolutionary army, and for destroying the dirty bomb in a manner that avoided excessive loss of human life. I was going to be given an honorable discharge and a promotion in rank to Major. I was assured that the families of my fellow soldiers who lost their lives would be provided for financially for the rest of their lives. I took solace in that last fact but that was the only thing."

"That explains why there was no official written record of the event. How did Trent find out?" Rich asked.

"To numb the pain and guilt, I started drinking pretty heavily after the war," Jasper responded distantly, remembering the torment of those months. "Trent confronted me one evening, obviously concerned. I ended up telling him everything. Trent soon became my confident on this matter. He helped me to move past it and to focus my activities on other things besides drinking. I could not have gotten through it without his help." Jasper finished and was silent.

Even though Michael's continence had softened, Jasper could tell that Michael was still upset about the situation. He couldn't blame him. Michael had risked his reputation for Jasper and now stood to be tarnished in the fallout from this scandal. Michael was a good man who had trusted Jasper. Jasper had taken that trust, stepped on it, and ground it into the dirt. It didn't matter that it was not intentional, the damage had been done. That thought rocked Jasper with remorse. All he wanted to do was the right thing and he had screwed it up again. It was the story of his life.

"Michael, please believe me, I am really sorry. I should have told you," Jasper said sincerely.

Michael removed his glasses and pretended to clean them for a minute before responding, "Jasper, this is not my first rodeo. Politics is full of surprises, some good, most of them bad. I'd be lying if I told you I wasn't disappointed." He let his comment hang in the air for effect. "But I always forgive everyone in time and I will forgive you too as soon as I deal with my anger. If you had leveled with me about this in the beginning, I would have had time to plan a contingency in the remote case that this story came out. Now, I am not sure what we do. Baldwin's campaign is going to use this to slam you. If there were any voters on the fence, chances are a story like this is going to push them into his yard. No one wants to elect a killer, even if that killing was justified or necessary."

"Michael is right," Rich said. "However, the people are also skeptical of the media and what is published as news. I should know, right?" Rich's attempt at humor was met with silence. "Anyway, we have to cast doubt on this story if we want to contain the damage. Who else knew about this other than Trent?"

"No one that I know," Jasper answered. "The Brigadier General whom I had debriefed at the base was killed six months later, a victim of a suicide attack. I have no idea if he ever told anyone else."

"We could assume that Trent was the source, which would mean he must have been blackmailed. I hope that was not the case," Michael frowned. "At this point, it does not really matter who the source was, the story has been released and now we have to control the damage."

Jasper looked at both of them, "I am at your mercy. What should we do?"

Rich clenched his massive hands together thinking through the question, there was a hint of perspiration on his forehead. "Look Jasper, it is obvious that someone has it in for you. Whoever it is, they are someone with a great deal of power. I admit that I am really intrigued by this development. This story has political scandal written all over it. That being said, it also makes me nervous." He picked up his note pad from his lap and began scribbling a note. "What you need is a game changer to turn the momentum back in your favor. You need to get offensive. You need a Hail Mary." He wrote another note on his pad. "Lucky for you, I think I can help," he said, closing his notebook.

"Go on," Michael said, his skepticism evident.

"Give me the evening to develop a counter story based on the facts that you just gave us," Rich said. "I will also make some initial inquiries into Trent's past. Maybe we can find out why someone was blackmailing him and that may lead us to who is behind it."

Jasper liked the idea of a counter story. The public needed to know the other side of the story. He wondered what Rich had in mind. "I like that idea," Jasper agreed, "but what will you want in return?"

"In return, I'm going to want a favor," Rich admitted, "but I don't know what it is yet. It will be above board, most likely an exclusive interview after the election, but I will let you know when I figure it out." Rich hastily rose to his feet, apparently eager to get started on his new assignment. "Until then, do not talk to anyone! You were already one of the biggest stories in the press. Now you are the only story!"

Jasper considered Rich's proposal for a moment. He never liked to be indebted to anyone, but given the circumstances, he didn't have another option. "You have a deal," Jasper stated firmly. Jasper rose to shake Rich's hand. Rich's grip was like steel and his hands engulfed Jasper. "I really appreciate it, Rich," Jasper added. "You're a good friend."

Rich turned to Michael, "Go easy on him. We all have skeletons in our past that we would hope never see the light of day." Michael nodded in agreement, closing the door behind Rich as he left the room.

Jasper looked at Michael expectantly, "Well, we have Rich on board and working to help us out of this mess. What else do we need to do?"

"The only thing we can," Michael responded slowly. "We tell the whole truth ... and we tell it to anybody and everybody that will listen."

Chapter 43

The entrance doors to the church opened and the crowd began to pour out from the evening service. Several people congregated outside, sharing conversation and exchanging greetings. Xavier had been waiting patiently in his black Suburban SUV in the parking lot. Exiting the vehicle, he made his way towards the church at a casual pace. Most likely, he would not even be noticed between all the people who were leaving the church, anxious to get home for dinner. He was just another parishioner who had decided to visit the church that day.

He made his way directly towards the courtyard and pretended to be waiting for someone who was still in the church. The truth was that was exactly what he was doing. A few moments later, Alexis Mills walked down the steps of the entrance way with her arm wrapped around a distinguished older man dressed in a dark suit. *That must be her father, the pastor,* he thought. He watched Alexis for a minute assessing the right time to make his move. She and her father were engaged in a conversation with an elderly woman. From the looks of it, the elderly woman seemed to be dominating the conversation. Now was as good of a time as any to execute his plan. He wasn't sure if his plan would work, but then again, he had contingency plans. He always did. He walked over to stand next to the pastor and interrupted their conversation.

"Excuse me. Are you the pastor?" He asked, feigning confusion.

"Yes, I am. I am Pastor Mills," the pastor looked at him quizzically trying to recall if he knew the man. "I don't think I saw you in church today. How may I help you?"

"No sir, I was not in church today. I am here to pick up my wife. She told me she was visiting a new church today, but I do not see her," Xavier responded, trying to sound concerned. "I'm worried I am at the wrong church. I would call her, but my cell phone battery is dead. I was hoping you may have a phone I could use to call her?" Xavier held up an antiquated cellular phone he had purchased at a Goodwill store in town just hours earlier.

The pastor shook his head negatively. But as he had anticipated, Alexis chimed in, "I have a phone you can borrow." She opened her pink clutch and removed a small phone that was covered in tiny pink rhinestones. "What is the number you need me to dial?" she asked innocently.

He gave her the number he had memorized just an hour earlier. It was the phone number for the Georgetown Chamber of Commerce. She dialed the number and handed him the phone. "Thank you so much," he said graciously.

Xavier stepped a few feet away and pretended to have a conversation with his wife while he listened to the digital answering service give him a menu of options to choose from. He made sure he spoke loud enough so that the others could hear him. "I can't believe I am at the wrong church. I am so sorry, honey. I will be right there." He hung up the phone and returned to Alexis' side.

"Thank you so much. She is at Faith Chapel a few miles down the road. I need to pay better attention to her instructions." He handed the phone back to Alexis. "Thank you again," he smiled broadly. "Well, I will be going. Have a blessed day."

Once back inside his vehicle, he removed a digital tablet from a velvet pouch lying on the front seat. He studied the tablet screen for a minute confirming that he was receiving a signal. On the screen was a three dimensional satellite map with a glowing red dot in the center. Yes, the micro bug he had planted on Alexis's phone was transmitting perfectly. Not only would he know her location, he would now be able to listen to her conversations and intercept any text or email messages. He returned the tablet to the pouch and proceeded to pull out of the parking lot. He shot a quick wave to Alexis who was watching him leave. *See you soon*, he thought. Only the next time he saw her, he doubted it would be under such pleasant circumstances.

Chapter 44

Charleston, South Carolina
October 30th

Jasper surveyed the deserted street through his office window and sighed. The rain flowed in heavy sheets of grey bolstered by a cold, strong wind. It was the type of weather that would soak someone to the bone in seconds. He hoped the weather was not going to be an omen of the day that lay before him. Sadly, the forecast indicated otherwise. He turned his attention back to the two men seated in the room with him. Michael and Rich each carried a solemn look of defeat that matched the dreary morning. Jasper was struggling not to follow suit, but he was slowly losing the battle.

"This is miserable," Jasper stated.

"Do you mean the weather or this scandal?" Michael asked, not really caring about the answer.

"Both. At least the weather will go away tomorrow," Jasper replied glumly. They were out of options at this point. All their hopes to save the election hinged on their ability to tell the public the truth behind the scandal. If their efforts over the next twenty four hours did not make the impact they needed to change public opinion, they might as well concede defeat.

The collateral damage from the news story had been significant, mainly due to the resulting media onslaught that followed. Within an hour of the story breaking, the scandal had become known as the Massacre on the Rhine. Multiple news channels had continued to expand on the story through the evening adding new details, some true, but most of them falsely exaggerated. CNN aired a hastily prepared biography of Jasper that mostly cited his emotional instability due to the tragic loss of his parents at an early age. It had concluded with a psychologist opinion that Jasper was unfit to hold any position of command in the military or in the government. Political pundits used the scandal as an opportunity to provide personal critiques of Jasper, bashing his performance in Congress and ridiculing his aspiration to be governor. The worst part of the whole situation was that the media had only half of the story. There was no mention in the news reports of the terrorist leader or the nuclear device that had the potential to harm thousands. The news was only about Jasper, the child killer.

Jasper recalled his conversation with Alexis after she heard the news of the scandal. At first, she had been angry that he had not confided in her about such a significant and tragic event in his life. She questioned her trust in him and wondered what other secrets he was hiding from her. When he had finally explained to her the entire story, she apologized for her reaction. But despite her apology, he could tell that she was still deeply disturbed by the situation.

"Blasted media!" Michael spit, his curls trembling in response to his frustration. "No offense," he said quickly, glancing at Rich. "I hate that we have given Baldwin a hammer to pummel us and wrapped it up with a ribbon and a bow to boot."

Jasper shook his head in agreement. Derrick Baldwin was taking every opportunity to discredit Jasper and position himself with the public as the only logical choice for governor. Baldwin's position was bolstered by several prominent congressman and senators who had publically requested Jasper's immediate resignation from Congress as well as an end to his candidacy for governor. The country wanted justice for the innocent lives that had been taken and Jasper had become the condemned perpetrator. The situation looked hopeless on all fronts.

"How is your story coming along?" Jasper asked Rich, hoping for a sliver of good news.

Rich looked tired. His eyes were bloodshot and it was obvious that he hadn't shaved that morning. "I spent all night working through the first draft of our counter story. It should be ready for us to review by noon." He scratched at the stubble on his chin as if it were a mask he was trying to remove.

Michael chimed in, "I have the press circuit schedule for tomorrow and we should plan to prepare for those as well." Michael had taken action early to arrange a series of interviews for Jasper with the top media networks. The interviews were to begin promptly at six in the morning and continue through the morning. The interviews would be followed by a general press conference where Jasper intended to dispute any misinformation as well as answer all questions that were asked of him.

"Any feedback from our constituents that differs from what we are hearing in the news?" Jasper asked, but not sure he wanted to know the answer. According to early media reports, there was a mixed response from the public about the story. All agreed it was a horrible tragedy, but the public was very skeptical about the media's implication of Jasper in the massacre. Jasper knew that the distrust of the media was the only saving grace in the situation. None of the news outlets were able to specifically identify the source of the allegations other than to say they came from high up in the government. Even so, very few people had come to Jasper's defense.

One of the campaign volunteers walked in, interrupting their pity party. Jasper did not recognize her. There had been an influx of people wanting to volunteer and work for the campaign in the last month. Of course, that was because he had been winning the race. He did not think anyone was thinking about volunteering now. The woman had a concerned look on her face. "Congressman, I am sorry to interrupt you. Trent Holloway's wife is on the main line. She is adamant she speak with you."

Jasper jumped out of his seat. He had been trying to reach Trent for two days. He had even taken the liberty to drive over to Trent's house earlier that morning and had knocked on the door, hoping someone would answer. Unfortunately, no one did. "Please, put her through," he said urgently.

The phone had barely rung before Jasper snatched it from the receiver. "Trudy, is Trent ok? I really need to speak with him," he pleaded. He had so many questions to ask Trent, so many things he needed answered. More than anything, he just wanted to understand what or who had driven Trent to betray his confidence. Trudy Holloway's response was short and not at all what Jasper expected to hear. He couldn't believe it. If he had any words to say in response, he wasn't sure he could say them. His best friend, the man who had been like a father to him for all these years was dead. Trent Holloway had committed suicide.

Chapter 45

Charleston, South Carolina
October 31st

Jasper relaxed on the couch in his hotel room, trying to steal a few minutes of sleep from the day, but not having much success. Even so, it felt good to have a moment of peace and quiet. A half-eaten ham sandwich lay in a Styrofoam container on the table beside him. He hadn't been hungry despite not eating breakfast. It had been a grueling morning that was both mentally and physically draining. Through it all, Jasper's heart was grappling with Trent's suicide and the grief he felt. Maybe it was a blessing that the day had been so busy.

The interviews were intense and the interviewers unyielding and merciless. The media had already convicted him as evidenced by the questions he had been asked. It had been challenging for Jasper not to lose his temper over the idiocy of some of the questions, not to mention the blatant lies couched as leading questions. Fortunately, Rich's counter story had hit the news wires earlier that morning and had been published on the front page of USA Today. The story had caused an immediate maelstrom of reaction from the press and public — accomplishing its intended purpose. The new information had forced the reporters from the major media outlets to seek further clarification from Jasper on what actually happened that day on the Rhine. Jasper utilized the opportunity to publically refute the allegations of the scandal and reassert his innocence in the death of any children. Luckily, Rich's story hadn't been killed. Rich had informed him that someone in Washington had tried vehemently to prevent the release of the story by pulling rank on the editor and every other senior executive at USA Today. Given the overwhelming importance of the story, and the fact that it contained an exclusive interview with the most controversial man in America, USA Today published despite the protests.

Jasper's mobile phone rang on the desk across the room. He had left it in the hotel room that morning and hadn't bothered to turn it off. He couldn't imagine the amount of calls he had received and the messages that were left in just the past six hours. Jasper checked his watch. His press conference was in thirty minutes, he would have to be downstairs shortly to prepare. The whole pace of this day was overwhelming.

Alexis got up from the bed where she had been editing his speech. "I'll get it," she said. He was tempted to tell her to ignore the ringing phone, but the look on her face as she picked the phone up told him otherwise. "Jasper! It's Trent?" she gasped.

He leapt off the couch and reached for the phone, taking it from Alexis. "Hello," he said cautiously. A momentary wave of expectation passed through him. *Could Trent still be alive?* Maybe it had all been a misunderstanding.

"I was hoping you would take my call, Mr. Thorne. Has it been a tough day?" The caller's words were crisp, and Jasper detected a slight Latino accent.

Jasper was immediately alert, "Who is this?"

"I know you feel guilty about all those children … beating yourself up that you couldn't save them. What a pity that they died because of the choice you made. I know you feel guilty that their blood is on your hands," the caller said calmly.

Jasper was not amused by the caller's statement or what it implied. "Who is this?" Jasper demanded.

"I'm just a messenger, Mr. Thorne, and I have a very important message for you."

"I'm not continuing this conversation until you tell me who you are?" Jasper said firmly.

"It is a simple message." The caller paused and Jasper thought he heard a chuckle from the other end of the line. "You need to drop out of the race, Mr. Thorne." From the tone of the caller's voice, it was a command, not a request.

"I don't know who you are, but you have some gall to call me and tell me that I need to drop out of the race," Jasper responded, beginning to pace the floor anxiously. There were so many questions going through his mind. *Who was on the line? What did he want? Why did he have Trent's phone?* Jasper knew that Trent's cell phone was missing according to the detective investigating Trent's death. He forced himself to focus on the conversation. "Why do you have Trent Holloway's phone?"

There was a seemingly long pause on the other end of the line as if the caller was considering how to best answer Jasper's questions. "Your dear friend Trent was a casualty of your prior actions, Mr. Thorne. He was a loose end that I had to snip, but his blood is fully on your hands too. Just like the children. In fact, he would not have died if you had not chosen to run for governor."

Jasper was taken back for a moment. "What do you mean he would not have died? What does Trent's death have to do with my candidacy?" Jasper asked bewildered by the caller's statement.

"I thought you were smarter than this Mr. Thorne? Trent died for one purpose, to motivate you to make a choice."

The thought exploded in Jasper's mind that the caller was implying Trent's death was not suicide, but murder. Jasper couldn't control his reaction. "You bastard!" he shouted. "Who do you think you are?"

The question was met by a mocking chuckle, "Mr. Thorne. I am exactly who I think I am." the voice said jovially. In the next breath, the voice became cool and unemotional. "I am your worst nightmare and my only mission is to see you fail, even if that means destroying everything you love."

Jasper wished he could strangle the person he heard through the phone, but knew that he had to contain his emotions. This voice was his only link to the truth about Trent's death. Even so, he decided to take an offensive approach. "You threaten me or anyone I know, consider yourself a dead man. I will hunt you down and find you."

The caller was unruffled by Jasper's threat. The caller continued, only this time, his voice was more demanding. "Maybe I am not making myself clear, Mr. Thorne. I think the last thing you want to do is make me angry. If you make me angry, I will have no choice but to take action against those who you hold dear. My wrath will pale in comparison to what happened on the Rhine." The voice laughed obnoxiously and then corrected itself. "Do you really want more innocent blood on your hands?"

Jasper was silent. He wasn't going to take the bait.

"Well said, Mr. Thorne. I am so enjoying this sparring match. But neither you nor I have time at the moment. Let's cut to the chase, as you Americans are so fond of saying." There was a long pause. "Mr. Thorne. You need to make a choice. "

"What choice is that?" Jasper challenged.

"It is a simple choice. All you need to do is make an announcement at your upcoming press conference that you are withdrawing your candidacy for governor. If you do that, I will disappear. I will go back to living my life and the name Jasper Thorne will be erased from my memory. Your life will no longer be any of my concern. Or ..." The last word trailed off hauntingly.

"Or what?" Jasper yelled. He was getting angry. He did not like being threatened but he hated being in a position that lacked control even more. Jasper's natural tendency was to fight, not to flee. Only now, he was uncertain about which option to pursue.

"Or ... what happened to your friend Trent will only be the beginning of your nightmare," the voice was sinister this time.

Jasper did not respond. Now, he was sure this person was a murderer. He didn't know why he had come to that conclusion, but his instincts told him he was talking to the man who had murdered Trent Holloway. Jasper stopped pacing as the impact of that revelation struck him. This caller was serious about his request and even more serious about his threat.

The caller continued, "Mr. Thorne, do you pay attention to the latest fashions?"

Jasper was perplexed by the question, what was the caller implying. He decided to remain silent.

"I will take it by your silence that you're not up on the latest trends from Paris. Between you and me, let's just say crimson red and hot pink are in style this week." There was another chuckle from the caller, only this one rambled on for several seconds.

Jasper gritted his teeth, understanding the implication of the caller's statement. The caller was referring to Alexis. He gripped the phone tightly in his hands, wishing he could smash it to pieces along with the mysterious caller on the other end of the line.

"Still nothing to say Mr. Thorne? You must be analyzing your options as any good chess player does. Very well – let's consider that the game has started. And I have already made my first move. Check!" A louder chuckle echoed in Jasper's ears followed by another long pause.

"You have twenty minutes to decide. Good bye, Mr. Thorne." The phone line went dead. Jasper stood there in silence for several seconds, pondering his next move. The thought struck him that he had just started a deadly game with the caller and he was at a disadvantage. How did he win a game when he didn't know the rules of the game or even how to play?

Chapter 46

"Jasper?" Alexis cried out. Her eyes were wide with concern. "What's wrong?"

Alexis had been by his side since the conversation with the mysterious caller had begun. Her face expressed the same things he felt; concern, confusion, and helplessness. But there was something else Jasper felt. Swirling through him, just below the surface of his emotions, was a tempest of rage directed at his unknown adversary.

He embraced Alexis for a moment, focusing his thoughts on her. He wasn't sure if it was the fragrant smell of her hair or the way she caressed him in warmth, he felt whole with her in his arms. Slowly, the rage he was feeling began to subside.

"Jasper, tell me what is going on. Please!" She was squeezing him tightly and would not let go.

He pulled away from her embrace, but only slightly, not willing to let go of the security he felt when holding her. "Alex, I don't want to alarm you." He spoke slowly, the words trickling from his mouth with difficulty. "That caller … I don't know who he was. I think he was involved with Trent's death. I think he might have even killed Trent." His words were cold and emotionless.

"You're scaring me … what do you mean he killed Trent? I thought Trent's death was a suicide?" Alexis responded alarmed.

Jasper turned away from Alexis and placed his face in his hands as the realization of the decision he had to make finally hit him. The caller had made a direct threat on Alexis's life. He had been trained to neutralize threats, only now; he didn't even know who his enemy was. He couldn't let anything happen to Alexis, but he couldn't drop out of the race. There was too much at stake for all of them.

He wasn't sure what to do. He slammed his fist into the wall, causing the entire wall to vibrate in response." Jasper, please tell me what is wrong?" Alexis asked confused.

Jasper made his decision. He wasn't going to allow anything to happen to her. "Alex, it is so crazy. I'm not exactly sure what is happening. There is so much going on and I don't have time to figure it all out." He turned back to her, "Even so, what I do know is that I won't let anything happen to you."

"What are you talking about?" Alexis asked, the fear in her voice was reflected in the tight lines of her face.

Jasper took a deep breath. He knew he had to tell her the truth. He hesitated a moment, searching for the right words "Alexis, I'm going to level with you. That man on the phone threatened to hurt you unless I drop out of the race. I believe he was serious about what he said he would do."

Alexis seemed to transform in front his face. In an instant, the fear was gone, replaced with a look that he could only describe as pure disdain. It reminded him of an animal that had been caged against its will staring at its captor. There was a pause before Alexis spoke. "Jasper, I want you to listen to me. There is no other choice here. This is not about me. You must stay in the race at all costs. To do anything else would be to give up on the principles and beliefs that we hold so dear. You can't drop out," she pleaded. "It would let evil prevail and justice to die. You can't … promise me!"

"Alexis, I can't let anything happen to you. I can't lose you too. I can't …" Jasper cried, his voice cracking. He cursed his indecision. She was right, he couldn't give up now. But he couldn't let anything happen to her either.

"Promise me," she demanded more firmly.

Jasper stared at her. *How could she be so strong?* Jasper thought. Her eyes were tearing up, but he also sensed the raw determination behind her request. "I promise. But we are going to take extra precautions so nothing will happen to you," Jasper said, though he wasn't sure he believed what he said.

"Listen to me, Jasper," she asserted. "We need to go to the authorities. In the meantime, I can handle myself. No one is going to hurt me or anybody we know. I am going to ask a couple of the church elders to come over to my parent's home to watch over them. If this guy wants a fight with some southern gentlemen, he is going to get the fight of his life. We will get through this together."

"Are you sure you want me to stay in the race?"

"I've never been more positive about anything in my life." she said, her face beginning to flush with a tint of anger. "I want you to focus on winning the race. The people of this state need a leader like you. You can't throw all of this away. You have worked so hard."

Jasper came forward embracing her in a hug. *How did she deal with things so calmly and self-assured?* He buried his head in her neck and whispered softly. "I don't know how you do it. I'm only surviving right now because I am not dealing with my emotions. Trent —" he stifled the tears that were forming. He squeezed her harder. "Please understand what I mean. I can't afford the weakness that emotions create in me, not now anyway."

She pulled his head up to look at her. "Honey ... please listen to me. My problems and my weaknesses are never too large for God to handle. Nothing I will go through in life will ever be too large for God. That gives me peace to be able to deal with anything."

"I guess that is really what I am asking of you. Please pray for us. I am beginning to believe that only God can fix this mess."

Alexis planted a long kiss on his lips. Jasper savored the softness of her lips. He pulled away reluctantly and checked his watch. He was running late. Jasper headed over to the closet to get his jacket. He threw it on, not bothering to look at himself in the mirror. He mind had already shifted focus to the speech he was to deliver in a matter of minutes to a crowded room of reporters. He headed for the door, but was interrupted by Alexis grabbing his arm.

"You're not going anywhere until I fix you." She proceeded to pull down on his shirt sleeves to expose them from under his jacket. She then adjusted his collar, and tightened his tie. She stood back appraising her efforts. "Now you're ready!" she said approvingly. She handed him the tablet that contained the speech he had hastily compiled only two hours earlier.

Jasper glanced momentarily in the mirror. He looked tired, but dressed for the occasion. He turned to face her. "Thank you. You are the most amazing woman, Alexis Mills. I don't deserve you," Jasper said appreciatively. A smile formed on her face at hearing his compliment. "By the way, I'm looking forward to tomorrow night, when we don't have anything scheduled. It will be just you, me, and a bottle of cabernet."

"That sounds amazing," she responded. "Just remember that tomorrow I am going home to check on my mother, but I will be back as soon as I can. Now get down stairs, the press conference starts in minutes." She marshaled him towards the door and then kissed him lightly on the lips. "Oh, and Jasper ... baby .... we deserve each other. Never forget that."

Jasper turned away reluctantly and walked out of the door with a renewed sense of confidence. Alexis always made him feel more confident about himself, no matter what the situation. Even so, he was having trouble concentrating on his speech as he walked down the stairs to the ballroom on the main floor. There were too many questions troubling him. Would the authorities believe him? Would Alexis really be ok? Did he really believe that God was the only answer? He pondered these questions as he made his way downstairs. Perhaps, the last question was the most troublesome of them all. Perhaps it was because he wasn't sure he knew the answer.

Chapter 47

Jasper was grateful the press conference was over and he could finally relax. The conference had been well attended by the media which was exactly what he and Michael had hoped for. His speech had only been five minutes long, but it had taken almost an hour to answer all the probing questions from reporters. When he finally left the stage, he felt confident that he had accomplished his objective of conveying the truth of what actually happened that day on the Rhine. His confidence had been bolstered by a reporter who apologized to him during the conference for making assumptions about his involvement without having all the facts. He just hoped the effort of the past days was worth it.

Immediately after the conference, Jasper confided in Michael and Rich about the call he had received and the threats of the mysterious caller. Like Alexis, they too agreed that he needed to go directly to the authorities and tell them everything that had occurred. Jasper didn't have to wait long to tell his story. On his way back to his hotel room, Jasper was intercepted by two agents from the Federal Bureau of Investigation wanting to question him about Trent's death. Jasper wasn't alarmed by the meeting; because he knew that the FBI investigated the death of any senior governmental official, even if the death was by all accounts natural. In fact, he was thankful they had saved him the time of having to contact them.

The two men were dressed like the typical agents he often observed on Capitol Hill. The older agent, who also appeared to be in charge, was named Bosco. He did not give Jasper his first name. He was a burly man in his early fifties and talked with a raspy voice. The other agent was a tall, lanky young man who introduced himself as Agent Kyle Parker. Agent Bosco conducted the interview, while the other agent remained silent, scribbling notes onto a tablet. The agents were surprised when Jasper told them about the mysterious caller who had threatened both him and Alexis. Thirty minutes later, the agents left armed with all the information Jasper could tell them about his relationship with Trent and the conversation with the mysterious caller. The agents told Jasper they would be in touch regarding protective measures for Alexis and him.

A few hours later, Jasper received a call from Michael on his mobile phone. The worry in his voice was evident from the first word. "Jasper, where are you?"

"Are you ok?" Jasper responded.

"Where are you?" Michael repeated.

"I'm just a few blocks away from the office at Starbucks having a cup of coffee with Duke Carroway."

"Carroway?" Michael questioned. "I don't have that meeting on my calendar."

"Relax," Jasper said. "Duke happened to be here when I came in so I figured I take the opportunity to chat with him. We have turned out to have quite an interesting discussion."

Jasper had met Duke Carroway on several occasions and each time he left the encounter more impressed with the man. Duke was the independent candidate for lieutenant governor and like Jasper, was behind in the polls. South Carolina, like several states, held separate elections for governor and lieutenant governor, so it was possible that these positions could be held by individuals with opposing political affiliations. Jasper knew that he would be dealing with that exact situation if he were elected since there was no republican candidate for the lieutenant governor position.

Fortunately, Duke and he agreed on many common points about state rights, what the government's role should be, and fiscal responsibility. Duke was also a vocal advocate for secession and had made secession a cornerstone of his campaign. Still, there were several areas in which they had different political beliefs. At least Duke would be easier to work with than the democratic candidate that was running on a combined ticket with Derrick Baldwin. That could prove to be a nightmare.

"You do know that he could be the next lieutenant governor of our state?" Jasper joked.

"This is not the time for jokes. I need you to get back to the office now," Michael demanded.

"Michael, what's going on?" Jasper was perplexed. *What could have happened since he left the office two hours ago?*

Jasper heard a long sigh of frustration from Michael, "You are going to have to tell me the answer to that question, Jasper."

"What do you mean?"

"I just got off the phone with Agent Bosco from the FBI. He has been trying to reach you for the last hour." Michael's voice was strained as he spoke his next words, "You, Congressman Thorne, are now a potential suspect in the murder of a U.S. senator."

Chapter 48

The room was hot, stuffy, and devoid of any character. The only feature of the room that was worthy of notice was the small camera in the upper corner. It was crawling past eight o'clock as the questioning continued, going into its third hour. Jasper could not believe that he was being subjected to an interrogation. *How could the FBI think that he was responsible for Trent's death?* It was absurd.

Though he had not been formally arrested, Agent Bosco and Agent Parker had been tag teaming him with questions all night. *Perhaps it had been a bad decision to allow this questioning to continue*, he thought. But it was too late to change his mind now. If he were to refuse to answer any further questions, he might provoke the agents to formally arrest him and force him to invoke his rights. He had to avoid that from occurring at all costs. His campaign would be sunk in an instant.

The questioning had started innocently enough. Both agents had been friendly and understanding of Jasper's confusion at being interviewed. They asked him the same questions they had asked him just hours earlier, only this time requesting more detail. But after an hour, Jasper was beginning to lose his patience. He challenged Agent Bosco, demanding to know why he was there. Agent Bosco proceeded to tell Jasper that the FBI had initiated a GPS trace on Trent's phone shortly after their recent meeting at the hotel. The trace led them directly to Jasper's house. After searching the house, they found Trent's phone inside a pocket of a blue sport coat that had been stuffed into a plastic bag and buried in a laundry bin. The sports coat had Jasper's name sewn into the inside liner.

At first, Jasper thought this story was a ploy. That was before Agent Bosco showed Jasper a few digital pictures of Jasper's closet, one of his sports jackets and a phone that he presumed must belong to Trent. Jasper was shocked by the pictures the agent was showing him. *How could any of this be possible?* His shock quickly turned to anger upon the realization that his home had been invaded without probable cause and without his consent. When he challenged Agent Bosco on the encroachment of his rights, the agent had only laughed and calmly informed him that his house was actually government property and Jasper had no say in the matter. That left Jasper seething, and there was little else he could do or say.

"We also found blood splatters on the coat that we positively identified as matching Trent's blood type. We have the lab conducting a formal DNA test at this moment," Agent Bosco rasped, sitting back in his chair, a smug look on his face. "I'll bet you a fifth of Scotch, that the blood is Trent's." Jasper shook his head in disbelief, but remained silent.

Agent Bosco tossed a picture of Trent on the table in front of him. Trent was face down on a white tile floor. A large pool of crimson blood surrounded his head. The picture made Jasper sick to his stomach. The caller's voice echoed in his head. *'He would not have died if you had not chosen to run for governor.'*

"The preliminary coroner's report indicates that Trent was killed by a single forty caliber gunshot to the head. We checked the national gun database. Guess who owns a forty caliber pistol?" Jasper didn't blink. He owned two pistols, both of which he had locked in his gun safe a few days earlier. One was a 9 mm Springfield XD9 that he had carried during the war. The other was his father's pistol. It was a forty caliber Smith and Wesson. "We confiscated your gun safe and opened it with the intent of conducting a ballistics test on any weapons found. The problem is we only found one gun in the safe and it was a 9 mm." Bosco leaned forward, his face coming within inches of Jasper. "So what did you do with the gun?"

"Both of my guns were in the safe the last time I checked it, three days ago. I swear," Jasper responded. Both agents shook their heads negatively, obviously they didn't believe him.

"Why did you do it?" Bosco finally asked. His tone was conversational, almost like he was asking Jasper if he thought it would rain tomorrow.

"Please understand. I am telling you the truth," Jasper pleaded. "Trent was my best friend and I would never do anything to hurt him. I was with my campaign advisor the entire day of Trent's death. Someone is framing me!"

Bosco shook his head. "Been there! Done that! Alibis are a dime a dozen and not worth the paper they are printed on. I'll answer my own question. You killed Trent in retaliation for releasing your secret about your war crimes in the Rhine to the media. Not only were you angry that he sabotaged your election hopes, you needed to make sure he didn't tell anyone anything about other secrets he knew about you, just in case. You must have done something nasty to him to make him turn on you like that?"

Jasper was now convinced he had made a mistake by continuing to allow this questioning to continue. It was time to tell Bosco he was done answering questions. Jasper stood up and leaned over the table, staring down at the agent. Before he could utter a word, there was a knock at the door to the interrogation room. Agent Parker, whom Jasper had grown to significantly dislike in the past hour, answered the door while keeping an eye on Jasper. Agent Bosco turned from Jasper, his face a mask of confusion as he recognized the man who entered the room. "What the hell are you doing here? This isn't in your jurisdiction."

"Good to see you too, Bosco," the man replied sarcastically. Though the man was short in stature, he carried himself with an heir of authority and self-assuredness. "Hear me out. Agent Roden briefed me in the hallway about your investigation or at least some of it. I believe Congressman Thorne is being set up and I know who is doing it."

Agent Bosco looked perturbed, most likely not liking this possible wrinkle in his investigation. "What proof do you have?"

"I have enough proof that I was willing to spend the last eighteen hours traveling to five different cities to get here," the man replied. "You know how many connections I had to make because government regs require I buy the cheapest ticket I can find." That comment must have resonated with Bosco because his mood seemed to lighten. He nodded his head and then closed the file.

"Go on," Bosco said.

"I firmly believe that the congressman's life is in danger. He is being stalked by a master criminal I have been investigating for several months," the man relayed with strong conviction. "This same individual is now in Charleston and was captured by surveillance video on three distinct occasions in the past week standing outside the congressman's home."

Jasper looked at the man and then at Agent Bosco. Though he was alarmed by the news that he was being stalked, he took comfort in the fact that the man's story corroborated the things he had been telling the agents. It was fortunate that this man had arrived when he did.

Bosco processed this new information reluctantly. It did align with the information Jasper had given him earlier that day and repeated multiple times during the interview. He glanced at his partner in the corner, but received only a blank stare. "Well here is the deal," Bosco said. "The congressman is a potential suspect in a murder investigation. As of now, I am planning on holding him in a jail cell until further notice. Since this murder was committed on federal property against a member of the Federal government, I can hold Congressman Thorne as long as I need to."

"Bosco, let's be reasonable," The stranger parried. "The election is in a few days. The congressman is not going to be a flight risk. Besides, holding the congressman is going to invite a tremendous amount of scrutiny on you from everyone. They are going to want definitive evidence of his involvement, which you don't have yet. Damn it, Bosco, you're not even sure yourself if he was involved, otherwise you would have already formally arrested him."

Agent Bosco was silent.

"Though I can't prove it yet, I can assure you that he was not involved with Trent Holloway's murder," the man said with conviction. "Give me forty-eight hours and I will get you the proof you need about who committed this murder."

Bosco was silent for several seconds longer as he mulled over the offer on the table. He and his partner exchanged a quick look, both considering the implications of holding a congressman and current gubernatorial candidate on circumstantial evidence.

Throwing his hands in the air in a symbol of surrender, Bosco acquiesced, "Ok, Reggie. I'll play. I need to get some sleep anyway as I am exhausted. I had three connections just to get here this morning and it has turned out to be a zinger of a day. That being said, I have conditions. First, I want a complete debrief from you tomorrow morning at seven am sharp. Second, I want to know everything you do while you are here. Everything! Are we clear?"

Not waiting for an answer Agent Bosco stood, taking his file from the desk. He stopped and looked at Jasper; he waved the file at him menacingly. "Congressman, you just bought yourself some time, but Reggie better have something good because as far as I am concerned, you're my prime suspect." With that, the agents walked out of the room, slamming the door behind them.

Jasper looked at the man who was standing before him. He rose from his chair and extended his hand is greeting, "I'm Jasper Thorne. I offer my sincere appreciation for your help."

Grabbing Jasper's hand in a firm grip, the man smiled, "I know who you are Congressman Thorne. It is a pleasure to meet you. My name is Detective Reginald Williams. Please call me Reggie." The detective's smile was quickly replaced by a solemn look. "Let's go get a cup of coffee. I have one heck of a story to tell you."

"Given the day I have had already, I'm not sure I want to hear it," Jasper responded glumly.

The detective tried to minimize the impact of his next statement by smiling slightly. He said in a somewhat enthusiastic voice, "Your right, you're not going to want to hear it. But on the bright side, you can at least look forward to a good cup of coffee."

Jasper didn't respond. For some reason he already knew the answer. This was not going to be a cup of coffee that he was going to enjoy.

Chapter 49

Jasper winced as the cold, bitter taste of the coffee filled his mouth. The coffee had been steaming hot when it had first been served, but that was before the detective began to tell his story about Scarface. Alexis and Michael were sitting at the table with them. They were the only people left in the small coffee shop with the exception of the staff. A waitress lazily pushed a dust broom back and forth across the worn wooden floor, not paying much attention to them, while a young man was busily restocking a matrix of square glass bins that covered a wall behind the counter with fresh coffee beans. The strong aroma of the beans permeated the air.

Detective Williams had spent the last hour weaving a harrowing tale of crime, violence, and murder. It was disconcerting to Jasper that the detective did not even know the terrorist's name, only what he looked like. The fact that this man was able to wreak so much havoc and then disappear meant he had powerful and well-connected friends. The detective ended his narrative with the recent events that had led him to make the trip to Charleston in hopes of arresting Scarface.

Jasper did not like hearing the last part of the detective's story. The thought that a murderer had violated his personal sanctuary made him angry. He did not like the feeling of being hunted, like he was prey. The only consolation was Jasper now knew how Trent's phone had ended up in a jacket in his closet. Scarface had put it there. *But what else had Scarface done while he was in his house?* This thought made Jasper uneasy.

Alexis was equally captivated by the story, though she was showing signs of visible distress as the implications of what she heard became clear. He could see the tension around her eyes. She was also biting her lip, something she only did when she was really nervous. Though he had been very concerned about the threat from Scarface, there had been a part of him who had thought it was simply posturing. Jasper now realized he had been wrong. Their lives were in real danger. Scarface was serious ... deadly serious.

Jasper relayed the events that had transpired earlier that day and had led to his interrogation with the FBI. It had only been a fortunate set of circumstances that Detective Williams had arrived when he did. It was even more fortunate that the detective had known Agent Bosco. Otherwise, Jasper felt confident he would be in a jail cell at the moment. "Detective, we owe you a great deal," Jasper said, placing his arm around Alexis. "Thank you for your help this evening. It is comforting to know that you are involved."

The detective nodded, his dark eyes showing the fatigue of a long day. "I am really sorry for the loss of your friend. I know what it is like to lose a good friend." A moment of pain flashed across the detective's face. "But you do not need to thank me. I am only doing my job. And tonight, well … it was just lucky that Agent Bosco and I have worked together before. He was originally the lead investigator for the FBI on the Santoro murders before being reassigned. We also spent a month together traveling across the United States as part of a racial relations task force," he smirked at the memory. "We would meet with Latino and African American community leaders in hopes of educating them on avoiding racial conflict. We both know each other pretty well and the pain and hassle of travel," he laughed. It was a warm and inviting laugh, one that you wanted to hear more. "Anyway, I only learned yesterday that he was in Charleston investigating that IPEA related murder in Florence from several months ago, so I came right to the office. And now here we are."

"IPEA? Now there is another interesting topic. IPEA has definitely made its impact here in South Carolina," Jasper said, glancing at Michael who was starting to doze off despite the coffee. Jasper was glad to take an opportunity to change the subject from Scarface. Not that he was ignoring the threat, only that he hadn't processed all the information yet and needed time to think. Jasper placed his hand on Alexis's leg and gave her a reassuring squeeze. "I don't know if you read the local paper this morning, but between IPEA and the President's Domestic Infrastructure Treaty, we have minted over 200,000 new citizens in South Carolina alone in the past thirty days. That is five percent of our population."

Reggie shook his head in disgust, "Ever since IPEA passed, it has only gotten worse back in LA. The Mexican drug cartel has utilized IPEA as a means to gain a strangle hold on Southern California and cement a U.S. distribution network. We have begun an investigation in conjunction with the FBI on a large distribution center in Los Angeles that recently started receiving truck shipments from Mexico, but it will be months before we have enough evidence to make any arrests." The detective starred at the bottom of his empty coffee cup for a moment before proceeding, "It was actually quite ingenious what the cartel accomplished. They opened legally licensed distribution warehouses in major cities throughout the country several months ago. The warehouses remained vacant until IPEA passed. From the federal documents that we were able to obtain, ten warehouses submitted official applications with the Department of Labor Equalization for one hundred union positions each. We don't know what these positions are for, but we can only assume that the cartel has sent key members into the country to fill these positions so they can become U.S. citizens. As a result, the cartel is in a strategic position of power that it has never held before. Not only that, the cartel is continuing to fuel the fire in the LA race war as drugs are the primary economic engine for both the Black and Latino ghettos."

"Where is it all going to end? We are destroying our country from within," Michael lamented wearily, suddenly coming to life.

"At one time, I would have disagreed with you," Reggie said. "But now, I can't agree more. It is a sad state of affairs," Reggie responded softly. "But on the bright side, there are still people like you folks in this country. I have been following your candidacy. I can't imagine what the past week had been like for you all." He stared at Jasper. "I was able to watch your press conference during a layover. Do you think you were able to change people's minds about what happened in Germany?"

Jasper pursed his lips. He hadn't really had time to think about it. The press conference seemed like it had happened days ago, maybe even months. He looked at Michael expectantly.

Michael stifled a yawn before answering, "The real key to changing people's minds is to make sure that the real story gets out to the broader audience in these last days. The latest poll reports and voter interviews seem to indicate that we were successful, but it is too early to tell to what degree. I definitely think the word is getting out that there was another side to this story that the press ignored," Michael offered hopefully. "Most Carolinians are wary of mainstream media anyway."

"What about the vote on secession?" Reggie asked. "I know your opponent had publically stated that he is against secession. Somehow, you've avoided taking a position so far. Do you think people are really going to vote to secede from the U.S.? It seems like an extreme act in this day and age."

Jasper glanced at Michael. It was the same question he had been asked countless times in the last few months. Jasper had avoided taking a stance for several reasons, opting to the viewpoint that as governor, he would do and support whatever the citizens of South Carolina decide. Michael had been driving him to make a decision one way or the other, but Jasper had resisted. The truth was Jasper wasn't sure what side he was on, but he didn't want Michael to know that. The last poll report he had read indicated that there was not enough support for Bill 122061 to become law, but the poll results were still tracking within the margin of error. It was still anybody's guess if South Carolina would secede.

The waitress came over to the table, slapping the bill down on the table with a loud thunk. "We are closing in ten minutes. Have a nice night, " she said then walked off leaving them in silence. It did not need to be said among them, but they were all glad this day was over.

"I suggest we all stay together at my place until things are safe again. I have plenty of room," Jasper offered somewhat adamantly.

They all nodded in agreement. "I will be over after I stop by my apartment and pick up my revolver. I will also get my hunting rifle," Michael stated.

"I have my pistol as well," Alexis added, referring to the small pink trimmed 380 she carried in her purse.

The detective nodded approvingly and rose from the table. "I forget about you southern people and your guns. I never thought I would say this, but I find something very comforting about that."

Jasper would have laughed if he had been in a better mood. He was not looking forward to tomorrow. Trent's funeral was in the morning. Though it had been a few days since his death, he hadn't had time to properly grieve. He knew there was a part of himself that still refused to believe Trent was dead. He hoped he could reach some sort of closure tomorrow so he could begin to deal with the emotions that were eating at him from within.

Alexis must have noticed the scowl on his face. "Jasper, is everything ok?" she asked concerned.

"Yes, just thinking about Trent," he responded. As they walked out the restaurant, Jasper placed his arm around Alexis and gave her another reassuring squeeze. He could tell she was exhausted, just like he was. "It will be a better day tomorrow," he said trying to lighten the mood. Alexis only nodded and stifled a yawn. For all of their sake, he hoped that his prediction would come true.

Chapter 51

The flicker of the television cast a sickly green glow across the serene face of Pastor Hank Mills. Serenity was not the expression that Jasper had expected to see given the circumstances. His eyes were closed, but Jasper could tell he was not sleeping. Jasper knew he was praying. The lights had been turned down in the waiting room almost an hour ago, on the chance that someone may want to sleep. There were three other people in the room, in addition to the two of them. On the couch behind him, reclined a mother and her young son. The toddler was sleeping in her arms as she unconsciously caressed his head, her mind obviously focused on someone else. An elderly, frail man was seated in the corner. He looked confused as if unsure what was going on around him. Jasper could only guess that the man's wife and probable caretaker was in surgery, leaving him without his help mate and alone in a strange place. That thought generated a momentary pang of compassion in Jasper for the old man. *Maybe he should go over and offer assistance*, he thought. But the urge passed as quickly as it came, replaced by thoughts of Alexis.

It was hard for him not to replay the phone call from Hank over and over in his head. There has been an accident. *Alexis is in surgery. Get here fast.* When he had arrived at the hospital, he had been ushered into the waiting room by a rather cold and portly attendant. The pastor was waiting there for him, but had no additional information to give him about the situation. Alexis was still in surgery, despite the six hours that had passed since her accident. Neither Hank, nor Jasper had received an update from the medical staff on her condition, despite Jasper's requests and in some cases threats. *Why couldn't they tell him something? Anything?* The uncertainty of the situation was killing him.

According to preliminary details provided by a police officer who had spoken with Hank, Alexis had been in an auto accident along Route 17 while driving back to Charleston. The accident had occurred just before the Santee River crossing. It had only been a miracle that a trained emergency medical technician had been traveling with his family a quarter mile behind Alexis. He had pulled Alexis from her vehicle before it completely submerged and provided necessary first aid until an ambulance had arrived. The EMT had also been able to provide police with critical information on the accident. He had seen a black SUV driving several hundred yards in front of him suddenly speed up and hit Alexis' car, causing it to spin out of control and veer off the road into the marsh. The SUV proceeded to leave the scene, forcing the technician to make a choice between Alexis and the fleeing vehicle. Fortunately for all of them, the EMT chose to try to save Alexis rather than try to be a hero pursuing the assailant.

Jasper knew that stretch of road very well; it had been the same area where his parents had died. Unfortunately, the details of Alexis' accident were way too familiar for him. He shuddered at the thought, cupping his face in his hands. He felt the sweat dripping down his face despite the cold air blowing on him from the vent directly above him. *How could this have happened? Why my Alex?* Jasper thought. He was having difficulty keeping his emotions in check. He felt so many things at this moment that he wasn't even sure what emotions he was trying to control. Worry, fear, doubt, anger, frustration, and helplessness cascaded over him at random intervals. Among the emotional chaos, there was one constant and one thing that was most familiar to him. The coldness generated from the mental void he created in his emotions. It was the mechanism he used to cope with his parent's death and later with the horrors of war. It was simple and logical. Use the coldness to isolate the emotions, ignore them and close yourself off to the pain. Don't let the emotions in. They can't hurt you if you don't feel them. It was what he had always done to protect himself. He didn't know why, but it had become part of who he was after their death. Though he knew his failure to deal with emotions was harmful, it had proven useful during the war to deal with the loss of friends and to deal with the horrors he had been exposed to. He had to be strong; he had to be a man. Emotions were a sign of weakness that had to be overcome.

Only, this time, the coldness was different. It was if another powerful emotion was battling the cold and he felt the

Chapter 50

Xavier watched as the red dot passed through the cross hairs on his monitor and drifted slowly away from his position. The monitor emitted a small chirp confirming that the target had passed within twenty five yards of him. He slowly pulled the black suburban onto the road and began to follow the white Volvo S60 now in front of him. The sun had just set, making the unusually cold day, even more miserable. There was a light mist forming in the air that added a dampness he detested. He scanned the horizon noting the last sliver of purple light fading in the distance, the only remaining indication that there had once been daylight. He was not concerned that Alexis would notice him. There was no moon out tonight. It would be a very dark tonight, indeed. *Perfect*, he thought, *all she would see was the Suburban's head lights*. He followed along casually, just another driver heading to a destination down the road.

He was feeling abnormally giddy tonight. Of course he should. Tonight was going to be a highlight of an assignment that surprisingly, had turned out to be much more enjoyable than he had anticipated. Jasper Thorne had proven to be more stubborn than he expected. Either that or he was a man whose heart was as cold as his own. Perhaps that was why he was excited about the next few days. Thorne would have to show his true colors soon, one way or another. He turned up the radio and began to wave his free arm in rhythmic motion as he conducted an imaginary orchestra to the song 'Ride of the Valkyries' that was emanating from the speakers. Yes, he felt good tonight. He kept conducting his orchestra as he turned onto Route 17 heading south towards Charleston.

Earlier that day, he had intercepted Alexis's call to Thorne and knew she would be traveling to Charleston that evening to meet with him. He also learned that the FBI was now seriously considering Thorne as a suspect in the murder of Trent Holloway.

That was more than he had hoped for, even though he suspected that his employer may have something to do with the FBI's suspicions. Of course, the evidence that Xavier had planted was all circumstantial. The authorities would never take Thorne to trial without first having the murder weapon. Good thing for them, Xavier would soon give them what they were looking for.

His planning for this assignment had paid off handsomely even though his activities had been slightly hampered because of the video surveillance net. He had chosen to take a calculated risk by showing his face at the church the other day, but it had needed to be done to lure Alexis into his trap. It had been worth the risk, no question. Besides, he couldn't resist the thrill he experienced from the direct interaction with an unknowing victim. People were so naive, so blatantly trusting of strangers. "You are all such stupid people!" he screamed in timing with the crescendo of the song. Yes, he was having fun tonight.

He checked the dashboard GPS. He was almost at his destination. His timing over the next few minutes would be critical in order to maximize the impact of his intentions. He stepped on the gas, causing the Suburban to lurch forward for an instant. Within seconds, he had closed the gap between him and Alexis and was riding on the bumper of the Volvo. The car looked so small in front of him, as if he could run right over it. The light from his head lights reflected back at him off the rear window of her car, casting a ghostly glow on the interior of his cabin. He drove behind her, his bumper only inches from hers for another mile, savoring the anxiety, fear, and frustration that he knew was occurring in the car ahead of him. He imagined Alexis gripping the steering wheel, the knuckles of her fingers white from the exertion. He wished he could see her face. He bet she was frantically shifting her focus from the road, to the rear view mirror and back again, searching for a way to escape from the possessed driver behind her. *What was she thinking about right this moment?* He wondered. Thoughts such as these were how he enjoyed passing time during the long days sailing at sea. It was so cathartic to daydream about the minds of his victims in their last frightful moments.

Out of the corner of his eye, he saw the headlights of an approaching vehicle in his rear view mirror, but it was still far enough away meaning that there was still time for him to act. He veered the Suburban to the right and onto the narrow shoulder. It was tricky as there was not much space between the road and the descending hill that led to the deep marsh that spread out over the horizon. As he anticipated, Alexis moved her vehicle slightly over into the oncoming lane in a defensive gesture. She was right where he wanted her. He nudged the Suburban forward with a quick tap on the gas pedal. He just needed a few more feet to position his front fender so that it was directly even with her rear tire well. It was a simple trick. One used all the time by law enforcement officials to end high speed pursuits. Pressing lightly on the gas, he slowly forced his left bumper into the side wall of the Volvo. The Volvo was so light in comparison to the Suburban that all he felt was a slight bump. With the bumper of the Suburban still in contact with the Volvo, he pressed on the gas and turned his wheel towards the Volvo, forcing the left front end of the Suburban into the rear of the Volvo. Instantly, the Volvo began to fish tail out of control spinning in front of his vehicle and then off the road to his right. He slowed down only for a few seconds as he watched Alexis and her car tumble end over end down the embankment, and into the black marsh below. *Parting is such sweet sorrow*, he thought, a small grin forming on his face.

Xavier stepped on the gas and sped south back towards Charleston. He was looking forward to getting back to Mt. Pleasant to celebrate. He had placed a bottle of Patron Añejo tequila in the freezer before he left just for the occasion. All he had to do now was lie low for a day or so and monitor the response of Mr. Thorne. The thought of Thorne made him angry. He had warned Thorne exactly what would happen if he made the wrong choice. Xavier had guessed incorrectly that Trent's death would be enough of a motivator to force Thorne to leave the race, but Thorne had not caved. But now, Alexis's accident would mean there was more innocent blood on Thorne's hands. If Thorne did not drop out of the race as a result of this incident that would mean Thorne would never yield, regardless of what harm Xavier would due to other people. If Thorne proved to be that stubborn, then Xavier would have no choice but to execute the next and final step in his plan. The thought of what that meant made him giddy and he started to laugh. Yes, he was enjoying this assignment. He was enjoying it tremendously.

emotion strengthen each time he pictured Alexis' face. The emotion was different than anything he had ever experienced and he could only describe it as a blending of anticipation, longing, desire, and acceptance. As he rationalized what he was feeling, the realization dawned on him that the emotion could be only one thing. Tears began to run down his face uncontrollably because he knew it was true. He couldn't fight it, he couldn't defend against it. Someone had finally found a way inside his twisted psyche. He was in love with Alexis and it was frightening and wonderful all at the same time.

Pastor Mills patted Jasper on the knee, "It is in the Lord's hands. Have faith in Him, whatever the outcome." Jasper glanced at him briefly. The pastor's blue eyes were clouded in concern.

Jasper wiped the tears from his face with the back of his hand. "Thanks for the comforting words, Hank, but the only outcome I will accept is Alexis alive and well. There is no Plan B, so the Lord better be on our side." Jasper's words solicited a slight frown from the pastor, who remained silent.

He looked at Hank again, studying him. He could not explain it, but the man emanated peace. *How could that be? Was he even concerned about Alexis?* Finally, Jasper decided to call the pastor's bluff. "How can you remain so calm?" he growled. "Your daughter has been in surgery for more than six hours!"

The pastor's response was slow and deliberate, "Jasper, I am calm because my trust is in the Lord and in no other place. Not in the surgeons, not in our medical technology, and not in anything I am able to do at this time. I also rest in the assurance that if Alexis should pass from this life, I will see her again in Heaven. Since she is saved, I know she will spend eternity in Heaven and that I will see her again."

"How can you know that with so much certainty?" Jasper challenged.

"I know it because of my faith in the Lord. It is a faith that has been confirmed over and over again in my relationship with God. I know that God is real because I see his interaction all around me," the pastor scanned the room, his eyes coming to rest on the small boy. "There have been times in my desperation that I have called on the Lord and he has answered my prayers. I have seen and experienced things in my life and the life of others that I can only accredit to the Lord. I have also found his word, the Bible, to be true. It is how he speaks to me."

Jasper frowned. "Michael tells me the same thing, but I don't really understand. The Bible is like a collection of stories to me. I don't feel it is speaking to me or providing me any magical insight."

"I trust in time, you will come to view the Bible just like Michael and I do," the pastor responded. "The Bible provides us with guidance, wisdom, support, and inspiration, among so many other things. It is hard to explain to someone who has never experienced it, but I tell you it is true. As one progresses in their relationship with God, they will see the reality of God more clearly. They will also see how the Bible is used by God to help us in our lives," he said, settling back in his chair. "I wish it were otherwise, because so many people go through life never having faith in God and thus miss a wonderful experience."

Jasper wasn't buying it, at least not entirely. "Look, you have spent most of your life in service to God. You have a different perspective and different experiences than me. For me, faith is something that does not come easy. Granted, I have learned a great deal about God, Jesus, and Christianity this past year, but faith ... faith is still an enigma."

Again, the pastor was slow to respond, but the clarity of his response told Jasper he had shared this same message many times before. "Faith is confidence in what we hope for and assurance about what we do not see." He patted Jasper lightly on the back. "Son, faith is not a destination it is a journey. It begins with hearing and understanding what you have been taught about the word of God. That means you must be listening and you must also believe what you hear. The Lord will build upon that belief and increase your faith in him through your experiences." The pastor took a deep breath and for the first time, Jasper detected small tears in the man's eyes. "Take this situation with Alexis. It is a trial that is occurring for the very purpose of building faith in us, for it is in trials that we are at our weakest. It is in the trials that the Lord desires you to lean on Him so that he can take care of you and by doing so, build your faith in Him, but also so that He can be glorified."

"Hank, if this is what it takes to build faith, I'm not sure I want it," Jasper said seriously. His frustration getting the best of him, he pounded the wood arm rest, soliciting a stare from the man in the corner.

They were both silent for a minute, momentarily lost in their own thoughts. Jasper glanced at the television set. The news station was airing a recent video of the standoff between the Texas National Guard and the U.S. Army. Under other circumstances, he would have been listening to the broadcast intently, only now he didn't care about anything but Alexis.

The pastor placed his hand on Jasper's shoulder, "Jasper, you have been a rock all evening. You've kept your emotions in check and kept a level head, at least from an outside perspective. It reminds me of how you were right after your parents died." Jasper was surprised by the comment. The pastor seldom mentioned his parents, but then again Jasper never talked about them. *It was just better that way*, he thought.

The pastor looked at him inquisitively, "I know you care for Alex very deeply. If you don't mind me asking, what is it that made you cry?"

Chapter 52

Jasper took a deep breath. He felt the tears welling up again. "Hank ..." he paused briefly, choosing his words carefully. Even so, they came out strained through the shroud of guilt that was covering him. "I was thinking about Alexis. I should never have let this happen to her. Not to the person who is most important to me."

Pastor Mills listened patiently, but remained silent.

"I should have dropped out of the race. She is all I want in life and I ... I caused this. " Somehow he found the act of telling someone else his feelings for Alexis a struggle. He clenched his fist as if to signal his defiance to what may come. "Oh, God!" he shuddered, "I didn't want anything to happen to her." He wiped his eyes to stop the tears running down his cheeks.

The pastor's hand came to rest on Jasper's shoulder and with it an expression that lifted his heart. It was a simple smile, but full of love and support. It reminded Jasper of how his father would smile when Jasper had done something to make him proud. "Jasper, you didn't cause this," he argued. "You are not in control. The sooner you learn to accept that fact, the easier life will be. I know it is tough right now. I can't imagine the pressure you are under. But I do know what Alexis would say to you right now if she could."

Jasper looked away from the pastor not wanting to meet his gaze. The pastor's voice was stern but supportive. His words cut through the cloud of despair in Jasper's heart. "Alexis would tell you that you are a stronger man than you think. She would tell you that you can't be selfish about your own needs at a time when so many need you. Lastly, she would argue that you can't give up, not when you are so close."

Jasper closed his eyes and nodded slowly in response. He didn't want to agree with Hank, but Jasper knew Hank was right. "Hank, it's just that my life has been an insanity trip these last few months," he acknowledged. "I have been fighting to stay ahead of it all, yet I feel I can't keep up."

The pastor shook his head in agreement. "We all have responsibilities that burden us, some carry greater responsibilities than others. That is by God's design." The pastor's voice suddenly became forceful, almost as if commanding Jasper to action. "Son, you need to come to the realization that you have a responsibility and an obligation to carry forth to the people of this state as their congressman, and Lord willing, as their future governor. The citizens of South Carolina need you. I need you. Alexis needs you."

Jasper stared at the toddler, sleeping peacefully on his mother's lap wrapped in the protection of her arms. "It is funny," Jasper said after a moment, turning back to face the pastor. "All of that stuff was so important to me just six hours ago. Now, the only thing I want is for Alexis to be alive and well. The rest of it could all go away, if I can just have her." His shoulders slumping as he finished the sentence.

Pastor Mills considered Jasper's last statement for a moment and then reached into his coat pocket. He removed a small pocket Bible from his breast pocket. The gold leaf words *The Bible* were barely legible on its cover, having been worn by the frequency of use by the pastor over the years. "Son, have you ever heard the story of King Hezekiah?"

Jasper was not really in the mood for a Bible lesson, but given the circumstances, he acquiesced. "No. Who was he?" he said.

"He was a young man who came into power over one of the kingdoms of Israel around 700 BC. Generations before his succession to the throne, God had broken the Kingdom of Israel into two kingdoms, Israel and Judah. God did this because King Solomon, the son of King David, had offended God by allowing other gods to be worshipped in the kingdom. Eventually, because the leaders of both kingdoms continued to do evil and offend Him, God destroyed them both. However, while these kingdoms existed, there where periods when these kingdoms were ruled by men who chose to obey God and rule under God's direction. These men became known through history as the good kings. Hezekiah was the last good king of Judah."

"Interesting story," Jasper said. "Why is it relevant to our discussion?"

Pastor Mills chuckled. It was good to hear him laugh given the circumstances. "Jasper, I don't think I am off base when I say this. I think there is a lesson for you in this story. In fact, the Lord had been bringing the events of Hezekiah's reign to my mind on many occasions in the last few months, particularly during my times of prayer. Now I think I know why." He opened the Bible and began to read.

"In the second book of Kings, the eighteenth chapter we read:

⁴ He [Hezekiah] removed the high places, and brake the images, and cut down the groves, and brake in pieces the brasen serpent that Moses had made: for unto those days the children of Israel did burn incense to it: and he called it Nehushtan. ⁵ He trusted in the Lord God of Israel; so that after him was none like him among all the kings of Judah, nor any that were before him. ⁶ For he clave to the Lord, and departed not from following him, but kept his commandments, which the Lord commanded Moses. ⁷ And the Lord was with him; and he prospered whithersoever he went forth.'"

The pastor closed the Bible and replaced it in his coat pocket. "Jasper, even though these verses were written twenty seven hundred years ago, do you see the significance of the message they convey to your situation today?"

Jasper considered the question for a moment before answering. "No. I can't say that I do," Jasper responded, trying to determine where the pastor was leading him.

"This man was no different than you or me, but what he was able to do was extraordinary. Hezekiah chose to rule in a manner that was completely different than the Kings that had reigned before him. He attacked the sacred cows of society and tore them down, literally."

"What do you mean by sacred cow?" Jasper asked.

"In this case, the people had taken a religious object from the past; a bronze snake fashioned by Moses, and made it an object of worship. They had stopped worshiping God and chose to worship something of their own making. By destroying the symbols of false worship in his kingdom, Hezekiah bucked years and in some cases decades of traditions – all in pursuit of what he considered was right."

Jasper reflected for a moment. "I would imagine a great deal of people disagreed with him and his actions?"

The pastor nodded. "I have no doubt that he faced criticism, hostile resistance, and retaliation in pursuit of his goals, but he persevered and became one of the greatest kings of his time. Hezekiah was a man committed to the laws established by God and took personal action to preserve those laws. He took a stand against society for his beliefs. Above all, he placed his trust in the Lord. Do you see the parallels that exist with you and your situation today?"

Jasper couldn't explain why, but the story the pastor was telling him about Hezekiah was resonating with him on so many levels. "I don't know why, but I believe I do understand," he said, sitting up in his chair. "In fact, I think I understand completely," he added, his voice beginning to build with confidence. "Today, society has chosen to place their faith in the government instead of God. The bronze snake is the U.S. Government, an institution that was designed to create good but has been corrupted at the hands of man. Our sacred cows are the systems our society had come to rely on such as Social Security, welfare, affirmative action, universal health care, IPEA, and many other government instituted programs. We have been led to believe that the government is supposed to protect us and to provide for us, when really it has been enslaving us. This is most evident in the recent actions taken by our government that have infringed and violated our rights established in the Constitution."

"Yes, you see it now." The pastor said nodding emphatically. He studied Jasper, his face showing the first signs of a smile all evening. The pastor paused for a moment, "Jasper, the people of South Carolina need a champion. They need a person who will stand up for them and make the tough decisions that no one else will make. They, – we, – I need you to make that stand, regardless of the adversity you may face in the process. I believe you can do it. You must believe the same. You must have faith in your direction and have faith that it is the direction the Lord wants you to go."

Jasper thought through the implications of what the pastor was telling him. *Could he really be the catalyst to create the change that was needed in the country? It seemed impossible. There was too much to do and too many obstacles stacked against him. Who was he, but just a single person?*

"I can tell by your expression that you may have doubts about this calling and that is very understandable. That being said, I do know one thing you can be sure of. If you let Him, the Lord will guide you on this journey."

The door to the waiting room opened. A man dressed in a light green smock and surgical cap entered the room. Both items of clothing were splattered with blood. The surgeons face looked fatigued and beads of sweat clung to his exposed forehead. "Mr. Mills?" the surgeon called out to those in the room.

Hank Mills stood up and walked slowly towards the man. Jasper heard Hank's question and it made his heart sink. "Doctor, is my baby girl still alive?"

Chapter 53

The miles ticked past in a blur as Jasper headed south down Route 17. He was too absorbed in his own little world to notice that he was almost to Charleston. He knew he was exhausted physically, but his mind was in overdrive. Old memories were surfacing with graphic images that he had thought he had conquered and suppressed a long time ago. He tried to stop the dizzying array of images, but they forced their way into his mind. He wasn't strong enough to resist them. The images blended with visions of Alexis's accident that he could only hope were nowhere near the truth. He tried to find the coldness of the void, to isolate himself from the pain and emotion, but it wasn't there. His only emotion was pure, unbridled anger. His stomach was a twisted knot of pain and distress. His head was throbbing as if his blood was boiling and the pressure building up inside needed to be released. He pushed the accelerator to the floor again as he crossed lanes to pass a car that was traveling at the speed limit. "Why?" he yelled. *Why did the people he loved have to suffer such tragedy?*

"Dad!" He stuttered out loud. "Mom!" He pounded his fist on the steering wheel again. He felt like ripping the steering wheel from the console. "Alexis! My darling Alexis! Why?"

He tried to stop the images and the piercing pain that accompanied them. "Why God? Why did you do this to me?" he yelled, the tears streaming down his face. It was the sole question that was fueling his rage, the question that he needed desperately to understand. *Why did God hate him so much that he gave him so much pain in his life?*

His mind flashed back to the bridge he had passed over thirty miles ago. It was the reason for all his pain. The bridge was where he had lost them. Alexis's accident had occurred at the very same spot as the accident that took his parents. He played through the memory of that fateful night in his head.

The noise of the crash was deafening. The spray of glass cascading across the seat, hitting him like thousands of tiny nails.

Suddenly, he was weightless as the car went airborne careening over the embankment. Time seemed to slow down to a crawl, only to speed back up as a wave of liquid surged into the car. The liquid was cold, so cold. His mother was in her seat screaming in agony, frantically tugging at something in her lap. His father was strangely silent, slumped oddly over the middle console. The coldness kept growing; threatening to consume him. It took him a few moments to realize that the coldness was water that was rapidly filling the vehicle. He hurriedly pulled himself out of the car through the rear window that had been smashed by the impact of the other vehicle. What was wrong with Dad? Why had Mom stopped screaming?

He swam over to the other side of the car to where his mother was still in her seat. She was crying now, cupping the head of his father in her hands. His father's eyes looked at Jasper, unseeing. The front side of his skull had been crushed when his head had collided with the steering wheel. Jasper didn't know what to do. He just stared at them, unable to do anything else. The lurch of the car, as it sunk further under the water, prompted him to action. He yelled forcefully at his mother, telling her to get out of the car. She ignored him. He reached into the car, frantically searching for her seat belt buckle, but couldn't find it. He kept yelling at his mother to help him, but she didn't respond. The water in the car had risen to her chest. Finally realizing the danger, his mother suddenly grabbed his arm, gripping it fiercely. She began pleading for Jasper to help her get out of the car. He finally found the buckle, only to discover it was jammed. His mother was screaming his name, over and over again, her arms flailing frantically. Jasper crawled half way into the car, his head underwater as he tried desperately to release the buckle. He had to save her.

Abruptly, there was no more screaming. There was no longer the sound of desperate hands smacking against the encroaching water in a futile attempt to keep it at bay. There was only silence. Suddenly strong arms enfolded him, lifting him to the surface and dragging him across the water. Jasper fought against his captor trying to get back to the now submerged car and to his

parents. He had to do more; he couldn't let them die. "Nooo!" he
screamed.

By the time Jasper pulled into his driveway, his anger had blossomed into full fledge indignation. Michael met him at the door, an anxious look on his face. "Jasper, I have been trying to reach you on your phone for hours." His voice expressing the concern ingrained in his face. "Is Alexis ok?" He asked tentatively, as if afraid of the answer.

Jasper huffed as he brushed by Michael and headed straight for the cellar. He wished for a brief moment that Michael would leave and go back to his own home for the evening, but then dismissed the thought. As long as Scarface was still a threat, it was better that they all stay together. Still, all he wanted right now was to be alone. At least the cellar would give him some privacy.

The cellar was dank and musty and the air smelt slightly of mildew. He hadn't been down here in a long time. Years ago, he had installed a punching bag, a bench press and a rack with free weights in the rear corner. The rest of the basement was taken up by his workshop which consisted of a large work bench, a drill press, disk sander, a table saw, and several shelving units containing tools, appliances, paints, stains, and other accessories. A long stave of hickory lay clamped in a vice on the work bench, one side roughly tapered to a narrow point from the center. It was a bow that he had intended to give to Trent last Christmas, but never made the time to complete it. The sight of it fanned his anger even more.

Removing his suit jacket and his shirt, he positioned himself in front of the punching bag. With a flurry of motion, he pelted the punching bag, yelling the questions that had been plaguing him as he delivered each punch.

"Why did I have to lose them?" Punch!

"Why did you do this to me?" Smack!

"Why are you punishing me?" Punch! Punch! Punch!

The frequency of his punching increased as if he expected the bag to eventually crumple under his relentless assault. "Why couldn't I save them?" Smack, Thump!

"Why Alexis?" Punch! "Why did you hurt her?" He executed a spinning kick sending the bag careening to the side. Whack!

With a wild howl Jasper released his rage with a final flurry of punches. He only stopped punching the bag when he noticed the patches of dark red forming on the bag. He fell to his knees exhausted. His breath came in ragged, short pants and he was soaked in sweat. His knuckles which were now bleeding heavily, the flesh and skin ripped away by the rough canvas of the bag.

Michael appeared holding a towel and took hold of Jasper's hands, wiping away the blood. He must have been watching him rant like a mad man. Jasper didn't care that Michael was there. He didn't care about anything right now. Though the release had been cathartic, Jasper's anger still smoldered, only temporarily dampened by his outburst.

"Anger can be a good thing, if it is dealt with properly," Michael said.

"What do you know about anger, old man?" Jasper quipped in between breaths as he pressed the towel against his left hand in an attempt to slow the blood flow. His hands were stinging with pain as the sweat mingled with the fresh wounds.

The smack of Michael's hand caught him off guard, sending a flash of bright light across his left eye. "What the —?" Jasper exclaimed bewildered.

"I have it on good authority that it is quite normal to be angry," Michael asserted. "God was so angry at the Israelites for their continued disobedience and sin that he punished them over and over again through history." Michael threw a second towel on the floor in front of Jasper, apparently done giving Jasper first aid. "But God also forgave them over and over again, eventually sacrificing his own Son, so that they would have a way to be forgiven eternally."

"I don't need one your biblical lectures right now! God did this to me. I don't deserve this!" Jasper struggled to his feet, but Michael pushed him back down forcefully. Jasper was taken aback by Michael's forward display of aggression, not really sure how to respond.

"Your self-pity is pathetic and you are weak," Michael chastised.

"Whatever —!" Jasper spewed back in annoyance, grabbing the second towel and wrapping it around his right hand tightly.

Michael looked down over him, his hands on his hips in a defiant gesture. "You know what your problem is ... you will never forgive. You are so wrapped up in your own conceitedness, your own selfishness ... there is no forgiveness in you." Michael's eyes were ablaze with anger. "You will never forgive yourself for an accident that was not your fault. You will never forgive yourself for failing to be there for those you love. You will never forgive yourself for things that you cannot control. It is sad that you are so screwed up."

Jasper felt his anger spark into a flame again upon hearing Michael's accusation, but he managed to quench it. He had never seen Michael so angry and there was a part of him that knew he deserved the verbal lashing.

Michael stabbed his index finger menacingly at Jasper. "You should be down on your knees thanking God that Alexis is still alive after such a horrific accident and has a fighting chance to survive! Instead you are on your knees wallowing in your own sorrow, mad at the world that you have hardship in your life." Jasper winced at the mention of Alexis. He knew Michael was right, but that didn't mean it was easy to listen to him berate him. Michael suddenly turned to walk away, apparently reading Jasper's mind, only to stop and turn back to face him.

"I was wrong about you, Jasper Thorne." Michael closed his eyes for a moment and shook his head. "I thought that you were going to be the leader that we needed. But to be a leader, you need to be able to forgive." He stooped down to pick up one of the bloody towels that Jasper had discarded. "For the leader that fails to forgive, who fails to show mercy to another when it is least deserved, is a leader who will never win the hearts of the people he governs." Michael approached Jasper extending his hand to help him up, but Jasper swatted it away.

Michael paused for a moment, staring at Jasper. When he spoke, the anger was gone from his voice. "Son, listen to me. You have two choices before you. You can focus inward and downward on your circumstances and choose to be a victim, or you can choose to focus upward and outward, and choose to be a victor. The choice is always up to you." He then promptly turned and walked up the stairs, leaving Jasper alone.

Jasper remained sitting in a pool of his own blood and sweat for several minutes. He slowly replayed the past several hours in his head, analyzing the events under the piercing light of Michael's comments. Slowly, almost like a trickle of water leaking from a crack in a dam, he began to laugh – soon a deep, hearty laugh was emanating from the pit of his stomach as the crack in his psyche expanded to become a growing fissure. It was a laugh born of true introspection. For the first time, he saw through the hypocrisy that had been so prevalent in his life. A hypocrisy that had begun the night of his parent's accident and that he had carried with him to this day, tightly protected by his pride and arrogance. All of the questions he had been asking himself the past hours where gone, replaced by a single, dominating query. *Was he a victim or was he a victor?*

Chapter 54

Jasper walked through the Intensive Care Unit at Georgetown Memorial Hospital searching for Room 426. It was easy to find it considering it was the only room with a burly state police man guarding the entrance door. He had Reggie to thank for that favor. The guard looked bored, his eyes buried in a copy of Good Housekeeping magazine that he must have borrowed from the waiting room. They exchanged greetings as he entered into the hospital room. Jasper closed the door slowly behind him, creating a small echo that reverberated from the cinder block walls within.

The overhead lights had been dimmed to provide an environment more conducive to resting, but he could see the layout of the room perfectly. It was devoid of any furnishings except a lamp that cast a small circle of light in the corner of the room and a hard plastic chair. Soft classical music played from an unseen speaker, the complexity of the melodic score wasted on the current listener. Despite the attempt to create an inviting ambience, the room felt cold and sterile. Maybe it was the occasional sound of a machine chirping as it measured the key vital signs of the patient. Most likely it was the fact that he knew Alexis was the patient the machine was monitoring.

He noticed a faded blue polyester blanket casually tossed over the back of the chair and a Bible resting on the seat. That must be where Alexis' father had been sitting as he kept vigil over his daughter. The pastor hadn't left her side since last night when she came out of surgery. The pastor had gone back home now, in need of a shower and to check on his wife. Hank would be back very soon though, of that Jasper had no doubt.

Jasper felt a tinge of guilt for not staying with Alexis and the pastor last night, only he just couldn't make it happen, not with the election only two days away. Jasper had spent most of the day with Michael reviewing the final activities planned for the remaining days of the election. Tomorrow, he was to embark on a statewide tour to rally last minute supporters. He would start in Charleston in the morning with a speech at Battery Park and then travel to Florence for another speech at the largest non-union manufacturer in the state, Carolina Medical Systems. The afternoon would find him in Columbia for a speech on the campus of the University of South Carolina. He would finish the day in Greenville at a potluck dinner event sponsored by the Greenville Republican Woman's Club. The women had opened the event to the public and had cooked an additional fifty pounds of bacon infused grits for the expected crowd, just in case.

It had been difficult for him to swallow his pride and to apologize to Michael for how he had acted earlier. Michael had accepted his apology routinely and simply returned to his work, leaving Jasper feeling even more like a fool. Michael was pushing him to make a public statement of his position on state secession in the speeches tomorrow and Jasper had finally agreed. The events of the last week had severed any ties of allegiance that he had been holding onto. He had made his decision about secession last night while he sat on the floor in his basement after his argument with Michael. He had also made other decisions that he had been avoiding for far too long, especially involving Alexis.

Jasper walked over to the bed where Alexis lay and stared at her unconscious body. He was shocked and taken back by her appearance. She looked so frail, so vulnerable. The usual vitality that radiated from her was gone, replaced by a pale shell of weakness. A mass of tubes extended from both her arms and an oxygen mask covered her face forcing air into her lungs. Her breathing was rhythmic but appeared difficult. He scanned the monitor that displayed an orange line that periodically peaked in a continuous pattern. *At least her heart rate was strong*, he thought, looking for something positive in her condition.

Her injuries had been so severe that the doctors had decided to induce a medical coma to speed healing. The head surgeon, Dr. Sullivan, told him she was lucky that she had not been paralyzed as a result of the accident. He surmised the forces within the car as it flipped over the embankment had been so severe that her neck had been snapped like a twig. Lucky for all of them, it had been a clean break and had not severed the spinal cord. It would heal in time. The main concern Dr. Sullivan and others had about Alexis involved mitigating the possibility for permanent damage from swelling of the spinal cord. The other concern was the possibility of the failure of key internal organs. She had ruptured her spleen and had severe bruising of her pancreas. The extent of her injuries were overwhelming, it was a miracle she had survived.

The idea of being away from Alexis tomorrow really bothered him. *What if something happened and he was on the other side of the state*, he thought. He couldn't look at her for long, the feelings of guilt quickly became more than he could bear. He pushed the feelings away, but he couldn't rid himself of them. He grabbed her hand searching for a response to his touch, but received nothing but a chirp from the machine. The guilt was eating at him, consuming him in despair. "I'm so sorry I did this to you," he whispered.

Last night, so much had become clear about his direction in life. Regardless of what happened in the future, he knew without a doubt that he wanted Alexis by his side. With her, the experiences of life had transformed from dull shades of mediocrity into the vibrant colors of adventure. She had become his best friend and the only person he truly trusted. She deserved to know how he felt about her. The pain the seized him when he thought that he might not get that chance was overbearing. All he wanted as to be able to hold her in his arms again, to hear her laugh, and to see her beautiful smile as she looked at him. He fell to his knees, overcome with emotion.

Jasper knew it was his fault. He knew that Alexis had been hurt because he had made a decision to pursue his personal goals over all else. It was a sobering thought to realize that his selfishness had created so much suffering. There was nothing he could do to change the situation. There was nothing he could do to help Alexis. He had failed her. The realization came over him that they were both in desperate need of help and there was only one person who could provide it. The one person he had been running from all of his life and blaming for all of his hardships.

The suppressed emotions he had stored away deep within began to explode to the surface. Waves of guilt and pain, cresting with anger, fear and frustration began to cascade over him in torrents. He began to weep in deep sorrowful sobs. "Oh God, it hurts ... it hurts so badly. I'm so sorry, Alex! I'm so sorry! God ... please ... please save her!" It wasn't really a prayer, but more of a scream. He continued to weep, as if an eternal reservoir of tears had been tapped and was going to continue flowing until it was empty.

Jasper didn't know how long he lay there at her bedside. He felt drained from the intense emotional outburst that had carried him back and forth between periods of crying, pleading, and prayer. He heard a voice speaking softly behind him and turned to find the pastor. Hank was standing against the wall, his head bowed in prayer, his hands enfolding his pocket Bible. Jasper did not know how long Hank had been there watching him.

A few moments later, the pastor raised his head and spoke softly, "Sometimes the Lord takes us into the pit of despair, to the lowest of the low, before he will raise us up. He does this because he loves us and it is only when we are at our weakest, when we realize how helpless we really are, that we discover how much we need him in our lives. Son, it is time to get right with the Lord. Jesus is calling for you to meet him. His gift is waiting for you to receive it. You only need to ask him for it."

Jasper nodded slowly. He knew Hank was right. He had been resisting for too long, his pride and arrogance fighting against the surrender that he knew must come. He met the pastor's gaze, "Show me."

Hank knelt down beside Jasper in response. "I can guide you, but this has nothing to do with me. This is between you and God." The pastor voice was soft and supportive. "Accepting Jesus as your Lord and Savior is a commitment of the heart, not an act. The heart only falls under conviction after the mind has understood and has come to truly believe." Hank placed his hand on Jasper's shoulder; his eyes were penetrating and commanded

Jasper's full attention. "But the desire in the heart must also be strong enough to overcome the will, because it is your choice and your choice alone to accept Christ or to reject him."

Jasper watched quietly as the pastor opened his Bible to a page that had a verse highlighted in bright yellow. Hank pointed at the verse. "Let's begin here with this verse, Romans 3:23. The verse reads *'For all have sinned, and come short of the glory of God.'*" Jasper remembered the verse from his lesson with Michael several months ago. Hank flipped forward a few pages and continued, "You, me, every one of us ... we all have sinned and as a result, we are separated from God." Jasper nodded, knowing this from his lesson with Michael.

"Now, Romans 6:23 teaches us about the consequences of our sin but also about God's gift, *'For the wages of sin is death; but the gift of God is eternal life through Jesus Christ our Lord.'* The pastor looked again at Jasper. "Our punishment as sinners is to spend eternity separated from God in eternal damnation. But, the good news is that God gave us Jesus Christ to be our savior from our punishment." He flipped a couple pages forward in his Bible and handed it over to Jasper, "We read in Romans 5:8 that the love God has for us is so strong that he sacrificed his own son so that we may have eternal life. The verse says, *'But God demonstrates His own love toward us, in that while we were still sinners, Christ died for us.'* In other words, God gave us his only begotten son that whoever believes on him should not perish but have eternal life."

"John 3:16," Jasper interjected, making the connection.

"Yes, exactly right," Hank affirmed. "Now do you know what grace is?"

Jasper shrugged, not sure of the answer, "I think I do."

"Grace is simply getting what you don't deserve."

"That makes sense," Jasper responded.

Hank continued, "Well since you and I are sinners, like all mankind, we deserve hell. But, it is by the grace of God through our faith in Jesus Christ that we are saved from that fate."

"But how is someone saved?" Jasper asked earnestly. This was the question Jasper had wanted to ask for so long but never felt comfortable bringing up.

"The moment you accept Christ, he gives you His righteousness. His righteousness is the only thing sufficient to get someone into Heaven." The pastor walked over and stroked his hand gently across Alexis' forehead. "As I told you last night, my trust is not in me, the things I do, my job as a pastor, or my religion. My trust is solely in Jesus and the righteousness that He and He alone gives me."

"How do I do it?" Jasper asked, somewhat anxiously. "Do I just ask for it?"

Hank smiled, "As a matter of fact you do. In the end, it is really quite simple." The pastor walked back to Jasper and handed him the open Bible.

"All that is required of each of us is belief in Jesus, a willful repentance of our sins and acceptance in faith of God's gift of forgiveness." Jasper looked down at the highlighted scripture on the page as the pastor spoke. "Romans 10:9 tells us *'that if you confess with your mouth Jesus as Lord, and believe in your heart that God raised Him from the dead, you will be saved.'*"

"Then, I'm ready to ask. I am tired of the doubt, tired of the struggle. I want to be saved," Jasper said firmly.

Hank placed his hand on Jasper's shoulder, "Jasper, do you believe that you are a sinner, separated from God and destined for eternal damnation."

"I do."

"Do you understand your need for a savior?"

"Yes."

Do you believe in Jesus Christ, the only son of God, who came to Earth as a man, lived a sinless life and was crucified upon a cross as penalty for your sins?"

"Yes."

Do you believe that God raised Jesus from the dead, an act that verified that Jesus had conquered death and created a path for salvation to those that believed in him?"

"I do."

"Do you believe you will receive the righteousness of Christ, your sins will be forgiven and you will spend eternity in Heaven if you accept him as your Lord and Savior?"

Jasper nodded, "Yes, I do."

"Do you want a relationship with Jesus Christ?"

"With all of my heart!" Jasper pleaded.

The pastor rose slowly to stand and gave Jasper a reassuring pat on his shoulder, "I've guided you as far as I can. You need to finish this with Jesus in prayer." He must have noticed the confused look on Jasper's face because he added, "Just talk to him, boy. Let him know what is on your heart. Tell the Lord you want the gift he offers and why you want it. Accept the Lord and the gift he gives you. The Holy Spirit will do the rest."

In a few seconds, Pastor Hank Mills had walked out of the room as quietly as he had entered, leaving Jasper and Alexis alone. The memory of the elderly man walking down the aisle of the pastor's church during the altar call came into his mind. Jasper knew he had changed on so many levels since that day, almost a year ago. He glanced at Alexis briefly. She seemed to be breathing more comfortably which was a good sign. He wondered if she could hear what was going on beside her bed this very moment. With that last thought, he gripped the side of the bed frame for stability, took a deep breath and began to pray.

PART IV

Chapter 55

Georgetown, South Carolina
November 2nd

The sliding glass door opened to reveal a blast of cold evening air. There was a faint smell of rain, but it was fleeting, quickly replaced by the aroma of burning leaves. One of the local residents nearby must have been priming their woodstove for the winter. It was late, but strangely, Jasper didn't feel tired as he left the hospital. He couldn't really explain how he felt. He felt lighter, as if a heavy weight had been lifted from his shoulders. A weight that he had been carrying all of his life and had not even known was there. Jasper walked slowly toward the parking lot, absorbing the atmosphere around him. He inhaled the air deeply, savoring the smell as it tickled in through his nostrils and out through his mouth in a smooth rhythmic motion. He felt vibrant and alive. His mind told him he was being ridiculous, but his soul told him something different. As odd as the feeling was, for the first time he felt truly at peace. Somehow, all the events of his life had become muted. It wasn't that they didn't matter anymore, it was quite the opposite. They mattered more to him, but now he felt he wasn't facing them alone.

The doctors had informed him and Hank that the next twenty four hours were going to be critical for Alexis and her recovery. If she could make it through, chances were she would fully recover from her injuries. He had not wanted to leave Alexis when she was in such a critical state, but he had no choice. He was committed to seeing this campaign to the end, no matter what the outcome. He had promised Alexis he would, no matter what. *It is funny,* he thought, thinking about his promise to her. *His candidacy for governor had become as much her mission as it was his.* Alexis had been such a rock of support these past months, encouraging him through the tough times. She had worked tirelessly to help him and his campaign. He never imagined he would have a woman like her by his side. She was everything that he desired and so much more than he deserved.

He took some solace in the fact that she would not be alone tomorrow. It was comforting to know that her father would be right there by her side. In the past few months, Pastor Mills had become so much more to Jasper than a friend from the past. He had become a father figure, a man who accepted Jasper for who he was and wanted to truly be involved in his life. Like Michael, Pastor Mills had become a spiritual advisor to Jasper as well, periodically coaching him, guiding him, and finally leading him to find his way down the narrow path. A feeling of satisfaction surfaced and rippled through Jasper. It was fitting that Pastor Mills, a friend of his father, had been there at the moment Jasper had finally seen the light of Christ, and surrendered after all the years of resistance. Jasper would have never have believed that by finally given up, he would also gain victory.

He and the pastor had agreed that they would spend some quality time together next week after the election was over. Jasper was looking forward to it, however for the next few days his focus had to be entirely on the election. Tomorrow was going to be another chaotic day of meetings, press interviews, and pressing the flesh with the public. It would be an exhausting couple of days, but necessary and important. With only two days left to the election, his schedule would be in overdrive. Regardless, he felt ready for the challenge. He did have an election to win after all.

Once inside his Jeep, Jasper reached for his mobile phone that he had left on his dashboard. He needed to call Michael and tell him what had happened. If he had to guess, Michael was still awake working through the details of their agenda for tomorrow. Michael will be thrilled with the news about Jasper's experience.

He started to dial the number but then stopped when he heard the click. A second later he felt the hard pressure of a gun barrel being pressed into his skull. There was no time to be startled. The comprehension of what was happening was instantaneous. He looked into the rear view mirror only to see a pair of dark, soulless eyes reflected back at him. The passing lights of a car highlighted the interior of the car, but only for a moment. It was enough time for Jasper to catch a glimpse of a large scar running down the man's left check. The man in the mirror began to laugh then abruptly stopped. He leaned forward slightly, his mouth coming near Jasper's ear. The man whispered softly, his voice carried a strong Latino accent.

"Hello, Mr. Thorne. It is so nice to finally meet you in person."

Jasper flinched unconsciously as a chill flowed through his body. He had heard that voice before. His nightmare had become a reality.

Chapter 56

Xavier kept the gun pressed sharply into Thorne's skull. He didn't want to take any chances. "Keep your speed to five miles below the speed limit at all times. Do not attempt anything stupid. I have no patience for heroes," Xavier said. Of course he didn't trust Thorne to do what he said. There was always the chance that Thorne would decide to accelerate and ram the Jeep into the nearest tree. Xavier would shoot without hesitation if he detected any such action, of that there was no question. He was prepared to deal with the outcome, even if it meant a car accident. He was not going to let his prey escape.

They arrived at the destination without incident. Xavier instructed Thorne to turn off the car, set the keys on the dash board and to keep his hands on the steering wheel. "Are you surprised where we are, Mr. Thorne?" he asked sarcastically.

"How do you know about this place?" Thorne responded looking straight ahead. *No doubt the man was trying to figure out how to escape,* Xavier thought. *Perfect*! He loved to see his prey resist the inevitable. It made the kill so much more enjoyable.

"It is amazing what one can gleam from spending a few hours in the house of a stranger. It also helps that I hacked into your girlfriend's phone and read her calendar. This was the first entry she had with your name in it. It must have been your first date, no?" Jasper appeared to ignore his question. "You two spent quite a deal of time together this past year. You must be in love," Xavier crowed. He smacked the butt of the pistol into the back of Thorne's skull, causing Thorne's head to plunge forward sharply in response to the impact. "How pathetic!" Xavier ranted.

Before Thorne could recover, Xavier stabbed the prongs of his Taser into the back of Thorne's neck with his free hand. Thorne groaned in response. Now that his victim was connected, he pressed the trigger of the Taser. Instantly, fifty thousand volts of electricity flowed through Thorne, causing him to convulse uncontrollably in the front seat. Xavier fought the urge to keep the trigger pressed and watch Thorne squirm into unconscious, but reluctantly released it. He wanted Thorne conscious and fully able to hear everything he had to say. This was just a taste of what was to come.

"Do you like the pain? You look like you are enjoying it. By the way, how is lover girl doing? That was quite some accident she had. I am sure it was very painful for her. It was hard not to stand around and watch her drown," Xavier laughed mockingly. He couldn't help it, he was having so much fun. "It is too bad she survived the accident I arranged. It would have been better for her not to have to deal with the sorrow of knowing that her boyfriend is dead."

Thorne was still recovering from the shock, but managed to gasp in response, "You're a dead man."

"No quite the contrary, Mr. Thorne. I believe you are the dead man," Xavier responded coolly. "You see Mr. Thorne, I told you that there would be consequences for ignoring my warning. You had your chance to drop out of the race, but you refused to take it. Now you have left me no choice."

"Why are you doing this?" Thorne responded alertly. Xavier was impressed by the man's ability to recover so quickly from the shock. Normally, most of his victims remained in a daze for several minutes after the first shock. He would have to be careful with Thorne.

"I am just doing what I was paid to do," he responded casually as he grabbed the pouch of items he had specifically prepared for the occasion. "Don't you get it Mr. Thorne? You are just a minnow in a sea of sharks. Your government does not want you to succeed." He giggled in delight at the double entendre his words implied. "They have larger plans in place for this country. It makes me glad that I am not a citizen. Where the current leadership wants to take this country is frightening, even to me."

"You mean the government is behind this?" Thorne rubbed his forehead, trying to shake the last remnants of the shock from his head.

"Hands back on the wheel, Mr. Thorne! We are almost ready to go," he threw the velvet pouch onto the seat next to Thorne. "Go ahead — open it," he commanded.

Thorne took the bag and opened it, spilling the contents onto the seat. The largest object was his copy of Atlas Shrugged that contained a hand written inscription from Trent Hollaway. Next to it was a small silver frame containing a picture he had taken of Alexis on their last trip to Savannah. Lastly, there was a laminated copy of his parent's obituary. The look of confusion on Thorne's face was evident, even in the darkness of the vehicle.

"I see you are confused. Maybe this will help clarify things." Xavier tossed a small object onto the pile. It was the Purple Heart medal that Jasper had received for his service in the war. Thorne was still silent.

"I thought you were a better adversary than this, Mr. Thorne. I would have at least expected to you to make the connection that I was staging your suicide." Xavier emitted a loud enthusiastic howl that reverberated through the inside of the car. He could tell that Thorne was still trying to figure out what was going on.

"Let me make the picture clearer for you," Xavier said, relishing the power he held over his victim. "The gun I am holding to your head is your gun. The one I presume you have now reported to the FBI as missing. It is also the gun I am going to use to kill you." He stifled a giggle at the abruptness of his statement. It was so hard not to laugh. He so enjoyed teasing his prey, it was disappointing that the fun would soon have to end. He noticed Thorne's hands clench tightly around the steering wheel in response. He had better be careful. Thorne could try to retaliate now that he knew his death was imminent. "These items I brought you will be found on your person, mementos of people who were important to you. The police will surmise that you buckled under the pressure of everything that has happened." Xavier watched Thorne for several seconds, expecting a response. He was disappointed when he did not get one. "Now put all of these items back in the bag. Let's get this over with." Reluctantly, Thorne complied and put the objects back in the bag.

"Since you know so much about me, at least tell me your name. Or should I call you Bastard for short?" Thorne asked.

Xavier pressed the trigger of the Taser again, this time he held it longer. A burst of spittle projected from Thorne's mouth as he thrashed helplessly. It was a good thing Thorne still had his seat belt on, otherwise he probably would be sprawled out across the front seat. "Above all, you will respect me, Mr. Thorne."

Xavier used the moments of Thorne's incapacitation to exit the vehicle, open Thorne's door and drag him out, throwing him to the ground in a heap. Thorne was writhing on the ground in obvious pain from the effects of the stun gun. In the darkness, Xavier caught a glimpse of the agony on Thorne's face. He wished he could see his face more clearly, to see his pain in all its glory, but the only light in the parking lot was a narrow cone cast from a lone street light on the opposite side of the park.

Xavier checked his watch. He needed to get this wrapped up. He hoped to be on his boat in less than two hours sailing out to sea under cover of darkness. He had made sure his preparations had been completed earlier that day to facilitate his departure. Everything was in order for him to make his escape, never to return to this forsaken land.

Thorne began to gain his bearings once more and was struggling to his feet. His recovery time really was impressive. *This man is really tough*, Xavier thought. He wondered what it would be like to physically fight Thorne. He was tempted to find out, but only for a moment. That would be inviting risk into the equation. Instead, he waited patiently for Thorne to make it to his feet. After all, Thorne could be faking his reaction to the stun gun, though he doubted it. Xavier laughed to himself. *He knew all the tricks. People were so easy to predict.* Next he expected Thorne to begin negotiating for his life, sensing the end was near. Maybe Thorne would offer him some ridiculous sum of money or just begin crying like a blubbering idiot asking to be spared. He had seen it all and it never failed to surprise him how people reacted. He watched as Thorne finally stood and turned to stare at him. Xavier was immediately surprised by how focused Thorne's eyes were. Xavier couldn't be sure, but it appeared that there was a look of indignation in his eyes. *Interesting*, he thought. He had not expected that.

He ordered Thorne to walk towards and into the park, while he walked five yards behind holding the Taser that connected him to Thorne in one hand and his gun in the other. There were several yards of coiled wire connecting the electrodes in Thorne's neck to the Taser, so Xavier was able to keep plenty of distance between them both. He expected Thorne might make a last ditch attempt to save himself. Perhaps try to die a hero versus a victim. Only, Xavier wouldn't give Thorne that chance. He wanted him to suffer. When they reached a large Magnolia tree, he ordered Thorne to stop. It seemed like a fitting spot.

"Get on your knees, Mr. Thorne," Xavier ordered. "Our time together is about to come to an end. No one can save you now."

Thorne shook his head, "You fool. You're already too late." Then, for some reason, he smiled.

Thorne's smile triggered something akin to rage but much more violent in Xavier. *How dare his prey mock him!* "I told you to get on the ground Mr. Thorne. Now!" Xavier shouted as he pulled the trigger of the Taser again. Thorne crumpled to the ground, but Xavier did not release the trigger. He was the one in control. He was the hunter. He was the one who deserved respect. Thorne continued to thrash on the ground, eventually going still before Xavier released the trigger. Still Xavier was not satisfied. He wanted Thorne to beg for mercy. He wanted Thorne to plead for his life. He wanted Thorne to acknowledge that he had lost.

He screwed the silencer onto his pistol as Thorne continued to lay motionless on the ground. The thought crossed his mind that he had made the wrong choice. Maybe he should have chosen to kill Thorne slowly, filleting him like a fish, versus staging his suicide. It didn't matter. Thorne was going to die either way. He just wished Thorne was awake to experience the end, but he didn't want to wait around for him to revive. It was time to end it.

He walked over to Thorne's prostrate form and bent down to place the barrel of the silencer against the side of Thorne's forehead, right above the ear. He was careful to angle the barrel so that it would appear Thorne had fired it. Even though he was sure that Thorne was unconscious, he couldn't help but gloat over his victory. Thorne had lost the battle and Xavier was once again victorious. "It is over Mr. Thorne. I have won. You have lost. I want you to know the name of the man who killed you. My name is Xavier. Good bye, Mr. Thorne ..."

Chapter 57

Jasper fell to the ground and thrashed uncontrollably for several seconds. He eventually stopped moving. He lay there on his side, simulating unconscious. He hoped his act was convincing enough, otherwise he was out of options. Only his instincts would keep him alive now. That first electric shock from the Taser had caught him by surprise. The second had been expected. He had forgotten how painful and disorienting the experience could be. Fortunately, he had been tasered many times while in the military so the experience was not unfamiliar.

Tasers were common weapons of control in European states where guns had been outlawed for decades. Prior to deployment to the European Revolution, Rangers and other elite military forces, were given extensive training on how to use Tasers to subdue a hostile foe, and how to resist an attack by a foe using a Taser. The key was to break the electrode connection at all costs, thus destroying the circuit of electricity. That one objective had been drilled into him over and over through the training process. Though heavily dazed from the second tasing, breaking the connection was the only thought going through his mind as Xavier had pulled him from the Jeep.

Tumbling to the ground, he had managed to dislodge one of the electrode barbs from his neck. The barb had lodged in the collar of his jacket, but was no longer directly touching his skin. The remaining barb was still firmly embedded in his neck and delivered a shock, but the shock was significantly reduced, allowing him to function without total disruption. That had given him the edge he needed to feign the third shock. It was a blessing to have the cover of darkness to keep Scarface unaware of this development. Now Jasper had the advantage of surprise.

With his peripheral vision, he watched Scarface fasten a silencer to his pistol and advance on his position. Strangely, Jasper was not afraid. He wasn't even nervous. Death did not scare him, but there was too much to live for. He couldn't let this mad man live to hurt Alexis or anyone else. He knew this would be his only chance to end the nightmare, once and for all.

Scarface stood over him for a moment. Jasper felt the barrel of the gun touch his head. He would only have seconds to act. He heard Scarface speak, it almost sounded like he was gloating. "It is over Mr. Thorne. I have won. You have lost. I want you to know the name of the man who killed you. My name is Xavier. Good bye, Mr. Thorne ..."

With all of his strength, Jasper kicked his leg forward towards Xavier. There was a loud smack as his shin connected into the legs of his assailant in a fluid motion, first one leg and then the other. He heard a sharp swoosh and felt the sharp pain of a bullet tearing into the flesh of his left shoulder. Xavier had fired his pistol but fortunately for Jasper, his kick had forced Xavier off balance and his shot had missed its mark. There was no time to assess his wound; Xavier was already scrambling back to his feet, bringing the pistol to bear on Jasper. There was an odd smile on Xavier's face as if he was pleased that Jasper was fighting back.

Jasper lurched at him, his left hand grabbing the wrist of Xavier's gun hand as he brought the elbow of his right arm down on Xavier's windpipe. Or at least that was what he had wanted to do — only his right arm was not responding. The bullet must have severed a primary tendon in his rotator cuff. His arm was basically useless. Jasper realized this too late as Xavier responded with a hammer punch that landed on Jasper's temple. The blow carried the force of a much larger man. The world around Jasper flashed brightly for a moment. Jasper instinctively pulled Xavier close to him, like a boxer wrapping up another boxer to make it difficult for the other to throw punches. He head butted Xavier with all the force he could muster, crushing the man's nose and causing him to squeal in pain. The force of the blow made Jasper light headed for a moment, causing him to open his guard allowing Xavier to fire another punch, this one smacking into Jasper's ear. It was enough to unbalance Jasper and cause him to loosen his grip on Xavier. Xavier wasted no time delivering a second strike to the same place. Jasper's ear drum exploded in pain.

Jasper instinctively released Xavier's wrist so he could use his free hand to block Xavier's next punch to his ear. One more punch like that and he would lose consciousness. Xavier used the opportunity to smack the other side of Jasper's head forcefully with the butt of the pistol. Jasper fell to the side of Xavier. It was going black around him. He couldn't focus. There was a strange sound, but it didn't make sense. The sharp ringing in his ear was too intense. It sounded like someone was laughing.

The kick to his head was so powerful it caused Jasper to flip over on his back. His face was exploding in pain. His mouth and throat were filling with liquid. He could tell by the taste it was his own blood. He coughed involuntary, forcing out a spray of blood. He tried to turn on his side, to get back on his feet, but he was so dizzy his body wouldn't respond. He watched as Xavier approached him, pistol extended and aimed at his head. *No, he can't win*, Jasper thought. He tried to get up, but the effort caused him to almost lose consciousness. There was nothing he could do but wait for the end.

He heard the shot. It sounded like it was far off. He tensed reflexively expecting the impact. It never came. There was another shot. This one sounded closer. He opened his eyes in time to see Xavier drop to his knees next to him, his eyes already lifeless as his body fell face forward on top of him. Someone had come to his rescue and not with a moment to spare.

Jasper rested for a moment, collecting his strength. With effort, he wrestled with Xavier's body, pushing it away from him before collapsing back to the ground. Jasper heard shouting, but the ringing in his ear was drowning everything else out. The next thing Jasper felt was the pair of strong arms pushing him to the ground. He struggled against them until he saw the concerned and panicked face of Reginald T. Williams.

"Jasper! Jasper! Where are you hit?" Reggie yelled, his eyes frantically scanning Jasper's body.

It was hard for Jasper to make out his words. The world around him was still spinning. He spit out another mouthful of blood. "What?" he responded groggily.

"Where are you hit?" Reggie yelled again, more urgently.

Jasper heard him this time. "Just my shoulder, but I think my ear drum exploded." He suffered through a fit of coughing for several moments. Reggie helped him to a sitting position and then ripped off Jasper's blood soaked shirt so he could inspect the bullet wound. A moment later, Reggie was shirtless as well, as he fashioned a make shift bandage from his shirt and began to apply pressure to the wound. Jasper's was still dizzy, due to losing so much blood.

"I didn't think I would get here in time," Reggie exclaimed. His face was still painted with concern. "After you triggered the alarm, the only thing I could do was hope and pray that I would find you alive."

Jasper looked over at the body of Xavier. He didn't feel anything but relief. "I'm glad you installed that cellular rescue beacon in my Jeep. Without it, I would be a dead man now." He spit more blood. It hurt to talk. He placed his hand on the side of his face; he could feel it was swollen. He hoped his jaw wasn't broken.

"I wish it had never had come to this. I'm sorry," Reggie offered sincerely.

"Don't sweat it. You did your job. I owe you, Reggie," Jasper grabbed Reggie's shoulder with his good hand, "I owe you my life."

Flashing blue and red lights lit up the night sky as several vehicles screeched into the parking lot. Several minutes later, Jasper found himself strapped into a gurney and being wheeled towards the open doors of a waiting ambulance. His head was finally starting to clear and the pain was receding thanks to an injection of pain killer from the medic. As they loaded him into the ambulance, Jasper looked back one more time at the lifeless body lying under the magnolia tree. Yes, it was finished. His nightmare was finally over.

Chapter 58

The Election Eve party, as it had come to be known by political insiders, was in full swing. Soft jazz tunes flowed in a random melodic pattern from the trio playing in the corner of the large ballroom. Members of Congress mingled with the White House executive staff and the occasional Supreme Court judge while waiting for the president to arrive for the executive toast. Service staff in white formal attire circled the room carrying trays of glasses filled with champagne, exotic wines, and specialty martinis. As had been the tradition, most of the senators and representatives in attendance were those who were fortunate enough not to be facing reelection. Mason Kelley noted that tonight the mood was much more jovial than parties of the past. He suspected it was because everyone there expected their absent colleagues to be reelected this year. That was unless they were a Republican.

Usually, the celebration was relegated to the relative obscurity of the Old Supreme Court room at the Capitol building. The president, however, had proposed the use of the East Room for this year's event, apparently adamant that the public needed to see the alignment and camaraderie between Congress and the Executive Office of the President. Mason knew it was just a political ploy of the president to remind his fellow congressman that he still held the power of the Executive Branch. Soon, that wouldn't matter. The Constitution was on its last legs and with it the structure of government that it had created. On account of IPEA, union ranks had swelled tremendously in the past few months, even exceeding the growth rates Mason had projected. The power was already transitioning to the working class. It would be the working class who would eventually usher in a new form of government for the country; a government that he and an elite few would lead and control.

Mason noticed Robert enter from the Green Room, trailed by Harry. *Perfect*, he thought, *he could talk with both of them at once.* He made his way toward the two men, passing the large portrait of George Washington that hung next to the fireplace. Washington appeared to be sneering at him. It was tough to resist the urge to sneer back. The portrait was a copy of the Lansdowne Portrait that had been commissioned in 1797 by the British Prime Minister, who had been a colonist sympathizer. Both the original and the copy had been painted by the same artist, Gilbert Stuart. Mason always thought it was an odd portrait of the country's first leader. Three books are resting at the feet of a standing Washington as he extends one hand in a gesture of parting while the other carries a lowered sheathed sword. *At least the books made some sense*, he thought, referring to the books titled General Orders, American Revolution, and Constitution and Bylaws of the United States.

Mason chuckled to himself. *You and I are not so different*, he thought. *We are both revolutionaries for our beliefs, only we have different causes.* He wondered if there would be a portrait of him hanging in a government building one day. One thing he was sure of, his portrait would not be hung in this building. The White House was a relic from another era. It didn't stand for the things it used to. It would probably be turned into a museum under the new regime. Either that or burned to the ground.

"Hello gentlemen, I trust you are in good spirits," he offered enthusiastically, shaking hands with each of them. The reaction he received did not mirror his enthusiasm. Both of the men wore dower expressions. *Crap!* Mason thought. The last thing he needed now was a crisis. Not when they were so close to victory. "What is it now?" he asked cautiously.

"You heard about Thorne, right?" Robert said, not bothering to hide his displeasure.

"Sure, it is all over the news. Unfortunate set of circumstance, both for him and for us."

"Robert and I were just discussing Thorne's decision to hold a press conference from the hospital later tonight," Harry said.

"Really? He is holding a press conference from the hospital?" Mason looked amused. "Is he looking for sympathy votes?"

Harry and Robert exchanged grave looks. "I wish that were the case," Robert said, the resignation evident in his voice. "I heard from the Director of the FBI that Thorne has filed a report with the Bureau implicating the federal government in a plot to murder him and his girlfriend. Apparently his girlfriend, who is a lawyer with the Christian Legal Association, overheard a member of Congress discussing a plan to take down Thorne. We think that the purpose of the press conference tonight will be to implicate the government publically."

"That is ridiculous," Mason snorted. "No one will believe that. The public will see it as a desperate man's last attempt to save the pathetic state of his candidacy. He will be digging his own grave if he does that."

"The race is still tight," Robert responded softly, lowering his voice as one of the White House waitstaff walked by carrying a silver tray jam-packed with long stemmed crystal glasses full of champagne. "Though we are leading in the polls, we don't have the margin of victory that we were counting on."

"Don't be so pessimistic. Pessimism is self-defeating," Mason retorted. "IPEA has done its job and will continue to. We will gain control of all the states, of that I am confident. Our plan is proceeding despite the complications that have occurred. That reminds me, in today's cabinet meeting, the president released his plans for dealing with our rebellious Texans."

"Oh really," Harry cut in. "Why haven't we heard about it?"

"I'm sure it is simply a matter of making sure that the plan does not get leaked," Mason said. "Basically, he is moving forward with our proposal. He is going to arrest the Governor of Texas and key state leaders. It will happen immediately after the governor's acceptance speech, since it is expected that all key members of the state leadership will be in attendance."

"What happens then?" Robert asked.

"Per the Texas Constitution, the Chief Judge of the Texas Court of Appeals will assume power." Mason motioned for a waiter who had just walked in to the room carrying more champagne. "Coincidently, she just happens to be an ardent supporter of the president. She will do whatever he tells her too."

He could see a measure of relief pass across Harry's face. *That was good*, Mason thought. Harry was always more anal about things than Robert. In the interest of keeping the mood positive, Mason decided against telling them about his conversation with Aaron Mandon the night before. At this point, Harry and Robert were better off not knowing, unsettling as the news would be.

Aaron had shared with him that a reporter from the USA Today had contacted his Senate office threatening to break a story on a government scandal involving Aaron and Jasper Thorne. Aaron wasn't sure how the reporter knew that he was involved, but wasn't going to take any chances. Their conversation had ended with Aaron threatening that he was not going down alone and that he would expose all of them if it came too it. Mason had hung up the phone without responding. Typical amateur, he scoffed at the memory. A weaker wolf never threatens the Alpha male of the pack. It is the surest way to end up wounded, or maybe even dead.

The lights dimmed and the music stopped. A loud speaker announced the president and his wife had arrived. Not bothering to wait for the president's toast, Mason held his champagne glass high in the air. "Tomorrow will be the beginning of a new era for our country," he said, his voiced booming with pride. "To the new regime!"

Both Robert and Harry echoed his words, thrusting their glasses into Mason's causing champagne to spill over the sides of their glasses. On the other side of the room, the president had begun his toast, his words filling the room over the hushed crowd. Mason took a measure of satisfaction in knowing it would be the last time the president would ever perform this toast. In honor of that thought, he held his glass towards the president and waved it slowly. Yes, tomorrow would be a great day. He was sure of it.

Chapter 59

Pete Janko settled down into his favorite lounge chair and placed the bucket of popcorn on the corner of the worn mahogany coffee table, easily in reach. He took a long sip of his beer and sat the half empty bottle of Coors Light on the end table as he picked up his tablet. He pressed a button on the side of the tablet and spoke into the device in a commanding voice, "Video on. Monday Night Football." Instantly the screen in front of him burst into light and his living room was filled with the sounds of a stadium packed with excited football fans. He was excited too. He had been waiting for this game all season. Tonight the Washington Redskins were playing the Las Vegas Chargers, a rematch of last year's Super Bowl in which the Redskins had won in the third overtime. Both teams were currently leading their respective conferences. This game had been the talk of sports networks for weeks. He grabbed a handful of popcorn as the team captains made their way to center field for the coin toss. Suddenly, to his irritation, the screen went black.

"Crap!" Pete yelled, thinking it was another power outage. Then he noticed that his lamp light was on. That did not make sense. He forced his large body out of the chair and walked over to the video screen. The screen was still on, only black. His first thought was that he had not paid the satellite bill, but the next instant the screen came alive again. The logo of the primetime channel covered the screen as a voice informed him that they were interrupting the normal broadcast for an important public announcement. The screen flashed brightly for a moment and then an image slowly came into focus. Pete found himself staring at a man dressed in a grey suit who was standing next to another man who was seated at a long table. Behind them, prominently displayed on the wall, was a blue and white emblem containing the name Georgetown Memorial Hospital. Both of the men looked familiar, but he could not place where he had seen either of them. The man sitting down was dressed in a white shirt with a tan sport coat. A navy blue sling on the outside of the coat held his right arm suspended. His face was severely bruised. "What the —," Pete mumbled.

The camera zoomed in on the man who was standing. "Ladies and gentlemen, I am William McAdams, current governor of this great state of South Carolina. First, I offer my apologies for interrupting your evening. I realize this is very unorthodox and an intrusion of your privacy, but I am doing this because of the importance and urgency of the situation that we all face as citizens of South Carolina. This is not an advertisement. This is warning to you and your families. The man beside me is Congressman Jasper Thorne, he is the Republican candidate for governor and he has a message that you need to hear."

The camera switched to the man sitting in the chair. Still standing, Pete grabbed his beer and took a long sip to wash down the popcorn he had just consumed. He couldn't believe that his football game had been interrupted for a campaign speech. He flipped through a couple channels using the tablet, but the congressman's face stared back at him each time. The right side of the man's face was deeply bruised, but his eyes sparkled and conveyed something that Pete wasn't sure how to describe. If he had been pressed to provide a description to someone, he would have to say the man's eyes reflected purpose and determination, maybe even hope.

The congressman began to speak, "Tomorrow, we will go to the polls to cast a vote that could change the history of our nation. On the ballot is a very serious question about whether or not South Carolina should secede from the United States of America. In 1860, the leaders elected by our state faced a similar decision. Only now, you the people will be the ones making this decision. This vote must be cast with the sincerest reservation and forethought for the outcome it will create. That is why I ask you to listen to what I have to say. Tonight, I am going to give you the grievous reasons for which we, as a people, must respond to our federal government and take appropriate action. Tonight I am going to explain why we must vote to secede from the United States."

Pete fell back in his chair, forgetting about his beer and popcorn. He had been thinking about skipping the polls tomorrow, but what this Thorne character had said had piqued his interest. *Tomorrow really could be a historic day*, he thought. If it was, he wanted to be part of it. Maybe he'd better listen and see what this guy had to say.

"Many of you may ask why pursue such a drastic course of action as secession? Why doesn't the state just refuse to enforce federal laws it believes are unconstitutional? The truth is, we have pursued nullification and we have failed. States have fought countless federal laws and executive orders in court in the past years and failed to overturn them every time. We have failed because our Supreme Court has chosen to interpret the laws of the Constitution versus uphold them." The congressman stared into the camera, his face stoic. "When the judicial branch of our government, or any branch of our government, no longer seeks to balance the power of the other two branches, then the people have lost their power. The only logical direction for us then, as determined citizens and as a sovereign state, is secession."

Pete had never heard of the term nullification, but it made sense to him what the congressman was saying. He remembered years ago the uproar that occurred in the states over nationalized health care and the legal battles that ensued for years after. In the end, the Federal government had won, despite the protests of the people.

The congressman continued, "So, many of you may then ask under what grounds does South Carolina have to secede from the United States? In response, I will provide you with five grievances I have against our Federal government. These grievances are direct reflections of the areas where our government has gone astray from its founding charter as established in the Constitution of the United States. The Preamble of our Constitution describes the purpose of the Federal government as our founders designed it. I quote, *'We the People* of the United States, in Order to form a more perfect union, establish Justice, ensure domestic Tranquility, provide for the common defence, promote the general Welfare and secure the Blessings of Liberty to ourselves and our Posterity do ordain and establish this Constitution for the United States of America.'"

"Given current events, we must ask ourselves this question. If our country's government was designed to establish justice for all, is it justified that this same government requires private companies to unionize their employees?" The congressman's question hung in the air for a moment. Pete turned the volume up by pressing a button on his tablet. Earlier that morning, his brother Jeff had called to inform him that the company he and his wife worked for in nearby Florence had been forced to unionize its work force. His brother was rightly pissed off about it because unionization had forced the company to reduce staff to compensate for the increased wages the union employees were going to be paid. As a result, Jeff's wife had been laid off along with several other friends and neighbors. Hearing that news had made Pete concerned. There were rumors flying around his own workplace that his company might unionize too.

"For the past decade, there have been more companies closing their doors each year, than companies opening them for business because of the cost of compliance with excessive governmental regulations, of which IPEA is the most severe," the congressman said. "When a business owner has to spend money and effort seeking to comply with governmental policies instead of using that money to invest in the growth of the business or to hire new employees, something is really wrong." The congressman leveled his gaze at the camera. "Let me be crystal clear on this point. Unionization increases the costs of doing business, which reduces the ability for a company to be competitive and reduces the ability of the business to generate profits for its owners, employees, and shareholders. IPEA is a harmful law that will create economic ruin for our country. This is my first grievance against the United States of America."

Pete thought for a moment about what the congressman said. The man had a valid point. The more he thought about it, the more it made sense and the madder it made him. Forgetting completely about the football game, Pete settled back into his chair. He couldn't wait to hear what else the congressman had to say.

Chapter 60

"Our Federal government is supposed to insure domestic tranquility. I ask you citizen, do we have domestic peace in our society today? The reality is our Federal government has failed miserably at preserving peace. In fact, one race of citizens is openly fighting another race in our neighborhoods and the government stands by seeking to resolve the issue through mediation and public service announcements?" The congressman paused for a moment to adjust the sling on his arm. Pete wondered what had happened to the congressman. The man looked like he had been in an accident or worse.

Jasper Thorne's voice boomed, interrupting his thoughts, "The government is not addressing this issue because it serves their purpose of creating divisiveness and disorder, which in turn allows our leaders to justify further governmental actions and policies that limit our freedoms and create dependence." His hand clinched tightly in a fist, the congressman banged the arm rest of the chair for emphasis. "When government policy spurns hate, it is wrong and must be rejected! This is my second grievance against the United States of America."

Pete watched mesmerized. He had never been captivated by a politician until now. Unlike other elected officials he had listened to, this congressman was direct, specific, and made logical sense. He felt like the congressman understood him and his own feelings about the government. Pete listened intently as the congressman spoke again. "Our Federal government is supposed to provide for our common defense. I ask you citizen, is our government providing for our common defense when it seeks to tear down what the people sanctioned to be built so that it would protect their property, their economy and their lives from the impact of illegal immigration and potential terrorist entering their state?"

The congressman reached into his jacket pocket and removed a small colored handkerchief. He unrolled it, revealing a miniature state flag of Texas. He held it up toward the camera so it could be plainly seen. There was a look of defiance on his face.

"Our government is systematically reducing our ability to defend ourselves through regulation. None of the recent actions by our government promote the security of the individual. No, on the contrary, they only serve to make the government stronger and in a more secure position of power. This is my third grievance against the United States of America."

Pete had been watching the news updates on the standoff in Texas and thought the whole situation was insane. Even so, he had to admire those people in Texas for fighting for what they believed in. He still didn't understand why the Federal government was tearing down sections of the border wall. It didn't make any sense. If anything it appeared to him it would only serve to weaken border security.

Pete's phone rang, but he ignored it. He would call whoever it was back after the speech. A few seconds later a text message scrolled across his video screen. It was from his brother. It said simply, *'I hope you're watching the speech. If not, turn it on, now!!!'*

"I ask you Citizen, is the government promoting the general welfare of the people when our president makes a treaty with foreign powers that benefits foreign citizens by providing them with jobs in the United States while our national unemployment rate is over twenty percent? Our government calls this diplomacy ... I call it treason!" The congressman's words echoed in Pete's mind. This guy had real nerve to publically declare that the U.S. Government had committed treason. Only a true leader or a real fool would take a risk like that and he didn't think the congressman was a fool.

"This is the fourth grievance I have against the United States of America," the congressman said finally. The congressman's voice became very solemn. "Lastly, and perhaps most importantly, our government was instituted to secure the blessing of liberty. Do we have liberty when a man's refuge, the place that offers him respite from the world, the pride and joy of all his efforts and toil, is taken away from him with a stroke of a pen? I and hundreds of thousands of other citizens lost our homes and property when our president implemented Proclamation

29230 in direct violation of our Bill of Rights. It is the most blatant attempt of our Federal government to usurp the rights of its citizens since Japanese Americans were interned against their will during the Second World War." The congressman's face tensed. "I ask you citizen, if the government can take away our rights this easily today, where will they stop? This is my fifth and final grievance against the United States of America."

After a thoughtful pause, the congressman continued, "But this vote tomorrow is not about my grievances. It is about yours. You are the citizens of this state and of this country. I ask you to evaluate the evidences of government intercession in your own life. Has the government been living up to its charter, its purpose, and its commitment to you? If your answer is no, then I urge you to vote for South Carolina's secession tomorrow."

Pete didn't hesitate with his answer to the congressman's question."No!" he shouted in response, rising to his feet.

The congressman winced in obvious pain as he struggled to his feet as well. He stood and faced the camera directly. "But, maybe you are still unsure. Perhaps you wonder what would be different if we had our own independent state. I regret the scope and breadth of that discussion is beyond the purpose of this speech. Suffice it to say, there are people actively at work preparing the foundations of a new government for our state." The congressman pointed at the audience. "However, those foundations will require the brick and mortar provided by you the citizens before the first shovel of earth is removed from the ground. That is because you are a designer of this new government, just like the rest of us."

The congressman's voice began to rise sharply in intensity. "Citizen, I have presented my case in support of secession, but I want to leave you with one last item to consider. If we choose to do nothing tomorrow, I fear a time will come in the near future when we will no longer have the freedom to act. It is thus even more imperative that we choose to act now, why we still can. That is why I am calling on you, as citizens of this great state, to vote for South Carolina secession. It is your responsibility to take action for yourself and for future generations. We are counting on you for our liberty, for our freedom, and for our lives!"

The congressman paused again, staring deeply into the camera, his hazel eyes vibrant green in the reflection of the surrounding lights. Pete stared back. He couldn't explain why, but he trusted the man. The camera zoomed out to show a large group of people had formed a semi-circle around the congressman. Several of the men and women were state officials, but there were also first responders, medical staff, business men, and a few military personnel. The congressman took a moment and surveyed the group behind him before continuing.

"In conclusion, I believe the state motto of South Carolina best expresses what I want to say. *Dum Spiro Spero*. It means, while I breathe, I hope. It is in the spirit of this motto that I make this solemn promise to you tonight." Pete moved forward until he was standing within inches of the video screen, face to face with Jasper Thorne. "With my every breath and with my every hope, I will apply myself to governing our state and serving you, its citizens. I will fight for you with all my strength and all of my spirit until I can no longer draw breath. Moreover, while I breathe, my hope will rest in our great God above and His divine providence for our new nation. I pray that God will bless you and our great state. Thank you and good night."

A moment later the screen went black only to be replaced by the broadcast of the football game. The Redskins were ahead by a touchdown with five minutes left in the first quarter, but the Chargers had the ball on the five yard line, in scoring position to tie the game. Pete ignored the game and stared at the floor. He didn't care about the game at the moment. The only thing he cared about was casting his vote tomorrow. A vote that he knew, deep down, would change the course of history.

Chapter 61

The bright light hurt, causing her to snap her eyes closed again. Not only was the light bright, it seemed to be spinning. She wasn't sure. She felt so groggy. *Where am I?* She lifted her hand to her head to move the hair that had been tickling her face, but there was something pulling her arm back. *What was going on?* She heard the sounds of a voice far off in the distance, but she couldn't make out the words. It was a strangely familiar voice that she found comforting even though she didn't know who it was.

She could tell she was lying on a mattress, but did not have any idea where she was. The mattress was not very comfortable and the sheets scratched against her legs when she moved them. There was something wrapped around her chest, it was constricting. She tried to open her eyes again, this time more slowly allowing them to adjust. At first she couldn't make out anything, just brightness. She heard the voice again, this time it was closer and louder.

"Alexis —."

Eventually, her eyes began to focus, but she was still having difficulty making out details of the environment around her. The bright light was coming through the window in front of her. She heard her name spoken again, this time the voice was very clear. She tried to turn her head towards the direction of the voice, but she couldn't. Her head wouldn't turn. A face came into view over her. Silhouetted against the bright light, it was hard to tell who it was. When her eyes finally came into focus, she found herself staring into the face of Jasper. He was smiling at her.

"Jasper?" she sputtered. It was hard to talk. Her throat felt like sand paper. *What had happened?*

"I'm here, Princess. I'm right here. Oh God! Oh thank you!" She suddenly felt intense pressure in her hand as he squeezed it. She had not realized he had been holding it. "Alex, I was so worried," he said.

"What happened?" she asked, trying to sit up only her body didn't respond. She was suddenly gripped with fear. *Where am I? How did I get here?* She squeezed Jasper's hand tightly for support. "Jasper, am I ok?" She was afraid of the answer he would give her.

Jasper said nothing but looked at her with tears streaming down his face. Finally he spoke. "Alex, you're going to be fine. You were in a car accident. You are really banged up now, but you will recover with time," he responded slowly. "Do you remember?"

"An accident?" she said, confused. Her head was slowly beginning to clear, but it was if her thoughts had to make their way through layers of mud. *An accident*, she thought. *That would explain where I am. I must be in a hospital.* "I don't remember anything."

"You've been in intensive care for several days. You gave your father and me quite a scare a few times."

"Daddy! Oh my! He must have been so worried. Is he here?" She struggled again to try to sit up, but again failed. She noticed the tangle of plastic tubing stuck into her arm. *That must be the reason my arm is restricted.*

"He will be here as soon as he can," Jasper said reassuringly. "The doctor thought you may wake up from your coma this morning so I wanted to be here when you did."

"Coma?" she said absently. Though she heard herself say the word, it did not register.

"Your injuries are severe. The doctors induced a coma to help your body stabilize and to start the healing process," he said stroking her hair softly. "The brace around your chest and neck is there because your neck was broken in the accident." She glanced down at the metal and plastic contraption that was strapped around her. *So that is why I can't move my head.*

Jasper continued, "You broke three ribs, suffered a punctured lung, shattered a clavicle and ruptured your spleen, in addition to general body trauma." The extensive list of injuries startled her. She didn't know what had happened during the accident, but the realization dawned on her that she was extremely lucky to be alive.

The concerned expression that suddenly appeared on Jasper's face alarmed her. *Was something else wrong that he hadn't told her?* He bent over her, bringing his lips to hers. "Alex, baby … I thought I was going to lose you," he said, his voice trembled. Tears were forming in his eyes. She could see he was trying hard not to cry. He caressed her head slowly with his fingers before continuing. "I wouldn't have been able to handle it. You're so important to me."

She imagined how worried he must have been about her. It was difficult to reconcile what Jasper had already told her. She was in a car accident of which she had no memory. She had been in a coma for days. Her neck was broken. She studied his face for a moment. The stress of the past week's events was evident; his eyes had tight crease patterns that were more pronounced than normal. She suddenly noticed that the right side of his face was discolored, a sickly collage of black, yellow, and red. *What else had happened since my accident?* She opened her mouth to speak but he put his finger to his lips, motioning for her to be quiet.

"One more thing," he paused. "This is something I should have told you much earlier, but I was afraid of how you would respond." His eyes locked on hers and he bent in close, his lips only inches from hers. "I'm in love with you, Alexis Mills," he whispered softly. "I love you and I have for a long time." The smile on his face slowly expanded to fill his face.

If she had been able to throw her arms around Jasper, she would have in an instant. She managed to raise her free arm to his face, cupping his cheek softly. "Oh! Jasper!" she exclaimed, the tears welling up her eyes as well. "I love you too! I love you too!" she repeated. He bent over and kissed her softly. How long she had waited to hear those words. How long she too had been afraid about how he would react if she said them first.

"You are an amazing man whom I respect and believe in. I thank the Lord above that he brought us together." She truly felt grateful to have him in her life. She realized now how much more joyful life experiences had become when she was able to share it with him. Jasper had not only become her best friend, but had become her first, true love. He gingerly wiped a rogue tear from her cheek with his thumb. They looked at each other in silence, enjoying the moment and the significance of what they meant to each other.

"There is something different about you, Jasper," she finally said. "But I'm not sure what it is."

"I will have to tell you about it later. Not now." He rose and walked towards the front of her bed. "I had asked the nurses to open the curtains each morning so you could see the sunrise." He closed the curtains of the window, casting the room into twilight. "But right now, I want you to concentrate on getting your rest."

When he turned around, she noticed that his arm was in a sling. "Your arm!" she shouted. "What happened? And your face ... Jasper, what did I miss?"

Jasper was interrupted before he could respond as the overhead lights to the room came on. A tall distinguished looking man in a white coat entered the room, a digital tablet in his hand. "Good morning. Ms. Mills. Good to see you up and about," the doctor said scanning the tablet in his hand. "Your vitals look good, but your heart rate has been all over the map the last ten minutes. How are we feeling today?"

"I am really not sure," she responded, suddenly realizing how tired she felt, as if she could drift off any moment. "Tired. A little groggy, I guess. I don't feel any pain?"

"We have you heavily medicated with pain reliever at the moment, but over time we will reduce the levels. Your grogginess is a side effect." The doctor looked at Jasper, "If you will please excuse us, Congressman." The doctor walked over to the side of the hospital bed and adjusted a dial on one of the machines. "I need to take Alexis through some cognitive tests while she is still awake. I expect she will only be up for a short time before she falls back asleep." He paused for a second and then looked at Jasper again a big smile forming, "Or am I supposed to call you Governor?"

"Governor?" Alexis gasped. She didn't understand what the doctor was referring to. She had forgotten completely about the election.

Jasper must have noticed her confusion. He bent over her and kissed her softly on the forehead. A brilliant smile dominated his face.

"Yes Princess, we did it!" he said proudly. "We won ... we won the election!"

Chapter 62

Mason Kelley was fuming as he paced back and force across the plush oriental carpet that framed the sitting area in Robert's Senate office. Robert and Harry sat on the ornate settee that Robert had purchased during his last business trip to China, watching Mason in silence, waiting for the outburst to pass. Despite talking frequently by phone, it was the first time they had met face to face since the election three nights earlier. Mason halted in mid-stride and pointed his thick index finger at Robert threateningly, "Your ineptitude screwed this up for all of us. You told me to trust you. You told me you had it all under control. Now we have complications that have greatly jeopardized our plan." He threw his arms into the air in frustration. "How in the hell did Thorne win?" he yelled.

Robert shot back, the redness of his face indicative that Mason was not the only one who was pissed off, "You have a lot of nerve to talk about trust. Why didn't you tell us about the situation with Aaron? We all could have been exposed!"

"But we didn't," Mason retorted. "I cleaned up my mess. Unlike you, I took precautions to make sure my loose ends didn't become tears in the fabric. You on the other hand, have put us all under the microscope with the FBI." Mason gave Robert a steely stare.

"That is a shame about your boy, Aaron. Terrible what happened to him," Robert remarked coldly.

Mason wondered what Robert and Harry really knew about what had happened to Aaron. Two days earlier, a trash collector had found Aaron's body in an alley just off 76th Street and Lexington Avenue in New York City, the apparent victim of a mugging. For some reason, there was no video surveillance footage in that block at the time of the crime to verify what happened, leaving the authorities in a quandary. As of now, any probable hypothesis on how and when Aaron Mandon died was pure speculation. So far, the police had concluded that Aaron had been walking to back to his apartment, located in the Carlyle Hotel, when he was attacked. Unless witnesses came forward, the case would be closed under the belief that Aaron Mandon had been the victim of another random act of violence on the streets of New York City.

Mason was positive that no one would come forward. He had made sure there were no witnesses. He hated losing Mandon after investing all those years training and mentoring the young senator, but Mandon had made a fatal screw up. There was no room for failure in the new regime.

"I can handle the FBI," Robert said flatly.

"It's not the FBI that I'm worried about. It's that damn reporter," Mason responded sharply. "He knows way too much and he is pushing hard to find additional answers. He must be Thorne's confidant or something close to it. The stuff he is publishing is not stuff you pick up at a press conference." Mason started pacing again. "You screwed up and we lost the damn election. Are you hearing me?" Mason screamed. "We lost that damn election!"

"Both of you need to calm down!" Harry growled, rising from the couch and placing himself between Mason and Robert. "What is done, is done. We can't change the election results and we're not doing any of us any good yelling at each other." He quickly returned to the couch. Harry could tell by the tightness in his head that his blood pressure was up. He massaged his temples slowly. "We need to be thinking through what Thorne's election is going to mean to our plan and any far reaching implications," he said slowly. "Agreed?"

Both Robert and Mason were silent and did not respond. Harry took it as an opportunity to move the discussion to events that had happened earlier that night. "I was able to connect with David Walker this evening, shortly after he had left the president's national security briefing. The news he provided me is not favorable to our situation."

Mason took a seat in an antique sitting bench that had large carved lion heads that served as the legs. *He hated that bench*, he thought, *it was so tasteless and just plain ugly.* He would never have it in his office or anywhere else for that matter, but he knew the lion was Robert's favorite symbol, the proverbial king of the beasts. He still refused to look at Robert. Finally Mason asked, "What did he tell you, Harry?"

"What I heard was more concerning than encouraging," Harry responded.

"What have I told you about being such a pessimist, Harry?" Robert chided. "It is all in how you look at the situation. So, what is happening?"

"Hold your judgment until you hear me out," Harry cautioned. "Tomorrow, the president is going to instruct his administration to begin preparatory steps to disassociate the state of South Carolina from the union. He has already ordered the Army to move troops into locations along the border on key highways that lead from North Carolina and Georgia. He is also planning to close all federal facilities and active military bases in South Carolina. Existing troops in those locations will be recalled to bases outside of the state unless they are originally from South Carolina. Troops native to South Carolina will be automatically relieved of duty and escorted off the bases along with all civilian workers."

Both Robert and Mason stared at Harry expectantly, waiting for him to provide more details on the president's plan. *At least they were paying attention to him instead of arguing with each other*, Harry thought. He hated the drama that was born when egos saturated with bravado conflicted.

Harry shrugged, "He did not establish a timeline for any of these actions. In addition, he is planning to offer the citizens of South Carolina temporary amnesty. They will have until the fifteenth of December to leave the state. He is pledging that the government will help them relocate and find employment."

"What about new citizens?" Mason asked.

"Any people who gained citizenship under IPEA will of course be offered the same privileges," Harry responded. "He also apparently wants to negotiate with the leadership of South Carolina before he does anything. From all indications, it appears that the president is planning for the full and non-confrontational secession of South Carolina from the United States."

Mason was obviously frustrated with Harry's news. He smacked his hand into the arm rest of the bench with a loud thump, soliciting a frown from Robert. "Are you kidding me? I can't believe he is given in to those traitors just like that?"

"Hold on, Mason. There must be some reason behind those decisions," Robert interjected. "Let Harry finish."

"I'm not so sure he is giving in or if he is just being cautious and not wanting to incite a civil war," Harry said. "Frankly, I think he is concerned that more states could follow South Carolina's lead. The president received a report last night that Texas lawmakers are considering legislation to secede and revert back to a republic. The citizens of Texas are really pissed off about what happened.

"Another screw up that is going to cause us grief," Mason sniveled, referring to the FBI's botched attempt to arrest the Governor of Texas and his staff the evening of the election. Someone had tipped the governor off in advance of the raid and he and his family had gone into hiding earlier that day. The massive manhunt by the authorities had yielded nothing, leading some to speculate that the governor may have left Texas entirely. Since the governor had not been formally arrested and was not in custody, he still retained his governorship and his power. Mason stood up, his anger returning, "This is really going to make implementation of the second pillar much more difficult."

The first pillar of their plan had been to implement widespread unionization as a means to control and influence the majority of the workforce and more directly, the citizens. By all indications, the first pillar had been established and was gaining strength. The second pillar's implementation was going to be more difficult because it would be in direct violation of the Constitution. Most citizens would resist having a constitutional right so blatantly taken away, whether they supported the intent of the action or not. That is why having state governors in place who were sympathetic to the cause was so critical. The second pillar involved repealing the second amendment and that had to start at the state level.

"I have no doubt that it will," Harry said. "The president is even considering pulling the troops back from the Wall until things settle down. If he is trying to portray the U.S. government as weak, then he is doing a damn good job of it."

"I think we just need to be patient and let things in South Carolina blow over," Robert said.

"What do you mean blow over?" Mason asked. "The ignorant people of that state just voted to secede. Their stupidity and misplaced loyalty is going to have ramifications across the country."

"Are you that much of a fatalist?" Harry exclaimed, somewhat surprised by Mason's comment. "The people may have voted to secede, but voting is a far cry from actually doing it. As soon as those people realize those are real bullets in the guns of the military poised along their border, they will concede."

"You may be right," Mason responded somewhat hesitantly. "But it does pose an interesting question. What happens if they actually go through with it? We could have another civil war."

Robert's face transformed into a devilish grin. "Then my friends, we will have exactly the catalyst we need to start constructing our second pillar. Better yet, we will have our opportunity to eliminate a thorn in our side at the same time." Robert rose and walked over to a cabinet on the far side of the room. "I think this revelation deserves a drink!" he said enthusiastically.

After a long pause mulling over Robert's comment, Mason began to nod slowly. Yes, it was becoming clear to him. As much as Mason hated to admit it, Robert was right. Civil war was exactly the type of traumatic event that they had been struggling to identify and so desperately needed. A second war between the states presented circumstances that could be leveraged to their advantage in implementing the second pillar. It would also give them a rare opportunity to dispose a sitting president.

Mason was starting to get excited. He could not think of a better opportunity to finally take power over the country. Still, there were questions that needed to be answered. *How would they actually do it? More importantly, how would they ensure that civil war would actually happen?* He pondered that question as Robert removed a bottle of scotch from the cabinet and began to pour each of them a full glass.

Mason's thoughts and the beginnings of Robert's celebratory drink were interrupted by a knock at the door. Harry rose and opened the office door, revealing a tall, dark skinned man in a three piece suit with a small black cap on his head. *Excellent*, Mason thought to himself, *Terrance was finally joining them.* The gang was finally all together. Mason took his glass of scotch from Robert and nodded in response. His anger at Robert would subside in time, and it was of no use to be angry over something he could no longer change. He had to focus on the future.

He glanced at Terrance who was had just removed his suit jacket and was hanging it on a polished brass hook on the wall. Mason caught a glimpse of the colorful tattoos that were peeping out from under Terrance's shirt cuffs. The tattoos clashed with the stark white cuffs that were accented with gold and opal cuff links.

Mason's mind returned to his previous line of thought. He knew that creating a war was not the real challenge they had to overcome. *Thrusting the country into another civil war would be difficult, but not impossible,* he thought. He took a deep sip of scotch, relishing the burn on his throat as he swallowed. The real challenge was to figure out how to make the public believe the president was the person who caused the war to happen. *Now that was a topic worthy of discussion.* Mason stood up an extended his hand to Terrance in greeting. There was no doubt that Terrance and his resources would be critical to their efforts to incite a war. At least now, the discussion could begin.

Chapter 63

Even though it had been only seven days since Jasper's world had turned upside down, the hectic pace of his days had made it seem like months since the election. His life, for all intents and purposes, had become a three ring circus with him as the center ring act. Worse yet, he was not the ring master and not in control of the performance. His days consisted of being pulled into one meeting after another. Most of the meetings involved Governor McAdams and other state legislators discussing urgent matters, the foremost being what form of government they should set up for the new sovereign state of South Carolina.

Several subcommittees had been hastily assembled to explore and recommend procedures for handling the urgent matters of defense, foreign trade, diplomatic relations, currency, banking, and domestic affairs. As governor elect, all of these matters were of vital importance, but he was most interested in the debate that was occurring over the design of the new state government. He was in favor of a constitutional republic with some minor modifications such as mandatory term limits for all officials and the ability for citizens to override any government law through majority popular vote. The discussion had been lively and thought provoking as other's had provided convincing arguments in support of nontraditional democratic structures that had only been tested in the classroom and not in reality.

Any gaps in his schedule had been filled with confrontational, sometime volatile media events. The national media was still in shock that the citizens of South Carolina had voted to secede and was still vetting how to spin that fact to the general public to the advantage of the U.S. government. Liberal pundits were incredulous to the reality that a group of citizens, let alone an entire state had actually stood up for its beliefs and thumbed their nose at the Federal government. These same pundits were ablaze with accusations that the citizens of South

Carolina were ignorant, prone to reckless endangerment of others and basically incompetent. Many questioned, under what authority, the state's citizens had to make such a monumental decision. Others called for the Federal government to nullify the vote as unconstitutional. Jasper did his best to stay above the fray, but he had become the poster child of secession and was in the crosshairs of every primetime reporter and journalist. With his inaugural ceremony scheduled to coincide with the official date of secession, he expected the media scrutiny would only get worse as they approached the twentieth of December.

The saving grace of the past few days had been the recovery of Alexis. Her vitals had now stabilized and her condition had been upgraded. The doctors expected to release her to recover at home by the Thanksgiving holiday. It was a miracle and he was truly thankful to God for it. He was looking forward to seeing her later in the day after he completed an impromptu meeting with the U.S. Secretary of State.

The Secretary of State had been hastily dispatched from Washington yesterday. Jasper and several ranking members of the state legislature were to meet with her, but no one was sure what she wanted to talk about. The consensus was it was simply political posturing by the president to appear that he was taking charge of the situation. Everyone knew the president hadn't taken any action yet and had barely commented on South Carolina to the media.

Jasper chuckled to himself as he imagined the chaos that must be occurring in the White House over this matter. States seceding from the nation was something from the history books; it was never supposed to happen for real. He imagined the president surrounded by an elite group of scholars he had corralled from leading universities, pleading for direction and insight in how he was to proceed. More likely, the president's actions would be based on appeasing political interest groups and wealthy campaign contributors than on doing what was right for the country.

Jasper slid a digital tablet across the table to Michael. "Take a look at this," he said.

Michael picked up the tablet and began to read. He and Michael were still in their campaign offices, which had become the ad hoc offices of the governor-elect. Governor McAdams had offered him a temporary office in the Governor's mansion, but Jasper had declined. He could handle what he needed to do from this office for now. He also did not want to be away from Alexis, not at this critical time in her recovery.

Jasper glanced at the overcrowded bookcase to his left waiting for Michael to finish the article. The shelves were piled high with books, papers, and random campaign paraphernalia. The top of the book case contained a variety of recent gifts given to him by foreign powers as gestures of goodwill and acknowledgement of South Carolina's future emergence as the world's newest country. Technically, they were still part of the Union, as the state's Constitution had not been amended, nor authorized by the state legislature, but that was in process. He glanced briefly at the yellow and green soccer ball signed by each player of the Brazilian World Cup championship team. It had become his favorite of the items, but he wasn't exactly sure why.

Though all the gifts were unique in their own way, there was one gift that gave him deep pause every time he thought about it. It was a gift that was veiled in possibilities, some good and some not so desirable. Delivered a day earlier by special courier, the gift had been packed in a small wooden crate the size of a shoe box. Inside the crate he had found a handwritten note that only said, "To your rise as a new nation – Demitri." The other thing he discovered in the box was breathtaking. Nestled inside a protective covering was a replica of a Faberge egg. It was beautiful.

The significance of what the egg represented was not lost on him. The egg symbolized the vast wealth Russia possessed. Shortly after the U.S. outlawed domestic oil production a decade ago, Russia surpassed Saudi Arabia as the world's leading producer of oil, become one of the few remaining financial powers in the world. Russia had wealth that a new nation could use. As tempting as that was, he knew that dealing with Russia would come at a hefty price and that is what gave him so much turmoil. The political ideology of Russia and his new state would be polar opposites. *How could he even think to align himself with a country like Russia?* He thought. Even if ideology was not an issue, he had reservations about what a military and economic power like Russia would expect in return.

Michael scanned the tablet quickly, his response indicated by an arched eyebrow and the cusp of a smile forming on his face, "Based on this article, it looks like we have some possible allies." The brief article from the New York Times detailed recent news from the United Nations. Yesterday evening, the countries of Russia, China, and Brazil petitioned the UN Council to install United Nations peace keepers in South Carolina. It was an indirect way of acknowledging South Carolina as an independent nation.

"Of course those countries are going to support us," Jasper said assuredly. "We have given them an opportunity that they could never have created themselves. We created a tear in the fabric, a chink in the proverbial armor called the United States. I have no doubt that whatever we are in need of, be it finances, food, arms, or anything else, these countries will stop at nothing to aid us. Particularly if they think it will give them a way to turn the chink into a divot and maybe a fissure in the strength of the Union."

They were interrupted by a loud tap at the door. It opened slowly and Detective Reginald Williams entered, looking somewhat perturbed.

"Reggie! Welcome. Is everything ok?" Jasper asked. "You look a little frustrated."

"Yes, fine. Just a little irritated that I got the third degree by your security staff outside," Reggie scoffed. A moment later, he smiled and said in a softer tone, "Then again, I guess you are a pretty important guy these days."

"My apologies for the rough treatment, Reggie," Jasper offered. "I have been receiving death threats from people all over the country that are unhappy with division in the Union. We are all a little nervous, but it is to be expected, I guess," he shrugged. "So, what can I do for my favorite person from LA?" Jasper and

Reggie had spent several hours together since Alexis's accident. At least to him, it felt like they were old friends.

Reggie smiled again, "I wanted to stop by before I leave and say goodbye. My business is done here and I have an afternoon flight back to Los Angeles."

Jasper motioned Reggie to sit in the chair directly across from him, but Reggie shook his head. "No thanks," Reggie said, "I prefer to stand. I am going to be sitting on my butt for the next several hours, as it is." Michael chuckled softly, but otherwise did not pay any attention to Reggie, intent on reading another political article on the tablet Jasper had given him.

"Did you enjoy your visit?" Jasper asked, somewhat jokingly.

"Some of the best food I have ever eaten, that is for sure. The people here are also really accepting and friendly," Reggie replied honestly. "Unlike back home where trust is rare, these people seem to trust first, entertain, and ask questions later. I dare say I could get accustomed to the pace of things around here. Part of me is actually sad to leave."

"The South has its own way of life that is for sure," Jasper responded. "So, have you made any progress in your investigation of our mysterious assassin, Xavier?" The mere mention of Xavier's name left a bitter taste in Jasper's mouth. Even though Xavier was dead, he still found it hard to come to terms with the anger he felt because of the carnage that man had created.

"Unfortunately, we have not," Reggie frowned and shook his head. "We hit a dead end on multiple fronts. Our best lead ended tragically with the death of Aaron Mandon. As you know, we did confirm that Mandon hired Franco Milano and that Franco was the man who discovered and leaked the information about your war exploits. The FBI in New York City has Franco in custody and is interviewing him." Jasper nodded affirmatively upon hearing this information. That incident seemed so long ago he had barely thought of it in the last week.

Reggie picked up the soccer ball from the shelf and stared at it for a moment before setting it back down. "Franco has a checkered past and appears to be involved in several other crimes currently under investigation. Hopefully, we will learn how he uncovered the information and why he did it. Even so, Franco is just a henchman and likely does not know who Aaron was working with." Jasper detected the frustration in Reggie's voice. He knew Reggie had been working long hours to make progress on the case, almost as if trying to work through a penance. It bothered him that Reggie had expressed on many occasions that he felt responsible for what had happened to Alexis and Jasper because he had not captured Xavier earlier. He appreciated the man's sincerity, but he wished Reggie would realize that some things were not always in a man's control. It was a lesson he had personally learned the hard way.

Reggie continued, "Xavier was carrying house keys that had a rental agency name on a keychain and an ID number. That led us to his house and his sailboat. The rental agency that managed the house was paid cash and the company that signed the agreement turned out to be bogus, so we struck out there."

"What about his boat?" Jasper asked, hopeful for some sort of lead.

Reggie shook his head, "Xavier's boat was registered under a false name so that trail is cold as well. On a positive note, we at least know how Xavier entered the country and more about him. We found a treasure trove of evidence on his boat that links him to crimes all over the country, including the pistol that fired the bullet that killed Trent Holloway."

Jasper remained silent at the mention of Trent's name. At least it was comforting to eliminate any doubt that Trent had taken his own life.

"For some reason, Xavier kept meticulous records," Reggie added. "He had every receipt, every hotel bill, and every bus fare ticket, basically any type of paper transaction you can think of, he kept a record of it. Maybe he thought it would protect him from those he was working for. I don't know, but the good news is we have more to investigate." His eyes narrowed with intensity, "Jasper, we will figure out who is behind this, one way or another. I assure you of that."

"That is really reassuring," Jasper said genuinely. "I know you will."

Reggie looked at the book shelf again, his eyes coming to rest on the Faberge egg. "So you guys are really going to go through with this?" he teased.

"We are just the servants of the people and the people have spoken. Now it is my job to lead them," Jasper said resolutely.

"I admire your gumption, Jasper. You are a rare man in this world today. Even so, I still think you and the whole lot are crazy," Reggie laughed, prying a smile from both Jasper and Michael.

Jasper rose and extended his hand, "Reggie, I want you to know that you have my sincerest gratitude for everything you did for me and Alexis. If I can ever repay you, you know I will. If you and your wife ever decide to leave Los Angeles, you know I have a position for you here as we discussed. We are always in need of skilled law enforcement professionals."

Reggie smiled and shook Jasper's hand firmly. "I will keep that in mind. I wish you luck as well, you're going to need it," Reggie said, as he patted Michael on the back. "Take care of him for me and try to keep him in one piece."

Michael snorted in response, sending a shock wave of curls through his white hair. He obviously knew that was a difficult chore. A moment later, Jasper and Michael found themselves alone.

"It's funny," Jasper said.

"What's funny?" Michael asked, giving the tablet back to Jasper.

Jasper pursed his lips, thinking about Reggie. "Have you ever met someone for the first time and felt like you have known them for much longer or maybe even a lifetime?" he asked.

Michael gave Jasper a hard look trying to discern where Jasper was leading him. He slowly began to smile, "I felt that way about you."

"Really!" Jasper said surprised. "Well that is what I feel about Reggie. I think, in fact I know, we will see him again. I just feel it in my gut. He and I have something great to accomplish, I'm just not sure what it is."

Michael nodded in agreement, but remained silent.

Jasper turned his gaze back to Faberge egg and admired the darkly colored blue enamel shell inlayed with random streaks of gold and white. The colors reminded him of the colors of the state flag. The egg was closed now, but he knew what was in the center. He cursed Demitri under his breath as he stared at the egg. *How could Demitri do this to him?* Inside that egg was a gift that properly used, would help South Carolina to rise again. Still, Jasper knew the same gift, if handled incorrectly, could destroy the state from within. As he reflected on Demitri's gift, it became more apparent to Jasper that *how* was not the question he needed to answer. The real question he needed to answer was *why?* And he needed to answer it soon. Time was running out, and with it, the hopes of a new nation.

Chapter 64

Georgetown, South Carolina
November 26th

The coldness of the air was invigorating. Jasper inhaled it in deep rhythmic breaths. For him, it did something that coffee could not — clear his head and revitalize him. He searched the night sky, thinking about the circumstances of life that had brought him full circle to where he was this very moment. The sky was midnight blue and punctuated with an endless sea of bright glittering stars. A blue moon was rising in the east, stealing the scene from the rest of the universe. It was a good feeling to be back at the Mills' home once again to share Thanksgiving dinner. He couldn't help but think that his parents would be proud of him. It was odd how he could think of them now and not suffer those sharp feelings of guilt and anger. Maybe he was finally beginning to heal after all these years.

Pastor Mills walked out on to the porch from the door that led to the kitchen. He was carrying two cups of steaming hot coffee. "That was some turkey you cooked. I ate more tonight than I have in years," he chuckled. He gave one of the cups to Jasper with a nod and proceeded to look up into the sky. "Your father and I used to spend nights on the porch staring at these same stars and talking about life. Every time I come out here, I can't help but think of him."

"Hank, did my father know the Lord?" Jasper asked.

Hank considered the question for a moment and took another sip of his coffee. "You know your father and I used to talk a great deal about spiritual things," he paused, reflecting on a distant memory. "Jasper, sometimes that question is not easily answered. It is not our place to judge the state of salvation of others, because our judgment is tainted by our own subjectivism. It is only our place to enlighten, encourage, and edify."

"But you did discuss spiritual things?" Jasper questioned again. "I recall several entries in my father's journal referring to conversations he had with you about Christianity." Jasper placed his hand on the Pastor's shoulder, "What does your gut tell you? Please — it is important to me."

Hank looked at the sky again for a moment before answering, "Yes, your father knew the Lord. Your father had a heart for God, but he was shackled to a religious system that sought to minimize that relationship in favor of tradition and rituals of man. Sadly, that is the situation of most religions these days."

Jasper was encouraged by Hank's comment about his father. "What would you and my father talk about?" he asked.

"We would mostly debate about the fundamental tenants of the Baptist and Catholic faiths," Hank said reflectively. "We had some great discussions that helped us both understand and to grow, even though sometimes we had to agree to disagree."

"Could you share an example with me?" Jasper asked.

"Let's continue this conversation inside. I'm getting a little chilled," Hank said, as he opened the door and motioned for Jasper to follow him inside.

They sat in the living room in front of the dying embers of a fire that had been in full blaze only hours before. Jasper and Hank had prepared dinner while Alexis kept her mother company. Alexis had been released from the hospital only the day before. She was recovering quickly, but she was still relegated to bed rest and was not to be overly active. Even so, it was a blessing to have her back home and out of the hospital.

Jasper and Hank spent the next hour in deep conversation discussing Jasper's parents. Hank shared stories of his father that Jasper had never heard before. He was memorized by Hank's tales of his father during their service together in the military and equally enthralled by the stories of his parent's courtship. Jasper found it comforting to talk to someone who knew his parents so well. At the same time, he felt a little remorse that he had neglected fostering a relationship with Hank for so long. Hank was a good man and someone he was proud to call his friend.

There was a brief lull in their conversation as they both sipped their coffee and stared at the now dark fireplace, their thoughts drifting to other things.

"Jasper," Hank's voice broke softly through the silence. His tone of voice carried an urgency of purpose. "I want you to listen to me and never forget what I am about to tell you."

"Sir?" Jasper responded, surprised by the seriousness of the request.

"Son, I believe that God has placed you here at this very point in time for a specific reason. All throughout history, God has used normal men and women to change the course of history. Moses was poor in speech, but God chose him to lead the Jews out of Israel. David was just a shepherd who eventually became king of a great nation. The apostle Paul was a persecutor of Christians who became the most influential Christian of all. You are no different than they were before God started to use them."

Jasper was confused by Hank's comments. *Why was Hank comparing him with such famous biblical figures as Moses and David?* Hank must have noticed the confused look on Jasper's face because he quickly added, "What I am saying to you son, is never doubt the power of God. In all matters, seek the Lord with all your heart, your soul, and strength. In your weakest moments, He will be your strength. In your darkest hours, He will be your light. And in the times when you don't know how to lead, He will be your guide and provide the path. Never forget the role that He wants to play in your life."

After a moment of reflection, Jasper said, "That is wise advice, Hank. I will do my best to heed it."

"There is something else I want you to know, Jasper," Hank said earnestly. "I am very proud of you. You have done well and become an honorable man in a society steeped in immorality. I know your parents would be proud of you as well." The praise from Hank was unexpected, but welcomed. Jasper felt both humbled and overwhelmed with affirmation.

"I really appreciate you telling me that," Jasper responded sincerely. "Thank you."

Hank reached over and patted Jasper's hand. "I am also proud that you have fallen in love with my daughter. You deserve each other," he said, a warm smile forming on his face. "I want you to know that I would be honored to have you as a member of the family."

Again Jasper was taken aback by the unexpected comment from the pastor, only this comment left him speechless. He didn't know how to respond. He simply stared back at Hank, who now had an amused look on his face.

Later that evening, Jasper stood on the back porch again starring silently at the sky. Hank had retired for the evening earlier, leaving Jasper to sleep on the living room sofa. Only, Jasper couldn't sleep. He was troubled by what the pastor has told him earlier. He wasn't sure he wanted to be God's next project.

The flashing moon beams reflecting off of the silver hood of a state trooper vehicle in the driveway caught his attention. He had forgotten that his personal security detail was there, keeping guard. As governor-elect, he didn't travel anywhere without official police protection. Like it or not, this was his reality now. Life was definitely going to be different. He couldn't help but wonder if this path through life was truly what the Lord intended for him.

He looked at the moon now directly overhead. It had shrunk in size and its color had changed from pale blue to icy white as it had risen. "Well Lord," he spoke out loud, "I guess there is only one way to find out what you want from me in this life — there is no sense waiting any longer. I'm ready. Let's go make history."

Chapter 65

Columbia, South Carolina
December 7th

President Dante Perez stared through the window into the courtyard, his finger slowly tracing the outline of a small circle in the frozen condensation that had spread across the window pane. The temperature had dropped below freezing in Columbia that morning, as it had across most of the South. A frigid arctic front had settled over the region unexpectedly, trailing the arrival of the president a day earlier, almost as an omen of the reception the president would receive from the small group of men assembled before him. The radiant heating system in the mansion was losing the battle against the attack winter had sprung on them, leaving a noticeable chill in the air of the historic home. The president didn't feel the chill. To the contrary, he was burning. Heated by his own rage towards the men he had come to see.

Though he was a man of average stature, he was powerfully built, a result of his years as a championship wrestler at Florida State. He paraded a full head of black hair that had only begun to gray at the temples, despite the celebration of his fiftieth birthday only two months ago. He had a kind face, with deep set cocoa eyes that matched the color of his skin. No doubt his persona was a main reason that the former governor from Florida had quickly risen to prominence to become the first Latino President of the United States.

To someone who was not in his inner circle, he appeared the genuine picture of a gentle, nurturing, yet strong parental figure. But to those who knew him, he was anything but gentle. Complaints from previous staffers had circulated for years about his chaotic fits of rage, belittling abuse of staff, and overall lack of respect for anyone who challenged him. The president had paid no attention to the allegations, dismissing them as defaming propaganda generated by the conservative front. He knew the real truth. There were very few who ever crossed him without suffering severe consequences.

The president turned abruptly from the window to face the twelve men huddled around the center coffee table. Jasper was among them, in addition to Governor McAdams, Senator Hardy, and Lieutenant Governor-elect Duke Carroway. Also present were the six other South Carolina congressman, the Speaker of the House and the Senate Majority leader from the South Carolina state legislature. They were seated in the large drawing room of the Governor's Mansion. The room had been a centerpiece of several historical events in the history of South Carolina since 1868, when the manor had been officially designated as the residence of the governor. Today, it would add another event of historical significance and become forever known as the room where the President of the United States made a last ditch attempt to save the Union.

"So have you had enough time to consider my offer?" the president asked hopefully.

There was no response from the men. They just stared in silence. Some of the men were not even paying attention to the president, their gaze cast on the ornate wood inlayed ceiling above. Obviously perturbed by the lack of response, the president's tone became more forceful. It was not overly blatant, but noticeable enough to get the attention of all those in attendance. "Listen to me gentlemen," he rapped his knuckle sharply on the wood mantle of the fireplace behind him, causing a shriek echo to expand through the room. A glimpse of agitation flashed across his face only to be quickly replaced by a look of concern and reservation. "Today we celebrate the anniversary of Pearl Harbor. Are you going to let the legacy of those brave men and women be in vain? I dare think not. You must see the logic in my proposal?"

Cole Hanson, the Speaker of the House stood up. Cole had diligently served as a member of House of Representatives of South Carolina for more than forty years and was still as vivacious as he was on his first day in the legislature. He was well respected for his knowledge of public affairs and envied for his wit and charm. He was tall stately man, whose distinguishing feature was a long silver mustache that extended outward more than two inches on each side. His friends would joke him that he had more hair in his mustache than he did on his head, which was not far from the truth. "Mr. President," Cole said slowly, "with all due respect, you and your predecessors of similar ideology have done more damage to this country than any foreign enemy ever did. Those men and women, whom we celebrate and remember today, fought and died for a country and a government that believed in freedom, hope, and prosperity for every citizen. We are not that country anymore ... we are not even close."

Several of the men in the room echoed their agreement with nodding heads. Jasper was one of them. He believed exactly as Cole believed. In fact, he knew that all the men in the room shared the same opinion about the president and his policies. Their disdain for the liberal agenda that the president supported had made it difficult to get consensus from their group to even entertain an audience with the president. Now, the president was asking them to negate the direct will of South Carolina's citizens by not seceding. In return, the state would receive economic favors and an unwritten agreement that the Federal government would rescind Proclamation 29230 for the state of South Carolina alone.

Jasper considered the offer ridiculous. Not a single man in the room besides the president would even consider entertaining the offer unless they wanted to commit political suicide. If the state legislature overturned the will of its citizens, then they would be exercising the same type of governmental abuse that South Carolinians had voted to be free of. To renege on seceding from the Union at this point would create irreparable damage to the citizens' faith in South Carolina's state government and invite outright revolt.

Governor McAdams stood up, "Now gentlemen, let's be hospitable to the president. He is after all, our guest. We need to treat him with respect, whether he deserves it or not." He emphasized the last word, letting it linger in the air for a moment before continuing. "The president has given us an offer to consider. What do you say to it?" Several people exchanged glances, but no one offered a response.

President Perez squared up against the men, standing before them defiantly. His cheeks had taken on a tone of crimson red. "If you do not put an end to this madness," he barked, "I will be forced to take direct control of this state in order to preserve the Union. Do you know what that will mean?"

Again, there was silence.

The president's entire face flared fire red. It was clearly evident to everyone in the room that he was angry. In a voice with the coldness of ice, the president issued his challenge, "Let me paint a picture of what an abomination your world will become. First, I will have the military close down your borders with the United States. People will be allowed to leave, but no one will be allowed into the state. There will be no exceptions."

Jasper could tell the president was trying to retain control of his emotions, but was losing the struggle with each breath. The president's clenched his fists as if he were a boxer preparing to send a knockout punch.

"I will have the military blockade set up along the entire state border including the coastline. All goods, supplies, and other trade items trying to be transported across the border will be turned away or confiscated. I will shut down your air transportation as all air travel to South Carolina originating from within the United States or from one of its territories will be halted and no flights originating from South Carolina will be allowed in U.S. airspace or to land on U.S. soil. You will be effectively isolated from your neighboring states and everywhere else in the U.S. and that is only the beginning."

Jasper and the others had expected the president would pursue that approach. It was a logical course of action. The quickest method of weakening a fortified enemy was to ensure that all supplies were cut off. Eventually, the enemy would be forced to either surrender or starve. They expected that the path before them was going to be difficult, that is why they had already taken preemptive measures of their own. The group of men continued to listen with passive expressions, unmoved by the president's dire threats.

The president apparently did not expect this reaction, or lack of reaction from Jasper and the others. He continued, only now his voice was abrasive and threatening, "All military bases and airfields in the state will be considered federal property. Any attempt to interfere with federal operations or troop movements in and out of the facilities and the state will be considered an act of war and will be dealt with accordingly. All official state bank accounts and financial assets held within U.S. banking institutions or off shore will be frozen so that you will not have access to any of these accounts. Furthermore, the bank accounts of all citizens choosing to remain in South Carolina will similarly be frozen."

There was an audible murmur from a few of the men in the room. They had expected the president to freeze the accounts of the state, but never the accounts of individual citizens. That would be inviting a violent response from the citizens.

Sensing an edge in the discussion, the president walked over to stand directly in front of Jasper and stared at him intensely. "I see that I have your attention," he said flatly. "One more thing I am prepared to do. So while your citizens began to starve, I will leverage our position on the world stage to paint your tiny state as inhumane, uncivilized, and a violation of the human rights accord. I will lobby for and secure global sanctions against your state. Any country continuing to conduct business with your state will jeopardize its relationship with the United States and the United Nations." He crossed his arms and waited, letting the severity of his statement sink in.

"Are you willing to test that premise, Mr. President?" a strongly accented voice challenged from the corner of the room.

The president's head snapped towards the direction of the voice. "Who are you?" the president asked, visibly disturbed by the interruption and somewhat surprised that the meeting had been disrupted by a stranger.

"Allow me to introduce myself," the distinguished looking man said as he walked over to the president extending his hand in greeting. "My name is Demitri Polanski."

Chapter 66

The president stared at Demitri, a bewildered look on his face. Demitri took the opportunity to complete his introduction. "I am the Correspondent of Governmental Affairs for the Federation of Russia. We have officially recognized South Carolina as a sovereign body, free and independent of the United States of America."

Jasper stood up. "Demitri, thank you for coming." He walked over to shake the hand of the tall Russian who had appeared from a door at the far side of the room. Jasper turned back to face the president. "Demitri is my guest, Mr. President. I asked him to join our meeting." The president looked confused, not sure what to make of this new development.

Earlier that week, Jasper had met with Demitri to discuss emergency funding arrangements for the state. At first, Jasper had been very reluctant to pursue this course of action. The last thing South Carolina needed was a foreign power possessing leverage over it. Even so, both he and Demitri knew South Carolina's options were limited, at least in the short term. The state needed access to funds and Russia could provide them. It would be a business transaction and nothing more. It had been a strange meeting, with neither individual very forth coming with information. Jasper was adamant that South Carolina and its citizens would not be comfortable with any type of political alignment with Russia due to the difference in ideology. Demitri did not see it as an issue.

"How do you Americans say it ... politics makes for strange bedfellows," Demitri had remarked during their meeting. "My dear friend, Russia does not want to colonize you. We only want to assist you to become a stable, independent nation. You and I both know that your state's biggest need will be money. You could print your own money, but it would be worthless on the world stage. Look at the United States dollar today! It is barely worth the paper it is printed on relative to Russian currency." His face suddenly turned deadly serious. "My government is not only willing to give you money, but we are willing to offer you protection."

Jasper had been slow to respond, "But why does Russia want to get involved? I can understand why you want us to secede, as maybe other states will join us and this could weaken the power of the United States. But then you would have to deal with two democratic countries versus one. That does not make sense to me."

"Sometimes the end does not always justify the means," Demitri had responded. "The end we seek is clear only to us and that is the way we want it. Your end is clear only to you, and is of no consequence to us."

"We are going to have to put this decision to vote before the people after secession is official. It is the only way," Jasper had stated, not expecting a response.

The meeting had reminded Jasper of a chess match, where each opponent was trying to guess his opponents next move. In the end, Demitri had proven to be a challenging opponent as his motivations for wanting to assist South Carolina still remained hidden, despite Jasper's best attempts to expose them. Their conversation had concluded shortly thereafter with Demitri simply stating, "In the meantime, you will have our support."

The president was obviously rattled by Demitri's appearance. "Russia? What business do you have here?" he snapped accusatively.

"That is none of your concern, Mr. President," Demitri responded politely. "Let's just say that South Carolina and the Federation of Russia are exploring mutually beneficial arrangements."

"What? You can't do that!" the president's voice cracked as he looked at Jasper and then back to Demitri.

"Who is going to stop me? Certainty not you!" Demitri challenged.

The last comment sent the president into a rage. Jasper lost count of the number of expletives issuing forth from the president's lips. Is was a demeaning display that confirmed what they all suspected about the president's behavior when dealing with a situation that he was not able to control. After a few more condescending comments aimed at southern people in general, the president regained his composure.

The president leveled his gaze at Jasper, "Is this what you want? An alliance with a communist? Do you know what you are doing? This is not a game. If you fail to accept my offer I will be forced to take action."

Jasper took the opportunity to engage the president directly. "Mr. President, you may speak like this in your house, but this is not your house. This house belongs to the people of South Carolina and you will treat us and our citizens with respect. I should toss you out of here for the filth coming from your mouth." The president looked confused, obviously unfamiliar with being challenged so directly.

"Regarding your offer, the answer is unequivocally no!" Jasper stated defiantly. "Those terms you want us to accept? Forget about them! Your terms mean nothing to us. You, however, and the United States of America will be expected to accept our terms." Jasper voice echoed inside the room as he spoke. He could tell the president was shocked by the blatant disregard for his authority and power.

Jasper continued, "Effective this twentieth of December, we no longer recognize the sovereignty of the United States over South Carolina. Federal law and policies will no longer apply to our state. Therefore, any federally owned facilities within the border of South Carolina will become our property. All goods, supplies, and assets found on those properties will also become property of South Carolina."

The president tried to respond but Jasper cut him off before he could utter a word. "Until that date, federal troops will be allowed unhampered access out of South Carolina. Federal troops pledging allegiance to South Carolina will be welcomed and allowed to stay and serve. Any other individual with federal ties remaining for other purposes will be arrested. We will also retain and control all property, facilities, and equipment of our National Guard." Jasper's tone conveyed the assurance of a man without fear. "Finally, any attempts to remove equipment or supplies from National Guard depots will be repelled with force. Believe me, we will use all necessary measures to protect our assets, our citizens, and our new nation. Are we clear?"

"You're a naive, pathetic man," the president shouted. "You and your ilk are stupid little worms. You think you can give me or the United States these demands? You have no idea what you are doing. Your refusal to accept my offer leads me with only one option. By my official decree, you are now considered domestic terrorists and a threat to the national security of the United States." The president scanned the room expecting someone to capitulate that his threat had become personal. "I now have the power to lock up each of you forever without due process of the law."

There was silence in the room as everyone exchanged glances, considering the implications of this development.

"You mean like you tried to do to those fellows in Texas. How's that working for you?" chided a voice from the opposite corner of the room. The men in the room turned to see a man casually leaning against the wall, dressed in blue jeans, a silk shirt with a sports coat, and wearing cowboy boots.

"Your timing is impeccable, Doug," Jasper said smiling. Jasper turned to the president, "I do believe you know the governor. He has a message for you that he wanted to deliver to you in person."

Governor Doug Whorter walked across the room towards the president in a slow gait, as if he were a lioness stalking her prey. "I bet you wonder where I have been hiding," the governor said, his eyes locked on the president. "These good old boys have given me and my family asylum since you have made things a little difficult for me back home." He stopped directly in front of the president, leaving only a few feet between them.

"I wanted to tell you personally what I think of your offer to these gentlemen," the governor said. After a brief pause, the governor spit on the ground at the feet of the president. Governor Whorter turned away from the president for a moment and then back again. With a quick action, the governor lurched toward the president, his full six foot four frame towering over the president. The president stepped back instinctively and crouched.

"One more thing I wanted to tell you. If you take military action against South Carolina or further actions against Texas, you are going to have a hornets' nest on your hands. Is that understood, Mr. Perez?"

In an attempt to recover, the president pressed himself into the governor, his head held up engaging Whorter's gaze. The president's eyes pulsed with contempt, "Are you threatening me, Whorter? Under federal law, you aren't even governor!" he scoffed, spiting back on the governor's shoes, "You're a fugitive!"

Not intimidated by the president's bravado, the governor held his gaze firmly, "I'm not threatening you. I'm telling you a statement of fact." Whorter jabbed a long finger into the chest of the president, "Maybe I need to simplify it for your tiny, little, elitist brain. You misjudged the people of Texas and you certainly misjudged the citizens of South Carolina. I can assure you with all confidence that if you take military action against either of us; you're going to have more than one state's secession as part of your legacy. I guarantee it." With that, the governor stepped backward, removed his hat, bowed his head slightly, and walked over to stand next to Jasper and Governor McAdams.

The president surveyed the room and the faces of the gentlemen staring back at him. He could tell from their expressions that he was no longer welcome.

Sensing an opportunity to end the meeting, Jasper stood up and approached the president, "Thank you, Mr. President, our discussion is now over."

Fury, from being dismissed so casually, exploded from the president. "What!" the president exclaimed, his face turning beet red with anger again. "You can't dismiss me! I am the President of the United States of America!"

Jasper motioned behind him, "Security! Please see the president out."

The president lunged at Jasper, his fist swinging in a wide arch towards Jasper's face. Jasper expertly deflected the blow and using the president's own momentum, tossed him forcefully onto a nearby couch.

Two state troopers helped the president back onto his feet and held his arms tightly at his sides. The president looked at Jasper with disgust, seething with anger. "You have no right to secede!" the president howled, "Your attempt will end in failure. I will personally see to it."

Jasper leaned in close to the president, so that only he could hear him. "Sir, unlike you, we listen to our people. Our course of action is set, because that is what the people have demanded. People will always seek to overcome oppression, even if it takes them centuries to successfully do so. If you want to keep the rest of the United States intact, then I suggest you start listening to your citizens and not your ambition. South Carolina does not want another civil war. We want to secede peacefully. But we will fight for our sovereignty, our people, and our freedom, if we are forced to. Are you willing to risk engulfing the entire country into civil war for just one state?"

The president didn't say anything and only stared at Jasper with contempt as two state troopers lead him out of the room. Jasper watched him leave before turning back to the two governors and the men in the room who were watching him. Their meeting with the president had come to an end.

Chapter 67

Charleston, South Carolina
December 20th

Jasper and Alexis stood hand in hand on the promenade surrounding Battery Park, watching the waves lap gently against the concrete seawall below. The sun was just overhead, casting a dazzling spray of broad silver beams across the sea and adding a layer of warmth to the day. It was not overly chilly but there was a brisk breeze that made Jasper thankful for the wool sports jacket that he was wearing. Alexis was draped in a pink cashmere scarf tucked into a tight fitting black overcoat that covered a stylish black dress. She caught him looking at her and she smiled as she squeezed his hand tightly. They were both excited about what they were about to witness.

He and Alexis were surrounded by several public officials, but the entire boardwalk was crowded with people who had come to view the historic event that was about to unfold. There was a vibrant energy pulsating through the crowd that could definitely be felt. It reminded Jasper of the anticipation he felt right before the kick-off of a college football game. He was anxious for the event to start, but uncertain of the outcome and how it would all transpire. There was so much at stake. There was so much at risk. But he expected nothing less from the journey they were embarking on. The path of historical significance was only established through brave people who took great personal and public risks in pursuit of what they believed.

Earlier that morning, he had delivered his inauguration speech to an enthusiastic crowd of thousands at the picturesque parade grounds of the Citadel. He had chosen the Citadel for its historical significance to South Carolina, but also for its personal significance to him. Much of his character had been forged as a student on the campus, along with many of his beliefs about government, the military and personal responsibility. Jasper's speech had been short, but relevant. He recalled looking over the crowd as he concluded his speech; their eyes were tightly trained on him, their ears listening to every word, their hearts eager for confirmation that he was the leader they so desperately needed.

"Our founding fathers envisioned a country were the Government served the people, not controlled them. A country where citizens are free to pursue their dreams, to benefit from their God-given talents, and to engage freely with others in a moral society. This dream inspired a document that was not only a Declaration of Independence, but a guide for all free nations to live by. The Declaration of Independence provides us with four key guideposts that we are meant to interpret, understand, and apply to the matter of government.

The first guidepost states that we, the people, are endowed by God with certain unalienable rights that are absolute and independent of any structure of man. These rights are not given to us by our Government, but by God and they existed before government existed. We must be wary of their sanctity because governments have the power to take these rights away.

It is for that reason; the second guidepost recommends that governments are to be instituted to safeguard these rights, deriving their just powers from the consent of the people. You see citizens, the people were meant to possess the power of our nation and to control the reaches of our government, not the other way around.

The third guidepost of our Declaration of Independence cautions us not to take action without just cause, as we should not change our structure of government for light and transient reasons. We, as citizens, are urged by our forefathers from their own experiences, to be completely cognizant of the path we pursue and the reasons we pursue it. There must be a solid list of past and current grievances that justify the actions we plan to take.

The fourth and final guidepost is unlike the other guideposts, as it is not intended to provide us guidance, but to call us to action. Simply stated, the guidepost commands us that whenever any form of government becomes destructive, abusive, overreaching, or demonstrating a consistent, long line of abuses of power, it is not only the right of the people, it is the duty of the *people, to abolish such government, and to institute a new one. In its place, we are to implement a government that preserves and promotes, among others, our unalienable rights of life, liberty, and the pursuit of happiness.*

Today, we find ourselves in the shadow of the fourth guidepost. We have heeded the warnings of our forefathers and we have identified the justification for our decision. We have taken action and we have been successful. Today, we step out into the light of our new free and independent state. That is why I am proud to be a citizen of the Palmetto state and that is why I am proud to be your elected servant. Together, we will provide new guards for our future security and together, we will create a nation like none other in history." His speech had ended to the deafening sound of cheers and applause.

He felt a hand grasp his shoulder and turned around to find Michael staring at him expectantly, holding a flare gun.

"It's time!" Michael shouted, making sure he could be heard among the noise of the crowd. Michael wore a grey three piece suit accented by a blue and red tie. On his lapel he had two pins, a Palmetto tree and a cross. His hair had been trimmed, but the curls still gyrated in random fashion in response to the stiff breeze. Jasper had never seen Michael so well dressed, but Michael was not the only one who had dressed for the occasion. Several women in the crowd of observers had donned replicas of banquet dresses from the Civil War period and many of the men wore Confederate uniforms. For the uninformed observer, it would be difficult to tell if the crowd had gathered to commemorate the passing of an old friend or to celebrate an important historical event with period dress. The reality was that both situations were true. Today was the end of an era in the history of South Carolina, but it was also the start of a new beginning for the Palmetto state.

A few moments later, a hush settled over the crowd. Jasper turned his attention to the small island in the center of the harbor. In the distance, he could barely make out the outline of Fort Sumter. He removed a pair of high powered binoculars from his coat pocket and trained them on the left side of the fort. It did not take him long to locate the small grouping of six flags that waved rhythmically in the wind. Each of the flags had at one time been raised over the fort to represent the government in power. The main flag, situated atop the tallest flag pole in the center of the others waved defiantly. It was the flag of the United States of America.

Michael handed him the flare gun and stepped aside. Jasper took a deep breath and surveyed the crowd that lined the boardwalk. He could feel their anticipation. It was time to make it official.

"To God be the glory and may He continue to bestow His blessings on the Palmetto state!" Jasper shouted as he aimed the flare gun into the sky towards the fort and pressed the trigger. In response, a bright red starburst exploded over the bay. The deep booming sound of a cannon firing reverberated across the bay acknowledging the governor's signal and calling all to attention. Many of the observers on the Battery scrambled to focus their binoculars on the fort. They watched as seconds later, the American flag was slowly lowered from the center flagstaff of the fort.

Jasper looked at Alexis, her face beaming in the sunlight. He knew what she was feeling. What they both were feeling. They were filled with exhilaration and hope. This moment was a culmination of so many experiences they had shared together over the past year. Their efforts, their hardships, and their triumphs had come down to this moment. A new flag would fly over Fort Sumter and all of South Carolina today.

The significance of raising a flag over the fort was shared by all those who had come to observe the event. On April 14th 1861, soldiers of the 18th South Carolina regiment had raised the Palmetto flag over the captured fort, making it the first Confederate flag flown over a captured United States' territory. It has also been the first official signal of the start of the Civil War. Jasper was thankful that war with the United States was not on his immediate agenda and hoped it never would be. However, he was not oblivious to war as an outcome of the secession process.

War was a very real possibility. The United States would not let South Carolina go without a fight, of that he was sure.

As the sun reflected off of the surrounding waters, a new flag began its ascent. It quickly reached the apex of the pole, hanging limply for a moment before capturing the prevailing winds of the harbor. It was a beautiful flag that commanded both respect and reverence. The flag was similar to the current state flag, with a white crescent in the upper left quadrant and a white palmetto tree in the center situated on a navy blue background. However, the designers of the flag had also incorporated elements of prior South Carolina flags into the design. On the left side of the flag, the word "Liberty" had been added to the crescent in bold block letters in honor of the flag designed by William Moultrie in 1775 that was carried by the South Carolina militia during the Revolutionary War. On the right side of the flag, a thick navy blue bar bordered by thin white stripes split a field of old glory red. Running vertically down the center of the blue bar were thirteen equally spaced white stars. The thirteen stars symbolized two historic moments in world history that involved South Carolina. The first being South Carolina's role as one of the original thirteen states that had fought for independence from Britain. The second being South Carolina's membership with the thirteen states that had seceded from the United States during the Civil War.

A large cheer arose from the crowd as the flag expanded to its full glory, proudly displaying the colors of the newly independent South Carolina. Several observers shared congratulatory handshakes, many with tears in their eyes. A man in the crowd broke out in song and was soon joined by several others. Jasper did not recognize the song, but it didn't matter. He felt it too. It was a feeling that had been lost for many of them years ago. Watching the new flag, waving gallantly, filled him with pride. A deep pride for South Carolina, its citizens, and the mission they had undertaken.

As thirteen cannon blasts sounded in congratulatory salute, Jasper placed his arm around Alexis and pulled her closely to him. Together they watched the flag in silence. There was nothing to say. For the second time in its history, South Carolina had seceded from the United States of America. Today, its future as a new nation had officially begun.

THIS ENDS BOOK 1 OF A NEW BEGINNING

####

www.ingramcontent.com/pod-product-compliance
Lightning Source LLC
Chambersburg PA
CBHW071200250626
47159CB00001B/151